Two Steps from Heaven

By J. S. Robinson

Published by New Generation Publishing in 2022

Copyright © J. S. Robinson 2022

First Edition

The author asserts the moral right under the Copyright, Designs and Patents Act 1988 to be identified as the author of this work.

All Rights reserved. No part of this publication may be reproduced, stored in a retrieval system or transmitted, in any form or by any means without the prior consent of the author, nor be otherwise circulated in any form of binding or cover other than that which it is published and without a similar condition being imposed on the subsequent purchaser.

ISBN
            Paperback   978-1-80369-523-5
            Hardback   978-1-80369-524-2
            Ebook   978-1-80369-525-9

www.newgeneration-publishing.com

Acknowledgements

My dearest Abi, thank you for being the person who rekindled my passion for writing. For pushing me to finally complete this book no matter how far away the end seemed. Without your constant support this would never have been possible, and I thank you from the bottom of my heart.

And to my family. Thank you for your encouragement and feedback, no matter how many drafts you received. I could always rely on you to give me the advice I needed to make this book the best it could be.

Thank you all.

Chapter 1

Death is a strange thing. We spend our entire lives doing everything we can to avoid it while at the same time trying never to think about it. Perhaps that is because we fear the unknown, fear the vast, timeless darkness of eternity. Or maybe it is simply because, as individuals, we cannot fathom the world without us. We can contemplate ages long past, or imagine distant futures, but never with the same clarity as the here and now. Instead, they are like dreams, abstract and intangible because we were not there to experience it. The idea that the world continues to exist without us is a disquieting thought best left undisturbed.

And yet this is the exact situation Nate found himself in. On his usual journey home there had been a sudden, brief darkness, followed by a blinding light. Now here he was, sitting in a small, windowless room with walls white as bone.

Across from him at a large desk sat Death, wrapped in a black cloak, his scythe resting casually against his chair. The desk itself was beautiful, or at least it would have been if any spare inch of its surface had not been smothered by stacks of paper. From what Nate could tell, it was mahogany, polished so finely that it cast a reddish-brown glow on the otherwise featureless room.

"Dead? What do you mean I'm dead?" Nate cried.

"I think the statement is pretty self-explanatory," Death replied without looking up from the mounds of paper surrounding him. "Human skulls and the front end of buses have never had a particularly healthy relationship."

"What bus? I didn't see a bus!" Nate cried in desperation – surely there had been a mistake.

"Hence why you're here," Death replied, seemingly uninterested in the new panicked soul before him as he continued to scribble away at some very corporate-looking forms with a white feather quill.

Nate's hands were gripped onto the edges of his chair so tightly that it was as if he was expecting it to take off. He blew out a long breath and tried to stop himself from heaving. Death continued to scribble, offering Nate only the briefest of glances. So far, he was taking this all exceptionally well.

As Death began shuffling papers around, he without warning began spouting, to Nate's ears at least, complete nonsense. Caught up in this whirlwind of events, only a fraction of Death's words made their way into Nate's head. Words like *Repentance*, *Sin*, and *Eternity*.

"Nate…Nate," Death repeated once he noticed his guest's absent, forlorn expression. Slowly, Nate's head stopped spinning and focused on the hollow eye sockets staring back at him.

"Sorry," he tried to say, but even that almost came out as a cascade of vomit. Death put down his quill and reached into one of the desk drawers. After some rummaging, he finally found what he was looking for. He extended out his arm towards Nate, a pack of branded cigarettes between his bony thumb and forefinger.

"Want one?" he asked. Nate shook his head, staring at the space between his feet. However, he looked up again just in time to witness Death placing a cigarette in his own mouth, lighting it with a flame that materialised from his fingertip.

The whole scene was so surreal Nate could have burst into fits of laughter, had he not been afraid it would cause him to faint. Death took a few drags from the cigarette, blowing the smoke which was not already escaping from his eye sockets into the air above their heads. Stubbing it out on his palm he spoke again.

"I imagine this is quite a shock. Even I was surprised, to be honest. I had you pegged for thirty years from now after trying to pet the wrong dog. Alas, nothing is ever set in stone."

Nate nodded and finally found his voice. "This really isn't how I planned to spend my evening." Death let out a small chuckle as he pulled another cigarette from the pack. That was it now, he would end up finishing them all, and he had been doing so well.

"You think you were surprised? You should have seen Marx's face when he got here. Literally begged not to be sent to Hell." The mere mention of the word filled Nate with an indescribable dread.

"And did you?" he whispered. Terrified of the answer and what that would mean for him, a man who had spent his life ridiculing the idea of God and the afterlife. Death shook his head, the smoke from his cigarette swirling around his skull.

"We don't really do that anymore, it's more about rehabilitation than punishment nowadays," Death reassured him. While promising, this statement was vague enough to keep the fear latched painfully to Nate's skin.

"So…. what now?" Nate asked sheepishly. Glad they had finally reached the subject, Death searched his desktop until he found the page he was looking for.

"It's quite simple really" he began, dipping his quill in its inkpot before leaving it hovering menacingly over a dotted line. "I have a few questions I need you to answer for me so we can submit your afterlife application form."

"My what?" Nate scoffed, the colour finally returning to his face. Death sighed, leaning back in his chair, crossing one bony leg over the other.

"Honestly, I've been pushing for us to move this whole process online for years, but upstairs is old fashioned. Are you ready?"

"I… I guess," Nate stammered. The whole situation was so bizarre he could barely keep up. He had so many questions he wanted to ask; which religion was right? Were his family back on Earth ok? And had his ancestors really been watching with disgust that time he ate twenty-four doughnuts in a single sitting?

But Death would not allow time for such questions to be posed, he had a job to do, and he preferred to do it quickly.

"Ok, first question. Did you live a happy life?" Death stared intently as Nate thought back. It seemed an easy question, he was sure his life had not been particularly awful. Indeed, he could think of no moment in which he could say he had been utterly miserable, lost in despair and desperate. Yet at the same time, despite scouring the depths of his memory, neither could he find a particularly happy moment, one where he had felt especially loved or even content.

The question made him realise that his whole life had been spent doing little more than sustaining himself. He had barely lived and had no happy memories or achievements to show for it. In the end, he could only answer Death's question with a sad,

"Not really."

"I'm sorry to hear that Nate," Death replied empathetically as he scribbled something on the form. "Did you live a good life?" he continued without offering time for thought or reflection. Although Nate was not listening, as he was still reeling from the realisation he had wasted his entire life. Chasing goals that in the end were meaningless. The whole time forgetting that life was for enjoying and appreciating.

"Nate," Death repeated. Nate snapped to.

"Sorry," he gasped. His head felt light, his palms were sweating, and his body ached under the weight of his thoughts.

"Don't apologise," Death replied. "Dying is no easy thing to accept. Very few people have sat at this table and been able to tell me they lived their lives exactly the way they'd hoped." The statement was little comfort and Nate nervously chewed the inside of his cheek until it was bloody.

"Did you live a good life?" Death repeated. Nate thought back once more. While he had never lived his life in accordance with any religious doctrine, he had never gone out of his way to be cruel or unkind to anyone. He had been no paragon of virtue either, never giving to charity and rarely helping those in need.

Altogether, he would not have considered himself to have lived an evil life. However, sat here now, before Death himself, Nate was worried this would not prove to be enough for whatever standards were expected of him.

"It wasn't a bad life," he responded, hoping this ambiguous answer would be enough. Death tilted his head as if in doubt as he scribbled once again. Nate picked up on this and instantly regretted his answer. This time there was a much longer pause as Death spent considerable time working his way through the page. Nate meanwhile sat in silence. Each moment that passed filled with the sound of quill scratching against paper.

"This is my final question; I want you to think long and hard about this one, understood?" Death asked, the seriousness in his voice making it evident that this question was of vital importance. Nate nodded and Death continued. "Who is your God?"

Crap, Nate thought. The one question he knew would come but had dared hope he would somehow avoid. He shifted uncomfortably in his seat as he pondered the best way to tell Death he had spent most of his life ridiculing those with faith. He tried to think of a diplomatic answer, one that would seem entirely reasonable for having no belief in a God until this very moment.

But the only thought that came was a memory from his university days as part of the debating society. How he had laughed as the girl with the cross around her neck had burst into tears as he'd informed her that her parents were not waiting for her in heaven, but were instead being eaten by worms as they spoke. Now it seemed, she would have the last laugh.

Nate sighed and shrugged his shoulders, there was no point in lying, for all he knew this was all a test and Death already had the answers. He may as well just tell the truth.

"I suppose…I suppose I don't have one." He wanted to be angry, to lash out at Death as an agent of a now clearly real God, who had allowed so much suffering and pain to happen unchecked. Yet all he could feel was a deep disappointment in himself as if he had let down someone he loved.

Death raised an invisible eyebrow; it was not often that he received such an answer. Even Nietzsche and Lenin had drastically changed their tune once they sat before him. Nevertheless, he could sense Nate was being honest. A strong aura of bitterness and anger seemed to hang over him like a cloud. Yet Death felt no contempt for Nate, for denying what was beyond all doubt. Only pity for a man who had lived his life with his back towards his creator, who had not felt the love he had been promised.

To Nate's relief, there was no sermon, no sudden burst of thunder as he damned himself with his own mouth. Death simply nodded at the admission. He noted the answer on the form, each stroke with a heavy heart. It pained him to see mortals who had lived with such a disdain for their makers. Most were selectively blind to their plight, eager to point the finger in accusation as long as it was not directed at themselves.

There were many more pages that Death had to complete before the form could be submitted, but they did not require Nate's presence. He, therefore, decided to press forward with his entry to the afterlife. He carefully placed the papers back into their respective drawers and leaned forward, resting his clasped hands upon the desk.

"Thank you for answering honestly. Now it is time for me to inform you of what happens next."

Nate sat forward also, worried his answers were not enough to guarantee him a place in Heaven. "Am I being sent to Hell?" he asked, his voice cracking. Death shook his head, slightly amused how nearly every human automatically assumed the worst.

"No, my boy, nothing of the sort" he reassured him. Nate practically ejected from his seat, he had done it, paradise here he came. "You will be going to Purgatory," Death continued. Nate immediately crashed back down from his high at the words.

"P…Purgatory?" he stammered. He imagined a flat, endless expanse of grey wasteland, swirling smoke, and the souls of the damned, doomed to roam for all eternity. Surely, he did not deserve this.

"Yes," Death continued. "Now I know it's not what you hoped to hear, but I promise it's not as bad as you think."

Nate held his head in his hands, he wanted to cry, he had been screwed over by the Almighty all his life, it was only fitting that once it was over, he would be delivered the mother of all screw yous.

Although, in the end, Purgatory was a much better deal than Hell. Probably. He straightened himself back up, his eyes red and stinging from holding back tears. "What can I expect Purgatory to be like?" he choked.

Death let out another long sigh, already itching for another cigarette. He had been asked this same question by every sentient lifeform since the beginning of time. And he was still no closer to providing a fully comprehensive answer.

"Well," he began, wondering which part of this monumental question he should start with, before deciding he would start at the same place he always did, at the beginning.

"Purgatory will be in many ways a world very similar to your own. You will know hunger and thirst, weariness, and pain, not even from death will you have respite." The cold, unflinching indifference in his voice was clear and left Nate feeling cold and abandoned, on the very cusp of a great unknown that for all he knew, he would traverse alone.

"It will be your task, as it is with all those sent to Purgatory, to atone for the sins you have committed. Once you have done this, that is when you will be allowed into Heaven," Death explained.

"And how do I do that exactly? Atone, I mean," Nate asked.

"That is for you to figure out. If I was to offer you all the answers what would be the point?" Suddenly Nate leapt from his chair, a great burst of rage erupting from him seemingly out of nowhere to his complete surprise.

Death had felt it coming, however. It had begun as a simmering cauldron of resentment, fear, and anger gradually rising in Nate's heart. Now, as it had been made clear there was no easy way out of his predicament, that cauldron had bubbled over and gushed out as a wave of insecurity masked by anger.

"What do you mean what's the point?! What's the point of making me suffer even more? Why does everything have to be some bullshit test?" Nate shouted. Death simply stared back in silence. Without waiting for a response Nate slumped back into his seat, his head in his hands once more. "I don't understand, why can't I just get a break for once?" he whimpered.

After a brief silence Death replied with, his tone stricter and less empathetic than before.

"Believe me Nate when I say that I would love nothing more than to send you to Heaven this instant. Your life has not been easy, and you deserve to be shown some compassion. But it is not my fault you are being sent to Purgatory. It is not upstairs' fault either, you made your choices. Now it is time you take some responsibility for yourself. Instead of blaming others for all that has befallen you, accept that you are here because of you and nobody else. Because the only one who can atone for your sins is you."

It was ironic really, Nate thought. His whole adult life he had told people to take responsibility for themselves. To not expect anyone to come and help them through tough times and to have no sympathy for others. Now here he found himself, in a situation entirely of his own making, desperately looking for a compassionate hand to guide him.

He knew there was no point in continuing arguing or begging, but that did not put him above sulking. So, there he sat, a fully grown man, his face wrapped in his arms, his knees up to his chest. He refused to accept what was happening to him and hoped if he sulked hard enough then God or Shiva or Zeus for all he cared, would send him back to his old life. Unfortunately for Nate, it seemed the will of the Almighty was greater than his own, and he soon gave up with a defeated sigh.

Death had waited patiently as Nate went through his childish act of defiance. He had been forced to sit through speeches and tirades from the worst creation had to offer. Heard them beg for forgiveness like their victims had done, all the while feeling no anger or hate towards them. Nate's sulking was a walk in the park compared to them. He understood humans were emotionally complex yet intellectually simple creatures. Few were prepared to own up to and repent for all they had done.

Nate let out another sigh and resumed a normal, albeit slouched sitting position. Without any comment on their short intermission Death continued with his explanation of Purgatory, although this time trying to sound less disinterested in Nate's plight to hopefully cheer him up.

It wasn't that Death did not care for those he was tasked with helping to move on. He had simply been doing this job for so long that it had become difficult to differentiate between one mortal and the next. They all seemed to suffer from the same excruciating know-it-all attitude, while at the same time being selectively oblivious to their own wrongdoings. Nevertheless, perhaps a change of tactic would help lighten the mood.

"Now, I am required to say that you can still die in Purgatory. We've watched far too many people jump off cliffs thinking they're invincible and now upstairs says we need a warning. Personally, I thought a sign on every elevated surface saying, '*don't jump dickhead*' would suffice, but upstairs didn't see the funny side." Nate gave a barely audible mumble of acknowledgement of what was clearly a hilarious joke. That would be the last time Death bestowed his comedic genius on a mortal if that was all the response he got.

"So, what happens if I do die in Purgatory?" Nate asked. Death waved his hand dismissively as he lit another cigarette. Where was he going to get another pack of these from? The planet they were manufactured on did not even exist anymore.

"Don't worry about it, you'll barely even notice. Your soul won't be erased or anything if that's what you're worried about, you will just have to start over." Death tipped his head back and blew a long pillar of smoke into the air before flicking the butt away.

"I suppose you have a lot of questions you want to ask me?" Death asked the sullen-looking Nate who was picking at the fabric of his chair. Nate nodded with the ghost of a smile.

"Just a couple."

"Well, too bad," Death replied jovially, jumping up from his own seat with unexpected energy for someone who was little more than a bag of bones. As he took hold of his scythe, the room around them melted away. The pristine white walls, now with the consistency of mud, slid down to the floor revealing a vast corridor that looked as if it belonged to a hotel.

Spaced a few meters apart on both sides were wooden doors, plain and unremarkable. Death immediately began walking confidently down the corridor, as he had done countless times before.

At first, Nate was dumbstruck by the way his concerns were utterly and remorselessly dismissed. But as he watched the tall, dark figure of Death gradually shrinking into the distance, he roused his body into action and started after him.

Nate followed silently, although his feet dragged along the smooth white floor of the insipid corridor. Once their starting position had melted into the horizon the two arrived at an intersection. The corridor continued in four different directions, seemingly forever, with no discernible difference between any of them.

"What's this?" Nate asked.

"This is where you make your choice," Death said with an unexpected excitement in his voice. "Behind each of these doors is a different land within Purgatory. Go to where your heart leads you." Death threw out his arm, gesturing to the paths along which lay countless doors. There were not many perks to his job, but he did so love to see where the mortals ended up.

"Right," Nate said, furrowing his brow. This whole thing seemed utterly ridiculous, which by this point was par for the course, and he decided to just go along with it. He examined the doors closest to him and could see no indication as to what lay behind any of them.

So, he set off down one of the paths, Death never more than two steps behind. Yet no matter how far Nate walked, each door was the same and he began to wonder whether it was all a trick, whether these doors did lead somewhere different, or if they would all end up in the same place regardless.

The whole time Death was silent. Of course, he knew what lay behind each door, but he could not afford to influence Nate's decision in any way. To do so would be a severe breach of the rules.

After what seemed like hours Nate finally stopped. Before him stood a door identical to the many hundreds he had already passed. Plain wood with a brass handle, it bore no significance to him, and he felt no otherworldly attachment. Yet this was the one he decided he would open. He turned to Death.

"So, I just walk on in?" he asked, certain it would not be so easy as walking through a door and finding himself in an entirely new world. Death tilted his head as if he had been found out.

"There is just the matter of purifying your soul," he conceded.

"I knew there would be something," Nate replied. "So, what do I have to do?"

Death was silent. If he had eyes, they would have been filled with visible sadness and pain. Nate could sense it however and he immediately understood.

"W...will it hurt?" he asked sheepishly, like a child about to get their vaccinations, edging away from the door as if it were something deadly. Death put a surprisingly warm and human-like hand on Nate's shoulder.

"It will be agony," he replied. Surprisingly, this did not instil Nate with a great deal of excitement as he turned to face the door. He wondered what hellish nightmare he could expect to find beyond its bland exterior.

Regardless, he stepped forward and rested his hand on the handle, his whole body shaking as fear began to overtake him. The most basic of human instincts is to avoid pain, to run in the other direction and hide. Despite all this, Nate took a deep breath and turned the handle.

The door swung open to reveal a swirling vortex, comprised of the most vivid and beautiful colours Nate had ever seen. They twirled and twisted into shapes and patterns beyond the ability of the greatest artists. At the same time, it was accompanied by a terrible roar, deep and rolling like thunder yet organised and harmonic like a choir. It was the epitome of power, vast and terrifying, orderly and beautiful. It stretched on for some distance, but at the end, a bright white light was clearly visible.

Nate turned to Death one last time in the hopes of avoiding whatever was to come. However, Death stood unwavering as he waited for him to accept his fate. Nate's mind turned at last to the life he had left behind. His family, friends, and all he knew to be certain. They were his only comfort heading into such an unknown. He still had so many questions he wished to ask Death but knew he had been told all he needed to know.

"Thank you," he said. Death nodded and gave Nate a reassuring pat on the head as if to say it would not be all that bad. At last, Nate took his first steps into the vortex, and as his feet left the corridor behind him, the world suddenly upended. No longer was Death standing behind him, but rather above, and the previously solid ground gave way. Suddenly, Nate was falling at great speed, the thunderous roar of the vortex filling his ears. The bright, swirling colours overwhelming his senses.

Then it began. Nate felt as if he was being pulled apart piece by piece, searing pain tearing through every atom of his being. He had no idea such pain was even possible as each one of his nerve endings screamed. He cried out for all he was worth.

Firstly, he cursed Death for forcing this upon him, for not giving him a choice. But the anger soon gave way to fear as the tortuous sensations continued to rip through his body and he began screaming for his mother, for God, anyone to save him from this torment. Soon, a new sensation took over. He felt his flesh begin to stretch and tear, and an overwhelming feeling of something trying to burst out of his skin took over.

As Death had promised, it was indescribable agony. To his horror, Nate watched as versions of himself began pulling themselves free from his flesh. At first, they were few, then they quickly turned into hundreds, then thousands. Before long there had been too many to count. They did not linger, however. Instead, they dissipated into nothingness as soon as they had wrenched themselves free from their host. They were not exact copies either, they were deformed, hideous, and evil-looking with grey, rotten skin and black eyes.

After what felt like years of unending torture, the apparitions stopped appearing. Nate was no longer in pain, yet he felt himself slipping out of consciousness. As his vision began to fade, he made out something below him: a vast sparkling sea and a green landmass, both stretching on into the horizon.

As the ground came up to meet him Nate passed out. He did not feel the impact, just a deep sensationless sleep.

Having watched Nate take his final step into Purgatory, Death shut the door behind him. He had no wish to hear the screams of pain as his sins were ripped from his soul. As he walked the long way back to his desk to meet another arrival, he could not help but ponder Nate's choice.

He had chosen that specific door, to that specific place, at this specific time.

Usually, he would not have offered this a second thought; however, this time something felt different. As if there had been a third guiding hand leading Nate towards his choice. The feeling was too subtle for a mortal to notice, but Death had felt it the moment Nate had arrived.

He laughed at his ridiculousness, he knew there was no way upstairs would get involved in such trivial matters, that's just not how things were done.

Chapter 2

Guard duty was by far not the worst punishment he could have received, but Marcus hated it all the same, if for nothing more than the fact that the boredom was intolerable. He stood outside the armoury door leaning against the stone wall, his spear lying neglected on the ground. This was a complete waste of his talents.

Although, it could be argued so was the tavern brawl he'd started which got him posted here in the first place.

However, Captain Ardell, Marcus' commanding officer, had been surprisingly lenient towards him. Six months of unpaid guard duty and a five hundred gold fine was a far cry from her usual punishments of lashings or border patrol. Perhaps she was finally developing a soft spot for him. Or more likely she had given up trying to discipline him entirely.

One would think a man who had spent most of his time alive in the Roman Legion would be a paragon of soldiering virtues. Unfortunately for Captain Ardell however, Marcus was not.

He lifted his head skywards; the sun was bright, as usual, and the clear skies made the heat unbearable. He had been used to hot weather when fighting in Syracuse, but at least back then he would have a task to take his mind off the heat. He undid his helmet straps and ran his hand through his sweaty black hair and wiped his brow with his forearm.

Exhaling loudly, so as to vent his frustration to nobody in particular, he dropped his helmet to the ground. It landed with a crunch as the side guard folded beneath itself, before springing onto its side. At least there was an upside to guarding the armoury. If he were careful not to be caught abandoning his post, he could sneak inside and get a glimpse of the vast array of weapons Ardell had accumulated over the years.

During his time with the Legion, he thought he had seen all the ingenuity and cruelty man had to offer. But these things were nothing compared to what he had witnessed here in Purgatory.

The weapons and machines he had seen amazed him; long shafts of metal capable of dispatching a foe further than any arrow. Huge ships that sailed through the air as if it were water. And of course, the beautifully crafted and intricate weapons with which he was more familiar. In the end, all his death had changed were the names of the places he fought in and the ways in which he killed, otherwise it was more of the same.

Eventually, the mix of boredom and curiosity became too much and he pushed open the armoury door (which was nonsensically always unlocked) and after ensuring there was still nobody coming to check on him, made his way inside. The armoury was huge, one of hundreds in the Vanguard alone. With three levels connected by spiralling stone steps, it stretched on for nearly a mile underground.

Every few meters were iron doors on either side of the room, behind which were held hundreds if not thousands of weapons. Marcus continued down the hall for about fifty meters before opening another unlocked door on his left. Once again checking nobody had followed him, he went inside and closed the door behind him.

Even with the door closed, there was plenty of light coming from a small square window at the top of the back wall, allowing Marcus to stand in awe at the beauty of what lay in front of him.

Propped up against the left wall were hundreds of musket rifles, beautifully polished, which gleamed in the sun like steel. On the opposite side were swords, axes, and spears, all made from a variety of different materials by hundreds of different craftsmen. But what made Marcus the most curious and excited were the machine guns, pistols, and other guns he did not know the names of, which were locked behind an ugly metal door and sharp wire fence at the very back of the room.

He would never forget the first time he saw them in action. A demonstration had been organised by one of the other captains. The most memorable moment was a machine gun mounted on a makeshift wall mowing down dozens of wooden targets in an instant.

However, firearms and the means to make them were exceptionally rare nowadays. They were only ever used in the most desperate of situations. Deep in his appreciation for the armaments on display, he did not hear the door open behind him.

"I didn't realise your job was to stop the weapons getting out of the armoury, Marcus." Marcus spun around to see Chion leaning against the door. Dressed in a thin leather breastplate, greaves and with a short sword at his side, he looked like a large stick insect with his tall, thin frame, tanned skin, and bald head.

"It's literally half of the job you imbecile. What do you want, run out of duties to avoid?" The smile on Chion's face disappeared immediately.

"The captain wants to see you; she's got a new assignment for you, I believe."

"Oh, gods," Marcus gasped.

"Oh, I do hope she sends you to the Great Wastes, then I'll never have to see your hideous Roman face again." Chion laughed as Marcus pushed his way past him and made his way towards Captain Ardell's fort.

Chion was one of Ardell's many messengers and had a deep personal hatred of anything even remotely Roman, including Marcus. Having lost his family when the Roman Empire of his own world expanded eastwards, Chion had made it his personal mission to make the afterlife intolerable for anyone associated with the empire which ruined his life.

Marcus had soon developed a mutual hatred. It was a difficult task to find another Roman in Purgatory, it was even harder when Chion was doing everything he could to get them killed. Lifesaving messages not delivered; incorrect orders being passed on. Marcus had lost his only two Roman friends to Chion's hate, and he'd be damned if he let himself fall victim.

Captain Ardell's fort was a two-hour walk away, but Marcus knew if he were not there within the hour, there would be hell to pay.

He scooped up his helmet and spear from the ground outside the armoury and recoiled in disgust as warm urine spilled over the edges of his helmet. Obviously, it was Chion, and Marcus was furious, but he did not have time to turn around and make him lick the helmet clean. It would have to wait.

He set off at a run in the general direction of Ardell's fort. He knew if he went through the streets at this time of day he would be held up for hours. So, he ran around them and through one of the many training yards that dotted the city. With any luck, his friend Joel would be there training with the cavalry.

Joel had arrived in Purgatory many centuries earlier than Marcus and the two had met in one of the city's most popular inns. One drinking competition and a fistfight later they had cemented a friendship that had lasted for decades.

Marcus had been especially interested in Joel's tales of his participation in what he called the Second Great War – a conflict which he claimed spanned the entire world, making use of metal ships and flying machines. At first, Marcus had refused to believe him, but after witnessing all the things he had seen in this world, he knew anything was possible.

"How's it going, Marcus?" Joel smiled, dismounting his horse.

"Not good," Marcus panted as he approached, the mixture of the heat and smell of fresh urine making him queasy. "Captain wants to see me for a new assignment." He gestured at Joel's horse with his thumb. "May I?" he asked. Joel swung out his arm motioning toward the animal.

"Be my guest, the last thing I want is for you to get sent off on some suicide mission for being late," he said only half-joking. Marcus mounted and gave Joel a thankful nod before speeding off.

After some hard riding, passing rows of poorly constructed shacks which loomed over the streets like twisted branches of a dying tree, Marcus entered a flat clearing with Ardell's fort ahead of him. It was an intimidating sight, three hundred and fifty feet across, with an arrow tower built into the side every fifty feet and a catapult on the roof. And that was just the keep. Wooden walls encircled the keep with thirty meters of space between the two. This was to make room for the guard's quarters, stables, armoury, and storehouse.

Ardell had overseen its construction personally, and each detail was meticulous in its design. She wanted a fort capable of sustaining itself for at least a year in case the city walls were breached. To top it off she had commissioned a dry moat to be constructed, six meters deep and filled with sharpened stakes for good measure. It had taken nearly three years to construct and was Captain Ardell's greatest joy. Nevertheless, it was still one of the smallest forts in the city, with the Citadel being nearly one thousand square kilometres across.

Marcus made his way across the drawbridge and past the guards into the fort. "Ardell is in the war room," one of the guards mentioned as he headed for the keep, "She didn't seem so happy," they added.

"When does she?" Marcus forced a laugh despite the crushing sense he was about to be sent to his death. Once he had passed through the gate, he hitched Joel's horse on the nearest post and walked the short distance to the keep's only door.

Upon entering Marcus caught a shiver up his spine; the keep was the only stone building in the fort, and it was always freezing. The building was split into three sections: firstly, the war room, kitchen, and reserve armoury on the ground floor.

From the war room, the captain held meetings with her advisors and planned operations both within and outside the city walls. She was not yet authorised to carry out large scale military manoeuvres, and so attempted to remedy this by working her men to near death on every job she could think of.

Below was a cellar containing up to a year's worth of food and an escape tunnel should the fort be breached. Finally, the top floor contained the captain's quarters, a small barracks, ladders to the roof, and archer towers. The barracks housed the captain's personal retinue, eight warriors handpicked to serve as her protectors, not that she felt they were necessary.

Marcus hurried to the war room, which was decorated with the expected spoils of war – banners of long-conquered enemies, maps of current ones, and dozens of weapons once belonging to fabled champions.

To his surprise, the captain was not there. This surprise quickly turned to dread as he realised she was waiting for him in her quarters. Everyone knew that unless you were a whore, if you were called to any captain's quarters, you were already dead. Ardell would simply make the death far more painful and drawn out than it needed to be.

Marcus stood at the bottom of a set of spiral stone steps that led to Ardell's quarters for a moment composing himself, quickly deciding he'd best get it over with before she had him stripped and beaten for being late, even though he was much earlier than would be expected.

Although his nerves only returned when he reached her door, where the medallions of dozens of long-slain heroes were arrayed like glittering stars around its edge. Marcus summoned up whatever courage he had left and knocked, which was met almost instantly by "enter."

Ardell sat at her desk in the centre of the room. Her usually straight black hair was knotted and unbrushed, her eyes bloodshot and accompanied by a set of bags.

She did not look at Marcus when he entered, instead she was shuffling papers into yet more stacks and furiously signing the seemingly endless work.

The state of the quarters was not much better than the captain herself. The bed which was draped in exotic animal pelts was unmade. Clothes were strewn about the floor and loose papers blanketed most of the room. The only semblance of order was mounted above the fireplace, Ardell's most prized and feared possession, her sword, Oath-Breaker.

It was said that not only had she travelled to the Imperium itself to have it forged from the bones of a dragon, but that its victims numbered in the thousands. The blade was long and delicate, yet quick and deadly like its master.

Just looking at it made Marcus uncomfortable as he wondered if the rumours that it was a magical blade were true. There were very few magically infused weapons left in the world. Although, if anyone were to have one, it would be Ardell.

Ardell had recently been given extra duties. On top of having to manage half a million men under her command, she was now also in charge of all anti-smuggling activity. She had volunteered for it, however, so Marcus' sympathy did not stretch very far.

The other captains and generals had been willing to divide the task between six of them, but Ardell had insisted it all be given to her. The others thought her mad, but she was desperate to prove her worth to Grand Admiral Lee. In the end, everyone decided it would just be less fuss to let her do it all.

After enough time had elapsed of complete silence, Marcus was starting to think the captain had not noticed him enter. He spoke up. "You requested to see me, captain?"

"No Marcus I demanded to see you," Ardell growled immediately in response, flicking her hair back from her face so she could see the quaking man before her.

She was an attractive woman by anyone's standards, with pale skin, small facial features and a thin yet toned frame. To look at her one would not think she was considered one of the greatest swordsmen of all time. The only blemish on her otherwise flawless face was three jagged scars running down her cheek beneath her left eye.

These could easily be removed by a healer, but for whatever reason, Ardell had seen fit to keep them. This was not an uncommon practice for those who had faced some great danger and lived to talk about it. Yet Ardell did not strike Marcus as that kind of person.

"Yes, Captain, apologies, Captain."

"I care not for your apologies, Marcus. I called you here because I have something I think you can handle for once," Ardell said looking back to her work. "There's no point having you guard the armoury when your skills can be used elsewhere."

"Thank you, Captain," Marcus interrupted.

"Shut up," Ardell snapped back, finally making eye contact. She leaned back in her chair, quill still in hand, pointing it menacingly in Marcus' direction. "Now this is still a punishment for your actions at the inn." She paused for a moment, allowing Marcus' mind to fill with images of a horrific death.

She enjoyed making the men under her command squirm, like a cat playing with its food. "We have a new recruit that I want you to mentor," she said at last. "So, you are going to teach them the way things work around here, and then in six months they will be sent on expeditionary assignments, do you understand?"

Marcus was both relieved and almost a bit disappointed, allowing it to spill out before he had time to think. "Respectfully Captain is there not a dragon you would rather have me slay?" he smirked, before quickly realising this was a terrible mistake when he noticed the look of amusement on Ardell's face. She laughed to herself. Not good. Ardell never laughed.

"You truly are an anomaly, Marcus. The first man I've had under my command I was not able to beat into submission. Life would be so much easier if you just did as you were told."

"Apologies, Captain, I'm sure it'll happen one of these days." Marcus was not sure why he always chose the hardest route, dicing with death at every available opportunity. He just could not help himself.

"Ok Marcus, if you're after a real punishment, I'll give you one," Ardell said throwing up her arms. "Just remember, this is going to hurt me a lot more than it's going to hurt you," she said sarcastically.

Ardell got to her feet and the two stood staring at one another for a moment. Marcus did not dare utter another word, as he was sized up like a turkey about to be carved. Finally, Ardell broke the silence. "Marcus."

"Yes, Captain," he said holding his breath.

"Fetch me my sword." Marcus looked first at her and then the sword which lay only a few meters away.

"Your sword, Captain?" he replied in bewilderment.

"Yes, Marcus my sword. Whenever you feel ready, no rush."

Not wanting to give the captain any more excuse to be angry he hurried across the room, stepping carefully over the clothes which littered the floor until he reached the fireplace. He reached up with his right hand and gripped Oath-Breaker's hilt tightly. For a moment Marcus felt a strange sense of pride.

He wondered how many others had been given the opportunity to hold this famous sword and smiled to himself as he admired its craftsmanship. The hilt was smooth and comfortable to hold, while the blade itself felt almost weightless. But then this thought shifted from the beauty of the sword to what Ardell was going to do with it.

As he tried to lift the sword from its perch, he felt a warm sensation emanating from beneath his hand. It was pleasant at first, like a sudden burst of sunshine on a crisp morning. But it rapidly grew until it felt as if his hand was amid a raging bonfire.

He tried to let go as soon as the heat had become painful but found he could not. The smooth leather binding of the hilt had come loose and had wrapped itself around his hand and wrist. Like a python it refused to let go, continuing to constrict, while the burning sensation intensified.

Before long Marcus' knees buckled and he hung there like some grotesque puppet, screaming in pain as Oath-Breaker refused to let go.

As the burning sensation reached Marcus' shoulder, Ardell slowly made her way over and stood over him. He looked up through tear-filled eyes, still clutching his right arm with his free hand, on the verge of reaching for his sword and cutting it off so severe was the pain.

Ardell lowered herself until she was eye-level with the poor wretch, a cruel smile across her face. "What is your assignment, Marcus?" she whispered mockingly.

"To…to train the new recruit, Captain," Marcus sobbed in response. Satisfied, Ardell reached out, her fingers mere millimetres from the burning leather which had now begun to climb Marcus' neck. They immediately responded to her presence and like a snake, struck out at her.

She quickly pulled her hand away and Marcus fell forward clutching his right side, cold sweat flowing down his back and forehead. The pain, while lingering, but nowhere near as severe, had left him exhausted and gasping for air. He looked up at Ardell, whose eyes were fixed on Oath-Breaker. It had returned to its previous inanimate state, its lust satisfied.

Ardell's face quickly contorted into one of disgust and she turned to face Marcus. "My God man have you pissed yourself?" she said half laughing, half gagging. Marcus wanted to explain that it was Chion's doing but was too exhausted to utter another word, so simply remained silent.

Ardell returned to her seat and began reshuffling her papers. "Get out, there's only so much of you I can stand in a day."

"Yes, Captain," Marcus replied, trying his best to rid the pain and embarrassment from his voice. Just as he was about to close the door behind him, Ardell called after him. "Remember Marcus, six months."

"Yes, Captain."

Marcus left the fort feeling a fool but relieved. He had lived to be terrorised another day. New arrivals were not a rare occurrence, thousands of people travelled to the city every day to serve under Grand Admiral Lee or to seek their fortune. But new arrivals to Purgatory itself were often limited to a few a year.

Training them was usually left to drill instructors and priests; after all, helping them adjust from their old lives to this new one was a delicate task. One Marcus was not sure he was capable of, he was more likely to mentally scar the poor soul than help. But evidently Ardell was determined to make him work for redemption.

Nobody was quite sure why, but those arriving in the city immediately after death all arrived in the same building. The very same building Marcus had found himself in after his own death eighty years earlier. It would take him a few hours to get there by riding but he decided he had best return Joel's horse and make the journey tomorrow. That hopefully would give him enough time to work out exactly what the hell he was going to do.

If he were lucky, this new arrival would be at best already a skilled warrior, at worst, willing and eager to learn.

Chapter 3

This time when Nate awoke there was no blinding light. In fact, there was nothing at all that seemed to indicate he was anywhere out of the ordinary. He found himself in a rather small wooden shack, flimsy and poorly maintained with rotten planks and mould everywhere. Just big enough to maintain about five people, with beds arranged in a row with a small window at each end.

Despite many days' recuperation, he was still exhausted. His muscles ached, and his head was pounding. Even blinking took more energy than he had to spare. A woman sat beside him, lost in a book, and dressed in a long blue robe that collected about her feet. Nate tried to say something to catch her attention, but his throat was dry, and the words came out as a cough. Nevertheless, this was enough for the woman to snap her book shut and quickly turn toward him.

She reached for a small cup filled with water and gently brought it to Nate's lips. With no energy in his arms, he could not take the cup for himself. He gulped the water down like a man lost in the desert, armed with only the memory of a satisfied thirst. He dropped his head back onto his pillow, letting out an appreciative gasp once he was done.

"Is that better?" the woman asked. Nate nodded in response. "Good," she smiled, revealing a set of perfectly white teeth. "My name is Daphne, what's yours?" she asked in a voice soft as silk.

"Nate," he replied with the little energy the water had provided.

"Hi Nate, do you know where you are?" she asked, softly dabbing his sweating head with a cloth.

"No," he replied.

"You will be ok soon; you just need some rest," Daphne cooed, still dabbing his head. She turned to another person who stood by the door whom Nate had not noticed until now. "Tell the quartermaster that we have a new arrival." The other person nodded and left without saying a word.

"What...what's going…?"

"Shhh, just sleep, you'll understand soon enough."

Nate did not bother pressing further, this short conversation had already taken his spare energy and all he wanted now was to heed the call of a deep and dreamless sleep.

Over the next few days, Nate slowly regained his strength. Before long he was able to walk around the shack unaided and was, much to his disappointment, also able to bathe himself without Daphne's assistance. Each day Daphne had returned with hot meals, changes of clothes and any information she thought useful. She had even cut his hair, albeit quite a bit shorter than he was used to.

Daphne had been the first port of call for new arrivals for many years and enjoyed the caregiving aspect of her job. She had discussed with Nate what he remembered being told about Purgatory, without giving away too much information herself too quickly. Adjusting to a new world such as this was a difficult task and Daphne did not want to give Nate more than he could handle. Nate was also forbidden from leaving the shack until further notice. At first, this had not bothered him, as getting regular delicious meals and clean clothes were enough to keep him content.

However, after the fourth day, curiosity and cabin fever started to eat away at him. He could barely sleep at night as he imagined what sort of world lay beyond the flimsy shack door. The windows were thick with dirt on both sides and so impossible to peer through. The only brief glance he had managed was the tiny fraction of the world visible when Daphne opened and closed the shack door, although this has not given much away either. Just a few trees located immediately outside, their foliage blocking any vision of what lay beyond.

It was on the sixth day of his confinement that Daphne arrived bearing good news. She had informed Nate that tomorrow he was to be visited by his new mentor. They would be responsible for guiding him during his initial time in

Purgatory. He had laughed when Daphne had asked whether he had been exercising during his time indoors.

That night Nate lay in bed unable to sleep once more. The woollen shirt he had been provided scratched constantly, although this was but a fraction of the reason for his restlessness. Tomorrow he would see with his own eyes the world that lay beyond. Hundreds of scenarios filled his head, each one more fanciful than the last. Eventually, he fell asleep, his final comforting vision a world where humanity had moved past its differences, actively working together to pay off their spiritual debt.

Marcus looked down at the sprawling mess before him. Nate lay fast asleep, one of his legs sticking out over the edge of the bed. The thin blankets were in a pile on the floor and the pillow resting upon his head. It was six in the morning, and most of the city had been awake for two hours. Immediately Marcus knew it was going to take all the patience he had just not to kill the poor sod, let alone train him.

"Oi, c'mon," he said, giving Nate's overhanging leg a nudge. Nate let out a series of unintelligible grunts as he turned over, still unconscious. Marcus rubbed his eyes with his thumb and forefinger and let out a frustrated sigh. His patience wearing thin, he walked over to the opposite side of the bed. Taking hold of the frame he quickly upended it, sending a confused Nate tumbling to the floor.

"What the hell?" Nate exclaimed as he scrambled to his feet. Although, upon seeing the Roman legionary who had so rudely awoken him, he quickly adopted a more conciliatory stance. Nate was by no means short, but Marcus towered over him, nonetheless. His muscles seemed to be barely contained by his thick steel armour. In complete contrast to Nate who, even with help, probably could not have lifted the bed as the legionary had just done.

"Can I help you?" Nate asked warily, not sure of the heavily armed man's intention. Marcus stepped forward and begrudgingly extended his hand.

"The name's Marcus; I've been assigned as your mentor."

"Nate," he replied, gingerly shaking Marcus' hand. His grip was like a vice and in less than a second Nate's hand had lost all sensation.

At last, much to Nate's relief Marcus released him and beckoned towards the door. "I suppose we had best get started," he said, already exhausted from the thought of the conversation he was about to have. As Nate pulled hard on the handle, filled with excitement to at last reveal the world beyond the bleak, rotten one he had come to know for the past week, Marcus' huge palm slammed the door shut once more. Nate looked up with confusion and betrayal.

"What do you know of the outside world?" Marcus asked. Nate's answer would greatly affect what level of pain in the arse this assignment would start with.

"Absolutely nothing," Nate replied. Marcus hung his head; he had hoped Daphne would have saved him at least some of the trouble he was about to go through. Removing his hand from the door he gestured for Nate to continue. Finally, Nate threw the door open and found that all the daydreaming in the world could not have prepared him for this.

Before him lay a sprawling city of unimaginable proportions stretching as far as the eye could see. Countless densely packed buildings, some relatively small and wooden, others huge stone towering monstrosities, filled the landscape. Surrounding this city were stone walls so tall and vast they looked as if the earth itself had risen to offer protection to the people below. Cutting through this landscape of urban sprawl ran glistening rivers of sapphire water, while on its flanks were wide green spaces full of meadows of colourful flowers and patches of woodland.

The most magnificent sight, however, was what at first appeared to be a mountain so massive and imposing that much of the surrounding area was perpetually blanketed by its shadow. Yet it soon became clear that it was no work of nature. A shapeless base of dull grey stone gave way to a brilliant mixture of white marble and glass which shone with the brilliance of a star. From it rose nine great spires, some as straight as arrows, others twisting and spiralling like warring snakes until at last they pierced the clouds like the points of a radiant crown. Nate could not imagine the time or effort it had taken to build such a feat of engineering.

"Where the hell are we?" he gasped squinting into the distance to see where the city ended. Marcus could not help but be swept up in Nate's wonder. Too often he allowed himself to get distracted by duties and his own interests. He rarely now took a moment to marvel at the world the gods had created and what man had built. In his heart, Rome was still home, but even he had to admit Rome was little more than a barbarian's pig pen in comparison.

"Tinelia," He replied, his arms folded, a slight smile on his face as he too took in the sight. "Named after our founding queen."

The two stood there for a moment just admiring the view before Marcus decided they had better get on with the task at hand. Nate had a lot to learn and only a short time to do so.

Nearby there was a bench, strategically situated for this exact situation. It was surrounded by rose bushes and offered an excellent view of the city. Marcus beckoned Nate to sit, but having done nothing for a week, all Nate wanted to do was stretch his legs, taking in the magnificent sight before him. With some coaxing, he took his seat but could not keep his eyes away from the view, everywhere he looked there was something new which defied belief.

Nate understood perfectly well that he was dead and in Purgatory, a fact Marcus was more than thankful for as it saved plenty of time. Over the course of the next few hours, with the bustling city below them, Marcus went over everything he thought Nate could possibly need to know. Everything he had been able to think of on the journey here anyway. It had been a long time since he had needed to consider the novelties of this new un-life.

Nate had taken quite a lot of things well; in fact, he quite enjoyed the notion that there was no ageing or reproduction in Purgatory. What he found hardest to wrap his head around, was what Marcus described as *alternate worlds*. After much questioning and contemplating, Nate mostly understood what Marcus was alluding to.

There seemed to be, at least to Nate's understanding, more than one version of history he knew to be correct. People from these *alternate worlds* were no different from himself but had simply lived in a different version of the world he knew, where history had taken another course. This was made clearest when Marcus had explained that he had only died roughly eighty years ago, at what he claimed was the height of the Roman Empire. To Nate of course, that had been nearly two thousand years prior in his own world.

And yet, this was not the most surprising of all that Marcus had to reveal. This honour was held for how Nate was expected to atone for his sins and eventually, get the hell out of Purgatory. Reaching for a small leather purse hanging from his hip by a delicate yellow string, Marcus produced a single golden coin and tossed it to Nate to inspect. On one side was an image of an angel, its wings outspread and its head facing skywards. On the other, a skull. After spending some time examining the coin Nate tossed it back, still none the wiser. "So, what, we have to pay our way out?" he said jokingly.

"Exactly," Marcus replied putting the coin back into his purse. It was not the response Nate had expected and he could not help but wonder which eccentric billionaire had bought up his spiritual debt.

"Ok how exactly does that work? I don't even know how many sins I committed."

Marcus tilted his head and raised his hand in acknowledgement of how ridiculous this whole situation was. "That's the hard part," he replied, "I don't want to dishearten you, but frankly I've never heard of anyone getting out."

"Getting out?" Nate asked.

"Moving on," Marcus clarified. Nate's eyes widened, a stunned silence overcoming him. Marcus knew it was a bitter truth perhaps better left unsaid. But remembering his own foolish optimism when he'd first arrived, only to be dashed after many years, he knew it was best Nate know now.

Such a devastating revelation made Nate feel like he had been hit by a train, which was ironic really. He did not know why, but he had expected this whole experience to be like some long seminary course. Months of praying and self-reflection ended with getting his dog collar and halo. Clearly, it was not that easy. If Marcus was still kicking around after eighty years, how long was it going to take for him to make up for his sins?

At first, Nate wanted to be upset – however, he knew this would do him no good. Reining in the negative emotions welling up within him, he made the conscious choice to be positive. After all, he was in a new world full of infinite possibilities, there was plenty to be excited about.

"Ok, so what is the best way to make money around here?" he asked. Marcus responded with a mischievous smile.

"Believe me, that's the only fun part about being in this world, but right now we should probably focus on more pressing matters." Nate was confused, what could possibly be more important than getting out of Purgatory as fast as possible? The sun was beginning to fade, like a dying fire casting an orange glow over the city, and nightfall would not be far behind. A cold wind made its way through the rustling rosebush, prompting Marcus to shiver and draw his cloak around him.

Nate, against his better judgment, looked at the dimming sun, perplexed. Despite them having sat there for many hours, the sun had not moved an inch across the sky. Yet still, it was getting dark. However, he stopped himself before asking a question he was sure would have an even less plausible answer.

"Do you have any questions?" Marcus asked. Nate looked back at the walls stretching off into the horizon. While they were tall and vast, their current hilltop position allowed him glimpses of further sets of walls both far into the distance ahead of them, and in the opposite direction towards the colossal fortress.

"What is this place?"

"Ah well," Marcus began, glad for a question he could fully answer. "That," Marcus said pointing at the gleaming fortress, "is the Citadel. It houses the Grand Admiral and other lords and knights. Basically, just all the rich and important people live there. The wall closest behind us (which even then was many miles away) separates us from the Warrens. We call it that because it's the most heavily populated part of the city.

"The level we are currently standing in is commonly referred to as the Vanguard. This is where you'll find most soldiers to be stationed. There are two levels further out from here. The Breadbasket we call them; they provide us with all our food. Last time I checked, I think there were over one hundred million people living here".

"Bloody hell," Nate gasped.

"It takes some getting used to, but after a few months, you will be dying to get out of this shithole just like the rest of us." Marcus smiled.

The sun had almost entirely faded, and it was almost dark. Nate pointed at it, unable to simply ignore it any longer. "Is that anything to be concerned about?" he asked. Marcus had become so used to this place he had almost forgotten how a real sun behaved. Indeed, he had spent more time staring up at this sky than the one in his own world.

"No that's totally normal," he shrugged. "From what we have gathered, this world has no end, so we simply get a set amount of daylight and then a set amount of darkness. It also depends on the season; I suppose it was designed that way to make us feel more at home than we really are."

Surprisingly, this made relatively more sense to Nate, well at least more than anything else discussed thus far. "Fair enough," was his response. He would be fooling nobody if he said he would miss the sunrise; he had never seen one in his life. Too busy sleeping in late, although the idea that he would never see the sunset again played on his mind. Something he had taken for granted as a certainty was now an impossibility. The idea that such a vital part of his own world was not present in this one made him uneasy, as he questioned all he had ever considered to be certain.

While he certainly had a much better idea of life in Purgatory than a few hours ago, there were still plenty of questions Nate wished to ask. However, Marcus was growing tired. It had been a stressful day for him also, the weight of this new responsibility already bearing heavily upon his shoulders. He knew when he first saw Nate's thin, chicken-like legs that he would have his work cut out for him.

Marcus swung his own muscular legs around and hopped off the bench, straightening his back causing it to produce several sickening cracks as the air pockets in his spine burst. "I think we have both had enough excitement for today, let's get some food and we can talk more," he said, his stomach rumbling in agreement.

Nate did not argue. It was cold now, and the prospect of a warm room and food sounded very appealing. The pair made their way down the steep steps cut into the hill and headed into the city. While Marcus had said that the Warrens were the most heavily populated level, the Vanguard was still crowded with shops and houses. The further into the city they went, the more extravagant the buildings became.

However, that is not to say that those on the outskirts were not impressive. No matter where he looked, Nate could not find a building fewer than three storeys high. The wooden structures were not uniform in their design either, each being unique. Some had twisting towers that jutted out from the sides, others were lopsided, their sheer height and weight fighting the forces of gravity. They loomed over the streets below like a twisted canopy.

The Vanguard, like most of Tinelia, had no centre due to its ringed shape. This had resulted in its outer edges being densely packed with buildings which hugged the walls to the upper and lower levels, whereas the long strip separating the two had been mostly left undisturbed, resulting in almost two entirely independent cities separated by a sea of green.

As they entered the city closest to the lower level, Nate marvelled at his surroundings. The more impressive stone buildings were usually found closest to the commercial areas. They were far larger than their wooden counterparts and many were ornately decorated with banners and flowers. Some had balconies that looked out onto the streets and there were more than a few with finely carved columns and archways.

The disparity between the rich and poor was put on display for all to see; the only shared aspect between them seemed to be the wide chimneys that bellowed thick plumes of smoke, leaving a gloomy haze hanging over the city. The streets were silent now, most shops had closed, and everyone was either already home or heading that way.

As they walked Marcus carried on explaining the more elaborate details of life in Tinelia. He started by trying to explain the tax system but gave up after realising the more he thought about it, the less sense it made. He then switched over to politics. Tinelia had been a military dictatorship for some five thousand years. New rulers were elected upon the death of the previous one, chosen from among the surviving members of their founder's original company. Now, however, only one remained, Grand Admiral Lee. From the way Marcus talked about him, it was clear he held his leader in high regard.

Despite Marcus' effort, Nate was only half-listening, his head was spinning. Trying to take everything in at once was just too much. He had held it together this long, but constantly being bombarded with information which made little sense to him, in a world which made even less sense was chipping away at his resilience.

He had not asked for any of this, he just wanted to be back in his house watching stupid TV, not traipsing round some fairy-tale land with a Roman legionary. But this was his life now, there was no house in the English countryside waiting for him anymore, no more TV. He raised his hand to his face and pressed his palm against his forehead, trying desperately to push all these unhelpful thoughts from his mind. Marcus stopped walking and looked at him. "Are you alright?" he asked, the concern in his voice genuine.

Nate stopped walking too, and just a few paces ahead of Marcus he sank onto the floor, his head between his legs, leaning against the wall of one of the many wooden houses. His earlier eagerness and confidence had vanished entirely.

Instead, he felt a stranger in his own skin, part of a world he did not recognise nor belong in. A world he had quickly learned, there was little chance of escaping. "I can't do this," he whimpered, trying his best to hold back tears.

Marcus had all the sympathy in the world for this boy – he too had once been in the same position. He approached and sank down onto one knee, the wet mud of the dirt road churned up by thousands of feet squelching as he did so.

"I know it's a lot to take in, and honestly, I wish I could just tell you that it's all going to be easy and if you don't like it here, I can just send you back where you came from. But that's not the case." Nate did not look up as Marcus spoke, he kept his head between his legs, so he could not see the tears running down his face.

Marcus continued, "The best advice I can give you, that anyone can give you, is to accept the way things are and move on. Things will never be the same as they were, but you can make a good life for yourself here and hopefully one day move on for good."

It had begun to rain slightly in the time the men had stopped. The only sound now came from the raindrops bouncing off Marcus' armour and the rooftops.

Still with his head between his legs Nate could see the mud beneath him become saturated and shapeless, oozing its way into his clothes and onto his skin. Suddenly he was uplifted by a great force until he was standing once more. The force had been Marcus, lifting Nate as if he weighed nothing.

"You're a good kid," Marcus said with a caring smile, "Let us get out of this rain and put some hot food into our bellies, I promise you'll feel better after that."

Nate nodded but did not speak; he did not feel up to eating anymore, but if he was stuck in Purgatory, he would prefer it be out of the rain. The two men continued along the street until they rounded a corner and directly ahead of them was the inn.

"It's the most popular place for scum like us," Marcus said without any hint of a joke. "So, prepare to see a lot of even stranger things than you have already," he continued, giving Nate a friendly slap on the back.

The inn was a huge four-storey wooden building, well maintained and sturdy, in stark contrast to most of the other bleak wooden houses and shops that seemed to be preparing for collapse. The inn looked to be very lively, both inside and out. Its large front garden was full of statuettes and rows of colourful flowers which seemed even more radiant against the bleak brown backdrop of the city. From the space above the doors hung a sign: '*The Hovel*'.

Inside, Nate could see shadows of people drinking and laughing through the windows on each floor. As they approached the inn's large wooden doors, Nate suddenly realised he had no money. He still had his wallet containing a few soggy five-pound notes but doubted they would be any good here.

"Don't worry," Marcus said sensing his companion's sudden realisation. "I'll pay for tonight."

Nate had been in plenty of bars before, usually in desperate attempts to pick up a girl, none of which had ever been successful. But this was like nowhere he had ever seen; hundreds of people filled each floor. Laughing, drinking, arguing, telling stories, and sitting by the huge fire pit in the centre of the ground floor, on which an entire pig was roasting.

The two had to almost fight their way to the bar. The building was huge, but even then, it could barely cope with the sheer number of bodies crammed within, all trying to find somewhere they could drink in peace. After much-concentrated effort, Marcus and Nate finally reached the bar and sat down on two wooden stools which by some miracle were empty.

While Marcus ordered two flagons of mead Nate surveyed the people around him. There was a group of four men who stood in the corner closest to him, dressed in traditional Japanese karuta, laughing over their drinks. Around the fire pit was a woman wearing a chainmail shirt and leather greaves over some green trousers with a crossbow resting on her lap. She was speaking with a man dressed in what seemed to be a friar's robe.

"Here you go," Marcus shouted over the hundreds of other voices, passing Nate his drink.

"Thanks, how much do I owe you?" Nate shouted back; Marcus laughed.

"Nothing today my friend but don't expect me to be paying for all of them in the future." Marcus took a huge gulp of his drink, with some spilling down his chin and onto his armour. Nate took a small sip and began to violently splutter and cough as the sweet yet strong liquid passed his lips. Marcus laughed and slapped Nate hard on the back. "Don't worry lad you'll get used to it." As Marcus carried on drinking, Nate continued to survey the room.

Looking upwards he could make out some of the people on the second and third floors as they leaned over the balconies, all with drinks in hand. Almost all were dressed as if going off to battle. Only the occasional one or two wore anything that even remotely resembled the kind of clothes Nate was used to. One man had a sword taller than he was, strapped across his back, while another wore a bandolier filled to the brim with knives.

Just what had Nate got himself into? Before he could begin to think of an answer, there was a tap on his shoulder, and turning around he was met by the smiling bartender. He looked to be in his early thirties, with long brown hair and dull grey eyes. His smile revealed yellow and broken teeth.

"Not seen you around here before, where you from?" the bartender asked. Marcus turned and replied before Nate could give an answer.

"He's fresh." The bartender at first gave a look of mild surprise, recoiling slightly and then offered Nate a hand.

"The name's Pedan, pleased to meet you." Nate took the hand and shook it.

"Nate," he replied. Pedan quickly turned his attention to Marcus.

"What are you doing with some newbie following you around?"

Marcus took a final gulp of his mead and tossed the mug back at the unphased barkeep who immediately began refilling it without averting his gaze.

"Captain's orders, I'm showing him the ropes."

Pedan slid the newly filled mug across the bar before addressing Nate.

"You're in luck my lad, not many more capable souls around than Marcus here, you're in good hands." Nate examined Marcus with renewed uncertainty. If Pedan had found his presence around Marcus strange, there was clearly something unusual going on.

"Have you had many apprentices before?" Nate asked, hoping this innocent question would not make clear his suspicion. There was a stifled choke from Marcus while Pedan laughed, slapping the bar with the palm of his hand. The jig was up.

"So, this isn't how things usually work then," Nate said as more of a statement than a question. It was hardly surprising when he thought about it. What sort of mentor takes their new apprentice straight to a pub? Marcus leaned on the bar and sighed. He had hoped to keep the ruse going for a few weeks at the very least.

"Not really," he replied at last after a long pause. "Usually, you get handed off to the priests or priestesses who help you adjust to this world. Captain decided I should train you up as a soldier myself."

Nate's ears suddenly pricked up; this was the first time anyone had mentioned the word '*soldier*'. What good were soldiers in Purgatory anyway?

"I'm confused," he admitted with a now pounding heart. "You never said anything about me being a soldier, I thought…" Nate stopped. In truth, he had no idea what he had expected, but being conscripted had not been high on the list.

Marcus was feeling increasingly awkward, and his ears had begun to burn a hot red. Nate shook his head and collected his thoughts. First things first. "So why are you my mentor exactly?" he asked, his suspicions now confirmed. Although it was Pedan who answered.

"Sounds to me like you upset the captain…again," he said, directing a smirk in Marcus' direction.

"I suppose you could put it that way," he conceded.

"Oh, fuck me." Nate despaired as he dropped his head into his hands. It hardly seemed fair that he was being punished for Marcus' mistake. He was no warrior; he could barely summon the courage to kill spiders. The thought of him being capable of anything other than dying immediately in battle was laughable.

Marcus was silent for a moment, studying Nate's reaction. It was clear training him would be an almost pointless task. However, maybe that *was* the point. He tried to console Nate with a gentle pat on the back, but Nate jumped from his seat and stormed out of the inn without a word.

"Off to a good start," Pedan said sarcastically as he wiped a mug with a filthy rag.

In the short time Nate had been inside, the temperature outside had dropped considerably. He stood with his arms wrapped around his torso, kicking at the ground as his frustrated breaths curled upwards into the sky.

He had not expected Purgatory to be fun, but this was just taking the piss. He looked up at the sky to see the sun had been replaced by a moon of pure white, its light gentle and soothing. The rest of the sky was set with an innumerable number of stars in a fantastic array of colours. Like the sparkling spray of the sea on a hot day, they filled the cosmos with their defiant light against the surrounding emptiness.

Had he not been so busy wallowing in self-pity, Nate would have been awestruck by its beauty. He looked around at the deserted streets, the imposing figure of the Citadel towering above him even at this distance. He thought back to all the books and television shows he had enjoyed back in his old life. He had always wished he could have lived in a more exciting world full of dragons and epic quests. Now that his wish had somewhat come true, he wanted nothing more than an escape.

The sound of laughter and chatter filled the air as the door to the inn swung open and Marcus emerged. He had two small objects in his hands, wrapped in cloth, steam fighting their way from beneath. Nate instantly recognised the smell of fresh pastry and his stomach grumbled violently in response. Marcus threw one his way, Nate caught it and without even a thank you, pulled back the cloth to find a comfortingly familiar sight. What looked like a perfect Cornish pasty stared back at him, begging to be eaten.

Without hesitation, he tore into it with his teeth and groaned with delight. Unable to place a single ingredient, he did not care. The sweetness of the vegetables mixed with the juicy tenderness of the meat dispelled any concern as to what any of it was. It was without a doubt the best pasty he had ever eaten. Marcus joined him in his feast and the two sat silently on the ground, resting their backs against a signpost in the centre of the street. Their meal lasted but moments, despite its searing heat burning both of their mouths. Marcus was busy licking his fingers clean when Nate spoke up.

"I'm sorry I lost my temper in there," he apologised. Marcus let out a sigh, his breath rising like a geyser into the night sky.

"It's my fault," he began. Marcus felt genuine guilt for his role in his companion's fate. Had it not been for him, Nate would probably be training as a clerk or some sort of official's assistant. He certainly did not have the look of a fighter, and, not for the first time, Marcus questioned his captain's judgement. This seemed more punishment for Nate than for him, and he saw no benefit in sending a good man to his certain death.

"I admit you don't strike me as the soldier type, but there is nothing we can do about it now. The captain is not known for changing her mind," Marcus admitted. Nate could not help but see the funny side, even despite the sense of dread clawing at him from within.

"I've never been in a fight in my life," he chuckled. Marcus smiled as he picked at the grass beneath him. He could try and console Nate with comforting words, but they would be lies, and Marcus was not in the habit of lying to those he had wronged. He also knew that in the long run, they would do more harm than good. The sooner Nate understood the world he lived in and what was expected of him, the easier he would find it.

Luckily, Nate was not entirely stupid. He knew that he was in no position to demand or barter for an alternate arrangement that better suited his skills. He would have to just roll with the punches, no matter how hard they came. He was just glad he had a friend to show him the way, even if that friend was only being ordered to do so.

"We should probably head off." Marcus groaned as he got to his feet and stretched his arms above his head. Nate nodded in agreement and climbed to his feet also.

"One last thing," Marcus said before they set off. "Tomorrow we will be starting your training, there's no point in postponing it any further, we have already lost a week. Once we are finished, we need to go to the bank. It's probably the most important building in the city, and we need to get you acquainted with it. So, make sure you are up early."

"I'm not really a morning person, can't we start after lunch?" Nate asked. Marcus answered with a groan and led his new companion back home.

Chapter 4

Nate awoke the next morning with a start as Marcus banged on the door with a clenched fist. "I swear by all the gods you had better be awake," he shouted. Rubbing the sleep from his eyes Nate rolled out of bed as Marcus made his way inside.

"What time do you call this?" Nate asked,.The sun was barely a glimmer in the sky and Marcus had already made the hours-long trip across the city.

"Time you were properly dressed and ready for the day," Marcus scolded. He could not help but be slightly repulsed at Nate's poor timekeeping or sense of duty. He would not have lasted a single day in the Legion. Nate quickly grabbed a washcloth and dipped it in the bowl of water which had been placed by his bedside the day before. Quickly washing his face and underarms he put on his clothes and made his way outside; it was raining slightly and there was a cold wind in the air that bit through Nate's thin shirt.

"God, it's freezing," he shivered.

"Yes, you'll need some better clothes," Marcus stated looking at Nate's woollen shirt, thin trousers, and brown pumps, all of which were already close to being soaked through. "I'm sure I can find you something that will fit."

Nate shivered the whole way down the hill and across the empty grassland between his home and the city as the pair made their way to the training ground.

This was the first time Nate had experienced the Vanguard during its waking hours and it surpassed all his expectations. Thousands of people packed the wide dirt streets; merchants stood by their wooden stalls bellowing for potential customers, and the clanging of blacksmiths' hammers rang out like the tolling of great bells. Overhead the hazy blanket of smoke from countless hearths was already thick, from which came the shrieks and black shapes of gulls searching for an easy meal. Flanking them on both sides were the tall, misshapen dwellings in which most of the Vanguard lived; uninviting and bleak, they bent over them like the victims of a foul sickness.

Turning his eyes from the structures to the people around him, it was soon impossible for Nate to ignore that virtually everyone was armed, from the loose columns of soldiers who hurriedly marched past carrying huge greatswords and spears, to the humble merchants who watched over their stalls with swords or axes at their sides. Even the prostitutes who were already hard at work soliciting potential clients had daggers visibly strapped to their thighs.

Nate could not help but wonder whether all these displays of willing lethality were necessary, and, if so, whether he would be expected to do the same. As the two men weaved through the throngs of people lining the streets, they passed a group dressed in dark leather smattered with green, evidently some form of camouflage. Either at their sides or slung around their shoulders rested a mix of long and shortbows. Speaking loudly, Nate could not help but overhear their conversation.

"These Ugars are a real pain in the arse," one man exclaimed. Immediately the woman beside him spoke up.

"I heard they slipped right past a patrol and nearly wiped out a hamlet." The rest of the group gave one another looks of concern and silently cursed their luck.

"Well, the captain wants them taken care of, so we had better get a move on," another said. The others all reluctantly agreed, and the party began moving out, all of them making some sort of adjustment to their bows as they walked.

After an hour of traversing the busy streets and glancing through shop windows at beautifully ornate armour and weapons, they arrived at the training ground. Roughly a mile from the more commercial and built-up areas, it was an open space with a two-storey wooden barracks. At one end about one hundred meters from the barracks were a set of ten round, straw archery targets, along with another three human-shaped ones.

Just a few meters outside the barrack's door was a raised circular platform. Weapon racks on two opposing ends contained various swords, hammers, and battle axes. At the far end, opposite the archery targets, was a long set of stables from which Nate could hear the whinnies and crying of numerous horses.

It was still very early. Nate guessed that it must only just be dawn and yet the world was already bursting with life.

"Go choose yourself a weapon," Marcus said pointing towards the raised platform. Nate obeyed and still shivering, walked over to the weapon rack closest to him and inspected the selection on offer. Marcus, meanwhile, made his way into the barracks.

Nate thought for a moment before rather optimistically attempting to pick up a Warhammer. One end of the head was a flat square and the other a downwards facing spike. It had not looked particularly heavy but once removed from the rack it took all of Nate's strength not to be dragged down through the earth with it. Having made it this far he pretended to inspect it before struggling to put it back with an exasperated grunt.

He quickly concluded that he was more of a sword type of guy and picked one which stood next to an ugly looking mace. It was not pretty but it was light. With a wooden handle and thin blade for piercing, it was thick enough to not be weak, and it seemed like it could still inflict serious damage if used for slashing.

Just as Nate made his decision Marcus reappeared holding a full set of leather armour. "You're in luck, put these on," he said, dropping the various components into Nate's arms, "then get in the ring." While Nate struggled with the various straps and buckles, Marcus stepped onto the platform and began stretching and slowly slashing at the air with his sword. Finally, Nate managed to get his armour on and made his way after Marcus with the sword he had selected. Seeing the nervousness on his face Marcus attempted to reassure him. "Don't worry, I won't hurt you, so give me everything you've got."

Nate had made clear his lack of fighting experience; nevertheless, he was determined to show Marcus that he could be ferocious when he had to be. So, he charged at him as fast as he could and swung his sword wildly, aiming for the head.

His opponent, however, did not flinch, instead, he swung his own sword at Nate's, knocking it from his hand. The force of the blow caused Nate to change direction and go flying off the platform into the mud below.

Suffering no injuries other than to his ego, he quickly pulled himself up. Wiping the dirt from his eyes, he retrieved his sword which had landed a few feet away. Making his way back up the steps onto the platform, Marcus was waiting. Without saying a word Nate charged again; however, this time he tried to be more intelligent with his movements, and zigzagged as he ran, hoping to confuse his foe.

It did not work.

By the time Nate reached the other end of the platform he was out of breath, and he raised his sword over his head with both hands hoping to strike Marcus once again on the head. There was no need to worry about Nate's sword; instead, Marcus focused on the fact that he had left his entire body open. He quickly brought his sword to Nate's stomach in a thrusting motion. Again, the force of the blow was so strong it sent Nate crashing to the ground.

"If this was sharp you would be picking your guts up off the floor." Marcus scolded as Nate writhed around, the breath knocked out of him.

"Great, thanks," Nate wheezed, slowly getting to his feet. Marcus walked over to where Nate stood, doubled over, gasping for air. It was clear he would have to start with the most basic of concepts before Nate could even be considered a novice with a weapon.

"Try to hit me without leaving yourself open, but don't come swinging like a madman, and don't do that zigzag nonsense either. Just take your time, look for weaknesses and strike quickly but hard, and always keep one eye on my sword, got it?"

Nate was more focused on desperately trying to get oxygen to his brain than listening to Marcus' advice. "Yeah…Sure…Great," he coughed finally getting his breath back. "I was always more of a lover than a fighter anyway." Marcus smiled and raised an amused eyebrow.

"Is that so?" he scoffed.

"Not really, no," Nate said with a grin.

"In that case, let's get back to it," Marcus ordered as he returned to his previous position at the far end of the platform. Nate held his sword out in front of him, clasping it tightly in both hands. This time he approached Marcus slowly, determined not to make any more of a fool of himself.

Hours passed and it was midday by the time Marcus finally called for a break. Nate was exhausted; thankfully the rain had stopped a few hours previously, although now his armour was fused to his skin by a layer of sweat. His whole body ached from the ferocity of the training and begged for rest. Marcus jumped off the platform and walked over to a pump beside the barracks. Sparkling, fresh water gushed out which he first splashed onto his face and then the back of his neck. He then placed his head directly underneath the nozzle and drank his fill.

Nate quickly followed suit and once both men were adequately hydrated, they lay on the grass breathing heavily from their hours of exertion.

"Right, swords are all very well and good, but you will need to learn how to fight from a distance if you want to survive more than five minutes. Have you ever used a bow before?" Marcus finally groaned as he pulled himself up and stood over Nate.

"Not even once," Nate sighed, begrudgingly getting to his feet. He started undoing the straps on his breastplate until Marcus quickly placed a hand in the way. "Leave it on," he said.

"But I'm dying in this thing, I feel like I'm on the inside of a cow," Nate protested.

"You're going to need to get used to it." Marcus pointed towards the wall which separated them from the outside world. "When you're out there you're in danger every second of every day. You'll be out there for weeks, even months at a time. You'll eat, sleep and bathe in your armour so it needs to become your second skin." Nate nodded and decided to change the topic from the unimaginable horrors that lay in wait for him.

"Tell me more about the world outside the city, are there other cities or countries, or is this all there is?" he asked. Marcus shook his head.

"Oh no, there are countless cities and towns spread all across Gaia, you just happened to turn up in this one," Marcus explained as they walked over to a rack which held four wooden longbows. They were situated underneath an outstretched section of the roof of the barracks so they could be kept dry.

"What's Gaia?" Nate asked, puzzled as he took the longbow from Marcus' outstretched arm. Marcus laughed as he took a bow for himself.

"It's just the name we gave the world we live in. Can hardly call it Earth, can we? Gaia seems more appropriate." Marcus nocked an arrow onto his bow and took aim at the target. The arrows were blunt and perfect for training but would be useless at penetrating armour.

Marcus released his arrow and watched it sail fifty meters to the target and thud into the red area near the centre. Nate scoured his brain back to the conversation the pair had had on the bench the previous day but remembered discussing nothing about Purgatory's physical attributes, only concepts which now either did or did not apply. Nate nocked his arrow and drew the string to his lips. With all that was going on, he was lucky he could remember his own name at this point.

"Good posture, just raise your elbow slightly," Marcus said, praising his apprentice's apparent innate handling of a bow. Nate could hardly believe how much strength it took just to hold back a piece of string. He could feel his muscles straining to keep the bow steady and he released the arrow before his arms gave in. Both men watched in astonishment as it flew almost perfectly into the centre, although Marcus did his best to conceal his surprise.

"Not bad, but you're going to need to learn to shoot from much further. Believe me when I say there are things out there you don't want any closer to you than this," he warned. The pair moved another twenty meters back and readied their arrows again.

"Wait." Nate paused, lowering his bow. "What do you mean '*things*'?" he asked, not at all liking the way Marcus had chosen his words. Again, Marcus released his arrow, which flew straight for a few seconds, before wobbling heavily, eventually hitting the inner blue area of the target. Realising he would need to have this conversation sooner or later, Marcus let out a long breath, wondering how to even begin.

Perhaps he should start with the fact that Purgatory was filled to the brim with horrific monsters and creatures from other worlds, not just people. Maybe then he would casually inform Nate that these monsters were a constant existential threat that he would be expected to hunt and kill after his meagre six months of training. Naturally of course Marcus would then end with the coup de grace, that monster hunting was the bedrock of the economy, and apparently, the only way to earn the currency which would get them into paradise.

Yes, that should go down fine.

At first, Nate refused to believe him, certain he was joking. That is until Marcus went into detail, far too great a detail for a joke. Nate stood still for a moment silently as he added this new information to the backlog of worries he had yet to lose sleep over. But then, curiously and with an unexpected air of indifference, Nate spoke.

"For future reference, perhaps you might want to lead with that the next time you have to mentor somebody". He raised his bow once more and took aim. He tried his best to concentrate on the target and the rapidly growing weight of the bow. He once again set his arrow free. It flew perfectly straight and thudded in the central gold zone.

This apparent shrugging off of such a monumental revelation surprised them both. Marcus wondered if perhaps Nate came from a world already inhabited by nightmarish creatures. And for Nate, maybe, just maybe, Marcus was still joking. Glad the conversation had gone down so well, Marcus turned back to his mentoring.

He was beginning to be impressed, but he knew that it would take more than a natural skill at archery for Nate to be able to survive outside the walls of the city. The men walked another eighty meters to the stables as a light rain began to fall once again. Squinting at the targets one hundred and fifty meters away, Marcus raised his bow as Nate began his usual annoying questioning for which Marcus never had a decent answer.

"I have to say, it doesn't make much sense to me. I mean, aren't we all here to make up for our sins, how does killing achieve that?" Nate had raised a valid point; one Marcus admittedly had considered on many an occasion. He lowered his bow and furrowed his brow as he tried to think of an answer – perhaps this time he would have a breakthrough. Alas, no great epiphany came, and he steadied his bow, letting out a laugh behind which hid deep discontent.

"No bloody idea." This left Nate feeling hollow and unsatisfied. To him at least, the idea of killing seemed totally contrary to their mission of repentance. But if such a blatant diversion from logic did not seem to bother Marcus, Nate decided to let it go for now. He had more immediate concerns anyway, like the sudden existence of bloodthirsty monsters that would rip him limb from limb.

He decided to change the subject and looked out towards the huge stone wall which separated him from the lower levels and, eventually, the outside world.

"So, when exactly will I be going out there?" he asked, the fear in his voice evident.

"It won't be for six months yet, Captain Ardell wants you adequately trained first. That's what I'm here for," Marcus replied as he drew back the string and focused on the target.

"And here I thought you just enjoyed my wonderful conversation and sense of humour," Nate joked as Marcus released his arrow. It flew straight for the first ninety meters but then wobbled and dipped, penetrating the ground a good fifty meters from its target.

"So, who is this Captain Ardell?" Nate inquired as he drew his bow and took aim.

"Well, if you're lucky, you'll never meet her," Marcus replied, deadly serious. "You're aiming far too high" he scoffed, "you will kill Sol himself." Nate was silent as he aimed, he stopped breathing and allowed his heartbeat to slow as the wind kissed his cheek gently. Then he released, and the arrow flew high and straight. Marcus gasped as he watched the arrow pierce the air.

While the arrow seemed to fly far off course with no hope of ever hitting its target, suddenly, its direction changed. It dipped heavily as the rain which had once again resumed, pushed it downwards and the wind nudged it to the right. With wide eyes, both men watched as it thudded triumphantly into the red zone of the target. "Gods," Marcus gasped, "you're a natural."

"Beginner's luck," Nate sniffed, wiping away a raindrop hanging from his nose, a grin etched across his face. Marcus was genuinely impressed, but Nate still had a long way to go before he was ready for a real fight.

"Ok, so you can shoot, but you swing a sword like a blind man in an earthquake." Marcus took the bow from Nate's hand and walked back over to the rack where they had found them. Nate could not help but feel put out by Marcus' critique.

"C'mon, I think I'm doing pretty well considering it's my first day and all." Marcus let out a frustrated sigh. It was true, for someone who had never fought a day in his life, Nate was learning extremely quickly. The issue was even if Marcus had double the time permitted, Nate would still not be up to Ardell's standard. He had no choice but to be ruthless, otherwise, Nate had no hope of surviving whatsoever. And that would just be with his first encounter with the captain, let alone outside the city.

Nevertheless, a small dose of encouragement could work wonders, and so Marcus gave Nate a smile as he returned from the bow rack. "You're doing well, but we need to up the pace, back in the ring." Marcus pointed towards the platform where they had been practising their swordplay.

"You're joking?" Nate despaired. "We've been doing this all day." Marcus could not help but give a taunting smirk.

"The day has barely started my boy, we will be doing this until nightfall, so pace yourself." He climbed the steps onto the platform with Nate following close behind. With aching legs, Nate took his previous spot and drew his sword. Marcus reached his end of the platform and drew his own.

"Ok, but I won't go easy on you this time." Nate groaned as he stretched his arms above his head.

After another intense six hours of training, Nate was certain he was going to die. Marcus had only allowed two breaks for water, claiming that in the middle of a battle nobody was going to stop just because you were tired and needed a lie-down.

Unable to keep himself up any longer Nate fell face-first into the grass beside the water pump while Marcus used it to fill two small metal bowls. Only just able to open his eyes as Marcus handed him the water, Nate noticed that his friend was not even out of breath, despite the scorching heat, heavy steel armour, and hours of beating the living daylights out of him.

"You're disgusting, you know that?" Nate panted, hardly able to form a coherent sentence.

"I don't smell that bad, do I?" Marcus joked as he sniffed under his armpit.

"How are you not tired?" Nate whined after draining the bowl dry in one gulp.

"Practice my friend, you'll get the hang of it eventually, but six months is barely long enough to teach you how not to cut your own head off."

Getting to his feet Nate's thoughts quickly turned from training to food. All he had eaten during twelve hours of beatings was a few slices of bread and some cheese that Marcus had brought with him.

Both men stood still for a moment, as the sun began to cast a golden glow over the city as it faded. From the relative privacy of the training ground, all the men could hear were the sounds of the horses in the stable still protesting at their captivity and the birds singing their high-pitched songs. For a moment Nate forgot he was dead, and that this place was designed to make him pay for his sins. The city was beautifully lit up in radiant gold and the quietness made it seem far more peaceful than it really was. Although the tranquillity was abruptly and violently disturbed by Nate's stomach which had, at that moment, decided to declare that it had never been fed once in its life. Marcus laughed as he undid the straps on his helmet and tucked it under his arm.

"We will get some food soon, but first we have to go to the bank; we need to create an account for you, don't worry it's not too far from here," Marcus reassured Nate, noticing the look of exhaustion on his face as they began walking away from the training ground.

Nate let out a huff. "I don't trust banks, they're all robbing bastards." Marcus pointed at Nate's small, leather coin purse dangling from his hip, in which was held a few useless five-pound notes.

"You really planning on keeping your entire fortune in there?" It was a good point, so Nate did not bother with a clever response, he was too exhausted to waste valuable wit when it was not needed.

There were dozens of banks in each level of the city. Curiously though, nobody had ever seen one being built, they would just appear one day out of nowhere. Before long entire districts would have risen around them. Nate and Marcus found this to be nothing but an annoyance as they had to force their way through the densely packed streets of shoppers.

The bank itself was quite distinguishable from the other buildings in the area. A two-storey building made of polished marble, it resembled a Greek temple. It even had a large marble statue outside; a naked man holding a handful of coins aloft, while his other hand gripped a knife which was pressed against his wrist, a snake wrapped around his leg. The doors to the bank were thick oak and intricately carved with depictions of coins, ledgers, and tall men in robes. Nate was inspired by the beauty of the place, even before the doors had been opened.

Within was a vast expanse of marble, so finely polished that it reminded him of the room where he had met Death. Although this time the floor was a huge mosaic depicting what appeared to be God, raining down golden coins on the naked men and women below, all of whom had their arms outstretched while sharing a look of mania on their faces.

The interior was completely empty, save for a single large wooden desk in the middle of the room, behind which a long trail of people queued. All around them wandered incredibly tall hooded figures with elongated limbs. Most were simply stood scribbling on parchment with excessively long quills. Others seemed to be just watching the long procession of people, their faces hidden by their hoods. In the corner near the door, there were four of these figures hunched together, as if plotting some scheme before quickly dispersing and seemingly floating across the floor.

Nate was snapped out of his observation by Marcus nudging him on the shoulder. "We need to get you registered, come with me." Nate did as he was told and soon found himself in the queue waiting to be seen at the solitary desk.

"Who are these people?" Nate asked. Marcus glanced at the hooded figures before whispering.

"We call them the Vault Keepers, they're in charge of managing everyone's accounts. Nobody knows what they are or where they come from, but they provide an essential service, so nobody really cares."

"We call them accountants where I'm from".

The minutes ticked by and quickly turned into an hour; they were now second in line but had been waiting for a good fifteen minutes while a man argued with the Vault Keeper attending the desk.

"I told you that I killed the Ember-Hound, I stuck my sword right into its heart!" the man screamed. The Vault Keeper simply sat there patiently, with its hands folded, its long, grey fingers tapping in a menacing rhythm. Once the man had stopped screaming and banging his fist on the desk the Vault Keeper spoke, its voice a soft hiss.

"I am sorry sir, but our records indicate that it was not you who struck the killing blow, but rather your companion."

The man had gone red in the face and was panting with anger.

"So, what if he got in one lucky hit? I did the work, all of it. I tracked the beast, I set the trap, and I fought it alone until they arrived. The kill is mine and I demand you pay me the bounty."

Again, the Vault Keeper was unmoved by the man's ranting.

"Once again, I apologise sir, but this establishment only awards bounties to those who struck the killing blow. While we at the House of the God of Man are all very grateful for your role in slaying the Ember-Hound, we cannot award a bounty if you did not strike the killing blow. Now if that is all, I would please ask you to leave as there are other worshippers waiting."

This dismissal tipped the man over the edge; in a blind rage, he withdrew a dagger. But before he could even think of what to do next, he had already been set upon by two other Vault Keepers who had rushed over seemingly out of nowhere. They grabbed his wrists and held his arms outstretched as the Vault Keeper at the desk rose.

It spoke but this time its hiss was menacing, akin to that of a snake about to strike. "Sir, this holy house does not tolerate violence. For your inexcusable behaviour, it has been decided that you shall forfeit sixty per cent of your accounts to the house as recompense. If you continue to act in this way, we shall close your account indefinitely. Is this understood?"

The man stood there, immobile, with tears in his eyes, brought on by a mixture of pain and the loss of sixty per cent of everything he had. His silence was met with the Vault Keepers on either end of his arms tightening their grip, and he yelped in pain and spluttered an apology. The Vault Keeper at the desk sat, and the other two immediately released the man. "Thank you, sir, now please have a good day and may the God of Man be with you."

The man did not even curse under his breath as he skulked away like an injured dog, avoiding the hundreds of staring eyes trained on him. Shocked by the scenes before him, Nate had not even realised that Marcus had already moved on and was communing with the Vault Keeper as if nothing had happened.

Nate stepped forward and was surprised to see despite all his pondering, that there was no face under the Vault Keeper's hood, just black emptiness.

"Good day and may the God of Man be with you, how may I help you today, fellow worshippers?" the creature asked. Marcus gestured to Nate.

"This one needs to open up an account." The black hood looked away from Marcus and towards Nate, peering over the desk, its wooden chair creaking as it did so.

"Ah Nathan, we were beginning to wonder," the Vault Keeper said in an amused tone. "If you would like to follow me, and please, feel free to ask whatever questions you wish." Nate looked at Marcus who nodded reassuringly.

The Vault Keeper led Nate through the empty bank and down a set of stairs, its seat being immediately occupied by one of its brethren. The staircase carried on for quite an extent and before long the way was lit by torches. So far, the two had travelled in silence, but Nate thought this was his best opportunity to annoy someone else for a change. But the questions he had been pondering since he had arrived had been replaced by more immediate curiosities.

"What are you exactly?" he asked as they continued down the seemingly endless staircase. The Vault Keeper answered immediately.

"We are the servants of the God of Man."

"And who's the God of Man?" Nate asked, certain he was about to receive a sermon.

"The God of Man is the true God of mankind, he who occupies all our thoughts, our hearts, and our desires. He who brings joy to all, he who has the power to level mountain ranges and raise cities. We all serve his will."

The response was hardly informative, but Nate decided not to press further, all religions were equally ridiculous to him, this was just another to add to the list. He was also not sure why, but he felt uneasy around the Vault Keeper. It was not entirely due to their terrifying visage, but rather a feeling in his heart he could not place, although they had been nothing but courteous, even when threatened. So, he assumed it was just his nerves at being led underground by a floating creature with no face.

At last, they reached the end of the stairs and found themselves halted by a huge, solid gold door. Even by the dim light of the torches, it radiated beauty. It was dotted with exquisite gemstones, some of which Nate could recognise, others were entirely unknown to him.

The Vault Keeper reached into its robe and withdrew a rather ordinary-looking key for such a magnificent door and inserted it into the lock. There were loud clatters and the sound of gears turning as the door swung open to reveal a huge yet very empty room, in the centre of which atop a pedestal rested a stone bowl. The Vault Keeper led the way and hovered by the pedestal as Nate peered into the bowl. It was empty. "What's this about?" he asked.

The response was once again immediate. "In order for the God of Man to bestow his blessings upon his worshippers, a sacrifice of blood must be made." Nate looked first at the Vault Keeper and then at the bowl. This is why he had never been into religion, far too many blood sacrifices.

"Well, of course, makes perfect sense," he said sarcastically.

"Please hold out your hand over the vessel," the Vault Keeper asked politely. Nate was hesitant, he knew as soon as he did that the Vault Keeper would pull out a huge knife and cut his hand open, he had seen enough movies to not be fooled. He, therefore, kept his hand firmly by his side.

"I understand your trepidation," the Vault Keeper said, its soft hissing tone being one of vague reassurance. "What you have requested cannot be done without an offering – after all, what is a bit of blood compared to the rewards the God of Man has to bestow?"

Wanting nothing more than to get this whole situation over with, Nate closed his eyes and held his hand outstretched, his palm facing upwards. There was a quick and sharp scratch as the Vault Keeper jabbed Nate's finger with the end of a pin and turned his hand over so that the blood could fall into the bowl.

Nate was embarrassed at the performance he had made but mostly relieved he had continued use of his hand, although he could not help but recoil at the touch of the Vault Keeper. Its grey hand was stone cold, devoid of all warmth and life. He withdrew his own quickly, as soon as the first drop of blood had hit the bowl and faced the Vault Keeper.

"Now what?" The Vault Keeper did not answer as it held its hand over the bowl.

"Lord please accept this offering by your loyal subject, may he receive the blessings of your bounty and his soul be forever enriched by your presence."

No sooner had the prayer been said than the bowl had erupted into flames. Nate jumped back in surprise, yet the fire extinguished itself as quickly as it had appeared. Nate, nursing his finger, was now certain that there was more to this performance than met the eye – even by his new standards this was weird.

"What the hell is going on?" he demanded to know.

The Vault Keeper looked back at him, but its answer did not come straight away, rather it seemed to think about it.

"Housed within these walls is the blood of every creature within this world and through the offering of your own blood a connection was made. Now, whenever you shed the blood of a creature, anywhere in the world, you will automatically be paid a bounty for its dispatching. Only now may you truly begin the work to repent your sins."

Nate stood there for a moment in silence, not entirely sure he believed what he was being told. But Marcus had assured him this was the only way out of Purgatory, and everyone else seemed to be on the bandwagon, so he may as well jump in too. However, that did not mean he was happy about it.

"Is there anything else I need to know about? After all, what kind of bank would this be if it weren't full of completely unreasonable terms?" Nate asked, only half-joking. The Vault Keeper chuckled.

"You humans really should be more trusting, but yes there are some rules in place. Firstly, you may only be paid a bounty if you are the individual who strikes the killing blow, there are no prizes for second place."

Yeah, you made that pretty clear earlier, Nate thought to himself.

"Secondly, the House of the God of Man will always agree to a loan, no matter the character of those requesting one, or their ability to repay. The size of the loan, however, *will* depend on the ability of an individual to repay. Those who are least likely to repay are allowed the largest loans while those capable of repaying more easily are given the smallest ones." Nate looked at the Vault Keeper with heightened suspicion.

"That seems counterproductive for a bank," he stated. The Vault Keeper chuckled again, but not a humorous chuckle, but a deep, unsettling one, like there was a joke it was party to that Nate was not.

"We are here to help humanity atone for their sins, not to act as an obstacle, we are a charitable organisation." The Vault Keeper paused and stared at Nate who was now positive that there was something it was not telling him. But the faceless glare forced him to look away, upon which the creature continued.

"Of course, the loan does not count towards an individual's atonement, and there are severe penalties for failing to repay. Finally, upon the death of the faithful, the House of the God of Man shall seize all goods present within the vault of the faithful in question."

There it is Nate smiled to himself. Suddenly the Vault Keeper's head shot upwards as it sniffed the air loudly, like a wolf detecting prey nearby.

"What are you doing?" Nate asked nervously – there was something about a faceless creature sniffing the air around him after performing a blood ritual which set off alarm bells in his brain.

"I can smell an offering, what have you brought to this house, Nathan?" the Vault Keeper hissed as it snatched away Nate's coin purse.

"Oi," Nate protested without putting up any real resistance. The Vault Keeper opened the bag and retrieved the few notes.

It hissed again, although this time it sounded different, like it was experiencing pure ecstasy.

"A glorious tribute, the God of Man shall be very pleased," the Vault Keeper said as it dropped the notes into the bowl. Before Nate could react, the bowl was immolated once more. He had to shield his eyes as the flames shot skywards, licking at the ceiling. As he removed his arms from across his face, determined to give the Vault Keeper a piece of his mind, he noticed the inside of the bowl. It was partially filled with gold coins.

"The God of Man thanks you for your offering, please take these tokens of his appreciation." The sound of ecstasy had been replaced by a more tamed hiss. The number of coins certainly exceeded the worth of the notes; however, Nate was not about to argue. He scooped as many as he could into his coin purse; however, there were still many remaining.

"What should I do with the rest?" he asked, concerned he would lose whatever he could not carry. However, the Vault Keeper was reassuring.

"The House will protect what is yours, feel free to take however much you wish from your vault whenever you like."

Marcus was waiting for him by the main door once he had finished with the Vault Keeper. Before either of them could speak Nate's stomach once again growled ferociously sparking Marcus to laugh. "Come on Nate, let's get some food in us before you start eating grass."

"Good idea," Nate replied patting his stomach. "Oh there was another thing I wanted to ask you," Nate said as they exited the bank. "Why can I understand you? I didn't expect many Romans to be able to speak a language which didn't exist for another few thousand years or so."

"Well," Marcus replied, "I'm not speaking whatever you think I'm speaking, you're speaking Latin".

Well of course, that makes perfect sense, Nate thought to himself as the pair went on a desperate hunt for food. Returning through one of the many commercial districts, Nate had time to examine his surroundings as the streets were beginning to empty. He soon diverted from his path to inspect a sword displayed in the window of a shop called *Cut to Ribbons*.

Placed on a slanted stone slab this sword looked to be the definition of master craftsmanship. The grip was smooth, polished ivory, and the pommel was round steel. The blade itself was thin and slightly curved upwards. About two thirds down the edge stretching down to the tip were razor-sharp teeth, perfect for causing multiple deep wounds.

The only thing that put Nate off the blade was the light green tinge that had been given to it. That was until he saw a thin string with a paper tag attached detailing the price. "Four hundred thousand gold?!" he gasped, spinning around to see Marcus standing directly behind him.

"Who has four hundred thousand gold, and who would want to spend all that on a sword anyway?"

Marcus folded his arms, an unimpressed look on his face as he too inspected the weapon. "Some people have a lot more money than you think, although personally, I've never understood the need for such things. I think anyone who spends that much on a sword is compensating for something." Nate nodded in agreement, turning around once more he replied.

"You must admit that it looks pretty cool though."

Marcus rolled his eyes and continued towards Pedan's inn.

"Come on I'm starving," he beckoned, giving the sword one last glance. Nate followed Marcus down the street. He had been seriously impressed by the mystery meat and veg pasty Marcus had procured the night before and he hoped for something equally as delicious tonight. His mouth watered as they rounded a corner and The Hovel stood before them, food now a very real prospect.

Once again, the sights and sounds of hundreds of merry drinkers filled Nate's senses as they entered the inn. Marcus declared it was Nate's turn to buy the goods as he found somewhere to sit. Making his way to the bar Nate saw many familiar faces from the night before, some of whom gave him a smile and others who refused to even acknowledge him.

Pedan had a reaction of mild surprise to see Nate again. "Back again already? I thought we would have put you off for a few weeks at least." He laughed as he cleaned a flagon with what looked like the same filthy rag from the night before.

"It will take more than forcing me into a life of servitude and monster-slaying without any prior warning to keep me away from here," Nate smiled back. Pedan laughed again.

"So, what can I get you?"

"Two flagons of your finest mead and whatever food you have," Nate replied passing over six gold coins.

"Right away my lord," Pedan snorted, giving a mock bow as he walked to the back of the bar where the kitchen door was situated from which furious shouting could be heard. In the meantime, Nate spun around on his stool to try and spot where Marcus had gone. It was difficult to see anything with hundreds of people filling the building. Yet he managed to spot the legionnaire thanks to his distinctive armour, sitting on a chair facing over the balcony on the next floor.

A few seconds later Pedan returned from the kitchen with two plates, upon which sat a slab of thick red meat, cooked rare, with the juices still oozing out. The rest of the plate was piled high with various vegetables, many of which Nate had never seen before, yet they looked delicious. "There you go my friend," he smiled as he placed down two fresh meads. "So how has your training been going? I've heard Marcus doesn't suffer any nonsense."

"You can say that again," Nate scoffed as he rubbed his bruised arms.

"Believe me, you'll be glad for it when the time comes. Don't want you ending up like the poor sods that go out there barely trained to wipe their arse," Pedan replied with a tinge of regret in his voice. Not wanting to open that bag of worms, Nate thanked him for the meal and set off. Navigating the densely packed room was a challenge, especially considering half the patrons were drunk and could barely stand upright. Nevertheless, by some miracle, he reached the stairs to the next floor, goods still in hand.

Luckily, the stairs were empty, and he breathed a sigh of relief. However, despite his delicate balancing act, by the time he had reached the second step from the top, a figure appeared. Looming over him was a large and imposing man with a thick black beard, bald head, and muscular arms covered in tribal tattoos. Nate tried his best to scoot over to one side of the stairway, but the other man simply stood unmoving, staring at Nate with furious eyes.

"Move," he said in a deep, commanding voice. Nate looked back down the stairs, there was no way he would be able to turn around and go all the way back without dropping his cargo. He looked back at the man, and then at the two steps that separated him from the next floor.

"Can I just squeeze past?" he asked as politely as possible, despite the rudeness of the giant towering above him.

"Move," the man repeated once again, this time his fists clenched as his patience ran out.

"C'mon I'm nearly…" Nate tried to protest before a vicious punch cut him short. He had been struck on the side of the nose, causing him to tumble down the stairs. Food and alcohol flew in all directions, spattering the patrons below who erupted in anger.

Nate lay at the bottom of the stairs in a heap, his face in agony. He watched helplessly and in a daze as the man who had punched him sauntered down the stairs and out of the inn without so much as looking at him. None of the hundred or so people who had observed the scene moved in to offer Nate any assistance. As he struggled to his feet, gripping the banister tightly for support, Nate noticed a steady stream of blood dripping from his face. He moved his hand up to touch it and recoiled in pain as his fingertips barely brushed against his nose. Even from the slightest of touches, he could feel that it was broken.

He struggled back up the stairs, his legs like jelly. He had never been punched before, and with such ferocity. He wondered how he was still alive. His head was ringing, and he felt as if he were about to be sick. At last, after much great effort, he reached the top. He was immediately met with a hundred pairs of staring eyes, some evidently disgusted at such a sight. Most, however, were totally indifferent to random acts of violence.

Finally dragging himself over to Marcus' table, Nate dropped himself into the chair exhausted. His face and neck were now drenched in blood as Marcus sat there in stunned silence.

"Bloody hell, Nate, you were supposed to buy dinner, not fight the whole town for it," he choked, trying his best to stifle a fit of laughter. Nate was too exhausted to utter a word and so half-heartedly shrugged. The sound of his hands slapping his thighs perfectly summed up his thoughts on the matter.

"Here," Marcus said passing Nate a clean handkerchief. Gently Nate raised it to his nose but recoiled again in pain.

"How much pain would you say you are in? Too much to eat?" Marcus asked, praying he would not be kept from his dinner for much longer. Nate shook his head, a mistake as the dizziness and nausea worsened. "Good, wait here then. I'll go get us some food and afterwards I'll take you to the temple to get that nose fixed."

Nate sat in silent agony, watching enviously as Marcus tore through his steak. Meanwhile, he could only manage the slightest of nibbles of his own. Eventually, he gave up entirely and pushed the plate aside. Marcus looked up at him in astonishment – missing a leg would not have come between him and his meal.

Without so much as a confirmatory glance from Nate, he snatched the discarded plate and wolfed down the entire thing in seconds. He then gulped down his mead in an equally rapid fashion. Once Marcus had finished gorging himself, he slapped his stomach and gave out a contented sigh. Turning his attention at last to his battered friend, he inspected his nose once more. It was hardly the worst injury he had ever seen. But it would take a priest's skill, nonetheless.

"Who hit you anyway?" he asked. Nate shrugged again.

"No idea. Big guy, bald, long beard, only knew one word." The description was immediately recognisable to Marcus.

"Sounds like Barrett to me. Doesn't surprise me, he always was an arsehole."

"Oh, so he's a friend of yours?" Nate slurred. Marcus had been down to the bar again and fetched them both fresh meads. Still not quite used to it, it barely took a few sips for him to become tipsy.

"Been here for over six hundred years," Marcus explained as he finished the last of his drink. "Fought more battles and been on more expeditions than most people his rank. He is a capable warrior, not many who face him live to talk about it. Count yourself privileged to be on that very short list."

"I'm honoured," Nate moaned as the mead finally began to dull the pain in his face.

"I actually went on an expedition with him once," Marcus said, leaning back in his chair, staring at the ceiling as he recounted the tale. Nate could not care less about Marcus' story while his face still looked like a partially melted waxwork. Yet Marcus continued, regardless.

"We were told by Captain Ardell to head north to Fort Sumnter, it's located just shy of where the Heartlands ends, where the ground begins to harden before what we call the Great Wastes begins. People there had reported seeing Imperial troops in the area, so Ardell put Barrett in charge of leading an expeditionary force to investigate. We set off with one hundred troops, and only three of us returned."

Marcus had been on numerous expeditions that had resulted in many companions being killed. However, the expedition to Fort Sumnter was one of the hardest to try and forget. It was the first time he had ever faced the true brutality of The Imperium. Decades under Ardell and he had still never seen such violence.

"What happened?" Nate asked trying to sound interested as his nose throbbed.

"It's well over two thousand miles to Fort Sumnter. So, we set off expecting to take one or two casualties along the way, nobody ever makes it anywhere with a full party. We eventually got to our destination after six months of travelling by horse. We lost twenty troops to Husks and an attack by a Drake."

"What's a Drake?! Nate interrupted. Marcus placed his hands on the table so that they were facing each other.

"It's a very, very big lizard that breathes fire," he replied, increasing the distance between his hands to emphasise its size.

"Oh, a dragon?" Nate was excited, mainly due to the mead, Marcus laughed.

"No, no we don't get dragons around here anymore, these things are babies in comparison. So anyway, we finally reached Fort Sumnter after about six months, only issue was that once we got there all the people were gone. Poof, vanished into thin air, not a single trace the place was ever inhabited.

"So, we set up camp and began investigating, we were all exhausted but we needed to establish what was going on, and we were honestly terrified. It is not every day a whole garrison just disappears. After a day of searching and finding absolutely nothing, we decided to head back the following day.

"That night hundreds of Imperial troops came pouring out of the forest to the east and attacked us. They used carts to block our exit from the fort and rained arrows on us before they used ladders to get over the walls. We lost half our men to the arrows alone and once they got over the walls, well, we stood no chance.

"But instead of running Barrett charged straight towards the enemy, we wanted to run but he…he just inspired us to fight." Marcus sounded full of admiration despite the fact he had just nearly killed Nate. The memories had come flooding back now, he could remember every detail of those events as if they had been only moments ago. "Barrett led us straight at them swinging his sword, cutting down anyone who opposed him.

"After an hour of fighting, we were down to ten men, that's when we decided to retreat. Barrett wanted to carry on fighting, we had to literally pull him away, he was knee-deep in bodies when we finally forced him to run.

"We climbed over the carts and made a run into the forest. We didn't even mount our horses because we didn't have time.

The enemy sent arrow volleys after us as we ran and brought down many more of us. It took us nine months to get back to Sundered Crown by foot, and we were attacked almost every night by Imperial troops. By the time we got back here only three of us were still alive. Ever since then Barrett and I have had mutual respect. Although, we haven't been on another expedition together since."

"What happened to the other guy?" Nate asked.

"Asked to be transferred to the navy after that, not much chance for action, but I think he had seen enough." Marcus sighed, leaning back on his chair.

"God," Nate gasped now finally somewhat more interested in the tale. "How do you cope? I mean after all these things that have happened how do you manage to get up and do it all again?"

Marcus was still leaning back in his chair as he stared into space searching for a suitable answer. It was a question he had asked himself so many times, even before he had died. In the end, there was only one answer. Still staring into space he almost whispered his response, as he tried to remember the faces of all the friends he had lost.

"Because we don't have a choice." There was a moment of awkward silence as the two reflected, Nate mostly on three words which had stuck with him. *Six hundred years*. Before long Marcus snapped to and focused back on the here and now. "Come on, we should get you to the temple and get that nose sorted," he groaned getting out of his chair and walking toward the stairs. Nate was still attempting to process what he had just heard, attempting to understand what Marcus had been through, but raced after him once he realised he was halfway out of the inn.

Before leaving Nate made sure to grab a pair of seasoned lamb shanks and a bread roll from Pedan as the effect of the alcohol was only making his hunger worse. The sun had been dark for many hours and in its place had appeared the moon, artistically pockmarked with craters of non-existent asteroids. Apart from its faint glow, the only light came from the many oil lamps and candles that adorned almost every window.

"Come on, the temple isn't too far away. If I keep looking at that nose, I might have to start telling people I don't know you," Marcus laughed. The pair walked along the narrow streets as people began to enter their homes and lock their doors. All the while Nate longed for the food he held wrapped in cloth, the delicious scent teasing his senses. After a few minutes of walking, Nate looked up and for the first time, noticed that the sky was absolutely filled with stars. More glorious than the most beautiful night sky back on Earth, they twinkled in every imaginable colour. Meanwhile, huge pillars of coloured gas streaked across the cluttered cosmos, like the strokes of a brush across a canvas.

It was as if every square inch of the sky had been meticulously designed to show the true glory of creation. Despite this awe-inspiring beauty, however, Nate could not help but ponder the question it posed. Were these the same stars he had seen when looking up at night back on Earth? If so, up there somewhere, was there his own home? So far away yet still very much real? Even Marcus, who had spent decades staring at the same sky, found new beauty with each new glance. It was not the sort of view that ever became tiresome.

The men passed a small barracks situated next to an inn which Nate thought was probably done on purpose. It did not look like much compared to the one they had been training outside of today. So, Nate was surprised when Marcus gestured towards it with his thumb and said, "That's where I live in case you ever need me." Nate knew that Marcus did not own his own home, yet to see for himself the sorry excuse for shelter filled him with guilt.

He had assumed that from Marcus' natural leadership qualities and confidence, not to mention his skill with a weapon, that he could at least afford to live comfortably. Marcus could sense exactly what Nate was thinking and spoke up once more. "Don't worry about me, one day I'll get lucky on an expedition. Then you can come round to my mansion and feed me grapes any time you like." He snorted at the very thought. Nate replied with an awkward smile – surely there had to be more to this life than sheer luck?

"That reminds me, we need to find you somewhere to stay, new arrivals can only stay at the palace for a few weeks before they have to move."

"The palace?" Nate asked, confused. Marcus rolled his eyes at having to explain the joke.

"Does it look like any palace you've ever seen?" he asked mockingly.

"Oh, right," Nate replied feeling stupid that he'd even had to ask.

"Now that I think about it, I think there is a new barracks near to the lower level, it's probably mostly empty seeing as most people only stay in barracks for the short term. I'll take you up there tomorrow so we can get you sorted with somewhere to live."

"Thanks, Marcus," Nate replied. He was genuinely shocked by Marcus' willingness to go out of his way to make his life there easier. He had only known him for two days and already he owed him everything. He just hoped that he would not disappoint him when it counted and that he would be able to repay the same kindness that had been shown to him.

Eventually, after walking for a few miles, they were on the outskirts of the city. Ahead of them was a hill like the one on which Nate's current residence was built, except atop this one stood a huge white stone building with multiple pillars and statues to the gods of various religions.

"That's the temple," Marcus pointed. "You have gold, don't you?" Marcus said raising his eyebrow at Nate.

"Ah of course, because why would healthcare be free in the afterlife?" Nate laughed.

"You're lucky it's just a broken nose, re-growing a limb can cost thousands," Marcus replied casually.

"What do you mean re-grow a limb?" Nate asked. Considering the most modern thing around seemed to be the wheel, he doubted the technology to re-grow limbs was just lying about.

"Ah, so you're from one of those places without magic then?" Marcus replied. Magic was such a common tool in Gaia that he had completely neglected to mention it.

"Oh, piss off," Nate said rolling his eyes; he was only just starting to believe the whole thing about monsters, but magic was pushing it too far. Stood at the foot of the hill Nate suddenly decided that his nose was not that broken, as he examined the hundreds of steps leading up to the temple's huge wooden doors. After twelve hours of exhausting training and his earlier altercation with Barrett, he really did not feel like climbing any more stairs, even if it did mean a fixed nose.

Nevertheless, despite his internal monologue begging him no, he began climbing, making sure that Marcus understood how much he hated each step, by grunting and groaning more and more loudly. Before they had even reached halfway Marcus turned around and growled, "If you keep complaining I will send you back down those steps on your head, now keep walking and shut up." He did not sound serious, but Nate did not want to test him, and so suffered the rest of the climb in silence.

After reaching the top of the hill Nate went down on all fours and rolled onto his back panting heavily, "How...do they...expect injured people...to get up here?" he gasped. Marcus looked down at his pathetic excuse for a companion and could not decide whether to laugh or join him on the floor in despair.

"We really need to get you in shape, my friend, the captain won't be impressed if she sees you like this." Nate was too exhausted to utter a response so simply lay there trying not to die. Marcus knocked on the temple door and waited.

By the time the door was answered, Nate had pulled himself together and was standing beside Marcus. However, he was still breathing heavily and the pain in his nose had only worsened. The door was answered by a tall, dark-skinned man whose face was littered with rings. He wore a white robe decorated with colourful patterns and what Nate assumed to be scripture.

For a moment there was an awkward silence as the robed man observed them, his eyes darting between them as if searching for some hidden danger. Once he was satisfied that these two men were indeed in need of aid, he swung his arm open and moved aside.

Marcus gestured for Nate to enter first, who jumped as the huge doors slammed behind him. Marcus carried on walking, but Nate was transfixed by how beautiful the interior of the temple was. The ceiling was a large dome with hundreds of tapestries and banners hanging from floor to ceiling.

The main hall was a huge circular room with hundreds of altars and statues filling every possible spare inch and crevice. Some statues were nothing more than a collection of sticks, while others were beautifully carved marble figures. Most looked human, but there were some animal-human hybrids and some that Nate could not describe with mere words. In the very centre was a spiral staircase. It led deep beneath the ground to the very base of the hill and beyond. This is where most priests and priestesses spent their time, in silent reflection and study of the arcane, undisturbed by the dull barbarians of the surface.

The room was dark despite the thousands of candles scattered into every nook and cranny, and Nate could barely see Marcus standing by an altar speaking to another robed figure. Marcus pointed toward Nate and the figure began moving towards him. Nate knew he was not in any danger but was still apprehensive of a tall man in a white robe and pointy hood heading towards him with purpose.

Once the man was a few feet away, Nate could make out his features. He was ginger with a pathetic excuse for a beard, multiple earrings, and a nose ring. He had a tattoo of a seahorse on his left hand and wore at least two rings on each finger. Nate was shocked, he'd expected the friar he had seen at the inn on the first night, or maybe a Dumbledore type character with a huge beard and a strange fascination for teenage boys. Alas, here he was being greeted by the hipster time forgot. The man held out his hand which Nate shook tentatively; this caused a grin to creep across the man's face as he sensed Nate's anxiety.

"The name's Kyle, I hear you've been introduced to our famous Tinelian hospitality. Welcome to the jungle, bro," he said in a deep southern US accent as he placed his hand under Nate's chin and inspected his nose.

"Did you just call me bro?" Nate replied. There was no way, even in an infinite number of universes that someone like this could really exist he thought.

"Well, we can fix the nose, but unfortunately the rest of your face will have to stay like that."

Nate's brain exploded into action attempting to deliver the wittiest response it could imagine. "Tough talk coming from a ginger" was the product of his effort. Kyle let out a laugh and produced a small green bottle from his sleeve. Instinctively assuming the bottle was medicine for his nose, Nate reached out his hand to take it. However, he was quickly slapped away as Kyle raised the bottle to his own lips and took a long swig.

"Oof," he said blinking rapidly as he hid the bottle back up his sleeve.

Nate stood there confused, wondering if it was common practice for priests to get hammered before the healing process. But before he could utter a word, Kyle simply waved his hand in front of Nate's face. There was a short, bright burst of blue light, followed by a sickening crack as Nate's nose moved back into place. The pain was immense and caused him to shout out and to drop to his knees, cupping his hands around his newly repaired nose.

"That'll be fifteen gold," Kyle said without missing a beat, his hand already outstretched by the time Nate looked up barely a second later.

Nate's immediate inclination was to punch Kyle for his sheer audacity. But realising he was in the afterlife, perhaps punching a priest in a temple of all places, whilst being watched by countless gods, was not the best idea. Furthermore, the fact that Marcus had indeed not been joking about the existence of magic was a far more pressing concern that needed addressing.

Struggling to his feet, Nate opened the coin purse at his side and handed over the requested amount. Already most of what he had taken from the vault was gone. "Thanks, bro," Kyle smiled as he walked away and shook hands with Marcus.

Marcus too then placed a hand under Nate's chin and inspected the product of Kyle's work.

"You won't be launching a thousand ships anytime soon, but it'll do," he smiled. "C'mon, it's getting late, we should head back. Otherwise, you won't have the strength to stand tomorrow," Marcus said as his own eyes began to feel strained. As the two left the temple Nate turned to Marcus.

"Well, he was fucking weird, are all priests around here like that?"

Marcus smiled. "Nah, Kyle is a bit of an anomaly. Most priests spend their time in total silence, studying new spells or reading their religious tomes. You should count yourself lucky if one even agrees to see you. Kyle is more of a people person." Over the years Marcus had built up a strong friendship with Kyle. He was a skilled sorcerer and his aid had proven invaluable on many an expedition. Above all, he was loyal to his friends, a trait which he had proved countless times and Marcus respected greatly.

"I can't believe it was that easy to fix a broken nose," Nate said, bewildered. "Where I'm from it takes weeks."

"Magic certainly makes life a lot easier that's for sure," Marcus agreed, as they began descending the temple steps back towards the town. However, Nate was not so convinced. From his vantage point, he could see much of the surrounding area. What were little more than shanty towns made up much of the city.

Meanwhile, the people all travelled either by foot or horse, there were practically no signs of modernity anywhere. He found this strange – after all, a world full of people from an infinite number of universes and time periods was bound to have moved on past the dark ages, surely? In the end, he posed the question to Marcus, hoping he could offer some sensible explanation.

However, Marcus seemed to have no quarrel with the current situation, and until now had thought little of it. Tinelia was not that much different from the world he had left behind; nevertheless, he tried his best to offer an explanation.

"Well, I suppose…" he began before trailing off as if he too had only just realised that the whole world seemed to be stuck in some sort of time loop.

He inhaled deeply and puffed out his chest as he thought, stopping a few steps below Nate. "Well, as long as you've got the basics, magic can do the rest, everybody seems happy enough with things how they are anyway." Satisfied with his answer he carried on with his descent. But Nate was struck by the sense of sheer complacency when things could be made so much easier and more comfortable. He quickened his pace to catch up and expressed his confusion.

"So, you're saying nobody has ever tried to change things, no mad inventors, or scientists around?" He found it hard to imagine the idea of Einstein sitting in a dingy wooden shack somewhere, sharpening a sword in preparation for his career as a monster slayer.

"Oh, we've had a couple, some tried to convince us we could harness the elements for energy. But in the end, nobody really cared enough to take their word for it. I think they work for the Citadel now anyway; Grand Admiral Lee probably has them working on some sort of superweapon." Marcus could not help but smirk at the ridiculous prospect.

Nate, however, was dumbstruck. To him at least, the need to create, the capacity humans had to change the world around them to suit their needs, was one of their most defining characteristics. Yet in this world, that seemed to be lacking almost entirely. For Nate this was a terrifying prospect, to be stuck in a world where nothing changed in a meaningful way. Like being forever trapped in the head of a politician.

By now the temperature had dropped considerably, and Nate's breath curled towards the starlit sky as his descent reached its end. By the time he reached the bottom his hands and face were frozen and numb. Rubbing them together did nothing but give him a horrible sense of pins and needles.

"I'm going to go to bed," Marcus announced with a yawn. "Training starts at six tomorrow, and I won't be coming to wake you."

The prospect of even more training was daunting, but Nate knew he did not have a choice. He was not about to set up an inn so training would have to do. He shook hands with Marcus and parted ways; hopefully, tomorrow would be easier.

The next day was in fact, much harder. It had begun with the usual routine where they further practised both swordplay and archery. However, Marcus was eager to teach Nate as much as possible to both prepare him for the world outside the walls, and more importantly for Marcus' sake, to impress Captain Ardell.

He had therefore attempted to teach Nate the basics of riding a horse which ended about as well as he had expected, although he admired Nate's determination to continue despite being repeatedly thrown off, much to the amusement of the others in the paddock. After a few hours, he had finally managed to stay on the horse and ride around at a steady trot. "I'm a natural," he smiled stretching out his arms from atop his steed. Marcus stood at the edge of the paddock with his arms folded.

"Aye, you'll be leading the cavalry in no time." As Nate gracelessly dismounted, he gave his newfound equine friend a pat on the neck, while Marcus took the reins and escorted her back to the stable. Sensing a rare opportunity for rest Nate exited the paddock and fell to the ground, stretching out his limbs.

The leather armour Marcus had given him was still alien and incredibly uncomfortable at the best of times, and the day's exertion had only made it worse as the leather fusing to his skin from his excessive sweating acted as further insulation. He tugged at the armour constricting his neck in the hope of some small relief from the heat. Alas, the sun was scorching, and he was resigned to his fate of being cooked alive by cow flesh, a cruel irony he thought. He ran his hand through his hair and yawned, as with all the excitement he was not getting much sleep.

Marcus returned shortly. Nate had never seen him in anything other than his legionary armour and was amazed that he never so much as broke a sweat, even during the most demanding of tasks. He passed Nate a bowl of water which he hurriedly gulped down, throwing it aside and returning to his starfish position once it was empty.

"I think that's enough for today," Marcus said as he sipped from his own bowl. Nate sat up in surprise. It was only just midday, and he had expected to keep training for at least four more hours.

"Why, what are we doing?" he asked. Marcus waited until he had drained his bowl before also discarding it.

"We need to find somewhere for you to live. I spoke to a friend last night and he said that there should still be ample room left for you in the barracks I told you about." Marcus offered Nate a hand who took it gladly, pulling himself up with an exhausted grunt.

"Thank you, Marcus, I really appreciate your help with everything." Nate felt incredibly lucky to have Marcus watching over him. From what he had seen so far, many would have just left him on the streets if they were able to train him and present him to Captain Ardell when their time was up.

Marcus replied with a warm smile, it was not often people thanked him for anything, and he had to admit it made him feel good to help this scrawny excuse for a man. He had dreaded his assignment to Nate at first, but over the past couple of days, while he acknowledged there was a lot of work to do, he had begun to like him.

"It's no problem, you're a good kid," he said, patting Nate on the back before changing the subject. "It's about two hours to the barracks, less than half that if you want to ride." Nate looked back at the stables. His few hours of practice had not instilled him with great confidence in his riding abilities, but anything was better than spending two hours walking in this heat.

Marcus had been right; it had not taken long to reach the barracks by horse. However, horses were not allowed through the city streets, so the pair rode around the outskirts while Marcus pointed out interesting places and the stories behind them. One such building was a five-storey stone structure with its own training yard and armoury. Initially assuming this was either the house of a well-to-do general or a barracks, Marcus had declared that this was in fact one of Tinelia's many monster-hunting guilds.

He explained how the captains rarely sent soldiers out to hunt monsters unless they posed a major and immediate threat to their interests. Otherwise hunting them was an entirely private enterprise. "I would personally recommend you consider investigating them yourself once you've finished your training," Marcus said over the panting of the horses. Nate squirmed slightly as he imagined some indescribable horror tearing his guts out.

"I'm not really sure monster-hunting would be my thing," he said shrugging his shoulders.

"You must earn a living somehow, plus they won't throw you in at the deep end straight away. They usually send new members on missions in groups, led by a more experienced member to show you the ropes. Only idiots go monster-hunting alone."

For the past few days, Nate had tried to avoid thinking about what was going to happen once his training ended in six months, rather hoping to burn that bridge once he got to it. But Marcus was right of course, he had to earn a living, and he was not entirely confident his degree in journalism would be in high demand. This whole world seemed to be built on blood. "I'll think about it," Nate sighed.

"Actually, there's something else I wanted to ask you," Nate said as they slowed their horses to a stop. They had reached the barracks situated just a few hundred meters from the gatehouse which led to the lower ring of the city.

"Ask away," Marcus replied, as they dismounted their horses and led them to the hitching posts outside the barracks' door. Nate made a hash of tying a knot with the reins which forced Marcus to take over with an irritated sigh.

"Give it 'ere.'"

Nate relinquished the reins and continued with his question. "Why do you think we have to kill monsters to make up for our sins? I mean, out of all the trials they could have chosen, this one makes the least sense."

Marcus rubbed his eyes in frustration, sick of the constant philosophical questions. "Listen, Nate," he began. "I don't know what you want me to say. I haven't been here that long, not really, so I've just been doing as I was told. Well, mostly," he admitted. "I'm not the right person to ask these sorts of questions. If you want to know how to swing a sword or please a woman, I'm your man, but existentialism isn't my area of expertise."

Nate rolled his eyes and at last gave up on expecting sensible answers from Marcus. The two climbed the steps onto the barracks' porch and Marcus knocked on the door. After thirty seconds of going unanswered he knocked again, but this time much harder and for longer. The door suddenly opened as Marcus was halfway through another swing.

Greeting them was a barely-dressed young woman with messy black hair and a dozy expression on her face. "Can I help you?" she asked, supporting herself on the doorframe as if she was about to collapse at any second.

At first taken aback by this woman's appearance and the fact she had been sleeping at midday, Marcus composed himself before replying, "We would like to know if there is any space available, my friend here needs somewhere to live." Marcus gestured at Nate who until now seemed to have gone totally unnoticed by the woman at the door. She looked him over with bleary eyes and then looked back to Marcus.

"Yeah, I have room, come on in," she said opening the door fully, stepping aside so Nate and Marcus could enter. The barracks was a single large rectangular room with beds aligned in rows along each side. It had a kitchen at the end of the left-hand wall next to the fireplace, and a medium-sized dining table in the middle of the room. There were rugs placed on the floor and racks for weapons next to each bed. The building had only just been finished yet the place was in a state. Clothes and food bowls were strewn about the floor, one bed was covered in knives and spears, and there were overturned tables and chairs everywhere.

"By the gods," Marcus gasped, "Is an army stationed here?" He could not believe the condition of the place. His years of rigorous training in being utterly immaculate in all aspects of his life were screaming at him to run before he become tainted with such apathy. Nate was equally shocked but remained silent. The woman looked around at the carnage and was unphased.

"Sorry, I didn't know I'd be getting visitors," she replied, irritated.

"Are you the only person living here?" Nate asked at last. The woman walked up to Nate with her hand outstretched,

"Chen, nice to meet you…?"

"Nate," he replied.

"Nice to meet you, Nate. To answer your question, yes, I'm the only person living here and I'm not a morning person. So, feel free to unpack and choose a bed," Chen said gesturing with her arm in a wide arc. "Just not that one," she said pointing to the bed covered in knives and spears.

"Noted." Nate smiled as he turned to Marcus who was still in awe at the mess surrounding him.

"Do you want to look for somewhere else?" Marcus asked, more interested in getting out of the barracks as quickly as possible than finding Nate somewhere suitable.

Nate smiled as he looked around. "It's just a little mess, I'm sure it'll be fine." Marcus nodded and shook Nate's hand.

"Well, if you need anything just ask, otherwise I'll leave you to get settled in. If that's even possible," he said shooting a glare at Chen who was already back in bed and asleep.

"I'll see you first thing tomorrow," Nate said confidently, feeling slightly more relaxed and grounded now he had somewhere to call his own.

"You certainly shall, tomorrow is when the real training starts." Marcus smirked as he closed the door, catching a glimpse of the sweet look of horror on Nate's face.

Chapter 5

The sky was choked with the smoke of the burning city below. The sun tried in vain to pierce the shadowy veil but was unable to break through its impenetrable stranglehold. The Emperor looked on as the empire he had built crumbled around him. The golden spires of the ornate temples in the district of the One fell from their perches while explosions rocked the rest of the city as fire rained from the sky.

Even from the palace, he could hear the screams as people were slaughtered in the streets like animals. He tightened his grip on the balcony rail, his knuckles white in anger. He was chosen by God, yet he was powerless to stop the carnage unfolding before him.

Suddenly, he found himself in the grand courtyard outside the palace, mixed in amongst countless faceless warriors, all still and silent, the only sound coming from the flames as they tore through the city. He pushed his way forward and upon reaching the front saw two figures in the distance, facing one another across the courtyard.

Like the warriors around him, they were faceless, more shadow than human. It was impossible to distinguish any of their features whatsoever, male or female, tall or short, they seemed to be everything at once. The two simply stood facing one another, staring intently at their featureless faces as if trying to work out the other's next move.

Then one of the figures began to speak, but their words were incomprehensible and distorted as if spoken from behind thick walls. The two figures spoke only briefly before turning hostile, and the warriors drew their weapons ready for yet more slaughter.

The figure furthest from the Emperor, standing with the towering Imperial Palace behind them, spoke as they held out their arm. A blue flame formed in their hand and suddenly there was a brilliant flash, accompanied by heat so fierce it burned the clothes from the Emperor's back. He threw his hands over his face to protect his eyes, but the firestorm lasted only a moment.

As he opened his eyes, he found himself in a different place. It was instantly familiar to him, but he could not recall ever setting foot there before. An endless, flat expanse of dried mud as far as the eye could see, there were no other landmarks at all and the earth itself seemed to have cracked open.

He coughed violently as the scorched air filled his lungs and he sank to his knees. Tears filled his eyes. This was it, he thought. He had seen the end of this world first-hand, and he knew nothing of how to stop it.

Waking with a violent cough, a remnant of his nightmarish vision, the Emperor was relieved to find himself back in his chambers. He sat there for a moment, breathing heavily, sweat running down his back as he tried to re-live what he had seen but moments ago. Who were the two figures cloaked in darkness? Who could amass an army capable of sowing such destruction? And why bring war to the Imperium?

These were questions he would have to raise with the Congregation. He threw off the bedcovers and shuffled to the bathroom, still groggy from his disturbed sleep. The sun had barely begun its illumination as the Emperor finished his bath and there was a sudden knock on his bedchamber door. "One moment," he replied. Believing it to be one of his scullery maids he quickly dressed.

Across his upper body he wore a purple tunic, embroidered with golden flower motifs and held together by a dozen polished silver buttons. Over his left shoulder, a white cape which hung just above the knee. His breeches matched his tunic if not for being two shades darker and somewhat creased. His boots were the height of imperial fashion, black leather with no less than five brass buckles along their sides. Then there were his gloves, the most delicate and expensive silk which could be found anywhere on Gaia. They too were white but unlike the rest of his attire, lacked any adornments.

Lastly, came the most hated part, his mask. Made from solid gold and engraved with dozens of patterns ranging from floral to religious, it covered his entire face. Only his cool blue eyes and a vertical slit between his nose and lower lip were visible.

The Emperor could not stand to be so overburdened with clothing, but Elias, the Grand Seeker, had told him that his divine image must be protected against the eyes of the impure. He thought it nonsense, but even the Emperor did not want to test the Seekers. "Come in," he ordered once he was fully dressed.

He was surprised to find not his maid entering, but his advisor, Nestor. He entered with a silver tray carrying the Emperor's breakfast and a stack of papers under his arm. "Good morning your holiness," Nestor smiled.

Nestor had been the Emperor's closest advisor since the birth of the imperium — he was a master administrator and true friend, guiding the Emperor through the most trying times of the Imperium's creation. Most importantly for the Seekers, he was a fierce believer in the Emperor's divinity.

"Where's the maid?" the Emperor asked as he removed the mask, tossing it onto the bed. Nestor placed the tray down and handed him the documents under his arm before speaking.

"I gave her the morning off," Nestor smiled. The Emperor picked up a piece of toast, chewing and pacing slowly while he flicked through the papers.

They ranged from reports from the imperial treasury to upcoming important social events. "That was nice of you, what's the occasion?" he asked, taking a gulp of apple juice while reading a document revealing the results of the imperial elections.

He was met with silence and averted his gaze from the page to see Nestor with a childish grin painted across his face, obviously barely able to contain his excitement. The Emperor was intrigued. "What's going on?" he asked. Nestor came close and whispered, at this distance his excitement palpable.

"They found something, your holiness, beneath the palace." The Emperor's eyes widened in shock. "The Arch-Sorcerer and master engineer await you in the Congregation chamber," Nestor continued as the Emperor put his papers aside.

"What have they found?" he asked both excited yet cautious, not wanting to get his hopes too high should they be dashed.

"They wouldn't tell me, just that you would want to meet with them immediately."

After once more adorning his mask, the Emperor dashed out of the bedchamber, Nestor close behind. Guards and servants all halted their tasks to bow as the Emperor rushed past. The Congregation chamber was only a few rooms down from his bedchamber, a design which had paid dividends since the palace's reconstruction.

Over the walkway, the Emperor could see hundreds of servants, civil or otherwise, also hurriedly going about their daily tasks. Ever since the palace had become the home of the elected officials it was more like a bazaar than the residence of royalty.

He had been reluctant to agree to such terms at first, but he had soon begun to enjoy the drama. Often, he would watch bemused as officials argued with one another over petty grievances, sometimes being escorted out by the palace guards. It had made the place livelier if nothing else.

Before long he was at the Congregation chamber doors.

"What is it, what did you find?" the Emperor gasped as he burst in. Adeneus, the Arch-Sorcerer and Tanish the master engineer stood close, talking in hushed tones but turned and bowed in the Emperor's presence.

"Your holiness," Adeneus smiled clasping the Emperor's hand tightly. "We found it, your vision was true, right here, below the palace." The Emperor could not believe what he was hearing.

"You're sure?" he asked, not wanting to commit to the jubilation he desperately wanted to express without absolute certainty.

"If your holiness would like, we can show you," Tanish chimed in, eager to get back down into the excavations and continue his work. The Emperor nodded and was escorted out of the chamber and into the very bowels of the palace, passing through the kitchens and servants' quarters as he did so, the residents of which could scarcely believe their eyes that their places of work were being blessed by his divine presence.

After nearly half an hour of hurried walking, they came to the entrance of the excavations. In what had previously been a storeroom, a shaft had been dug at a 45-degree angle into the north wall, wide enough for two men standing abreast to pass through. Tanish and Adeneus took the lead with the Emperor and Nestor close behind.

The shaft grew in both width and height the further the men pressed on and every few meters a new torch had been placed on the walls to light the way. Despite the plentiful room to manoeuvre Nestor was becoming increasingly agitated at being underground, a mere tunnel collapse away from a slow and painful death in the dark. "Can we hurry this along please?" he pleaded with those ahead of him, a hint of desperation in his voice.

"Nearly there," Tanish groaned as he had to duck under a dip in the ceiling the excavators had evidently deemed too laborious to bother doing anything about. For the remainder of the journey, the men walked in silence, each preoccupied with their own thoughts of what this discovery could mean for them or their field. After another fifteen minutes, the men came to a crossroads.

"Left," Tanish whispered, his voice echoing down the tunnel. The men continued along the winding passage for another few minutes. All the while Nestor became increasingly agitated, cursing with each new step until finally, they came to a set of iron gates which Tanish pulled apart, beckoning the others to stand beside him.

Once the men were all past the gates Adeneus pulled a lever and with a jolt the men began to descend further into the depths as the floor lowered.

After another few minutes in the lift, the cavern below them began to fill with a gentle blue light which grew in intensity until torches were needless. Meanwhile, the sound of striking tools and the barking of orders became clear and echoed as if the stone itself were speaking. When the lift finally came to a stop the four men, even those who had already known what awaited them stood, mouths agape in amazement.

The lift had brought them into a huge structure with the walls and ceilings carved from pure white stone, and at the centre, carved into the back wall was a truly marvellous image. It was a man, well-aged and bearded, his eyes closed, and hands held out, his palms showing.

At the base of the carving was a pool of water, blue as the sky, sparkling like gems seemingly giving off its own glorious light. All around men were striking at the walls with their tools to no effect, their pickaxes and shovels would bend or snap upon impact with the unknown material, much to the fury of the chief excavator.

Tanish opened the gates once more and the men stepped out, almost in a trance gliding across the immaculate floor. It seemed as if neither time nor nature dared touch this place for fear of desecrating its beauty. The light emanating from every corner of the room seemed to have its own presence, hanging in the air, singing like a ghostly choir.

"It's incredible," gasped Nestor turning to the Emperor. "Is this what you saw in your vision?" The Emperor, whose eyes were fixated on the carving's face replied with a simple

"Exactly."

"This is not all your holiness," Adeneus whispered, "please, this way." He led the Emperor and Nestor forward, around the pool and up a set of stairs that were almost invisible at any angle other than when climbing them.

Meanwhile, Tanish, with a bow to the Emperor broke off to oversee the workers who had halted their tasks out of respect. At the top of the stairs, it was clear what Adeneus had meant to show them. In the centre of the carving's palms were two mirrors, their image so clear that even at his current distance the Emperor could see specks of dirt on the overalls of the workers far behind him.

The Emperor moved closer to the mirror on the right palm until only he was visible in its reflection. Gently, as if reaching out at a new-born babe, he touched the mirror's surface.

Running the tips of his fingers down its edge, afraid that at any moment it may shatter.

Suddenly, the smooth surface at the end of his fingertips became something more. He looked down and saw a handle, shaped like a diamond which had been invisible to him until the moment he had touched it. Behind him a crowd had begun to form, none of whom had previously noticed the handle themselves.

Excitement and nerves filled everyone in the room, not least the Emperor himself. After all, this was as far as his vision had taken him. He knew nothing of what may lie beyond this door, and for a long moment could not bring himself to grasp the handle.

No one uttered even a whisper as they watched, eyes glued to their Emperor. The only sound was that of the room itself, its ethereal whispering almost daring them to open the door. The Emperor's mind was swimming, his heart pounding. He swore he could feel something behind the door, something ancient, something of immeasurable power.

Its presence was tangible, flowing through him like blood. It was reaching out to him, but unable to pass, like a whisper in a hurricane. At last, the Emperor breathed deeply and grasped the handle firmly, and with his mind and heart still racing, turned it.

Locked.

There was a collective sigh as some were relieved, others disappointed. The Emperor however was furious. Why would the Lord give him such a vision if he were unable to fulfil it? He tried again, twisting the handle harder this time, but still with no luck. He took a step back, the faces of concern and confusion of those behind him clear in the door's reflection.

He turned and pointed to the largest of the excavation crew, a burly man with a bald head and thick moustache. "You, come and help me with this." The man could not believe he had just been personally addressed by the Emperor and stood, frozen in place, the blood draining from his face.

"Now, man," the Emperor scolded. With a nudge from his fellows, the man snapped out of his daze and rushed forward.

The Emperor turned so that one hand was on the handle and his shoulder faced the door. "On three, understood?"

"Yes, your holiness," the man squeaked, positioning himself.

"One. Two. Three." The Emperor huffed as he turned the handle and used all his strength to push the door, to no effect. Incensed, he turned away and storming past the crowd behind him, grabbed one of the many pickaxes which had been left scattered across the room.

Nobody dared speak as the Emperor struck blow after blow against the door, sparks flying, with each strike being more desperate than the last. Until, eventually, the pickaxe shattered entirely. Panting, the Emperor threw down what remained of the tool and to his dismay found that there was not so much a speck of dirt on the door, let alone any visible damage.

At this point, Adeneus stepped forward.

"Your holiness, perhaps we should retire now." The Emperor turned to face him, reaching up under his mask to wipe sweat from his brow. "I will send some of our brightest academics to conduct some experiments, for now, there are other matters which need attending to, I'm sure?"

"Yes, your holiness," Nestor added. "We have much to do today, the newly elected Prelates will be arriving, and you must bless Parliament before the day is done." The Emperor nodded, frustrated yet filled with a new purpose.

"Fine," he said begrudgingly. "I want every mind you can spare working on a way to open these doors, Adeneus."

The Arch-Sorcerer bowed. "Of course, your holiness, we shall work night and day."

The Emperor turned to Nestor. "I want the Congregation to convene today, after the blessing of Parliament." He turned again to Adeneus. "I expect to see you there." Adeneus nodded in submission. "Right, let's get this over with," the Emperor sighed as Tanish led them back the way they had come.

Hours later the Emperor was stood facing two huge doors which led into Parliament's main chamber. One made of solid gold and decorated with the crests of the Imperium's nobility, the other wooden, bare except for the words "All are equal in his house" carved across the centre.

The Emperor shifted uncomfortably where he stood as he waited for his cue to enter. "We really should get somebody to do this for me. We do with all the fun engagements. Why not the dull ones too?" he complained to Nestor who stood by his side.

Nestor bowed apologetically. "I'm sorry your holiness, but you know how important this ceremony is. The last thing you need is Elias breathing down your neck accusing you of not taking your duties seriously." He made a good point. The Emperor's relationship with the fanatical Seekers of the One had been strained since Elias had assumed its leadership nearly a century ago.

His extreme puritan views on the behaviour and role of the Lord's favoured had put them at loggerheads on more than one occasion. The Emperor found it ironic. As an emperor one would expect to be entirely free from the judgement and control of others. As he had found early on in his reign, the truth was in fact the opposite.

Suddenly, the doors were pulled open revealing the main chamber. Hundreds of bodies, both sitting and standing, packed the room, all wearing the robes of their faction and eager to catch a glimpse of their master. A man in bright yellow robes stood beside a golden throne situated atop a small platform. It was evident that he who sat there was above all others in the chamber.

The man raised his arms and began his speech as the Emperor entered, timing his footsteps so that they were perfectly in sync with the man's words.

"Please stand for his holiness. The Lord's favoured. Emperor of the Imperium. Defender of the faith. Guardian of the people. Our Imperator!"

There was rapturous applause as the Emperor took his throne. Many of those present, even those who were veterans of Parliament, had tears in their eyes. To be blessed by the Emperor's presence was an honour beyond words. The applause lasted far longer than scheduled and already the Emperor was beginning to sweat.

The windowless chamber packed with hundreds of overdressed people was stuffy at the best of times. Now it was almost unbearable as the Emperor begged the Lord for this to be over quickly. Once the applause had died down the Emperor rose, his ornamental armour and robe weighing him down making it a struggle.

Silence gripped the room.

"Friends," the Emperor boomed in his official engagement voice. "It is my pleasure to welcome you on this auspicious day to this holy place. Now, before we can begin, I ask this house to bring forth its representatives so they may swear loyalty and be blessed."

As rehearsed, the leading members of Parliament's three factions took leave of their seats and kneeled before the Emperor. Meanwhile, a small man in a white robe approached from the side, a silver platter in hand upon which rested a silver goblet.

The Emperor took the goblet in his left hand and with his right gestured towards the man in silver robes kneeling on the same side. "Do you Elias, Grand Seeker, pontiff of the clergy, swear loyalty for both you and your brethren to the Lord's favoured and Imperator?" Keeping his eyes fixed straight ahead Elias responded.

"Aye, for my brethren and myself do I swear undying loyalty unto you. The Lord's favoured and Imperator." The Emperor handed him the goblet.

"Drink then, and should you speak truth be unharmed. Have you any doubts or false allegiance in your heart may this poison strike you down." Without hesitation, Elias drank from the goblet, not a sliver of doubt in his mind.

Once he was finished there was silence as the room waited to see the effects of the poison, the death of the Grand Seeker being a scandal the likes of which the Imperium had never seen. To the disappointment of more than a few, Elias remained, steadfast in posture and faith, his loyalty proven.

The Emperor took the goblet and spoke once more, his right hand hovering over Elias' head, addressing both him and his faction.

"Your hearts have been tested, and you have been found loyal to your God. Go now unto the world. Be my right hand and spread word of his divine grace throughout its many lands. Knowing that the light of the Lord shines on your backs always."

There was applause across the chamber as the Emperor moved to the man kneeling to his left. Robed in black with the Imperium's military crest emblazoned upon it, a sword of pure white wrapped in a red flame, a golden crown resting upon its crossguard. This time, taking the goblet in his right hand and gesturing with his left, the Emperor repeated his question.

"Do you Sir Bryce, Imperial Knight, commander of my armies swear loyalty for both you and your brethren to the Lord's favoured and Imperator?"

"Aye, for my brethren and myself do I swear undying loyalty unto you. The Lord's favoured and Imperator." Sir Bryce repeated as the Emperor handed him the goblet.

"Drink then, and should you speak truth be unharmed. Have you any doubts or false allegiance in your heart may this poison strike you down." Once again Sir Bryce drank without fear, knowing in his heart his loyalty to be absolute.

Silence filled the room once more, followed quickly by applause as Sir Bryce remained very much alive. The Emperor took the goblet and held his left hand above Sir Bryce's head.

"Your hearts have been tested, and you have been found loyal to your God. Go now unto the world. Be my left hand and bring destruction to my enemies. Root out and destroy those false gods and idols who pervert the true faith. Protect the faithful and all that is mine and know the wrath of the Lord guides your arm."

At last, the Emperor stood over the man in the centre, his robes a dull brown and representing the common folk of the Imperium. Not long ago it would have been a capital offence for one either not of noble blood or a member of the clergy to be in such proximity to their Imperator.

Nevertheless, the near defeat of his armies during the peasant uprising which had gripped the Imperium a century ago had forced his hand to adopt a more democratic approach to ruling his vast empire.

Having spent so many millennia speaking down to peasants he counted his capitulation during the crisis as his most humiliating moment. It was no surprise, therefore, that the current situation left him with a bitter taste in his mouth.

This time he did not raise his hands in blessing, but simply spoke, meanwhile examining the faces of the commoners who were seated at the rear of the chamber.

"Do you, Abraham, elected representative of the common folk of the Imperium swear loyalty for both you and your brethren to the Lord's favoured and Imperator?"

"Aye, for my brethren and myself do I swear undying loyalty unto you. The Lord's favoured and Imperator."

This time the Emperor was slow in handing over the goblet. While the other two had been confident in their commitment, there was an evident tinge of fear in Abraham's voice. Perhaps, the Emperor wondered, it would prove to be that his loyalty was not so unquestionable.

Eventually, he offered Abraham the goblet who took it with trembling hands. There was a long pause before he finally raised the courage to take a sip, memories of him and his friends fighting to rid the Imperium of the Emperor's rule flooding back.

He closed his eyes and held his breath, expecting at any moment his disloyalty would be discovered and put on show in an agonising display. He wondered what would happen to the others in his faction. Would they all immediately be taken outside and shot, to ensure no disloyalty remained?

However, these thoughts turned out to be unnecessary, as much to Abraham's own surprise, the poison had no effect on him. Filled with relief he raised his hands to offer back the goblet to his Imperator and unintentionally looked upon his face.

The two locked eyes. A wave of emotions rushed through Abraham – anger, humiliation, but mostly fear. Whether these were his own feelings, however, he was unsure. He quickly bowed his head as the Emperor took the goblet and offered his blessing.

"Your hearts have been tested, and you have been found loyal to your God. Go now unto the world and do good works. Be ever faithful to me and one another, and thou shall be protected by my hands." He took a step back and raised both arms addressing the room. "Go now all of you from this place and do as I have commanded. And know that all are equal before me in this house."

The room erupted into applause for the final time as the Emperor took his leave. Parliament would now sit for the next decade, debating and proposing laws for the Emperor to decide upon.

"Well done your holiness," Nestor praised. "I have called a meeting of the Congregation as you requested, the members will be on their way now."

"Thank you, Nestor but I want to make a quick detour first," the Emperor replied. "Do you have any idea where my wife is?"

Nestor let out a small chuckle. "I'll give you one guess, your holiness".

Chapter 6

The Imperial Palace library was the most renowned place of learning in the known world, second only to the Imperial University. Located in the westernmost wing of the palace, students from across the world would flock to read its rare manuscripts, some of which dated back to before the wars of liberation when the human kingdoms revolted against their dragon overlords. Its bursting shelves were like pillars of pure knowledge supporting the very foundations of civilisation itself.

So long had the library stood, that it had gone through dozens of aesthetic changes to fit whatever architectural and philosophical trends were popular at the time. Now was no exception. As works and ideas pertaining to man's coalescence with nature had grown in popularity, the library's new form had begun to take shape. No longer were the floors of polished wood or sheen marble. Now when one perused its vast collection they would feel the touch of soft grass beneath their toes, barefootedness being greatly encouraged.

But that had only been the beginning; soon whole trees had been planted. Hundreds of them acting as both artistic reminders of man's part in nature, and as markers, denoting the next section of the library. Beneath each tree were ponds filled with a plethora of the most beautiful and colourful aquatic life that could be found in the Imperium, around which were rings of flowers in every shade and colour.

This gallery of nature was only made possible by the long glass ceiling which filled the whole building with the sun's life-giving rays. And of course, the army of gardeners who worked tirelessly to keep it fresh and orderly.

Beside one such pond sat a woman, with long blonde hair and a slender frame, her delicate fingers gently turning the pages of a book, as old and worn as she was young and beautiful. The Emperor watched from afar as she tucked her hair behind her ear and bit her lip in concentration, fully immersed in her research.

The Emperor had met his wife millennia ago, back when he was little more than a commoner and she a lecturer of zoology at what was now the Imperial University. He remembered each detail of the moment they met with perfect clarity. He had been tasked by the council to provide information pertaining to a beast which had been causing havoc across the republic but was at the time unknown to science.

While frantically scouring shelf after shelf of the university library with no luck, a beautiful woman approached him, the same beautiful woman who now sat before him, lost in her work. Introducing herself as Sarah, she had been trying to conduct research of her own, but his frantic cursing and raving had made it impossible.

After listening politely to his incomprehensible ramblings, with the occasional giggle as he lost his temper with whatever book he was holding, she took his hand and led him to another section of the library. The two had spent hours together, poring over manuscript after manuscript, book after book, letter after letter. Anything that could lead them to the answers they needed. All the while they talked. They discussed their work, their past and what they hoped for the future.

It had been during these moments that he had become captivated by her. While her beauty had been obvious immediately, it was her mind and dry wit which had pushed him over the edge. Less than a month later they were married.

As he watched her, Sarah's nose still buried between the old musty pages, he thought to himself how lucky he truly was. To have found a creature of such unadulterated perfection whom he loved with every fibre of his being.

Already his heart was yearning to embrace her, he could not stand for them to be apart for but a moment. Without realising, he had already covered the distance between them, and he stood but a fraction away, her back facing him. He reached out his hand to touch her but hesitated, as if she would fade away like a dream should he get too close.

"I'm a married woman I'll have you know," Sarah sighed nonchalantly, still reading. Behind his mask, the Emperor was grinning from ear to ear and decided to play along.

"I'm sure your husband isn't the sort of man who gets jealous over a casual conversation," he grunted, lowering himself beside her. Still not looking up from her book Sarah smiled, sending his heart into a flutter.

"Clearly you don't know my husband."

The Emperor tilted his head to one side as if lost in thought.

"I think I have a pretty good idea. I bet he's tall, devastatingly handsome." He paused to gently caress Sarah's cheek before continuing. "And he's a fool to not be spending every waking moment by your side."

Sarah at last looked up from her book to face her husband. A bright smile illuminated her face. Her deep green eyes brimming with overwhelming love and longing that was only for him. "I've missed you, my love," he whispered.

"And I have missed you," she said, gently kissing his palm, squeezing his hand tightly with her own. But her face soon changed to one of disappointment. Her eyes now filled with sadness as she too reached up to touch her husband's face, but was halted, the cold, unfeeling mask acting as a barrier.

"I wish you did not have to wear this ridiculous thing," she sighed. "I cannot remember the last time I saw your face."

"The one thing that has kept us going this long," the Emperor teased back, trying to change the mood. Sarah shot him a look of disapproval that he had become all too familiar with and decided not to push his luck. He may be favoured by God, but like any sane man, he was still afraid of his wife.

"Where are your guards?" he asked scanning the room. It made him uncomfortable to think of his beloved in such a vulnerable state, at the mercy of any passing man with a grievance. She casually glanced around, squinting between the seemingly endless rows of identical stone bookshelves.

"They are here somewhere. I sent them off to find some books I needed."

"Are they for your next paper on the hunting habits of ground-nesting lizards?" the Emperor asked, gently swirling his fingers in the cool water of the pool. "Because I've been excited ever since I finished the last one," he teased once more. Sarah rolled her eyes.

"Not that I am not happy to see you my love, but have you visited me for the first time in months just to mock me?" Sarah sighed in frustration.

"Perhaps," the Emperor grinned. Sarah rolled her eyes again and stood to leave, her many books and papers clutched to her chest. As she turned away the Emperor's hand shot out and grabbed the hem of her dress. "Wait, I'm sorry, please sit, I promise I'll be good. I wanted to speak with you about something." he said, genuinely apologetic.

Sarah was both suspicious and intrigued. The last time her husband had made such an effort to speak with her, he had informed her of Elias' demand they live apart. She had held very little time for optimism since. The Emperor, sensing his wife's suspicions, took her hand. Although this served only to further fan the flames of fear in her heart.

"I was wondering," he began before stopping to reword his request. "I was hoping," he continued. "That you would retake your seat in the Righteous Congregation." He waited for Sarah to reply, studying her face for any sign of an answer.

At first, Sarah was shocked, her face clearly expressing this. But then as she realised her husband was not playing a cruel trick on her, her face lit up. "Are you serious?" she whispered, barely able to believe her ears. "What about Elias, won't he throw a fit?"

The Emperor simply shrugged. "Let him, I think it's about time I started exercising some authority around here anyway." He had barely finished speaking when Sarah threw her arms around him in a tight embrace.

The Emperor wanted nothing more than for this to last. It had been so long since he had felt her warmth, he had forgotten how much he missed it. He buried his face in her hair, the sweet smell of her perfume filling his nostrils. "I've missed this," he sighed.

"Me too," she sniffed, countless memories of happier times swimming through her mind. "I won't let you down my love," she whispered.

"That's good," he said, "Because the next meeting is in an hour." Sarah quickly pulled away.

"You're joking?" she gasped. "I am hardly dressed for such an important event. I cannot have the Congregation seeing me like this upon my return." The Emperor quickly examined his wife's attire. A red silk dress with golden trim, adorned by a variety of floral patterns intertwining with one another. Unblemished and handmade by his personal tailor as a gift no more than a year ago.

She was the visage of perfection to any man. "My love. If anyone dares comment on your appearance, apart from calling you the most wondrous and beautiful creature the Lord has ever made, I will personally deal with them," the Emperor reassured her.

"Well, I suppose that will do for now. But a new dress wouldn't do me any harm either." Sarah smirked. It was the Emperor's turn to roll his eyes, there was no way he was going to start that conversation.

"I was hoping we could walk together," he said as he climbed to his feet and offered his hand. Sarah smiled once more as she took it and stood.

"We had better hurry my love," the Emperor said as they linked arms. "You know what Nestor is like if I'm late."

The pair arrived at the Congregation chamber with five minutes to spare. All the while they had talked, although it had been Sarah who did much of the talking, and mostly about her research. She would throw her arms around and gesticulate wildly as she explained the physiology of whatever creature she had recently been studying. Meanwhile, the Emperor could do nothing but laugh at his wife's excitement.

It was in those moments, where Sarah's brilliant mind and passion were so evident, that his love for her seemed to overcome any doubt or fear in his heart. The Emperor worshipped her like the people of the Imperium worshipped him, although where there was fear and obedience in their worship, his reverence of Sarah was comprised of nothing but genuine awe and wonder.

He needed not to be chosen by the Lord to feel blessed, as the greatest blessing that could ever be bestowed upon a man was already his. Frantically explaining her latest theories to him as he looked on, hypnotised. Even before becoming empress, Sarah had been somewhat of a celebrity. Having discovered exactly how and why animals but not humans were able to reproduce in Purgatory, she had answered questions which had plagued farmers and scholars alike for eons.

She finally halted her lecture as the pair arrived at the chamber doors and took a deep breath before following her husband inside. She had been banned from all formal engagements and matters of state since Elias had assumed the title of Grand Seeker after the peasants' revolt a century ago. To openly defy his orders was a dangerous act of rebellion, even for the Emperor. Nevertheless, she trusted her husband utterly and felt no fear, even as all eyes in the room fixed themselves upon her. Some were filled with pleasant surprise and in others, anger.

The room was a testament to the glory and achievements of the Imperium. Upon the walls hung banners of now long-conquered enemies. So numerous were they that many overlapped like feathers, giving the room the appearance of being at the heart of some monstrous bird.

Along the walls were dozens of display cases, within which could be found priceless artefacts the Congregation deemed too precious to be trusted to the Imperial University. Among such treasures were daggers cut from dragon's teeth. And Ancient tomes older than the known world brought from lands beyond their comprehension, containing magic only the greatest of sorcerers could hope to understand but a fraction of.

The floor was itself carpeted by the hide of a single massive creature, slain by a great hero, long before the Emperor's ascension, upon which rested a large table. It was big enough to sit perhaps twenty people comfortably, yet only eight chairs were present, spaced an equal distance from one another.

At the table's head sat the Emperor. On his throne of dark ebony, where his back would rest, was carved a pair of angels, swords crossed. This was meant to represent his holy crusade against those who would deny his divine mandate, led by the forces of the Fallen One.

To his immediate right sat Sarah, silent and poised with the grace befitting an empress. Her throne was a pure white, to represent her purity and sanctity and until now had remained empty for almost a century, a ghostly reminder of the Emperor's weakness. Before them sat the other members of the Righteous Congregation. Comprised of the most loyal and influential members of Imperial society, they were the final piece of the bureaucratic jigsaw which allowed the Emperor to govern.

Closest to his right sat Elias, the Grand Seeker, leader of the fanatical Seekers of the One, the religious order which had brought the Emperor to power in a coup over a millennia ago. He was a short, wispy fellow with a common military-style haircut and a worn, creased face. The only man the Emperor truly feared.

Beside him was the empty seat of Cardinal Praxus, Lord of the Uncharted. He was charged with leading expeditions into unknown territory and bringing back detailed information on the world beyond. Currently, he and his men were heading north. Their orders were to reach the end of their maps and then keep going. They were only allowed to return after ten years of exploration.

Beside his chair sat Rohm, the Eyes of the Lord. He was the Emperor's spymaster, charged with gathering information on the Imperium's enemies. locating powerful magical artefacts and dealing with plots against the Imperium.

He was himself the least inconspicuous of people. Always dressed in the most flamboyant colours with a booming voice and a dozen times the weight of a healthy man he required a specially made chair to accommodate his mass. Nevertheless, his discretion and army of informants were unparalleled in the known world. If one of the Emperor's enemies were to catch a cold, Rohm would know before they started developing symptoms.

These three men were colloquially known as the Emperor's 'right hand'.

Opposite these men sat the Emperor's 'left hand'. First was Sir Bryce, Commander of the Emperor's armies – a mountain of a man, easily seven feet tall. He sported a long yet fashionably braided, black beard which accommodated his tanned skin, earned from countless hours of training in the sun.

The Emperor had never seen him not dressed as if about to wage a one-man war. Even now, in the safest room in the Imperium, he sat fully armoured, a sword on his belt and another on his back for good measure.

Beside Sir Bryce sat Nestor, the Emperor's most trusted advisor and chief administrator. He, along with his army of clerks, kept the Imperium running on a day-to-day basis. Dressed in the lime-green robe of his office, he sat twirling his thin moustache between his thumb and index finger, skimming over the multitude of papers before him.

Finally, there was Adeneus, dressed in his iconic purple robe and white cape, the Arch-Sorcerer of the Imperial University. His arcane knowledge was beyond compare, and second only to his expertise in ancient history.

He was a tall, slender man, his pale skin reflective of the little time spent outside of his laboratory. Even now, in the presence of his Imperator, he was more preoccupied with trying to solve mathematical and arcane equations, unconsciously scratching his thought process into the table.

The Emperor removed his mask, much to Sarah's delight. This was the signal for the meeting to begin.

"Your holiness, your majesty," Nestor said as he raised himself from his seat to bow. "I am glad you could both attend this session. It has been so dull without your radiant presence, your majesty." Nestor smiled as he shot Elias a disapproving look. Sarah smiled back.

"It is good to be back, although I am sure everything has been running just as smoothly in my absence. After all, there is no man in the Imperium better suited to the task of keeping this country ticking."

Nestor blushed at the compliment and did his best to retain his composure. Before he could continue Elias spoke up.

"While no one is more delighted than I to be blessed by your presence your majesty, I must admit I am surprised you have seen it fit to return to these boring meetings. Surely there are better ways you would rather spend your time than listening to us drone on?"

The Emperor was about to interject but Sarah spoke first.

"Thank you for your concern, my lord. However, I can assure you that there is nothing I would rather do than make sure my country is being run effectively. Of course, if you believe these meetings to be little more than dull inconveniences, I would be delighted to introduce you to the ladies of my crochet club?"

There were snickers all around, even the Emperor had to try his best to stifle a chuckle. Elias's face was blood red with embarrassment and rage. However, an outburst at the Emperor's wife would do far more harm than good. So, he gave a gentle bow and sat without another word. He might be powerful, but that power came from his subtleties and quiet scheming, not open insubordination. Sarah had only vented a fraction of her intense hatred for Elias in her remark but was proud of herself, nevertheless. She turned to her husband and gave him a subtle wink.

Nestor stood once more and began circling the table, handing out papers which his clerks had spent all morning copying by hand. "While I know we were not supposed to convene for another few days, this means we can get through this backlog of issues ahead of time. Afterwards, I believe his holiness would like to raise his own issue with the Congregation."

The other members quickly turned to look at the Emperor. It was highly irregular for him to raise a personal issue; it must therefore be a matter of great importance. Each man wondered whether it concerned him directly. The Emperor began flicking through the papers in front of him. *Boring, boring,*

boring, he thought to himself, unsure if he would be able to cope for the next few hours. Then Sarah, leaning close so she could see the papers for herself placed her hand on his. Suddenly, his whole mood changed.

Simply being in her presence was intoxicating and seemed to dispel all doubt and negativity from his mind.

"The first order of business," Nestor said returning to his seat. "I have received a letter from Cardinal Praxus."

"Did he finally discover a way to remove his head out of his own arse?" Sir Bryce interrupted. Once again there were scattered laughs across the room. Nestor, however, simply stood with a look of disappointment and disgust upon his face. He had never been a great admirer of Sir Bryce and his vulgarity but had learned long ago to just let him have his moment before pretending it never happened. He simply tutted and continued.

"In summary, he claims the area north, past the Borderlands to be arable and sparsely populated. After that, it becomes little more than huge open plains where beasts roam wild. He also claims to have discovered little more than the occasional farmstead, yet states the peasants swear loyalty to a great prince by their reckoning a year's ride west. He requests permission to change course and head west to see if the peasants speak the truth, and what are his orders in case they do happen upon this princedom?"

"How many men does Praxus have behind him?" Sir Bryce asked. Nestor scanned the letter again for the finer details.

"He left with two thousand," the Emperor answered, "however, no doubt some have perished on the journey."

"Ah," Nestor exclaimed having found the page he was looking for. "He reports that while some of his men have succumbed to the wilds, they are well below expected losses. He also says he has been able to recruit a good number of peasants and adventurers with the prospect of riches beyond our borders. He states his final troop count is nearer double than what he set out with."

"Not enough to conquer this princedom if it's indeed as great as the peasants say," Sir Bryce grunted. For the first time,

Rohm spoke, his deep, guttural voice an unpleasant product of his size.

"Perhaps violence need not be the answer, Sir Bryce. Maybe offer them vassalhood or an alliance. Invite this prince to the Imperium where we can get a good measure of him and act afterwards?"

"Typical, you've got no balls, Rohm," Sir Bryce scoffed. "I say order Praxus to find the princedom and raid it for all it's worth. Burn every farm, plunder every treasure, and send this prince a message showing him what we are capable of."

"I admire your gusto, Sir Bryce," Sarah chimed in, to which he could not help but puff out his chest and shoot the other men at the table a look of smug victory. It was short-lived however as Sarah continued. "However, I worry it may turn out poorly for us in the end."

"How so, your majesty?" he replied. Sarah stood and began slowly wringing her hands together as she spoke.

"Let us say we go with your plan. For the first few months to a year, it is a blinding success, riches flood into the Imperium the likes of which we have never seen. But after such a time has elapsed for this great prince to amass his armies, he crushes our expeditionary force. Then in his rage, travels all the way south to the very heart of the Imperium."

"Our armies are the largest in the world your majesty, they would stand no chance against us," Sir Bryce replied, a hint of hurt in his voice at the very idea his forces could ever be defeated. Sarah nodded and continued.

"In the known world certainly, but we have no way of knowing the full strength of this prince. Also, what if he has allies, of which we know nothing, all of whom rush to aid him in his journey south? If this were to happen, do you imagine our enemies to the west would simply remain neutral?"

By this point, Sarah had moved and stood with her hands resting on the back of her chair, a habit she had picked up over her countless years as a lecturer. "I imagine they would rejoice at such an opportunity to destroy us. Do you believe your armies could defeat an entire world united against us Sir Bryce?"

Sir Bryce did not respond and simply sat in silence with his face resting upon his clasped hands. There was a sudden, slow clap as Rohm smiled with delight.

"We are truly blessed to have such wisdom in our midst, your majesty. If only we were all so wise at this table," he said, shooting Sir Bryce his own smug grin back at him.

"What course of action would you suggest then, your majesty?" the Emperor asked. Sarah was suddenly thrown off guard, not by the question, but rather who was asking it.

"Well," she stammered before pausing. Her eyes darted from person to person. A disapproving look from Elias, as if questioning her ability or right to be present caused her now clenched fists to shake in anger. She cleared her throat and sat once again.

"I believe Lord Rohm has the best plan. Let us not make enemies when it is not necessary, let us instead invite this prince here to the Imperium. We can show him what he stands to gain by allying himself with us, and what he stands to lose should he oppose us.

"Over time we can gather information on both his strength and those around him. We should see this as a golden opportunity for us to expand without bloodshed, giving us a major numerical advantage over our enemies."

"I agree with her majesty," Nestor added, "why make enemies when we can make allies?"

"I agree," Elias said to the surprise of all, not least Sarah. "It is far easier to spread your word amongst allies than foes, your holiness."

The Emperor tapped his fingers on the table, weighing up the arguments he had so far heard. He then realised there was one voice which had not yet spoken.

"Adeneus, what is your opinion on the matter, do you agree with Sir Bryce or her majesty?"

This entire time Adeneus had been mumbling to himself, occasionally scribbling notes on the papers which he was supposed to be reading. So lost in thought was he, that he did not hear the Emperor's question.

"Adeneus!" Elias shouted, "Answer his holiness." At last, the Arch-Sorcerer looked up, dazed and confused as if woken from a deep sleep. All eyes were on him, a hideous scowl drawn across Elias' face.

"Apologies, your holiness," he stuttered. "My mind was elsewhere."

"We were discussing whether to adopt Sir Bryce's plan, or her majesty's regarding a potential new princedom to the north-west," the Emperor explained.

"Ahem," Adeneus said clearing his throat. "Well, I am sure her majesty's plan, whatever it may be is infinitely more well thought out and sensible than whatever Sir Bryce has suggested."

"Kiss arse," Sir Bryce huffed.

" I suppose that settles it then," the Emperor sighed in relief. "Nestor, please draft a letter to the Cardinal informing him of his orders."

"At once, your holiness." Nestor nodded as he began scribbling the reply on a new piece of paper.

"What's next?" the Emperor asked, hoping against hope for something exciting. This time Elias stood and addressed the room.

"If you could all please find the pages regarding the recent parliamentary election results by province, you will see some issues." The Emperor found the pages and skimmed over them with a bored huff. Nothing but page upon page of numbers which meant nothing to him. Until at last, he found what he thought Elias meant.

Highlighted in red were six towns and villages, all of which had a total vote count of zero. "So, what, some people didn't vote, is that not a good thing?" the Emperor asked tossing the paper back onto the table. Elias, still standing, removed his glasses and placed his papers down gently.

"If they were in protest at the democratic system in favour of your rule, I would agree, your holiness. Unfortunately, upon further investigation, it seems they are protesting your role in politics entirely."

"Preposterous," Nestor riled in shock. "These peasants were lucky to get the concessions they did in the peace treaty. Now they refuse to partake in their own ridiculous system?"

"It seems, your holiness," Elias continued ignoring Nestor's outburst. "They refuse to participate in a system where their representatives do not actually rule. They want to install a republic with an elected head of state."

There was an immediate uproar from across the table, each man voicing his displeasure at once. All their points drowned in a single wave of noise. The Emperor raised his hand signalling for the commotion to die down. Elias produced another piece of paper from his pocket and handed it to the Emperor. He unfolded it and read carefully as Elias continued speaking.

"I have already drawn up plans for the response, your holiness. My Seekers will raze the villages to the ground and burn all the inhabitants as heretics. It just needs your signature."

There were murmurs of agreement and the banging of fists on the table at the proposal. Rohm, however, rolled his eyes. He had never been a subscriber to the belief barbarity could solve all of man's ills. But when it came to the Seekers there was no arguing. Brutality was their trade and to them, reason and heresy were often one and the same.

The Emperor shrugged his shoulders; what were a few burned towns to cement his authority? He moved to pick up his quill when Sarah's hand shot across him and grabbed his arm, a look of pure horror across her face.

"My love, surely you do not agree with this insanity?" she asked, her voice filled with disbelief. She dreaded to think what else her husband had been coerced into over the last century without her knowledge.

"Your majesty, you forget yourself, please address his holiness as such," Elias scolded, his voice like venom. She turned to him in anger.

"No, my lord, it is you who forgets yourself. My husband is no tyrant, and you will not poison his mind with such insidious plots against his own people." The Emperor placed his hand upon Sarah's in the hope of calming her but did not speak.

"Well then, perhaps her majesty would like to enlighten the Congregation on how else to resolve this matter?" Elias asked mockingly. Sarah thought for a moment before turning back to face her husband, who was looking at her with wary eyes, begging her not to push Elias further. Suddenly she had an idea and turned back to the Congregation.

"His holiness and I will travel to these towns and villages. We shall show ourselves to the people not as tyrannical overlords but as compassionate protectors, willing and eager to listen to their concerns. I honestly believe this will strengthen our bond with the people without the need for violence."

The other members of the Congregation looked at Sarah with complete disbelief. Most of them had never even considered the idea of treating the people with anything other than contempt. Now, for many of them, her idea resonated, perhaps a gentle touch was indeed what the Imperium had been missing all these centuries. Elias however began to laugh hysterically, doubled over and clutching at his chest. All the while the rest of the room was silent, Sarah's face reddening with each passing second.

Finally, Elias' laughing fit relented, removing his glasses yet again, and wiping his eyes with his handkerchief.

"I am truly sorry your majesty and I mean no disrespect, but perhaps the Righteous Congregation is no place for delicate and ladylike creatures such as yourself?" This taunt was the final straw, Sarah could no longer contain her rage and she unleashed it with all the ferocity of an artillery barrage. She shot up from her throne and roared.

"How dare you speak to your empress in such a way you impudent little worm. If you dare address me like that again you will find yourself hang..." Sarah's tirade stopped abruptly as the Emperor's hand crushed her own. The pain was excruciating, yet she did not let even a fraction of it show. She looked at her husband, tears of pain and betrayal in her eyes. Nevertheless, Sarah understood she had gone too far and turned back to Elias.

"My apologies my lord, perhaps you are right. I believe my female weaknesses may have affected my judgement." The Emperor released her hand which was now badly bruised with at least one of her fingers broken which she quickly hid from view.

"I will take my leave now my lords, I thank you for entertaining me thus far. I trust you shall make the right decision." She quickly rushed from the room nursing her injured hand, tears beginning to flow freely down her cheeks. The Emperor meanwhile remained in place, an ocean of guilt welling up inside him.

Never had he intentionally hurt his wife and he could not help but feel the fires of rage burning hot upon his skin. He slammed his fist upon the table causing it to crack and splinter beneath him. Everyone else jumped in their seats, Elias almost stumbling back over his chair onto the floor.

"Elias," the Emperor growled. "Her majesty may have spoken out of turn, but if you ever insult her in such a way again you will see how far the protection of your office extends." This was an entirely new situation for Elias. He had become so used to being able to manipulate and abuse the Emperor's will through fear. Yet now, for the first time, he was the one who was afraid. The Emperor too could not believe he had finally taken such a stand. His heart was racing, and he wondered if perhaps he too had gone too far.

Yet his gamble seemed to pay off – Elias apologised sheepishly and returned to his seat, his body trembling. Realising now was the perfect opportunity to further undermine him, the Emperor stood.

"I have decided we shall go with her majesty's plan. Perhaps she is right, after all, had we been more sympathetic to the people to start with, we may never have had a rebellion in the first place."

There was an awkward silence as nobody wished to incur the Emperor's newfound wrath. As a final act of defiance, the Emperor tore Elias' order in half and tossed it back at him.

"Furthermore, from now on her majesty will be returning to all of her official duties." The Congregation all looked to Elias, expecting some sort of objection. But he was silent, still lost in the new reality he found himself in where he could no longer rely on fear alone to achieve his aims.

"If it is acceptable to you Nestor, I would like to raise my issue with the Congregation now. I don't think I can stomach any more of this today," the Emperor stated, his displeasure obvious.

"Of course, your holiness," Nestor replied, glad Elias had finally been humbled. The Emperor recounted his vision to the Congregation. Sparing no details, he described the city burning, the seemingly endless army of shadows, and finally the two figures whose battle resulted in such destruction. When the Emperor had finished, the room was deathly quiet. Each man was shaken to his very core by what he had just heard. At last Sir Bryce broke the silence which was hanging thick in the air like fog.

"And you are sure this was a vision your holiness, not just a dream?"

It was Adeneus who responded, jumping from his seat with great anger.

"Of course, this was no dream you fool! Unless you think his holiness's visions of the Vermindom spewing forth upon the earth was just a dream? Or perhaps the eruption of the Jaws of Vendaag which turned an entire civilisation to ash. Was that just an unlucky coincidence perhaps? No, it is quite clear his holiness has once more seen a cataclysmic event and we must do what we can to stop it."

Elias was quick to speak, his previous fear now replaced with overwhelming joy. "Your holiness, this is what we have been waiting so long for. Evidently you have foreseen your final confrontation with the Fallen One, at the end of which we are all lifted to paradise." Elias was practically squealing with excitement at the prospect. "We need do nothing at all, simply allow events to unfold and all shall be according to the Lord's divine plan."

Rohm shook his head slightly, trying to think of a more rational explanation. "Perhaps, your holiness, it is a warning that our more physical enemies mean to bring us harm?"

"Either way," Sir Bryce added, "from what you have described your holiness, I do not believe even we have strength in numbers to defeat such a foe."

The Emperor thought long and hard while the others argued amongst themselves. While the prospect of finally reaching paradise was very appealing, he believed Rohm was probably right, that this vision was of no more than his enemies waging war against him.

"Sir Bryce," he began, causing the room to fall silent once again. "I want you to start preparing our armies. Begin by conducting reconnaissance upon our neighbours and let all our people know that all raids against our enemies of a small scale have automatic royal approval."

Sir Bryce rose from his seat and bowed "At once your holiness." He marched from the chamber with purpose in each stride, eager for a chance to get his sword bloody once again.

"Sir Bryce," the Emperor called after him.

"Yes, your holiness?" he responded, half out of the door. The Emperor raised the papers with the election results so Sir Bryce could see them clearly.

"There were five villages."

Sir Bryce nodded in understanding. "Yes, your holiness," and with that, he left.

"Lord Rohm," the Emperor continued. "Get your spies to work, whatever our enemies are planning, I wish to know about it before they do." Rohm struggled with his massive frame out of his seat and bowed as low as his body would allow him.

"Immediately, your holiness," he wheezed before waddling out after Sir Bryce.

"Your holiness," Elias said, jumping in before the Emperor had a chance to speak once more. "May I please ask that you authorise an inquisition. Let my Seekers root out and destroy all the unfaithful in your realm. This will surely please the Lord before our ascension."

The Emperor swatted away the request. "Your Seekers will be working under Rohm and Adeneus. Rooting out spies and doing whatever Adeneus demands of them."

"But, your holiness…" Elias protested.

"Enough Elias, you have your orders, now go and see to them," the Emperor snapped back. Elias's face contorted into a scowl as he bowed and slithered away. Once Elias was out of earshot the Emperor groaned and nursed his aching head, a common by-product of even a short conversation with that man.

How long had it been since he had been able to sleep in the same bed as his wife? Or spend an evening walking the streets of the city like he used to without it causing a theological debate about his divinity? It was at this moment he realised, he had been addressed as '*his holiness*' or '*Imperator*' for so long, that he could no longer remember his own name.

"Your holiness," Nestor said interrupting the Emperor's train of thought, as if on cue. "Do you have any demands of Adeneus and myself regarding your vision?" Lost in his sad thoughts the Emperor had almost forgotten about his vision of impending doom, although it was now back, front and centre in his mind.

"Yes, Nestor, I would like you to gather our allies for a summit so I can inform them of the situation personally. Also, invite the less hostile powers in the east, perhaps we could persuade them if not to join us, then at least to stay out of the coming conflict."

Nestor rose and bowed, leaving without a word, determined to do as his Emperor had commanded to the best of his ability.

"And then there were two," Adeneus smiled.

"Oh, I wouldn't raise your spirits too high if I were you," the Emperor warned. "You have the toughest job of all."

"Whatever it may be, your holiness, I promise you I am up to the task," Adeneus assured him.

The Emperor was not so sure, he was not even certain his plan was even possible. Nevertheless, if any man could make it a reality, it would be Adeneus. He hunched himself over the table, hands intertwined. Adeneus did the same, excited about a potential new challenge.

"I want you to find a way to increase the strength of our armies one hundredfold," the Emperor revealed. Adeneus could not help but feel slightly disappointed, he had expected something more suited to his talents than a recruitment drive. He puffed out his cheeks and scratched his head.

"Well, I suppose we could tempt some rival lords and their armies to defect to our side. It would take some concessions on our part though. Perhaps even start training up the peasants. I'm sure with some help from Nestor we could reorganise our agricultural sector to be more efficient with less manpower."

The Emperor shook his head and could not help but feel a fool for what he was about to ask. "You misunderstand, my friend." Adeneus sat back in his chair, arms folded and now thoroughly confused.

"I don't want peasants or lords with allegiances as fickle as the wind. I want unquestioningly loyal soldiers with unmatched ferocity and in unprecedented numbers...I want you to restart the Phoenix project."

It took a few seconds for Adeneus to realise what the Emperor was suggesting, but once he had, his eyes lit up and his mind began swimming with ideas. He jumped up from his seat in excitement, tripping up over his words as his mind tried to both form a sentence and write formulas at the same time.

"Y-your holiness, such a task would rewrite entire fields of both magic and science. That's if it can even be done of course." Adeneus then began rambling incoherently about magic, psychic tethers and other things the Emperor did not understand.

"Adeneus," the Emperor said holding up a hand to cease the unintelligible noise that was now spewing forth from his mouth. Adeneus, who was at this point hunched over the table, furiously scribbling notes onto any spare paper he could find, stopped in his tracks.

"Apologies your holiness, I get carried away at the thought of revolutionising magical theory."

"I noticed," the Emperor smiled back. "Whatever you need to complete your task will be made available to you. Speak with Nestor whenever you need funds, spare no expense."

Adeneus bowed low, filled with pride that he had been chosen to make such a bold step that would reverberate with the intellectual community for centuries. He rushed quickly from the room, his cape billowing behind him, descending two stairs at a time – every moment away from his laboratory was a moment of potential greatness wasted. At last, the Emperor sat alone. Letting out a tired sigh he wondered if his plans would be enough.

Chapter 7

Three months later.

Slowly, Nate edged his way towards Marcus who stood at the opposite end of the platform with his sword at the ready. Peering over the rim of his shield Nate could see that while Marcus' stance was strong, his left flank was exposed. Once he was within range, Marcus quickly brought his sword down, aiming for the head. Nate had become used to Marcus' tactics however, and quickly brought his shield up, the sword bouncing harmlessly off. While this left Nate with an exposed midriff, Marcus was left in a similar position. Seizing the opportunity, Nate lunged forward with his sword aimed at his opponent's belly.

Marcus had anticipated the move but was not able to dodge it quickly enough. The tip of Nate's sword caught his left side causing him to stagger backwards. Seizing his chance Nate charged forwards. He ducked as Marcus took a wild swing, now with a perfect angle to bring up his sword into his stomach. With cat-like reactions, Nate was able to hit his target with full force. Again, Marcus stumbled backwards violently, this time falling onto his back, his armour making a deafening crash as he hit the floor.

Hoping to finish the fight, as Marcus lay like an upturned tortoise in his metal shell, Nate jumped towards him, sword raised. This time however, Marcus had the advantage; he rolled to the right just a second before the tip of Nate's sword crashed down into the spot where his head had been. Seizing the moment, Marcus quickly got to his feet and launched a strike aimed at Nate's chest. Before Nate could react, he felt the power of Marcus' blade against him, the blow sent him spinning out of control and over the edge of the training platform onto the ground below.

He lay there momentarily, winded and nursing his bruised ribs. He rolled onto his back to see Marcus sitting on the edge of the platform smiling.

"That was good, very good, if those weapons had been real, I'd probably be dead. Once you stop with the theatrics you will be a capable fighter."

Nate smiled back. "Well, I felt bad for kicking your arse, I thought I should give you a free shot." Marcus jumped off the platform and gave him an affectionate slap on the back of the head.

"Let's go and get a drink." However, before the men could make their way to the water pump a voice called out.

"Marcus!"

Both men spun around and saw Chion walking towards them. Nate had heard plenty of tales about him and did not have a favourable opinion. If the stories were to be believed, then he was not to be trusted.

"You know it's strange Chion, I never see you unless you're wanting me for something, I'm starting to think you don't like me very much." Marcus laughed which Nate could not help but join. Chion was stood just a meter away now, dressed in his usual leather armour and sporting a hatchet at his side. Ignoring the comment, he examined the sweaty Nate before him and was unimpressed. He gestured at Nate while looking at Marcus.

"Is this it, three months and this is the result?" Chion again looked Nate up and down with contempt before adding, "Captain Ardell won't be impressed." Marcus, slighted by the comment, replied angrily.

"What do you want?"

Chion smiled at the hurt his tongue had caused.

"The captain wants to see you, both of you," he said meeting Nate's gaze for the first time. Nate and Marcus looked at each other in shock before Marcus turned again to Chion.

"What does she want?" Marcus asked. Chion smiled revealing an extremely asymmetrical row of teeth, one side of which was completely white and straight, the other yellow and broken. It was as if he only had enough cash for a priest to fix one side.

"She wants to see what you have managed to produce with the ample time she has given you."

A stone suddenly dropped somewhere deep in Marcus' stomach. Nate was doing well but he was nowhere near ready to face going on an expedition, he would need the next three months as a minimum to train, it might even take longer.

"I would get going if I were you, the captain is not a patient woman." Chion smiled before walking back the way he had come. Marcus' mind was now swimming the dangerous waters of presupposition. The best-case scenario would be that the captain simply wanted a report on how the training was going, in which case he would happily report that everything was on schedule and that Nate was shaping up to be a capable addition to their forces.

Of course, that was the best-case scenario, and anyone who knew anything about Captain Ardell also knew your best-case scenario was in fact, whatever would have been your worst, and you had better pray she hadn't dreamt up something even more horrifying in the meantime. The worst-case scenario Marcus could think of was that Ardell would send Nate on an expedition straight away, without Marcus there to back him up. However, all this thinking was taking up valuable walking time and Ardell would have expected them in her quarters before even sending Chion with the message.

Marcus and Nate both ran to the stables and straddled their horses. Nate had never met Captain Ardell, but the horror stories he had been told by both Marcus, and his friends at The Hovel had certainly painted her as the type of character you did not want to disappoint.

The two rode hard towards Ardell's fort, the whole while Marcus listing off everything Nate should or should not say or do. In the end, they both agreed Nate would just keep his mouth shut unless spoken to. Nate was certainly nervous about meeting his commanding officer for the first time, but like the blissfully ignorant fool he was, he played down most of the horror stories as little more than natural friction between those higher up the chain of command and those beneath them. Surely the stories could not all be true.

After riding their horses to exhaustion Nate and Marcus found themselves outside Ardell's keep. Marcus was visibly distressed, wrangling his hands together repeatedly as if unable to cleanse them of the fear seeping through his skin. They had stood outside the door for a good minute before Nate questioned whether they should make their way inside, to which Marcus hastily agreed. After finally braving the doors into the keep Marcus became more visibly shaken the closer he came to Ardell's quarters. Nate, meanwhile, was humming tunelessly and admiring the banners which decorated the walls when he spotted the large map lying on the table in the centre of the war room. Walking over he was amazed. "Is this Gaia?" he gasped, turning to Marcus, amazed at the sheer enormity of the world. Marcus did not need to see the map; he had seen the same one hundreds of times.

"It's what we've found so far," he replied.

"So far?" Nate asked confused.

"I thought we'd already had this conversation?" Marcus replied hastily. He did not have the brainpower to spare while he was hard at work overthinking. Nate vaguely recalled something about this world being apparently endless and picked up the pace, meeting Marcus at the bottom of the stairs.

"What are you so worried about? She can't be that bad" Nate smiled. Marcus sighed as he forced himself up the stairs. Nate quickly followed, resting blissfully on a cloud of ignorance.

"Whatever you do…" Marcus warned.

"Marcus, chill out," Nate smiled. "I know how to handle myself around a lady."

"Gods have mercy," he whispered as he knocked on the captain's door, which was as always, answered immediately.

"Enter."

Marcus instantly stood to attention upon stepping inside, looking straight ahead not daring to glance at Captain Ardell who was in her usual spot, stooping over her desk studying a map. Nate on the other hand was transfixed by her beauty, her long black hair falling over both shoulders and resting on the desk. Her pale skin reminded him of the moon and her small, slender figure made her look almost elf-like. Why on earth had Marcus neglected to mention their captain was so hot?

Ardell looked up from her work, her deep, blue eyes bloodshot after so many sleepless nights. Marcus immediately spoke up. "

Reporting for duty Captain."

Without a word, Ardell shifted her attention to Nate, who immediately lost all sense of seriousness as their eyes met and his brain functions shut down one by one. All that remained now was his animalistic desire to get laid.

He saw Ardell's lips move, but he heard nothing. His mind was too busy imagining scenarios which saw the two of them alone, in various stages of undress, although, the sudden addition of Marcus' voice as he desperately tried to snap Nate out of his daydream quickly brought him unwillingly back to reality.

Ardell was furious, she *never* repeated herself and she looked ready to break Nate in half. "Sorry Captain, Marcus has told me so much about you, meeting you in person was just a bit overwhelming."

Ardell's furious look fell away, as disarmed by the compliment she fought back a smile, but even she could not stop her cheeks from turning red. Marcus, meanwhile, could not believe what he had just witnessed. He had a better chance of convincing people he had seen the Imperial Empress dancing naked in the streets than what had just transpired before his very eyes. Sensing her mask to have slipped, Ardell quickly got back to business.

"I asked whether you have been making decent progress these last few months. Has Marcus been an adequate mentor?" Nate nodded.

"Yes, Captain. It was a culture shock at first, but Marcus has been relentless, I feel I've come a long way." Ardell was surprised, this was the first time she had heard Marcus praised for anything other than his ability to drastically subvert her expectations.

"Is that right?" she asked, eyebrows raised and nodding slightly as if she did not entirely believe it. "High praise indeed Marcus," she said, her attention shifting now to him.

"Thank you, Captain, Nate is a fast learner. Although, there is still a long way to go before I would say he is ready for an expedition," Marcus replied.

Ardell quickly rolled her eyes. "Well, luckily Marcus, that is not up to you. I have an assignment I want the two of you to carry out."

Such a blatant disregard for his assessment shocked him and Marcus could not help himself from interrupting.

"Respectfully, Captain, Nate isn't ready, we have only just had half the time you promised to train, he isn't prepared for the outside." Despite the unheard-of interruption, Ardell smirked.

"Nobody is ever ready for the outside, the sooner he gets first-hand experience the better. Besides, I imagine it's getting a bit expensive for the both of you, cooped up within these walls."

Nate was not sure how much he liked being referred to as if he were not right there in the room with them, but he was too busy internally screaming to care. Marcus wanted to protest but he knew it was hard enough to change the mind of the average captain let alone Ardell.

So instead, he simply asked, "Is there a specific task you want us to carry out?" Ardell beckoned the two to come closer until they were also leaning over her desk. She shuffled a stack of papers until she found what she was looking for amongst the hundreds piled to head height.

She quickly scanned over it before placing it so the other two could see. Up until this point, Nate had done extremely well as far as first impressions went. However, he was so impressed with himself, that he did exactly what Marcus had expressly forbidden him to do. He was himself. Filled with a new arrogance he leaned on the desk, supported by an outstretched arm. Infringing upon Ardell's sacred workspace not being enough, he decided to fuck up like nobody has ever fucked up in the history of fucking up.

Before anyone could warn him, Nate spoke with a sly grin and mischievous eyes pointed in Ardell's direction.

"I don't suppose you would like to go out for a drink after all this?" he half-joked.

It was then as if time itself had been so shocked by Nate's words that it had decided to stand still. Nobody moved, even the air was still. Marcus stood, open-mouthed, his skin white. The ghostly whisper of "by Jupiter" escaped from his lips like a dying breath. Ardell was stone-faced, her eyes wide in both surprise and rage, this being a situation she was not familiar with. Sensing he may have just made a mistake Nate quickly wiped the smirk from his face and tried to compose himself. Ardell had another idea in mind, however.

With lightning-quick reflexes she swatted Nate's supporting arm from the desk and in a single motion, placing her hand on the back of his head, slammed his face into the desk. While Nate lay on the floor clutching his face trying not to scream in pain, Ardell sat back in her chair and raised her hands in confusion. "What the fuck, Marcus?" she half laughed. This calm was a façade however and Ardell could not hold back her fury. "Get out," she spat with such venom Marcus could feel his skin begin to burn.

"Yes, Captain" Marcus replied, terrified. He walked over to Nate and lifted him off the ground, helping him to the door. Still clutching his face, he whispered, "What a bitch."

"Nate…shut up," Marcus growled, as they descended the stairs back to the war room. Marcus knew he was not free to leave, Ardell would want him back up there immediately. By the time he returned Ardell had moved from her desk and was pacing furiously by her fireplace. She didn't see Marcus enter but she heard the door close behind him and immediately began to vent her anger.

"I knew you were completely useless; I gave you an assignment that I thought even you couldn't fail. Instead of giving me a capable soldier you give me…" she paused, "you give me whatever that is," she shouted pointing towards the floor.

"Forgive me, Captain, Nate is an imbecile, but he has the makings of a good soldier," Marcus apologised. Ardell was about to continue her rant again but paused, taking a deep breath – this was not worth the hassle of getting worked up. She stomped over to her desk, retrieving the letter she had intended for both Marcus and Nate to see. Snatching it up she walked over to where her terrified subordinate stood. Marcus winced, expecting another violent outburst, but was lucky to get away with the letter being pressed hard against his chest.

Wasting no time, he began reading, and by the end was both disappointed and relieved. "A missing...cow?" he puzzled.

"Yes Marcus, a missing cow," Ardell replied so condescendingly she could have made Stephen Hawking feel like an idiot. "Finding the cow isn't important. No, this is about preventing civil unrest." She sat down and leaned back in her chair, calm at last.

"It started out with as you see, a cow going missing. Not much of a problem in itself, but things have escalated. The farmers took to accusing one another and the other day the disagreement ended with a farmhouse being burned down."

Ardell paused while Marcus processed the information. "So why not just send the troops in, bash some heads together and resolve it?" he asked. Ardell scowled, and Marcus realised he should have kept quiet.

"Naturally, that was the first thing we did," Ardell continued. "But the farmers soon banded together and fought back. Now we have a situation where they're refusing to do their jobs and demanding compensation from the Citadel."

Marcus studied the letter again before speaking.

"How many farmers are we talking about?" He knew a handful of filthy peasants would not cause that much of an issue, after all there were millions of them in the Breadbasket. So, the captain must be speaking of a sizeable force if she was this concerned.

"Fifty-four," Ardell replied. Marcus looked at her with a look of puzzlement. "Wipe that stupid look off your face Marcus before I do it for you," she snapped.

"Sorry Captain, I'm just confused as to why this is an issue. Give them a few weeks of not getting what they want, and they'll be forced back into work by necessity surely?"

Ardell paused for a moment and stared at Marcus, the frustration evident in her eyes.

"If only all my problems were as simple as you Marcus, I might actually get a day off for once." She sighed. Marcus shuffled uncomfortably in place as Ardell did the same with her papers. She pulled out a parchment around half the size of the others. It was horribly stained and stank of alcohol. She handed it to Marcus who read it quickly.

The parchment was a letter of demands – despite evidently being written in a pub it was articulate and precise in what it hoped to achieve. Marcus scoffed as he read the full list. Ardell nodded silently upon hearing Marcus' response.

"They can't be serious?"

"Unfortunately, they are." Ardell sighed again as she proceeded to recount the demands in the letter. "Fifty thousand gold as compensation for the trouble caused by our men. The reconstruction of the burned down farmhouse, along with any other improvements to nearby farmhouses and structures to be carried out by the city guard.

"A ten per cent decrease in crops surrendered to the Citadel. Increased night patrols in both the lower levels to deter crime, then to top it all off, a fucking letter of apology to be signed by both myself and Grand Admiral Lee."

Ardell put her head in her hands, her dark hair falling over her face obscuring the look of fatigue across it. She took a deep breath and regained her composure, flicking her hair to one side. "They're threatening to start rioting if they don't get their demands met. Look here," she said, leaning forward and jabbing at a particular name at the bottom of the letter.

Marcus went back over the letter and was shocked at what he saw. It had been signed by fifty-five people, none of whom meant anything to Marcus, except for one. The name Ardell was pointing to was none other than Lord Massah.

"What in Venus' tits has he got to do with this?" Marcus asked, completely flabbergasted that such a high-ranking member of the Citadel elite would get involved with such a trivial matter.

Ardell clicked her tongue in frustration. "Massah is a snake. He has no loyalty to Tinelia or the Admiral. I imagine he is doing whatever he can to make the current leadership seem weak and unjust." She paused and threw a crumpled piece of paper across the room, missing the fire by some way. "We need to sort this problem out before it turns nasty," she said, staring at the weak tongues of flame. Marcus nodded.

"What are your orders, Ma'am?"

Ardell turned to face him, crossing her arms, and leaning on her desk.

"Get down there and talk to them and yes, I mean talk, no roughhousing. We can't afford to let this get violent. Convince them to withdraw their demands and get back to work." Marcus could not help but laugh, despite Ardell's foul mood and the potential dangers of this course of action.

"Do you really think it will be that easy, Captain?"

Ardell laughed back; a rare occurrence Marcus felt privileged to witness.

"I will be willing to concede the increased patrols at night and the rebuilding of the burned down farmhouse, but the other demands must be rescinded, understood?"

"Understood, Captain. Nate and I will make our way down there immediately."

"Good, now get out of my sight and make sure that fool goes with you," Ardell growled, returning to her paperwork. Marcus did not linger, descending the steps two at a time. Upon reaching the war room, he noticed Nate was once again fawning over the maps from earlier. He did not even get the chance to say something idiotic before Marcus slapped him less than playfully around the back of the head.

"You're fucking unbelievable, has anybody ever told you that?" Marcus asked both angrily and relieved at the same time.

"Well yes but probably not in the context you're referring to," Nate smirked. Marcus pushed his thumb and forefinger into his eyes and sighed, it was all he could do to stop himself from slamming Nate's head into the table himself.

"You got off unbelievably lucky there, if you try anything like that again I swear Ardell will scoop your eyes out with a spoon." Marcus threw down the letter Ardell had handed to him detailing his and Nate's task.

"I'm guessing this isn't an invitation for a drink after all," Nate said skimming the words as quickly as his headache and blurry vision would allow.

"First assignment," Marcus responded, perching himself on the edge of the table. Nate could not help but be bitterly disappointed.

"Is this a joke?" He laughed half-heartedly, desperately hoping Marcus was just messing with him.

"I'm afraid this is as deadly serious as it gets. If we screw this up, you can guarantee we will be stuck guarding empty rooms or cleaning toilets for years."

Nate brought the document closer to his eyes and re-read it, hoping maybe he had missed some crucial exciting detail. But no, the words had remained the same. It seems his first task in this incredible world of limitless possibilities was indeed to locate a missing cow.

"It's not what it seems, this is about preventing a possible riot or worse, it's serious stuff," Marcus added.

"Hmm, well we best get to it then." Nate smiled through bloody teeth.

Chapter 8

The sun was bright in the sky on a new day, a day brimming with possibilities. A day in which Nate and Marcus had already spent hours trying to locate a single building in an endless sea of identical-looking farmhouses and fields. After many failed initial inquiries with the local farmers, many of whom did not trust soldiers or simply had no idea what the pair were talking about, they were finally able to find someone who could point them in the right direction.

Once they had narrowed down their search area, it was easy to make out the charred remains of a building against the backdrop of golden fields and green meadows. As they approached down a path well-beaten by all manner of cattle, they were greeted by a crowd of people hard at work removing the charred remains of the structure.

The crowd saw them approach and quickly halted their work, huddling together, some grabbing hold of wooden planks or shovels, evidently expecting further violence on behalf of the benevolent Captain Ardell. Marcus held out his hands trying to diffuse the situation before it could escalate.

"We aren't here to cause trouble my friends; we've been sent to help." The crowd looked at one another, unsure how to take this apparent change of tactic of the city's higher-ups who only a few days ago were trying to kick their heads in.

"Who sent you?" shouted a voice within the crowd. Reluctantly, Marcus replied, knowing the answer would win him no friends.

"Captain Ardell."

Immediately upon hearing the name, the crowd turned more hostile, shouting their anger and contempt for the captain who had ordered their failed suppression. A stone suddenly flew from the crowd towards Marcus who noticed just in time to avoid it striking his face. This small act of violence caused a rush of blood to his head, and he placed his hand on the hilt of his sword. Nate, who had been up to this point happy to let Marcus deal with the rabble, was about to reach out his hand to stop him from taking things too far when a man stepped out of the crowd with his hands raised.

"Stop!" he shouted, placing himself an equal distance between the crowd and Marcus.

"Violence will not get us what we want," he said facing the now-silent crowd. He then turned his head to face Marcus and Nate while still addressing the others. "If these men are indeed, as they claim, here to help, we should listen to what they have to say. No matter who sent them, dialogue is the only way any of us are going to resolve this."

Marcus removed his hand from his sword, relieved at the de-escalation he had had no part in. Nate stepped forward, equally glad his first official action as a member of the army was not against their own people. He withdrew the letter of demands Ardell had given them and presented it to the man he assumed must be the group's leader.

"I'm assuming you're the one who wrote this then?"

The farmer took the letter and withdrew a small pair of beaten-up spectacles from his pocket. It only took a second for him to recognise it as his own handiwork.

"Aye, it was indeed me who penned it, but the demands are shared by us all," he said sweeping his arm in the direction of his fellows. "Dragging me off to the dungeon won't stop us, so I hope you're sincere about wanting to help us. Otherwise, we will have no business with you or that monstrous Captain Ardell."

Nate nodded in confirmation and held out his hand which the man shook, grateful that there seemed to be no beating in sight.

"Nate."

"Michael."

Nate patted Michael on the shoulder and addressed the now passive crowd behind him who had inched up closer to their leader.

"Captain Ardell has admitted that the route she initially took to resolve this little dispute was a bit harsh. She is eager to have this resolved peacefully and amicably, we are here to negotiate and see how else we can help."

The farmers began to excitedly whisper amongst themselves; never had the prospect of change ever felt so real. Michael smiled to himself, it was good to see his friends and neighbours finally optimistic about something, no matter how unlikely it was they would ever get what they were promised. He pointed down the dirt track towards a large farmhouse, smoke rising from the chimney.

"My farm is just down the road; what do you say we do all our negotiating there?"

"Sounds good to me," Nate replied. As the farmers, still grouped together, began walking down the road, Marcus placed a hand on Nate's shoulder.

"Nice work there Nate, I was about to start bashing some skulls, glad you were with me to keep the peace." Nate's heart rose in his chest, glad he had finally found a way to make up for his earlier transgression with Ardell. Michael lagged behind the other farmers, keeping pace with Marcus and Nate.

"Thank you for keeping hold of your senses back there, most soldiers don't have time for the people who keep their bellies full and make sure their mead doesn't run dry."

"No problem, we just want to make sure this all gets sorted without anyone getting hurt," Marcus replied. Michael chuckled.

"Well, I think you're a bit late for that, but the sentiment is appreciated all the same."

"How long have you been farming here?" Nate asked as they passed by golden shafts of wheat nearly ready for harvest. Michael rubbed his long, tangled beard as he tried to come up with an answer.

"To tell you the truth, I've been doing it for so long I can't even remember. A few centuries at least, but what really matters is that this is the first time I have ever seen my friends so angry. They aren't just going to give up this time as they have before, we need real change otherwise things are only going to get worse from here."

Nate nodded. "That's why we're here; the captain doesn't want things spiralling out of control. We all need this mess to be sorted quickly and with as few hiccups as possible."

"Easier said than done my friend," Michael sighed as they reached the front door of his farmhouse, all the others having already entered.

The sitting room where negotiations would be held had ample room for the thirty or so people who were now taking their seats around a large table. A fire roared in the hearth despite the heat outside – for what reason everyone had a fire lit regardless of the weather Nate could not fathom.

Michael took his seat at the head of the table while Nate and Marcus squeezed in beside some of the other farmers. The room itself may have been large enough to accommodate everyone but the table was evidently only designed for a maximum of ten, and everyone was eager to be a part of this historic moment.

This of course only made the heat even worse as all these sweaty bodies were piled in against one another. Nate had to stifle a gag as a man reeking of manure and sweat took his seat next to him. The was a lot of chatter while everyone took their places and waited for the negotiations to begin.

Nobody would make eye contact with Ardell's representatives, either quickly averting their gaze or turning their backs to them completely. Evidently there was still a great deal of mistrust between those at the bottom and the top which Marcus and Nate were only experiencing a fraction of. There was a sudden and loud metallic clanging as Michael banged a great dirty mug on the table. Almost immediately all chatter had ceased, and all eyes were on him.

"Good day, my friends," he began. "Today is an auspicious day, the great powers of the upper city have finally recognised our toil and strife and have sent emissaries to negotiate their surrender to our just demands."

There was a mighty cheer and the banging of fists on the table at Michael's announcement. An announcement which could not have been further from the truth.

Marcus and Nate looked at one another, realising that they were being played off as nothing more than an arm of an oppressive regime. Michael's assurance of total victory would make any move they made to whittle down the farmer's demands practically hopeless. Marcus cleared his throat and stood, the clamouring quickly falling silent as eyes pierced him like darts from every corner of the room.

"I am afraid it is not that simple; Captain Ardell has agreed to meet some of your more reasonable demands, but only if others are repealed entirely."

There were angry shouts and more banging of fists; meanwhile, Nate tried his best to appear invisible should said fists start flying.

Now it was Michael's turn to stand.

"Surely you cannot see our demands as unreasonable?" he asked. "Fifty thousand gold to cover the physical pain and suffering caused by your comrades. That is nothing compared to the profits unjustly stolen from us by the Citadel every harvest. Repairing the damage to our homes caused by centuries of neglect by the Citadel. At the very least an apology from your superiors – after all, they were the ones who caused all this ruckus to begin with!"

Michael grinned as his supporters cheered. The ball was firmly in Marcus' court, and it was clear Michael was enjoying perhaps his first taste of power in his life. However, Marcus had been sent here with a job to do and he was not leaving until it was done, partly because he hated losing, but mostly because he was terrified of what Ardell would do if he came back a failure.

"Captain Ardell is willing to accept an increase in patrols throughout the lower levels and will spare some men to repair and rebuild any damaged structures. But that is all. I suggest you accept these terms now as any future negotiators will not be so accommodating to your demands."

This announcement was followed by a mixture of laughter and anger as some took Marcus' warnings as a threat. Even Michael could not help himself from laughing at the offer.

"You truly have no idea how we suffer down here do you?" one of the farmers opposite Nate asked. He was dressed in little more than rags and his nose was badly broken, evidently caused recently as the swelling was still present.

"We break our backs down here every day and night toiling in the fields. We pay mages extortionate sums to make sure our crops grow twice as fast all year round and for what? So that you lot up there can go out on your adventures and spend your nights singing and dancing. Have you ever once thought about the people down below you who make your lives so comfortable?"

Nate and Marcus were both silent. Naturally, this question resonated far greater with Marcus as he realised that for all his time in Purgatory, for all his adventures and desire to protect those who could not protect themselves, he had not once thanked or even acknowledged the plight of those who lived separated by little more than a wall from himself. Michael spoke once more.

"We understand that none of this is you lads' fault, you weren't the ones who came down here kicking down our doors and breaking our faces. But surely you can both understand that down here millions of people, good people, are suffering. It is not just us; we are simply the ones who decided to say something about it, and what do we get for our trouble? Some empty promises and violence if we don't comply. Those demands aren't just a wish list, we need them to survive."

Marcus raised an eyebrow. "You need an apology to survive?"

There was a collective groan as he completely missed the point.

"If Ardell and Grand Admiral Lee apologise it will show people that we are not just a rabble to be walked all over and ignored. We will get the respect that we deserve – after all, how many of you up there would be willing to come down here and do an honest day's work just to feed yourself if we suddenly stopped working?"

Marcus grunted in reluctant agreement and sank back into his seat. He knew the farmers were right, but he was in no position to agree or disagree with anything he had not been given express orders to do so by Ardell.

Suddenly Nate stepped in with a question of his own. "Why do you need the fifty thousand gold then? If as you say it's nothing compared to what the Citadel takes in tribute what's the point? Why not instead ask for a smaller tithe?"

The room fell silent, there was no clever or philosophical response, just the tense silence of a room full of people withholding an embarrassing truth. Luckily for Nate and Marcus, one man was brave enough to defy the silence of his peers.

"To pay off the bloody smugglers," an angry voice spoke up.

"Jonah, silence!" Michael shouted, but it was too late, both Marcus and Nate had heard, and their interest was piqued.

"What smugglers?" they asked in unison. Michael shot Jonah a truly evil look before realising that the cat was out of the bag and there would be no benefit in keeping their struggle a secret. He ran his hand through his thick, muddy hair and let out a strained sigh.

"The last few years have been tougher than usual; some smugglers have been threatening to kill us or burn down our farms if we don't pay them every month. They said they would do the same if we told the guards so we just thought it would be easier if we complied."

"Problem is we have nothing left to give," Jonah added, his voice cracking and eyes stinging as the pain of so many tormenting months finally caught up with him. Marcus stood once more, filled with renewed confidence that he could resolve this situation after all.

"What if we get rid of the smugglers permanently, will you consider accepting the captain's offer?"

The room fell into another bout of whispers directed towards Michael who, after a few moments, raised his hand in a call for silence. "You know they're a problem now so there's nothing I can do to stop you from telling Ardell short of killing you both but that will hardly make the situation any better."

Nate and Marcus looked at one another, unsure how to react to such a statement.

"Fine, if you can rid us of this plague of criminals, we will accept the Captain's offer. Truth be told they're a far greater pain in our backsides than you Citadel lot," Michael smirked. Marcus smiled and reached over to shake Michael's hand. Michael clasped it firmly.

"Just understand that if you fail, all our blood will be on your hands." Marcus gave a solemn nod of understanding and the room suddenly filled with applause and the obligatory banging of fists on the table. Marcus strained to raise his voice over the noise.

"First things first. What can anyone tell us about the smugglers? What are they smuggling, how do they get into the city, where do they go once they're inside?"

A woman sat near Michael spoke up.

"I heard they bring in stolen gems and treasure." The man next to her snorted.

"Don't be daft, they're bringing in exotic animals to sell to the university for their experiments."

"Oh yeah, and I suppose you've seen these exotic animals, have you? Can't see where your own hedgerow ends," the woman retorted. The room suddenly burst into a frenzy of arguments and Michael signalled to Marcus to head for the door, Nate in tow.

Squeezing past the angry and stinking bodies the men emerged back outside the farmhouse, the clamour still clearly audible, even once the door was closed. Michael sighed and cracked his knuckles before rubbing the back of his neck, clearly stressed.

"I really wish we could have avoided this whole smuggler business."

Marcus folded his arms.

"Your friends seem to be happy that we are doing something about it. Why aren't you?" Michael shrugged.

"It'll probably only cause more trouble in the end. The smugglers will find out we helped you and we will suffer the fallout. If I thought the guards could do anything about it, I would have said something years ago. You'll only end up making a mess of it."

Marcus grunted, "Obviously, you don't know Captain Ardell. If she finds out there are smugglers running rampant, threatening people on her watch, she will hunt every single one of them down and hang them from the ramparts by their balls. Believe me, these smugglers won't be bothering you again once we are done with them."

Michael smiled. "I hope you're right," he said before a long pause as he stroked his beard. "The smugglers are using a tunnel that comes out on the outside of the city and leads to an overgrown field just a few miles from here. From there they go to the docks and stash their loot in one of the storehouses."

"Any idea what they're bringing in?" Nate asked.

"Weapons and potions, I believe mainly, although my friend was right about the gems, we've found a few in the fields over the years."

This was enough for Marcus to report back to the captain, and he thanked Michael for his help, assuring him once more that he and his friends would not have to worry about the smugglers for much longer. Walking back up the way they had come towards the Vanguard with a slight spring in their step, the two men could not help but feel proud of themselves. They had secured a deal with the farmers as they had been tasked, in what must have been the shortest negotiation in history. But they now also faced the more difficult task of tracking down and dealing with the smugglers.

Marcus and Nate had both been waiting outside Captain Ardell's quarters for over an hour. At first, they had been excited to disclose what they had uncovered. But now, with each passing minute without an audience, doubt was further creeping into their psyches. What if they were being made to wait because the captain was angry with them? No, that was ridiculous, of course Ardell was angry with them, but she would have already chewed them out by now if it was regarding their mission.

Were they going to be punished for failing some secret test she had set? What would the punishment be? Just as Nate was about to speak up to raise the likelihood of his concerns being valid the door opened. Before them stood a man unknown to Nate, but very familiar to Marcus. He was unusually tall, having to duck as he passed through the door. His face was covered in scars and behind him trailed a blue cloak, a white sailboat emblazoned upon its centre.

"Lord Massah." Marcus bowed, Nate quickly following suit. Massah did not bother acknowledging their existence and strutted past them, his nose upturned. The two remained bowed and silent until Massah had descended the staircase and the slam of the keep door was audible. As the two straightened themselves they were met with an even more unpleasant sight.

Leaning against the doorframe was Captain Ardell, dressed in a dark blue doublet adorned with gold buttons and the most hideous ruby brooch either man had ever seen. But what was even worse was the look of absolute disgust and rage upon her face.

"I pray to all the gods you have good news, for your own sakes."

Nate could not help but feel pleased with himself and stepped forward with a grin. "Even better, Captain, we have excellent news."

Ardell raised her eyebrow in surprise and turned, beckoning the men to follow her back to her chambers.

She practically threw herself into her chair and let out a pained sigh. All the while she tugged at the doublet which seemed to tighten around her neck when it sensed she was getting too comfortable. "Come then, let me hear this excellent news and I may even credit you with brightening my day," Ardell grumbled. Marcus thought it best for him to take the reins now as he doubted the news of smugglers would delight Ardell no matter how proud Nate seemed of the fact. Yet Nate once again beat him to it.

"The farmers have agreed to your demands captain," Nate beamed triumphantly; his arms folded in admiration of his own greatness. Ardell could hardly believe her ears and was about to jump to her feet with joy until Nate cut her short. "As soon as we deal with the smugglers that have been harassing them for the last few years." Even with this admission, Nate had lost none of his triumphant enthusiasm. However, Ardell's face had immediately soured once more.

"Your definition of excellent news appears to differ from my own," she said through gritted teeth. For once she just wanted to be able to get through a day without having to deal with complete fuckwits. It was not too taxing a wish, yet the gods seemed to deny her even this nicety.

This time Marcus was able to step in before Nate inserted his foot any further into his mouth.

"Rest assured, Captain, Nate and I will deal with them immediately."

"Damned right you will, and you will make sure not a soul finds out about this. The last thing I need is the Citadel finding out smugglers have been running rampant under my nose." Marcus nodded in understanding before Ardell continued, frustration and exhaustion clear in her voice. "What do we know about these smugglers so far?"

Marcus shook his head.

"Not much I'm afraid, Captain. The farmers couldn't seem to agree on what exactly was being smuggled, nor did they know how many the smugglers were in total."

"Great," Ardell exclaimed angrily. "So," she began, placing her hands at equal lengths across her desk, emphasising exactly how little this information helped. "They're somewhere between smuggling absolutely nothing, and the Empress' dirty underwear. They're also either as few as two, or we are the only people in the world not in on it." Ardell folded her arms and leaned back in her chair which creaked unnervingly. "This is far too easy, lads, perhaps you should go out looking for them while blindfolded, that will at least give the poor bastards a chance."

Nate and Marcus both shifted uncomfortably on the spot, neither meeting the captain's gaze should they be turned to stone.

"We do know where they're getting into the city though, if we follow them without getting spotted, they should lead us straight to their stash," Marcus replied sheepishly. Ardell took turns examining them carefully before she replied.

"Do you think you're both capable of such a godly feat?" This time it was Nate who replied.

"Assuming you will hang us by our balls if we don't, I would say we don't have a choice." Despite her awful mood this could not help but bring a smile to Ardell's face.

"Maybe you're better at mentoring than I thought, Marcus." she smirked. "Get to it then, I don't want to see either of you until you have good news. *Actual* good news this time," she said throwing a darting glance at Nate. The two men bowed and turned to leave before Marcus had a sudden thought and stopped, turning once more to face the captain.

"May I ask, Captain, what was Lord Massah doing here earlier? He never comes this far from the Citadel."

Ardell exhaled loudly through her nose and rubbed her forehead; she could feel another migraine coming at the mere mention of the name. At last, she brought herself to answer.

"He's currently doing the rounds of each district, hoping to pilfer away the best soldiers we have for his little adventures. He is setting out west again in six months and so is trying to raise as much hell as possible before he goes. Prick. But don't worry, as I said, he only takes the best, so we get to enjoy each other's company for a good while yet." Marcus could not help but smile.

"Wouldn't have it any other way, Captain."

Chapter 9

Two weeks later Nate and Marcus found themselves crouched beside the ruins of a farmhouse gutted by fire. The sky was illuminated by a dazzling full moon, yet this did little to make the pair's task of spotting a single figure within an ocean of overgrown grass and brush any easier. They had once again visited the farmers who had first informed them of the smuggler route and they had been shown exactly where to expect them.

Yet they had been sat wrapped in their cloaks for nearly three hours without incident and the cold was beginning to rob them of all sensation in their extremities.

"This is beginning to feel like a colossal waste of my valuable time Marcus," Nate complained. Marcus scoffed in response; his eyes still trained on the small spot where the smugglers were supposed to emerge.

"Valuable, eh, is that what you call it?"

"Hey, I have a life outside of work you know, places to go, people to see." Marcus turned to face him.

"You're not even allowed out of the Vanguard without me and it seems to be the only person you spend your time seeing is that roommate of yours," Marcus grinned. Nate was physically repulsed by this insinuation and recoiled in horror. Yet before being able to offer any kind of retort something quickly caught his eye and his horror turned to disbelief.

"Marcus, look, I think it's them," he said, pointing excitedly. Marcus turned his head only half believing him but was ecstatic to see Nate was telling the truth. From an insignificant patch of grass, the hatch to a tunnel had opened and two figures had emerged. One stayed close to the ground, keeping an eye out for any unwanted visitors, while the other was hunched over the tunnel busy lifting a large sack, which Nate assumed held all the illegal goodies.

It would have been comical seeing this man carrying this sack over his shoulder like a cartoon villain, had he not stood over six feet tall when seemingly doubled over as the weight of the sack pressed upon him.

"Ok, follow me, do exactly as I do and for the love of Minerva don't open your mouth," Marcus instructed.

Nate was about to protest when Marcus shot him a death glare which advised him otherwise. For the next two hours, Nate and Marcus stalked the smugglers. Keeping well back and low so as not to be spotted, at one point Marcus went chest-first into an old cow-pat, much to Nate's amusement. The ordeal was especially difficult when considering the smugglers were also doing their best to remain unseen and had far more practice than their pursuers.

More than once, Marcus despaired as he lost sight of his targets, only for them to re-emerge at a far greater distance than he had thought possible in the time that had elapsed. The chase had so far consisted entirely across farmland while keeping well away from the city wall where guards were patrolling with torches. By the time the third hour had elapsed, the sounds of chirping and buzzing insects had been replaced by the gentle lapping of waves, while the air had accumulated a distinctly salty smell. There was a sudden crash of metal as the smuggler hauling the sack had stumbled and dropped it.

Marcus and Nate both dove behind a nearby willow stump as the smugglers argued as loudly as their work would permit them. Having now significantly decreased the distance between them, Nate could make out some of the argument.

"That's it, wake up the whole bleedin' city why don't you?"

"I tripped," the second smuggler hissed as he hurriedly picked up the sack and hauled it over his shoulder once more.

"Trip any louder and we'll be hanging from the gatehouse by morning," spat the first smuggler, indeed in no mood for mistakes. As Nate peered into the dim light hoping to catch a good look at his prey, there was something definitely off with the second, larger smuggler.

His height notwithstanding, his fingers were unnaturally long and thin, while his chin seemed to protrude a good six inches from his face. However, the limited light made it impossible to tell for sure what the men looked like. After securing their loot once more and checking (poorly) that nobody was on their tail the smugglers set off once again in the direction of the docks.

The docks, after the Citadel itself, were the pride and joy of Tinelia, the known world's foremost naval power. Taking up the entire southern quarter of the city's lowest level, barely a single inch of shoreline was not occupied by ships, machinery for loading and unloading cargo, or vast warehouses which stored exotic goods beyond Nate's imagination. Indeed, the docks were so vast and wealthy that they required their own governor and dedicated police force to manage.

After a short wait in the long grass to allow a guard to pass barely a few meters ahead of them, the smugglers ran as quietly as they could to the side of a warehouse, pressing themselves into the shadows so they were nearly invisible. Marcus and Nate also had to wait for the guard to pass in the opposite direction as being caught now, while they were doing nothing illegal, would blow their cover.

"C'mon you sonofabitch, move," Marcus fumed as the guard took his time admiring the starry sky. Meanwhile, the smugglers had slipped around the back of the warehouse and were out of sight. At last, his thirst for existential questioning quenched, the guard moved on, although by now the smugglers had been out of sight for well over a minute.

Marcus and Nate rushed forward, leaping over the wooden walkway which stretched down to the sea so as to not make any excess noise. However, once they had rounded the corner of the warehouse where they had last seen the smugglers, there lay before them a seemingly endless labyrinth of deserted streets, each leading to more identical warehouses.

"Shit. We lost them." Nate panted as his body struggled with the sudden change of pace. Marcus too was ready to start panicking until he noticed a strange set of footprints in the sand. Much larger than any normal man's and paced far enough apart to indicate the owner had no trouble running on such a surface. Beside the footprints were what he assumed were the much smaller footprints of the other smuggler.

The realisation suddenly hit Marcus and slowly he drew his sword. Nate, surprised at this rapid change of tactic, tried to question what Marcus was doing. Yet he was halted as Marcus held up his palm to indicate silence. Knowing exactly when Nate was going to open his mouth and make a situation infinitely more difficult was a skill he was, luckily, picking up rather quickly. Carefully, the two followed the footprints down several alleys until they abruptly stopped at the back gate of one of the warehouses, a gate which was conveniently unlocked.

From within Nate could hear voices that he recognised, those of the smugglers, although what they were saying was muffled through the wall. With their backs against it, Marcus turned to Nate, a look of fear yet determination in his eyes. He was already breathing heavily, and his heartbeat was rapidly increasing its tempo as he prepared for the inevitable.

"Listen," he whispered before needing to catch his breath. "Once we go in, leave the big one to me, try your best not to kill your man though, understand?" Nate nodded but the clear stress in Marcus' voice had rattled him and now his own nerves were causing his sword hand to shake. Marcus closed his eyes and rested the back of his head against the wall while he caught his breath.

He hated rats.

"Ok, here we go," he said barging the door open with his shoulder, Marcus ran in with Nate close behind. The warehouse was huge and dimly lit save for a few torches placed upon long rods away from any flammable materials. All around were thousands of crates stacked upon one another. Most were plain, but others were marked with the seals and emblems of noble houses and private companies alike.

In the very centre of this orderly jungle, stood the smugglers who had until now been busy unloading their own cargo into pre-prepared crates. They quickly spun to face this intrusion and upon seeing Nate and Marcus drew their swords.

Nate however, had stopped in his tracks the moment he had seen the second, larger smuggler in the light.

Unburdened by the sack he stood at seven feet tall and having removed his hood and cloak was clearly no man at all. Instead, Nate was face to face with the largest rat he had ever seen. His long bony fingers were rather claws which looked sharper than the blade they were holding, while his protruding chin was in fact a long, scarred snout, upon which dark, thick whiskers twitched.

Rather than immediately devouring them both however, the rat held out its palms and spoke. A weak, almost childlike tone completely contrasted to its huge and imposing frame. "Hold on there, fellas, no need to get rough. I think it would perhaps be best for everyone if we just forgot everything we saw here and went our separate merry ways."

Nate, thinking this sounded like a grand idea, looked at Marcus who wore a look of disgust.

"Vermin like you don't give orders here," Marcus snapped back. Without even allowing for the remotest possibility of the smuggler's surrender, he charged forwards.

"Suit yourself," the rat squeaked back as their swords clashed. Nate, meanwhile, was still transfixed by the creature before him and almost too late noticed the other smuggler who was significantly less interesting, dart at him. By barely a fraction of a second was Nate able to duck as his foe swung with all his might at his head.

The man was quick, however, and delivered a kick to Nate's chest before he had a chance to recover. This sent him tumbling backwards, his back connecting hard with a wooden beam. Pain shot up through his spine and the resulting spasm caused him to drop his weapon. At that moment Marcus was thrown violently across the room as if he weighed nothing, landing close to Nate. Recovering far sooner and recognising the perilous situation of his ward he threw his body forwards, tackling his would-be killer to the ground. However, the rat was soon upon him, once more launching him across the room, leaving a large gash where his claws had pierced Marcus' thin leather armour which had replaced his usual steel.

Realising this was a true life or death situation Nate quickly came to and retrieving his sword from the sand slashed at the wildly flailing tail of the rat. There was an ear-piercing shriek accompanied by a flash of blood as the tip of his tail was severed.

The rat instantly turned his attention to Nate and, abandoning its sword entirely, swung at him with its claws. He swerved to the side and luckily for Nate, the other smuggler had decided to rush forward and in attempting to skewer him received the full force of the rat's blow. The smuggler fell to the ground, his torso little more than shredded flesh.

The rat let out a mournful wail at the sight of his comrade's fall and with burning, animalistic anger in its eyes moved to pounce at Nate. However, at that moment Marcus had regained his composure and despite his wound, thrust his sword into the rat's leg. This time the rat let out a pitiful squeal before it too fell to the ground.

"I surrender, please, no more," the creature cried. Marcus and Nate both stood over it, panting and covered in the blood of various donors. Marcus examined the rat's wound; it was little more than a scratch and there was no risk of it bleeding out before the guards arrived. He then looked over at what remained of the other smuggler and flicked his blade in Nate's direction.

"I thought I told you not to kill him," he panted. Nate wiped his brow which left behind a long streak of blood.

"Well, technically I didn't," he coughed trying not to be sick. Marcus rubbed his eyes and blinked rapidly; he had already lost enough blood to feel faint but could not afford to let his guard down around such a dangerous creature.

"Now tell me," he said striking the rat's wounded leg with his foot which resulted in another yowl of pain, followed by a whimper. "What's vermin like you doing above ground?" The rat was silent.

"You know what we do to scum like you when we catch them out of their holes?" Marcus continued. The rat trembled; he had heard from his people of the barbarity of humans but had so far been lucky enough to have never been on the extreme end of it.

When no answer came Marcus took express delight in informing it. "We skin them alive and wear them like coats." The rat did not answer and just sat there trembling; it was a pathetic sight, a far cry from the terrifying creature it had been only moments ago.

Nate watched the spectacle from a distance, unsure what to make of it. The creature had tried to kill them both, yes, but Marcus' clear delight in inflicting pain and terror on it shook him.

"Ardell is going to enjoy getting answers out of you, vermin," Marcus smiled as he limped his way over to Nate, the wound on his back still bleeding.

A few hours later Nate and Marcus sat in a dingy inn on the periphery of the docks. It stank of fish and unsurprisingly, they were its only clientele still awake. Nate had quickly alerted nearby guards once their battle with the smugglers was over and a healer had attended to Marcus. The guards took Nate's statement and promised to deliver it to Captain Ardell exclusively, for a price. They also dragged off the rat, who screamed and begged all the while not to be tortured. Nate was unsure whether this plea would be heeded.

Furthermore, Nate could not shake from his thoughts the image of the other smuggler, lying dead on the ground, his body torn to pieces. That had been Nate's first true experience of death, let alone combat and the idea that there would be much more to come made him queasy.

So queasy in fact that he could not manage more than a sip of his mead, which he handed to his companion. Marcus let out a burp as he finished Nate's drink, stretching his back which was still sore from their earlier adventure.

"You did better than I thought, you know," he said, a tinge of pride in his voice.

"Huh?" Nate replied, his head still filled with gory images that he was unable to shake.

"During that little scrap back there, you did alright." Nate rubbed his eyes; he had been awake for twenty hours and was exhausted.

"I nearly got us both killed."

"And yet here we are." Marcus grinned as he held out his arms. But Nate was right, his distaste for real, bloody violence was clear. Luckily, Marcus knew exactly how to remedy this. After spending what little remained of the night in the fishy inn, the two set off at first light. It would still take at least three days before they were back home, but the last thing they wanted to do was keep the captain waiting.

During their journey back Nate took time to marvel at the sights around him. While the lowest levels of the city were designed to be used entirely as farmland, this had not stopped small villages from popping up. Tiny communities isolated within a sea of fields and pastures. So far were they from any other form of civilisation they may have well been their own countries. Yet each was connected through vast and twisted stretches of road which ensured the lifeblood of trade could flow freely between all.

This had also been the first time Nate had entered the Vanguard through the main gate, by which all visitors and merchants had to travel. Despite thinking he had now become used to the sheer size of both the structures and the land itself, Nate was astounded by not so much the size of the gate leading into the Vanguard, but the endless line of people waiting to get in. It stretched on for miles and he assumed, all the way to the outermost ring of the city.

Marcus, noticing Nate's look of puzzled amazement, informed him that this was by no means out of the ordinary. In fact, for so long had such numbers of people queued to enter the city that buildings had sprung up on either side of the road hoping to take advantage of the travellers' gold and goods – everything from inns and bathhouses to theatres and general goods stores had opened beside them. After all, the wait to enter each level of the city could take as long as a month and these weary travellers would need beds to sleep in and food to fill their bellies.

Indeed, the main road leading to and from the main city gates looked like an almost continuous stretch of a high street.

"It used to be a lot easier when they could just come by train," Marcus said matter-of-factly. It took a moment for Nate to process what he had just heard.

"Wait, what?" he asked utterly astounded. "You mean we haven't always had to get saddle sores every time we wanted to go for a pint?" Marcus shook his head and grinned.

"The last train stopped running about two years after I got here, not a single scrap of coal left anywhere in Tinelia," he explained. Nate was utterly amazed by this revelation which Marcus had for some reason decided to keep to himself until now.

"Wait, so when did everything become so…so…" Nate paused as he tried to think of the right word.

"Shit?" Marcus laughed.

"Well, yeah," Nate replied. Marcus simply shrugged.

"I know that the oil ran out about five thousand years ago, or maybe it was six. Anyway, it was before my time, but I do remember all the factories being torn down. Although we had stopped using them decades before the coal ran out anyway.

"Only the railroads and a few weapon manufactories stayed open until the end. We used to get the odd coal shipment from Iletta, over the Shroud Sea to the west, until a few years ago when theirs ran out too."

However, this explanation did little to satisfy Nate's curiosity.

"Surely if this world is infinite, we could just go and find some more, get the world back into the 20th century at least?"

Marcus could not help but laugh at Nate's naivety.

"Sure, I'll let the captain know you've signed up to travel tens of thousands of miles across the Great Wastes and then through the Borderlands into lands uncharted where nightmarish creatures roam just to dig up some coal which you can then carry all the way back again."

"Hmm," Nate began, "Well when you put it like that, it does sound less than ideal."

"Believe me, Nate, people have been trying since long before I got here to solve our resource problems. The distances and dangers are just too great for anyone to risk it."

Nate let out a defeated sigh, for a moment the prospects of air conditioning, refrigerated food and convenient travel had been so tantalisingly close.

Finally, they had reached the open gates of the Vanguard and were waved through, both thankful they did not have to wait in line like the countless poor sods behind them. As they passed there was a commotion at the front between a guard and merchant.

"Miss, weapons not intended for personal use are prohibited inside the city unless you have an arms permit." The merchant pulled out a scruffy and torn piece of parchment from within her cloak and handed it to the guard.

"I think you'll find I have the permit right here," she replied snootily as if the three seconds this conversation had taken had been some monumental inconvenience from which she would never recover. The guard took the parchment and examined it closely before replying.

"Miss, this permit was signed by Captain Vernius."

"Yes," she scoffed. "Is that a problem?"

The guard sighed and wondered what she had done to deserve this posting.

"Captain Vernius retired eight years ago; you're going to need a new permit." The guard nodded to her nearby colleagues who moved in to confiscate the weapons.

The merchant was shocked and leapt between her cart and the approaching guards. "Wait, it's fine, the weapons are for personal use anyway. I'll just get a new permit while I'm in the city for next time."

The guard checked the inventory list the merchant had presented her with and raised her eyebrow.

"You have thirteen greatswords, twenty-five longbows, nine cudgels, fifty-seven daggers and two thousand threehundred and seventy-one arrows for personal use?"

"I like to be prepared," the merchant replied, her nose upturned. The guard looked back at her colleagues who once again moved in, confiscating the contraband despite the shrill protests of the merchant.

"How did she even get in with these?" the guard asked herself, looking at the expired permit as the next person in line stepped forwards.

"Busy morning, Jenna?" Marcus called. Jenna smiled, instantly recognising the friendly voice. She turned to see Marcus riding slowly past.

"Hardly," she said rolling her soft, brown eyes sarcastically. "See you at Pedan's later?"

"If the captain permits me to live that long, sure," Marcus called back as he continued onwards.

"Do you know absolutely everyone in this city?" Nate remarked.

"Only the ones worth knowing," Marcus winked back. Nate then spent the next hour trying to work out what he meant.

At long last, the two arrived at Nate's barracks, a whole day ahead of schedule too. "You go and get some rest, we can see the captain tomorrow, she won't be expecting us until then anyway," Marcus said, still rubbing the spot where the rat had wounded him. Nate nodded.

"Pedan's later?" he asked, doing an awful impression of the girl from earlier. Marcus replied with a thumbs-up as he too trotted homewards. Nate let out a long, pained groan as he lowered himself from his horse, making sure to hitch her around the back of the building.

Horses in the Vanguard were, unless expressly stated so, property of the state. This meant that any legal citizen could take and use a horse for as long as they needed. Well, so long as they did not venture outside the city without permission and the horses were well looked after. Nate had never owned a horse before, yet he enjoyed taking care of one. At least for now it felt like he had a definite purpose, even if that purpose was as insignificant as ensuring the welfare of his equine companion.

Despite Marcus' warning not to name her in case someone else came along in desperate need of transport, Nate had decided to name his new friend Bob. After removing her saddle and ensuring she had plenty of water and hay to keep her content, Nate finally made his way inside.

Despite his best efforts to install at least some modicum of pride in his home, Nate found that his roommate Chen had once again turned the place into a battlefield. Weapons and armour were strewn about with no semblance of order anywhere, despite the presence of multiple weapon and armour racks, which all stood unused.

Plates were also piled high in the kitchen while the fireplace contained enough ashes to bury Pompeii. Chen meanwhile was lying on her bunk, reading, like she always did if she was not sleeping.

"Took you long enough," she teased without looking away from her book. She knew exactly who she was speaking to, as Nate had been the only person mad or desperate enough to have bunked with her in years. Nate ignored her and collapsed face-first into his bunk, not even bothering to change out of his armour which now reeked of both week-old fish and blood. "How was your first little adventure?" she teased again, this being how the two communicated ninety per cent of the time.

"You wouldn't believe me," Nate groaned as he rolled himself onto his back. This caught Chen's interest enough to pry her eyes away from her book.

"Try me," she replied. Nate let out a huff, not sure why he was even bothering, he knew abuse would be his only reward.

"One of the smugglers was a rat, I mean a really, really, really big rat." Chen sniggered loudly. "Told you," Nate said rolling back onto his front and burying his face in his pillow. Chen raised herself from her bunk and stretched, her joints cracking one by one.

"Oh, I believe you," she yawned, "I just thought you were going to say something actually interesting for once." With renewed vigour, Nate pushed himself up.

"Oh yeah, like you've ever seen one. You would have shit yourself I guarantee it," he said, launching his pillow at her as he did so. She caught it and launched it back at him twice as hard.

"You blind and stupid?" she laughed, pointing at the wall furthest from the door.

"What are you talking about?" Nate said barely dodging the pillow. Following Chen's arm, he found to his horror, the hides of no less than three huge rats mounted above the bunks.

"Jesus Christ," was all he could manage, with no idea how he had not managed to notice the hides before now. "Did you do that?" he gasped.

"Sure did," Chen replied puffing out her chest as she admired her work. "Killed them first though, because I'm generous like that."

Dumbstruck, Nate had no idea how to continue such a conversation. Luckily, Chen was already bored and had moved on.

"More guard duty tomorrow, yippee," she sighed as she made some effort to tidy up the carnage.

"If you hate it so much why not just go out on an expedition? You're always telling me how great they are and all the things you've seen."

"Believe me, if it were that simple, I'd be gone already," she replied, a bundle of swords in her arms.

"Well, what's stopping you then?" Nate asked. Carefully, Chen placed each blade into the slots of the rack and began on the dirty dishes.

"Well," she began, in a tone that made Nate think this was going to be more of a lecture than a genuine reason.

"First, I need to submit a report on the objectives of the expedition to Ardell. If that's accepted, I must go out and find a party to go with me. I then need Ardell's permission to leave the city. After that, I must wait at least a week for any equipment requests to be reviewed. If any of these things fail, it's a six-month wait before you're allowed to submit another expedition request."

"Hmm," Nate replied. He had no idea that going on an expedition was such a strict process. "Why not just tag along with an existing expedition? Or go with one of the guilds, Marcus says they don't answer to the captains." Chen huffed.

"Firstly, those guilds are a scam. Not only do they not allow you on any expeditions until you've reached the right 'rank'", she said making quotation marks with her fingers. "But their cut of the profits is extortionate, even worse than the captain's. It's also not as easy as you think to find expeditions to 'tag along with'. Would you rather risk your neck for a stranger, or someone you've known for years?"

"Fair point." Nate shrugged. "Ok, how about this…" he began. Chen stopped mid-scrub of an especially filthy plate to hear his proposition. "When I get sent on an expedition, I'll make sure you come along too." Chen gave a thin smile.

"Oh yeah, like they'll ever send a useless lump like you anywhere," she teased turning back to her dishes – although, in her heart, she appreciated the gesture and had only turned around so Nate did not see the huge smile lighting up her face.

A few hours and a bath later Nate felt better than he had done in weeks. While living with a stranger, and a woman at that had been extremely awkward initially, the two were forced to reach an agreement of no wandering eyes and no comments of any sort after the smell had become unbearable. Drying himself off with a towel Nate slipped into his civilian clothes which had not been worn since the day they had set off after the smugglers. Curiously, Nate felt naked without the tight squeeze of his armour. As Marcus had said, it now felt like his second skin, and to be without it was a strange sensation.

"Any plans for tonight?" Nate asked as he put on his already worn-out leather boots which he had owned for less than three months. Chen shrugged.

"Probably just read until bed, you?" Nate rolled his eyes.

"All you ever do is read," he complained "What are you reading this time?"

"If you must know, it's the first volume on the nesting and feeding habits of ground-dwelling reptiles," she replied, annoyed that her week-long un-interruption had ended. Nate could not help but laugh.

"Are you serious? There's no way you're serious. Wait, the first volume, you mean there's more than one?"

Chen turned her eyes from the pages at the end of her nose and towards the ceiling, taking deep breaths, reminding herself that this book was far too expensive to beat Nate to death with.

"Is there a problem?" she asked through gritted teeth, knowing she would have to re-read the whole page.

"No no, not at all, just never thought that would be what you were into. I expected dragons, princesses, monsters, you know, that crap."

"Pfft, if I wanted that I could just go for a walk outside. I want to actually learn something, seeing as you know, we are stuck here forever."

This made sense Nate supposed, however, why anyone would spend so much time reading in a world of literally endless possibilities was beyond him. Chen seemed to read his mind and answered.

"Killing monsters is fun and all, but once you have been wading through guts up to your waist a few times, you start to think of alternative lifestyles. I for one want to go to the Imperial University, become a professor of zoology and spend a few centuries in the lap of luxury. At least then I'll be able to have an intellectual conversation for once."

"Ouch," Nate replied clutching his chest in mock pain. "But fair enough, I won't make fun of someone following their dreams." He jumped from his bed and stretched before putting on his cloak, as it was about time he left for Pedan's. As he reached for the door he looked back at Chen, still horizontal, the book having returned to just centimetres from her nose.

"You know," he started, a mischievous grin creeping across his face. "Where I come from, going out and getting absolutely plastered is an integral part of one's higher education." Slowly Chen lowered her book, revealing a grin of her own.

"Well now, how could I argue with a system that produces esteemed scholars such as yourself?"

"How indeed?" Nate replied as they both headed towards town.

"So, what's so great about the Imperial University, don't we have our own?" Nate asked as the pair walked side by side through the crowded streets. Thousands of shoppers were still busy perusing, even as the sun began to fade.

"Oh yeah, the world-famous Tinelian University, great if you want to learn how to shoot fireballs out your arse or build a bomb," Chen replied sarcastically. "Half those degenerates spend their time trying to turn wood into gold."

"I dunno, all those things sound pretty useful to me, well, maybe not a fireball out the arse but I'm sure a hand would do just as well," Nate replied, trying to lighten the mood. Chen, however, shook her head in frustration.

"Honestly, all anyone in this city thinks about is war, war with the Imperium this, war with the Imperium that. It's no wonder the Imperium is light years ahead of us." She suddenly stopped and stood motionless in the street, her arms folded crossly as she examined the shops which towered over them on both sides.

Nate stopped too, much to the annoyance of the other shoppers who had to take a whole step out of their way around them. "I mean, look," Chen continued, determined to continue her tirade until she felt her point had been sufficiently expressed. "One, two, three, four, five, six, seven, eight, nine," she said counting off the shops around them.

"Nine shops out of twelve within about twenty feet, all selling something used for killing." Nate had never really paid close attention to the shops seeing as he never had any money, but he realised now Chen had a point. Everywhere he looked, including further down both ends of the street, the majority were selling something of a militaristic nature.

Although this made sense from what he had been told and seen first-hand – this world was not exactly a picnic, something was always trying to kill you. He expressed this to Chen, bringing up that she too had been part of the whole system, going off on expeditions, helping fuel the industry. This, surprisingly, did not help settle her mood.

"But it doesn't have to be all there is!" she moaned. "There's so much to learn and all we do is kill each other instead."

Nate simply shrugged in response.

"There's nothing we can do to change it, may as well just roll with it."

Chen looked at the ground, defeated. The mud churned up, shapeless and senseless. The perfect analogy for this world, she thought.

"Yeah, I guess you're right, like we could make a difference," she replied solemnly. The rest of the journey was made in awkward silence, Chen embarrassed by her outburst, and Nate unsure how to change the topic. Luckily, it was not long before the familiar sight of The Hovel came into view, although they had heard its unmistakable din of laughter and singing long before.

As usual, it was heaving, the warm night having attracted yet more drinkers, many of whom sat outside, not willing to risk life and limb trying to find a table indoors. Squeezing their way through the crowd of patrons was no easy task, especially for Chen whose size made her easy to miss.

After being stood on several times they managed to reach the fire pit at the centre of the room. There was simply no way of getting to the bar at this point. Nate scanned what little he could see of the ground floor and the balconies above them, yet there was no sign of Marcus.

"What should we do?" Nate asked, turning to Chen in search of some sort of leadership.

"Let's wait here for a bit, till it's quieter." Nate nodded in agreement and turned his attention to whatever mystery meat was roasting over the fire tonight. Whatever it was, it smelled delicious. At that moment, a man who sat immediately opposite Nate across the fire pit began to speak. It was clear that he was extremely old. Despite like nearly everyone else looking barely out of his twenties, there was a clear aura of wisdom and antiquity which surrounded him. This was clearest of all in his eyes, they did not shine with the same youthfulness as his body. Rather, they seemed as weathered and lashed by time as a ship in a storm.

"What tale do you wish to hear tonight my friends?" the man asked. His voice was deep yet gentle, like that of a schoolteacher. This was one of the reasons why Pedan's was so popular, nowhere else could you hear tales and histories told with such verve and detail.

"The age of liberation," one voice called.

"Oh, come on, everyone has heard that one, do the rise of the Vermindom instead," called another.

"Are you serious? Half of us were there for that, tell us about the age of strife."

"The Dual Monarchy," said Chen speaking up excitedly. There were no protests from the other patrons as the old man smiled.

"The Dual Monarchy it is, although I warn you all, this tale is one of tragedy and woe and is not for the faint of heart." The old man took a sip from his flagon and leaned back in his chair, resting his feet by the edge of the pit to warm them up after a long day's travel.

"Millenia ago, two brave warriors by the names of Arda Tinelia, and Sabel set upon our very shores. Here they found the ruins of a great keep, long abandoned after one of the endless wars that plagued our lands, as this was still the age of strife. For many years did they and their companions toil to rebuild the keep, and when it was finished it was the greatest fortress this side of the Forked Rivers."

The tale had barely started and already Nate was enthralled. The combination of the crackling fire and the old man's natural gift for storytelling had already drawn him in until even the bedlam around them seemed but a distant whisper.

"However, word of their great deed had travelled far and reached unfriendly and jealous ears. Before long many petty kings and tribal warlords had descended upon their fair keep to conquer it for themselves. And for our fair heroines, well one shudders to imagine what designs lay in wait for such beautiful and capable a pair.

"Yet when all seemed lost as the savages besieged the walls, suddenly, our heroes and their company were saved. A king from a nearby land had also heard the tales of the pair's exploits, but more interested in their beauty was he than any stretch of land or fortress strong. A king I refuse to name so despicable were his crimes."

Nate looked to Chen who stood beside him – she too was enthralled, her hands clasped together against her chest, her eyes wide with wonder and excitement. She had read the history of the Dual Monarchy a hundred times, yet it never ceased to inspire her and put quick to her heart notions of heroism and valour. The old man continued, having stopped for another sip of beer.

"Once the savage warlords and petty kings had been routed, our fair ladies presented themselves before their rescuer and bid him to choose any prize he wished as his reward. Yet this king was interested in no gold or jewels as his fortune was far beyond that which our heroines could offer. So instead, he chose Sabel as his reward, to be his wedded wife.

"Now Sabel was no distinguished lady, any of whom throughout these lands would have jumped to be offered such a proposition. No, Sabel was strong of will and rejected him without hesitation.

"Enraged the king threatened to behead them both there and then and raise their fortress to the ground. Yet stubborn Sabel still refused him and instead presented to him her neck for chopping. However, quick-thinking and lovely Arda in fear for her friends' lives presented a counteroffer. Instead, she would marry the king, but only if he would spare the defiant Sabel.

"The king, who was both cunning and cruel, agreed to Arda's offer... upon one condition. Sabel must slay the evil Virion, he who had betrayed humanity to the will of the dragons during the age of liberation."

There were some hisses and boos from the crowd at the mere mention of the name. Nate had no idea what the old man was talking about but continued listening intently, nonetheless.

"Sabel feared the clutches of Death not, yet her loyalty to Arda and the love she bore her compelled her to undertake this perilous quest. A quest which would take over half a century to complete. Along the way, however, she became close allies with many lords and kings having aided them with their own troubles until eventually, she had a whole army of loyal allies she could call upon to support her in her endeavour.

"Meanwhile, back in our glorious homeland where the foul king had taken new residence, shrewd Arda had been hard at work herself. While her royal husband had been despised by his subjects, she came to be loved by noble and commoner all. She built a kingdom of unmatched wealth and power from her seat in that high place, that glorious Citadel. Her fetid husband, meanwhile, squandered his days hunting and whoring and inflicting dreadful abuse upon the peasants of the land.

"Then one day the king, that foul and loathsome wretch, returned from a hunting trip in a drunken stupor while the lovely Queen Arda hosted court. He hurled abuse at the gathered lords and ladies and when her glorious majesty attempted to intervene, for although she despised her husband, she was a loyal and dutiful wife, the king, such a cur was he, struck her across the face".

There was an audible intake of breath as the crowd could not bear to hear how their revered queen had been abused. The old man waited, allowing the words to settle amongst the crowd before he continued, a smile across his lips.

"The court, so outraged at the wanton violence against their beloved queen seized the king and cast him out. Like a foul rat, he scurried back to his former lands, with only his most loyal henchmen in tow.

"Most revered Arda immediately sent word across the breadth of the world, calling for Sabel to return. Back to that warm and familiar bosom of Tinelia which she had once called home so many years ago.

"By the month's end, our queen received an envoy, dressed all in black who presented himself as the ambassador of Sabellion, who had been sent by his queen Sabel to offer news of her triumph against the evil and dark forces of Virion. Overcome with joy did Arda set off immediately for Sabellion, to see her dear friend once more, the only wish of her boundless heart.

"At last dear Arda arrived at Sabellion, that city which we now call the Imperial City, where the Forked Rivers meet and become one. Like those rivers, Arda and Sabel too became

one; reunited at last after so long they showered one another with many hugs and kisses, so long and cruel had their parting been.

"On that very day, the Dual Monarchy was proclaimed, one nation, with two capitals, bright and reverent Tinelia, and dark but majestic Sabellion. From those two capitals ruled its two queens: fair and gracious Arda, and beautiful but proud Sabel. For a century, these two queens ruled the lands stretching from this great city to Sabellion and beyond, as Sabel was often prone to wars of conquest. Yet never had such peace and prosperity been so widespread, the people were fat and wealthy, while peace was the norm. For the most part."

The old man winked at the crowd. There were stirs of laughter while the old man finished his beer.

"Yet fortune smiled not on our dear queens, as yet more woe and misery were to be their ultimate prize. For you see, that cowardly king who had retreated in disgrace had for a century plotted with malicious heart against our most lovely heroines.

"One night, he was spotted by a maid sneaking into the palace of Sabellion. For despite all these years in the arms of the most beautiful Arda, it had been Sabel whom he had coveted. That night, with dark magic and ignoble trickery he kidnapped fair Sabel, leaving only a few drops of blood behind as evidence of their struggle.

"Then before the week had passed, his former wife, the God-like Arda, was found slain in her bedchambers, the culprit, wicked poison of the king's own design which had burst her heart asunder.

"That my dear friends is where our tale ends, for never again was Sabel or that dastardly king seen. While our perfect lady now lies atop the citadel which she built, betrayed by the one who had once professed to love her above all."

The old man stopped, the reactions from the crowd worth more to him than any fee he might charge for his time. So vivid had the descriptions been that Nate had seen the whole story play out in his mind as if he himself had been there. He turned to Chen, only to see her cheeks were wet with tears.

Yet before he could speak a stifled sob turned his attention to the rest of the crowd. Almost all were sobbing, and those that did not have moist eyes quickly excused themselves. While there were none present who had lived through these times, the cult-like worship of Arda Tinelia was profound amongst her people.

Worship which had been encouraged by Grand Admiral Lee, the last surviving member of Arda Tinelia's original company. There was a sudden, heavy tap on Nate's shoulder. He turned and was glad to see Marcus towering over him. "Having a history lesson, are we?" he smiled. Nate crossed his arms.

"Not sure how true it all is, it'd make a great book though." Marcus laughed; he had never truly believed all the claims peddled about Arda Tinelia. Mostly because they could never seem to keep the stories straight.

"Come, we have a table upstairs, plus there is someone I would like you to meet," Marcus said as he turned to walk away. Nate tapped Chen on the arm and instructed her to follow him, the sight of her bringing a low groan to Marcus.

Carefully, the trio navigated the crowded hall up to the very top floor, Nate making sure to give anyone coming down the stairs a wide berth. Marcus led them over to a table with room for five, situated near the back wall.

Sat at the table already was a handsome man with dark curly hair and a fashionable goatee, his skin tanned by many years in the sun. He wore a set of leather armour very similar to Nate's, although far more comfortable-looking and expensive. Noticing their approach, he offered a smile and raised his beer in greeting.

"Nate, Chen, this is my good friend Joel," Marcus explained as he took his seat. Both Nate and Chen shook Joel's hand which was strong and coarse after many years of manual labour.

"Nice to meet you both," he said with the hint of an Australian accent.

"Likewise," Nate replied.

"So, Marcus tells me you're a tad squeamish about this whole blood and guts thing?" Joel inquired. Nate was surprised at such an abrupt conversation starter with a complete stranger. Marcus meanwhile placed his head in his hand.

"So much for bringing it up casually," he sighed. Chen and Joel both laughed – evidently, Marcus had not yet been around long enough to appreciate the advantages of a direct approach to get the ball rolling. Things took long enough already in the afterlife, no need to drag anything out that did not require it.

"On that note, I think I'll get some drinks, evidently you boys have some issues to work out," Chen added as she rose from her seat.

"I'll join you," Marcus added. Chen smiled – while the two might not see eye to eye on matters of discipline, navigating the drunken masses would be much easier with him in tow. This left Nate and Joel alone for the first time, an awkward silence filling the void between them as Joel examined Nate closely. Nate tried to pretend to be looking around the room to avoid Joel's gaze, but Joel quickly spoke up.

"So where are you from? You sound like a pommy to me," he smiled.

"Guilty as charged." Nate awkwardly smiled back, failing awfully at settling into the conversation.

"I'm guessing your world is pretty peaceful then, most people you'll meet round here were used to violence before they arrived. Didn't take much convincing for them to join in on it," Joel replied. Nate shrugged.

"It wasn't perfect but relatively peaceful, yeah."

"Hmm," Joel hummed, resting his chin on his fists. "Well, I hate to be the one to tell you this, but to survive in this world, you're going to need to learn how to kill pretty quick." This was not news to Nate, and he wondered why he was having this conversation at all. He had not been around for six months yet – were Marcus and Ardell expecting him to have slaughtered a village by now?

"I have been in a fight already," Nate responded, unsure why he felt so compelled to prove to Joel he was capable of violence.

"Yes, Marcus told me you handled yourself pretty well. You didn't strike a killing blow though, and you seemed a bit put out at the sight of a little blood." *A little bit of blood? The guy was basically mincemeat,* Nate fumed internally. Joel could sense Nate was becoming tense which would make the next part of the conversation even harder.

"That's why Marcus has asked me to help you in the Wailing Pits."

Nate was not sure whether it was the part about the wailing or the pits which made him feel the worst, but either way, he did not like the sound of it at all.

"Do you really think I should be going on holiday in the middle of my training?" Nate laughed uneasily. Joel too let out a chuckle, he could tell the pair of them were going to get along well.

"The Wailing Pits are where we take people who have trouble with killing. I promise you it is completely safe; Marcus and I will be watching the whole time." It was at this point that Marcus and Chen had returned with an armful of drinks each.

"How are we getting on?" Marcus asked. He had been too cowardly to have the conversation with Nate himself and so had roped Joel in as his accomplice.

"Oh great," Nate huffed, "Joel was just telling me about how lovely the Wailing Pits are this time of year."

"Oof," Chen began, drawing the eyes of the three men as she took a long gulp of her drink. "Don't worry, the first one is always the worst, you'll be over it in no time."

"First what? I mean I'm taking a wild stab in the dark and guessing the Wailing Pits isn't a spa, but I feel like you guys are doing this to me on purpose."

This time it was Marcus who spoke.

"The pits are essentially where new fighters get used to what is expected of them out on an expedition. You'll be faced with a creature which has been chained and rendered passive and it will be your job to kill it."

Nate shook his head.

"Sorry, I don't want to kill some helpless animal just because I'm being told to," he replied angrily.

"Oh boy," Joel said downing his beer.

"Sorry Nate, but the Captain has already signed off on it. If you don't do it, you and I will both be regarded as deserters, that's how serious this is," Marcus lied.

"Christ," Nate said pushing his thumb and forefinger into his eyes. "First of all, I don't even get asked whether I want to be a soldier, and now I'm being forced into blood sports."

He took a long gulp of his mead to show his annoyance, something he immediately regretted as he was barely able to swallow a mouthful before he began to choke. Chen slapped him on the back, whether to stop him from choking or as a consolation he did not know until she spoke.

"Try not to worry, if anything I wish I had gone to the Wailing Pits during my training. But for now, how about you show me this critical part of education you were talking about?" She raised her second drink to her lips and downed it in one.

"I'll drink to that," Joel smiled, raising his flagon once more. Nate was not fooled by this attempt to divert his attention from whatever he had been signed up for. Then again, perhaps a drink or two would make processing the whole thing easier.

For the next few hours, the four drank merrily. Joel would tell amusing stories such as when he was stationed at an outpost only to spend three months there before realising he had accidentally been living amongst bandits entirely unnoticed.

Chen and Nate would tease one another mercilessly about their bad habits. Marcus, meanwhile, was simply happy to be in good company once again. As he was finishing what must have been his sixth or seventh flagon of ale, he noticed Jenna smiling at him from across the room.

It was nearing midnight and the inn was much quieter now, enough for him to notice that she was sitting alone, casually flicking glances in his direction every few moments. Filled with liquid courage he stood and bid goodnight to his companions. For a few moments, they were confused as they watched him struggle to make it to Jenna's table in a straight line. He had barely been sat down and chatting for a minute before Jenna rose and led him away by the hand.

He quickly shot his friends a drunken smile as he allowed himself to be taken. "At least he will be in a good mood in the morning," Joel grinned as he brought his final drink to his lips.

"God why is everyone getting some but me?" Chen sighed in drunken annoyance. Nate shot her a disgusted look and decided he had had enough of drinking for one night. After parting ways with Joel, Nate and Chen staggered home, supporting one another most of the way. Luckily, by the time they had reached their barracks the crisp night air and exercise had sobered them up somewhat.

However, it still took three or four attempts to insert the key into the lock. Once inside they threw off their cloaks, Nate lit the fire and Chen sat on her bed struggling with her clothes. The sudden burst of light and warmth made the room much cosier, and Nate stopped for a moment to warm his hands.

There were a series of frustrated grunts as Chen tried and failed miserably to take off her boots, her double vision making the task immeasurably difficult. Nate laughed and stumbled over, dropping to his knees and making quick work of the laces.

"Thank you," Chen slurred as she dragged herself into bed. "Now don't you get any ideas of taking advantage of me, I'd still kick your arse, even if there are two of you." Nate laughed as he struggled over to his own bunk.

"Oh please, I'm way out of your league."

Chapter 10

The next morning Nate found himself stood in the freezing rain, his cloak tight against his skin. Before him was a metal gate held shut by a long, iron bar. Beside him stood Marcus who was fiddling with a loose strap on his chest plate. They had travelled only a few minutes ride from Ardell's fort, in the opposite direction of home before they had arrived at the pits.

Dug straight down into the ground there were two entrances, one for spectators which led to seating areas around the circumference of the pit, the other for trainees, which led to a crude lift which required an operator on the surface to use. This laborious process was to ensure no escaping creature could make it to ground level.

Nate had protested for the duration of their journey that this exercise was unnecessary, but his complaints fell on deaf ears. His attention now turned to what hellish creature he would be faced with and whether he believed Joel's claim that it was all completely safe.

"Sorry I'm late lads," Joel called as he descended the lift and jogged over to where they were stood.

"No rush, please take your time," Marcus said sarcastically. Even with the three of them, it was a struggle to remove the iron bar keeping them from the pit's interior.

"Right, off we go," said Joel with an enthusiastic nod of the head. The inside was mostly flattened earth, damp and muddy from the rain, although the perimeter was defended by wooden stakes which pointed inwards. Meanwhile, the walls themselves were coated with some sort of black adhesive should something try to scale them.

All these security measures did little to calm Nate's nerves. The trio kept walking until they were in the very centre of the pit.

"Right, you wait here and get ready, I'll go get our friend," Joel instructed. Marcus nodded and removed his cloak; Nate did the same but was visibly shaking. Playing it off as the rain he placed his hand on the pommel of his sword. This small act was a comforting reminder that he was not entirely helpless.

Joel, meanwhile, had disappeared through a large door at the opposite end of the pit. "Try not to panic," Marcus advised. Nate looked at him. As usual, he was calm and looked just about ready for anything. Knowing Marcus was also there for him should anything go wrong further began to ease Nate's pounding heart.

That was until Joel re-emerged, trailing behind him was what appeared to be a woman, held in bondage by a collar onto which Joel held with a long metal pole. "What the hell?" Nate cried in both horror and anger, about to rush forward to help the poor soul. Marcus quickly shot out his hand and held a firm grasp on Nate's wrist.

"Wait," he demanded in a gruff voice, offering no chance to protest. Nate simply had to stand still until Joel and his captive were within spitting distance. Now that they were closer and Nate could see them both clearly, he let out a horrified gasp and almost stumbled backwards into the mud.

It was indeed some sort of woman at the end of the pole, except her skin was grey and visibly rotting, her eyes black and dead. Furthermore, her hands had been removed and from within her grey lips, from which strings of rotten flesh hung, came a quiet but unmistakeable sobbing.

"Marcus…w…what?" Nate began but was unable to finish his question as the words died in his throat.

"We call them Husks," Marcus replied, his voice tinged with pity and regret. He pointed directly at her soulless eyes. "This is what the embodiment of human sin looks like." Nate was dumbstruck and was shaking twice as hard as before. He tried to take a step backwards, to try running away, but once again Marcus grabbed hold of him roughly. This time Nate tried to fight back, to break free and make for the safety of home, but Marcus was too strong.

"This is insane!" Nate shouted. Marcus let go of his wrist and Nate fell back into the mud, cold, slimy water oozing between his fingers. "I can't do it, I refuse," he cried once again. Marcus sympathised, he too had once failed to see the difference between a Husk and a human, but that was a long time ago, and he was under no such illusions now.

"Nate…" he began, but Nate would not hear it.

"No," he sniffed, getting to his feet, his anger now replaced by fear, fear of what it would mean if he were forced to kill this defenceless woman. "I'm sorry Marcus, I'm not a murderer, this just isn't right." The Husk had watched the whole spectacle with her un-feeling eyes, all the while continuing with her low sobbing. Joel decided to keep quiet and let Marcus take charge.

"I know what it looks like, but I promise you, this thing," he said pointing back at the pitiful creature. "This thing is not human, she does not feel pain, she does not feel love or have memories, she probably doesn't even know she exists beyond her own hunger."

"Hunger?" Nate asked, his voice but a squeak, mere seconds away from cracking. Marcus nodded.

"All these things want is blood, human blood, they roam the world looking for people to devour. They are the epitome of evil, that is why we have brought you here. Not to be a murderer, but to learn how to recognise evil, and to do what is necessary to stop its spread."

Nate looked at Marcus for a moment and then at the Husk, and he took a step forward, hoping to see something which the others did not, something to confirm her humanity. Suddenly the Husk lurched forwards, its arms outstretched, hoping to reach Nate with hands that were no longer there. Joel held firmly onto the pole and yanked her back, stopping the Husk just inches from Nate's face. Nate jumped back, his heart on the verge of bursting.

"No, I'm not doing it," he said resolutely, continuing to take steps back.

"For fuck's sake," Marcus said grabbing hold of Nate by the scruff of the neck and throwing him down into the mud.

"Marcus!" Joel protested, but Marcus ignored him. Before Nate had been able to recover Marcus had secured hold of him once more and held him down, the left side of his face pressed against the cold ground.

"Listen to me Nate," Marcus said in a mixture of anger and desperation. "I don't care if you don't want to be a killer. The captain does not care either, but if you don't kill this fucking thing, we will both be out of this city and no clever comment is going to save us. Once we are out there, we are on our own, and that may be fine for you, but I for one want to be able to sleep in my own bed at night not having to worry about having my entrails eaten. So, do as you are told before you fuck both our lives up."

With his outburst concluded Marcus stood, releasing his hold on Nate.

Slowly, he pulled himself up, caked in mud and soaked as he fought off sobs. He looked at Marcus, then Joel, and finally the Husk. Marcus may have been right, but Nate hated him for it, and he would never forgive him for what he was about to go through.

Nate drew his sword, barely able to keep it from falling from his grasp as he was shaking more than ever. "Good," Marcus said, "now go for the chest, that's the quickest way." Nate looked back at him once more, loathing and anger clear in his eyes. Breathing frantically, he tried not to look at the Husk as he raised his sword into a thrusting position. Yet despite his best efforts he made eye contact. Its eyes were void of life, yet her endless crying could not help but seep into the memory of his heart.

He would never forgive himself for this. With an agonising cry Nate plunged the sword deep into the Husk's stomach. She let out a shrill shriek and fell to the ground, black blood dripping from the blade as it was pulled free. Panting like an animal Nate hurriedly turned to walk away, his grisly mission complete. However, he was stopped in his tracks by a harrowingly familiar sound. A low, distorted sobbing, as if the victim were in immense pain. He turned, tears already on the verge of spilling over the corner of his eyes. Marcus and Joel were both looking at him, Joel still holding a firm grip on the pole.

"Nate," he said softly. Nate looked at Joel's feet where the Husk lay – she was still very much alive, lying in a pool of her own blood, sobbing unrelentingly. With feet like lead Nate dragged himself over to where she lay, stopping just short of her arm's reach. He looked at her face, she could have been beautiful once, had a family, children who loved her. Yet here she was, nothing more than a practice dummy for the amusement of sadists.

Slowly, he raised his sword so that its point was above her heart. The blade cut through her flesh easily, as if she had been butter. The sword's tip pierced her heart and the Husk let out a quiet, prolonged sob, before at last the crying stopped.

"Well done, Nate, you did it," Joel consoled, finally letting go of the pole and placing a reassuring hand on Nate's shoulder. However, the toxic mix of the smell of the Husk's foul blood combined with the sound of her sobs echoing through Nate's mind and the previous night's alcohol was too much for him. He vomited, dropping his sword as he fell onto his hands and knees.

Joel kept his hand on Nate's back as he emptied the contents of his stomach onto the already disgusting mixture of blood and mud. His skin had gone deathly white, and a cold sweat had broken out across his whole body. The vomiting had done little to help, and he remained there, on his hands and knees, the tears finally breaking over his face. Suddenly, Marcus spoke up.

"Joel," he said, "go fetch another."

Chapter 11

Thirty-six. Nate had stopped crying after the fifth. His arms had stopped shaking after the tenth, and after the fourteenth, he felt nothing at all as he slid his blade into the hearts of the Husks.

But Marcus pressed him on until the ending of Husks' lives was as routine a motion as brushing his teeth. Thirty-six was where it stopped. By the end, Nate's hands were black with Husk blood and his whole body felt numb. Even the torrential rain and piercing wind could not rouse him to shudder. As Joel piled up the last of the corpses for burning, Marcus approached Nate and offered him water. He had not allowed for a break until he was satisfied, and it was now well past midday. Nate took it but could only manage the most meagre of sips before handing it back.

Marcus began speaking but Nate could not hear him, the cries of the Husks as he killed them drowning out even the pounding rain. With wide and emotionless eyes Nate turned and walked out of the pit, ascending to ground level and riding home without a word, while all the while Marcus and Joel called after him.

The journey itself was a blur and before he knew it, he was back home. Smoke rose from the chimney, a welcome sight. He did not bother hitching Bob to her usual post and shuffled inside. Within he found Chen stood over the fire, book in hand, turning as she heard the door open. She wore a warm smile and was about to speak when she noticed Nate's face, devoid of life, and his hands covered in blood.

She stood frozen as Nate approached her slowly, and for a moment she was terrified that he had been critically injured. Yet before she could reach out to him, Nate collapsed to his knees, wrapping his arms tightly around her waist. What followed were the most harrowing cries of pain Chen had ever heard.

She lowered herself until she was sitting on the floor, Nate's head on her lap, his eyes streaming with tears.

"What did they do to you?" she asked, but no answer came. Seeing Nate in such a state soon brought Chen close to tears also. For the remainder of the day and all through the night she sat with him as he sobbed, holding one another as if they were the last people in the world.

The next morning there was a knock on the door. Chen knew exactly who it was and leapt from her place at Nate's bedside. She flung the door open and before Marcus could even register who he was looking at, Chen threw all her strength into a punch aimed at his jaw. Taken by surprise Marcus did not try to defend himself and received the full force of the blow knocking him from the porch to the ground. He could not believe what had just happened and lay there for a moment, dazed.

"You son of a bitch!" Chen cried as she advanced on him. Marcus quickly stood and dodged as Chen attempted to strike him again, this time catching her arm mid-swing.

"What the hell are you doing?" he shouted, adrenaline now coursing through his veins. Chen was not listening, however, as incensed with rage she wrenched free her arm and pushed him away.

"Why would you do that to him?" she asked, her whole body racked with anger.

"Chen what are you…" but she cut him off.

"You know damn well what I'm talking about," she snapped. Marcus sighed and bowed his head.

"I had to, if I hadn't the captain would have punished us both," Marcus replied. Chen nodded.

"I understand, you were just trying to save your own arse," she sniffed. "Well, I hope it was worth it, you've broken him."

Marcus shook his head, thinking she was exaggerating.

"The captain wants to see us both, I need to take Nate with me," he explained as he took a step towards the barracks. But Chen jumped between them, clearly eager to take another swing.

"He's not going anywhere with you, and if Ardell has a problem with that she can come and tell me herself," Chen spat as she slammed the door in his face and locked it. Marcus remained in place for a moment, shocked that such anger could come from such a small woman. He thought about what to do next and perhaps for the first time, Captain Ardell was not the person he was most afraid of right now.

Chen returned to Nate who was now sitting upright in his bunk. "What was all that about?" he asked. Chen took several deep breaths before she was composed enough to speak without sounding furious.

"Just that bloody soap salesman again, I told him there's no hope for you," she said trying to force a laugh. Nate was exhausted in both mind and body – his effort to sit upright had used up all his accumulated strength from the night before. He had only managed a few hours of sleep as each time he closed his eyes he was haunted by nightmares.

Chen too was exhausted, having spent the entire night either by Nate's bedside while he slept or on the floor beside the fireplace consoling him. She moved over to the fire where a cauldron was boiling and poured two bowls. "Sorry, we are all out of sugar," she said as she handed him the bowl of plain porridge.

"Honestly, what do I pay you for?" he smirked, the spark of life slowly returning to him. Chen lightly thumped his leg and ate her porridge, smiling for the first time in what felt like forever. A few hours later there was another knock on the door. Chen awoke abruptly. The sun was dimmer now, casting a soothing orange glow across the room. She once again expected it to be Marcus and leapt up, although approaching the door with less haste this time, her muscles not yet ready for another fight.

Nate too had been woken by the noise but did not have the strength to raise himself up again. Chen readied herself for another altercation – there was no way she would let Marcus take Nate away in this state. When she swung the door open, however, standing before her was perhaps the last person she had expected. Tall and elegant, and with the distant sun resting atop her head like a halo stood Captain Ardell. Behind her, Marcus looked as if he might melt into a puddle of shame at any moment.

"Is Nate here?" she asked. Chen could not find words to either express her shock or answer the captain's question.

"I...I..." she stammered. Ardell looked back at Marcus and repeated her question. He replied with a sheepish, "Yes, Captain."

With that, Ardell pushed her way past Chen and into the barracks. The three of them gathered around Nate's bedside in silence. Nate was awake yet he was both too weak and surprised to react to Ardell's presence and wondered if it was just a fever dream. Immediately upon seeing Nate's almost transparent skin and still trembling hands, Ardell turned to Marcus in a fit of rage.

"Is this what being a mentor means to you?"

There was no answer from Marcus who simply stared at the floor, too embarrassed to see with his own eyes what he had caused. Ardell squared up to him until their noses were just a centimetre away from each other.

"I gave you permission to use the Pits under the express condition that you did not push him too far," Ardell spat. She forced Marcus to look as she pointed at Nate. "Is this not far enough for you?!" she screamed directly into Marcus' face.

"I'm sorry, Captain," was all Marcus could summon. At this point Ardell was shaking with fury, her fists clenched so tight her knuckles were white. For a moment she remained just shy of Marcus, her breathing heavy as her blood boiled.

"The last time I checked I was the captain here; do you know what that means, Marcus?" she asked. Marcus played the dangerous game of remaining silent. "It means the only person allowed to abuse my men, is me... You will be severely punished for this," she concluded.

Again, Marcus remained silent, although a satisfied scowl had crawled across Chen's face – she hoped whatever awaited Marcus would make him suffer. Ardell then turned to Nate.

"Nate, you have my sincerest apologies, this is by no means how I intended for you to be treated." She turned and gave Marcus a filthy look before turning back. "In light of this, I am recommending you be transferred from under my command to a position more suitable for your skills." Nate's eyes widened at the thought of never having to lift a sword again.

"Once you have recovered come and see me at the fort, we will go over your options then, in the meantime get some rest, you've been through hell." Nate managed the slightest of nods to indicate he understood. Ardell then turned to Chen, much to her surprise. "Anything he needs let me know, I will cover it."

"Thank you, Captain," Chen replied with a bow. With her business concluded Ardell forced her way past Marcus and back towards her fort – this little excursion had already cost her far too much valuable time.

There was an awkward silence as the others remained. Marcus desperately wanted to apologise, he recognised his mistake but both pride and embarrassment kept the words lodged in his throat. As the silence grew ever longer and Chen's laser-like stare burned through him Marcus finally swallowed his pride and spoke.

"Nate, I…"

"Get. Out." Chen growled; she did not want to hear a single word more from him. Defeated, Marcus bowed his head in shame and left – whatever punishment Ardell had in store for him, it could not be worse than how he felt now. Nate was slightly disappointed; he would have liked to hear Marcus apologise so he could put the whole thing behind him. At present, however, he had larger concerns, his eyelids were heavy, and all the recent excitement had taken its toll.

Determined that by tomorrow he would have regained his strength, he drifted off into a sleep beset by nightmares. Chen returned to her own bed, picked up the book she had left open and carried on from where she had left off. *Chapter eighteen: Changes to hunting habits during warm winters among tree-dwelling reptiles.*

*

Nate rubbed his eyes and rolled over, the familiar sight of Chen asleep in her own bunk, her head buried beneath her pillow and her leg sticking out informing him that all was well. The sun was just beginning to brighten, and slim rays of light crept their way slowly across the floor. It had been three days since Captain Ardell's visit and like a fire slowly being fed more fuel, his strength had returned.

Today was the day he would meet her in the fort to discuss his future and he already felt apprehensive. He had made up his mind some time ago on where he felt his future lay but was unsure how the captain would respond. Nevertheless, he could not keep her waiting and so he dragged himself from bed, the warm sheets practically begging him to remain. Outfitting himself with his leather armour, which he had not worn since his day in the Wailing Pits, he hurriedly stuffed his pockets with as much fruit as he could for his journey before venturing outside.

Despite the deceivingly warm sun, it was bitterly cold, and Nate's breath sped away from him as if it too were in desperate search of warmth. Rubbing his hands together he circled around the back of the barracks where Bob stood patiently, having awaited her master's arrival for days. Patting her affectionately on the neck and offering her some of the fruit spilling out of his pocket, he hauled himself into the saddle as Bob broke into a gentle trot in the direction of Ardell's fort. As Nate rode along the outskirts of the city, he could see the people spilling out of their homes or stumbling out of the taverns as a new day dawned.

Even from a distance and at such early hours, the already bustling streets easily put New York or Tokyo to shame. As he watched merchants open their shops for a day's business or blacksmiths hammering away at their forges, their red glow keeping the frost at bay with a moat of heat, Nate wondered if he was making the right choice.

After all, once he had informed Ardell of his decision, he doubted he could return to her whenever he felt like it and swap careers again. Once he had made his decision known, he would be stuck with it. By the time Nate had reached Ardell's fort, his former confidence had been shattered and all he could think of was what a huge mistake he might be about to make. Despite his best efforts to shake such thoughts from his head, they kept returning in greater numbers and with more convincing arguments.

The fort remained as dreadful as ever; no matter how many times he had seen it Nate could not help but feel a shiver run up his spine as it came into view. He passed over the stake-filled moat and under the iron portcullis which was primed to drop at any moment. Stuck outside the fort at the mercy of a besieging army, or trapped inside with Captain Ardell – Nate could not decide which fate would be worse.

Hitching Bob beside the other horses on the east side of the keep, Nate pushed the heavy iron doors open and made his way inside. As per what had now become somewhat traditional, he spent a good ten minutes ogling the many maps spread about the main table of the war room.

As the world was so large, a single huge map was useless tactically, and so stacks upon stacks of maps covering the known world blanketed nearly every inch of the table's surface.

In this instance Nate found himself examining an extremely detailed map of what claimed to be the Imperium's imperial palace. He marvelled at its magnitude, and complexity. There were thousands upon thousands of rooms, all expertly labelled and measured to the inch.

Something of such importance must have been hard to come by, he thought before deciding he had best move on. Greeted once again by the dazzling array of medallions which decorated the door to Ardell's quarters, he announced his presence with a gentle knock. Hopefully Ardell would not hear him, and he could leave citing the captain had been busy.

There was a pause after the knock which was filled with silence. This gave Nate hope he could indeed head back home and think over his decision for another week or so. Unfortunately for him, the unmistakeable grumpy voice of Ardell called out for him to enter. Reluctantly, Nate did so, pushing the door open, and he was so shocked to see Marcus already present that he forgot to stand to attention before the captain. Marcus was stood firmly with his arm raised in salute and looked as if he had been there all night. He did not turn to Nate as he entered and kept his eyes fixed forwards.

Captain Ardell, meanwhile, was not in her usual hunched position over her desk, which for once, seemed to be immaculate, as did the rest of her quarters. Instead, she was by her dressing table, furiously brushing the knots out of her hair with a pained expression on her face and with what had to have been the most obscenely ornate hairbrush Nate had ever seen. Not a single centimetre was not covered with some sort of sparkling gem or gold and for a moment Nate wondered if it was indeed Captain Ardell he was beholding.

Ardell wore her usual cloth shirt and hide trousers, but her face was plastered with makeup and her hair, as unruly as it was, shone with beauty and health. She was without a doubt the most enchanting woman Nate had ever had the displeasure of meeting.

To his even greater surprise, she gave him a warm smile as he entered and beckoned him to sit opposite her desk where a chair had been pulled up just for him. "I'll be with you in a moment," she said as she brushed the last few knots out with a grunt of discomfort.

While she was distracted Nate felt this was a good opportunity to make some sort of communication with Marcus and turned in his chair. Marcus noticed this and his eyes darted to Nate and then quickly back to staring directly ahead.

Nate had lacked the time to offer the slightest glimmer of reassurance but had still felt a strong, piercing sorrow as their eyes met. This was enough to assure him that Marcus was indeed deeply sorry for the pain he had caused. This briefest of glances and their ensuing silent apology were enough for Nate to be confident in his decision.

"Ahh. Right," Ardell sighed as she finished with her hair and took her seat. "I'm glad to see you well," she smiled sweetly. An expression which seemed to fly in complete contrast to everything she represented and unsurprisingly, therefore, it sat upon her face as naturally as an elephant.

"Th…Thank you, Captain" Nate replied, unsure whether Ardell was about to slam his head into the table again or offer him freshly baked cookies. Ardell leaned back in her chair and rested her intertwined hands upon her stomach.

"Well, no need to drag this on," she said withdrawing a fresh parchment from her desk and dipping her blue-feathered quill into the inkpot while still precariously keeling on her chair.

"So, have you made your mind up on where you would like to be transferred?"

Nate remained silent; his eyes glued to Ardell's quill which hovered like a hawk over the parchment. With a flick of her wrist, she could drastically change his life, for the better or worse, and for the first time, he was in control. Once more Nate looked back at Marcus who through the corner of his eyes had been watching the proceedings eagerly.

Nate may not have known it, but his was not the only fate which he currently held influence over. Ardell too shifted her gaze to Marcus and reacted with mild surprise as she had completely forgotten he had been standing there for the past two days.

Nate gave Marcus a mischievous wink which set Marcus' heart pounding for fear he was about to do something incredibly stupid. A sound assumption. Nate turned back to Ardell and cleared his throat.

"If it is ok with you, Captain, I would like to remain under your command."

Marcus practically choked on his own spit upon hearing these words. Ardell meanwhile sat in disbelief, blinking as if Nate had just transformed into some mythical creature before her very eyes. Capitalising on the awestruck captain Nate added, "and I would like to be put back under Marcus' tutorship."

Marcus was now doubled over in a coughing fit and Ardell, having come to terms with what Nate had said, rested her quill gently beside the blank parchment. She leaned in closely, ignoring Marcus' spluttering and spoke softly.

"Are you sure about this? There's no changing your mind or special treatment if so."

Nate nodded, a resounding yes. Ardell's eyes shifted over to Marcus, who having now recovered stood back to attention albeit with red, streaming eyes and heavy breaths. "And him?" Nate grinned impishly.

"I don't think I would make it without him, Captain."

Marcus had heard little of the conversation due to his own desperate struggle to draw breath yet could not help feeling both honoured and undeserving of Nate's forgiveness and trust.

Realising now that she was completely free of any sort of legal threat which could have bankrupted or demoted her, Ardell did away with the false niceties and returned in an instant to her usual brooding self.

Her smile disappeared and was replaced by the hard impatience which Nate loved to hate. While she would never admit it, Ardell was impressed by Nate's resolve and refusal to take the easy way out. Perhaps he would turn out to be an asset after all. Marcus, meanwhile, still drew her ire.

Pointing a delicate yet menacing finger in his direction she addressed him. "You got lucky this time Marcus, but I swear by all the gods if I see your name in a single report from now on, you're done. That includes the good ones" she fumed. Neither man was sure if she was serious, just the way she liked it.

Ardell leaned back once again and cast her eyes over the sorry pair before her. She wondered whether it was worth punishing Marcus anyway but quickly opted against it. Instead, she had another idea and withdrew a report which had been delivered to her by her chief inquisitor, whose job it was to extract information others may be less than willing to divulge.

"Now I could leave you two to have a heartfelt moment of reconciliation and reflection on how this experience has brought you closer together," Ardell huffed. "But I really don't care so we may as well get back to business, both of you come here and look at this." She slid a parchment over to Nate's side of the desk. Marcus joined them and quickly scanned the words over his shoulder.

"Jupiter's beard…" Marcus began, the excitement springing forth as if he had not just spent the last two days stood in place without rest or water. The parchment was a confession which detailed a huge network of smuggler camps scattered throughout the country. As the men read, Ardell withdrew a map which had already been dotted with the apparent locations of these camps, the largest of which was barely a whisker from the city itself.

"The vermin was especially talkative once we threatened to skin him alive," she smirked. Nate was not sure whether it was the idea of the act itself or Ardell's sick enjoyment that made him feel the queasiest.

"How do we know he's telling the truth?" he asked. Ardell shrugged.

"Torture always works eventually, it's just a matter of when not if. I also sent scouts out to check and they confirmed all these locations to be accurate."

"Damn," Nate whispered, impressed with the speed at which all this had been achieved. Ardell once again took her quill and pointed at a black blob used to denominate the camps.

"There are apparently as many as fifty smugglers in this location. We expect this is the main hub of their operations." Nate shook his head in confusion.

"Why would they put it so close to the city? I mean that can barely be a day's walk," he said. Marcus then chimed in.

"Exactly, the last place we would think to look." Ardell nodded in silent agreement.

"That's not all," she added, and the men looked at her with anticipation. "Did either of you notice exactly what the vermin was smuggling? Or who the warehouse belonged to?" she asked knowing full well neither of them had, otherwise their demeanour would have been far more serious.

Nate and Marcus shook their heads, guilty as charged. Ardell brushed a strand of her glossy hair from her face, which wore a mixed expression of irritation and intrigue. This time when reaching behind her desk she did not return with a third piece of paper as the men were expecting, but a sword which clattered loudly on the table as she dropped it. Nate jumped in his seat at the noise while Marcus folded his arms.

"Weapon smugglers," he grumbled.

"Wrong," Ardell scolded as she brought her fist down hard on the blade, much to Nate's horror as he expected to witness a self-inflicted mutilation first-hand. Instead, the blade shattered into splinters as if it were made of glass. Now even Marcus was confused.

"Wait, I don't understand," he complained as if this were some sort of test where the answer did not fit the question. "Why smuggle fake weapons into the city, any smith or merchant worth his salt would notice the difference." Ardell shook her head at the question and continued, biting the inside of her lip in frustration.

"These weapons were being smuggled into Lord Massah's warehouse, the contents of which go straight into the Citadel's stockpile, not into general circulation. Our prisoner said his job was to remove the real weapons and leave fakes in their place."

Both Ardell and Marcus frowned as their thoughts swirled trying to make sense of it all.

"But why?" Nate asked at last.

"That's what we are going to find out," Ardell replied. She rose from her seat which Nate also did out of habit. Running her hand across the map Ardell inwardly rejoiced at her first chance at action for decades.

"I have assaults planned on all the camps within a two-hundred-mile radius, you two idiots are going to join me in the assault on the smuggler's base, but first I need to convince Grand Admiral Lee to agree." Marcus' eyes widened and his mouth swung open slightly with surprise.

"You're coming too, Captain?" he asked, double-checking he had heard her correctly the first time. Ardell responded with a snarl.

"Do you think I'd plaster this shit over my face if I wasn't about to go begging ass in hand to the Citadel?"

"I think you look great Captain," Nate interjected. Ardell shot him a deathly stare which could have turned Medusa to stone before pinching the space between her eyes and letting out a calming breath.

"It seems to me discipline has gone to hell around here. A little reminder of who's the captain and why should set the issue straight," Ardell said, a hint of gleeful malice in her voice indicating that was only partly the reason. Marcus nodded.

"When do we set off, Captain?"

"Tonight. I want you at the outer gate in a week. Everything should be ready by then." Ardell then shooed them away with a limp hand and the two bowed low before leaving her alone with her thoughts. Marcus was practically bouncing off the walls with excitement, his first chance at a real fight for nearly a year. Nate meanwhile was less enthusiastic. He had barely survived the last hostile encounter, how would he cope against a small army?

Alone in her quarters, Ardell sauntered over to where Oath-Breaker lay suspended above the fireplace. Slowly and delicately, like a lover, she ran her fingers across its central ridge. Memories, more like agonising nightmares flooded her mind, taunting her with past mistakes and futures which could have been had she been stronger, better. She quickly moved her hand away and the memories vanished; its time would come, but this was not it.

Marcus' excitement had died down once they were back outside and the cold wind bit through their armour and frosty grass nipped at their ankles. He turned to Nate, his face screwed up as if he had just eaten a lemon as he tried to apologise. Nate immediately realised what Marcus was attempting to do and waved him away.

"Let's not talk about it, I was angry at first but now I understand. Don't worry, I won't hold it against you."

Marcus let out a relieved sigh and wiped the nervous sweat from his forehead.

"Come," he said. "We better get packing."

Marcus and Nate split up and headed home. Their plan was to meet at the Vanguard's main gate by midday. Marcus had strictly instructed Nate to bring only the essentials; his sword which was strapped to his side as always, a bow and a quiver full of arrows which he could borrow from Chen, and, of course, some cash.

There was, however, one factor which Nate had foolishly overlooked when making his decision to stay under Captain Ardell, and that was lying to Chen about it. Chen currently believed that Nate was midway through telling Ardell where she could shove her soldiering and that he would be much happier as an administrative assistant at the docks or the Citadel.

His rushed confession as he quickly pilfered her bow and quiver while slipping every coin he had hidden in his mattress into his coin purse did not go down well.

"You did fucking what?!" Chen screamed, unable to believe the words coming from Nate's mouth. She did not even attempt to question why he was 'borrowing' her bow let alone do anything to prevent it so severe was her shock. She shook her head vigorously to restore some movement to the rest of her body.

"What the hell are you doing?" she gasped as she moved in hoping to end Nate rushing around the room like a madman. Nate simply darted around her as he picked up anything he thought he would need, whether they fitted the description of 'essential' or not.

This included spare socks, underwear, and of course food. He did not get paid as a trainee and the funds given to him by the bank when he'd first arrived were nearly spent. Any cost that could therefore be avoided would be. Nate ducked under an outstretched arm which meant to grab him by the collar and sped towards the door.

"Ardell wants me on a mission straight away, I don't have time to explain," he said as he flung the door open. As he stood in the doorway he glanced back at Chen, clothes and perishables bundled in his arms. He looked her dead in the eyes, hers filled with confusion and hurt at being lied to.

"I asked for Marcus to remain my tutor too," he said as the door slowly swung back. Chen's eyes and face lit up in a sudden burst of rage. Her mouth ajar, and her neck muscles strained as she prepared to lose her shit entirely, were the last Nate saw of her as the door slammed shut.

He could hear her unintelligible screams as he quickly mounted Bob and set her off at a run in the direction of the agreed-upon gate. Never was the size of the city of Tinelia more apparent than when trying to leave or find something specific. As most people lived in their own semi-isolated towns the two-week journey from the outermost level to the Citadel was rarely made. He had often wondered during his first few weeks how such a massive city could be effectively managed without collapsing in on itself in total anarchy.

It had made much more sense once Marcus had explained that each level was split into districts, with each district overseen by a different captain with an equal force of men under their command. The captains and their armies kept order in their districts while the Citadel passed down commands and concerned itself with more important affairs. Still, he thought, something like this would never have worked in his world. Someone would have burned the place down within a week.

Once Nate was certain he was too far for Chen to send a spear after him he slowed Bob to a gentle trot. The air was still cold enough to stab at his throat and lungs with each intake of breath, but the sun was beginning to amplify, and so he made sure to ride Bob in its gentle, warming rays. While still fearful of the danger he would soon be subjecting himself to, not turning up at all would have been a much worse fate.

He took his usual route to the gate, passing the city's outskirts before following the main road which led out of the Vanguard. He had on occasion taken alternate routes through what was commonly known as the 'countryside' but which was just large, empty expanses of land away from the city which separated the countless other small towns and villages.

As the Vanguard was designed as the main line of defence for the city should the enemy besiege her, the plan was to have not a single inch of land idle. Ardell and the other captains had enacted a huge infrastructure project just under two decades ago which sought to turn every available space into either living quarters, industrial centres, or rings of further defences.

Yet even with engineers and builders working around the clock, they had barely scratched the surface of the Vanguard's immense size. Ardell's megalopolis would have to wait a while longer it seemed.

The journey to the gate would not take long so Nate decided to use the time wisely. He knew no matter how much he wished to the contrary, that in just over a week he would be thrust into his first real battle. Therefore, he tried to remember everything he had learned during his training sessions with Marcus. Back on that raised platform or in the mud below, where he had spent most of his time, real combat seemed so far away.

He had hoped the day would never come, the same way a student wishes for the summer to never end, holding out that tiniest sliver of hope that a miracle may occur, and they never have to return to school again. Nate knew this would not happen, and so replayed every sword swing, every dodge and block of the past few months until the motions were as familiar to him as breathing.

The gate was bustling with activity as usual. Merchants and travellers all queued into the horizon for their chance to peddle their goods or find work in the city, although this time there were far more people exiting through the gate than Nate was used to seeing.

Large, unorganised columns of men and women armed to the teeth chatted excitedly as they passed under the portcullis. There did not seem to be any captain or commander leading them and Nate's first thought was that the farmers had been causing trouble again and Ardell had decided to knock some heads together after all.

That was until he drew closer and saw the insignia of one of the city's largest monster-hunting guilds emblazoned on their shoulders. It depicted a golden knight standing upon the slain carcass of a dragon, his spear thrust deep into its skull. The sons of Karridon traced their lineage back to their founder

Karridon the Brave, who during the Age of Liberation slew the great dragon Ulviir.

Over the ages they had grown into one of the world's largest monster-hunting guilds with a reputation for reliability to get the job done, no matter the cost. Nate wondered to himself as he watched them pass by, their exquisite armour glistening in the sun, whether one day he would be skilled enough to join such a guild and make his fortune.

They certainly seemed to have an easier time of it than the average soldier; with no internal leadership each member was free to follow their ambitions, which obviously paid off as even the scruffiest of them looked to be wearing boots worth more than the barracks Nate lived in.

Pushing such depressing thoughts from his mind he ventured on, carefully weaving Bob between the mess of hunters who either rolled their eyes or gave him clear looks of superiority, as if they were so much better than the average citizen just because of the patch on their arm.

One particularly boorish fellow held out his arms, pushing his companions to the side as he sidestepped out of Nate's path. "Make way lads," he jested "one of our brave heroes is on very important business, best steer clear." His friends laughed as Nate rode past, his face red with embarrassment. He spurred Bob on faster which the hunter noticed and called after him. "Save some for us!"

The relationship between the various monster-hunting guilds and the average soldier was frayed at the best of times. The hunters saw themselves as superior in every way, fighting the real threats out in the world whereas the soldiers were little more than a glorified and untrained rabble. The soldiers meanwhile just saw the hunters as a bunch of arrogant pricks. But that did not stop nearly all of them from secretly wishing to join them.

Nate had often wondered why more people did not just quit being a soldier and sign up to the guilds, especially those who had to deal with strict or cruel captains. Chen however had informed him that the entry requirements for the guilds were extreme. Not only did you have to be vouched for by an existing member, but you also had to have killed a variety of monsters single-handedly. Only then could you pay the fifteen-thousand gold entry fee. This last obstacle was usually the greatest barrier for most prospective members.

Marcus had been waiting just outside the gate and Nate found him talking with Joel who smiled awkwardly at Nate as he approached. He still felt guilty for his part in Nate's ordeal in the Wailing Pits. However, Nate bore him no ill will and nodded his head in acknowledgement. It was not much, but it was enough to disperse Joel's sense of wrongdoing.

Taking a quick glance at Nate, Marcus spoke. "Right, we'd best be off." As the three trotted down the dirt path Marcus said something to Joel that Nate did not catch while nodding in the direction of the waiting arrivals to the Vanguard. Nate instinctively followed the cue and inspected the long line of people. There did not seem to be anything out of the ordinary at first, until he noticed large numbers of people, perhaps as many as one in ten, carrying no belongings at all. Many of their faces were weary and covered in dirt, some clearly injured, their limbs wrapped up in bloodied and spoiled rags.

Tinelia was no stranger to refugees or those simply down on their luck. Yet to see this many, one would assume there was a war on. Nate could see a scowl crawl its way across Marcus' face as he too wondered what would cause such a sudden desperate influx, but none of the men spoke anything of it.

Sometime later Joel asked, "Did you hear Ardell is coming along on this one?" His tone was as surprised as Marcus' had been when Ardell had declared it. He shook his head in amusement.

"I know, I can't believe it. This smuggling business must have really pissed her off."

"Even more than usual," Nate added. Joel scratched his chin which was beginning to show the first signs of a newly forming goatee.

"I dunno, all those years behind a desk, I'd be itching to kick some heads in too. With her temperament, I'm surprised she hasn't done it to one of us already."

"We came pretty close once or twice," Marcus laughed. Joel's mind jumped back to the multiple occasions where he and Marcus had been stood in Ardell's quarters while they were berated for doing one stupid thing or another. Ardell had threatened to do everything from whipping them in the town square to ripping their legs off and beating them both to death with them. But she never did, and Joel began to wonder if she was truly as bad as she tried to make everyone believe.

"I for one would love to see her in action, they say only the Emperor is better with a blade."

"Oh?" said Marcus, raising an inquisitive eyebrow. "And who are they, exactly?"

Joel shrugged.

"Just people, her bodyguards and former captains mainly." Marcus, for all the fear he held of his captain, was not one to believe rumours without solid proof. Perhaps she had been skilled once, but decades behind a desk with nothing but a quill to swing would dull even the best warrior's abilities.

"I bet you she spends the whole assault sitting on the sidelines," he replied confidently.

"Oh, you're mad if you think I'm not taking that bet. I say she gets three kills, at least," Joel responded immediately, holding out his palm to officially seal the deal.

"Ten gold." Marcus grinned as they shook hands.

"You're going to regret this one my friend," Joel said straightening himself as he imagined the many pints he would spend his winnings on. Marcus rolled his eyes.

"You've got more chance of her shagging Nate than getting off her arse for a real fight," Marcus quipped, jerking his thumb in Nate's direction.

"God, I wish," Nate grinned, visualising the idea with every spare neuron his brain could fire. Marcus and Joel produced a mixture of groans and theatrical gags.

"She'd eat you alive," Joel laughed. Nate simply shrugged.

"You guys can keep your monster-hunting, she's the only beast worth slaying." The three men laughed, partly at the ridiculousness of their conversation, and partly at the idea of the shit they would be in if Ardell had heard them. They decided to call it a day once the sun had begun its slow transition into the moon. They had only stopped once for a toilet break, and all were famished. Except for Nate of course who had eaten almost every provision he had brought along during the first two hours. Despite this, however, Marcus refused to allow them to stop until he had found a very specific boarding house.

Nestled away from the main road, behind a row of shops, it was not much to look at. Compared to what Nate had become used to, it was relatively small. Only three storeys tall with a thatched roof on one side, and tiles on the other, as if they had been halfway through a renovation before running out of cash. The walls too seemed half-rotten and verging on collapse, while a single lantern hung above the doorframe, the universal sign of a room for rent.

"This is the place," Marcus said cheerily as he led the way to a small stable with room enough for five horses around the back. Nate and Joel looked at one another; sure, they were not expecting luxury, but this place seemed dire even by their standards. Marcus saw the unimpressed looks on their faces and waved them away. "I promise you'll love it, c'mon," he said pushing open the moss-covered front door. Nate responded with a shrug to Joel's unsure look.

"At least it'll be cheap," he said feeling at the mostly empty space in his coin purse. The inside of the house, however, could not have been starker in contrast to its outer appearance. Nate had expected a dark and damp-smelling dive of a place with rats scurrying around the floor and beds like stone. Instead, he was met with a sensory assault of colours and smells. Bright red carpets led their way to a large and beautifully decorated living room. Curtains of blue, green, and yellow hung from the ceiling to the floor, while exquisite portraits and other works of art adorned the walls.

The furniture too was luxurious, mostly hand-carved wood and plush recliners set around a roaring fireplace, for which the men were thankful after their long journey in the cold. "This is not going to be cheap," Nate gasped as he felt his coin purse scream.

"Bloody hell, it's like a palace," Joel added. "How'd you find a place like this?" Before Marcus could answer a woman appeared, descending the spiral staircase which stood near the back of the living room. She wore a long ball gown of royal blue embroidered with silver flowers, which Nate thought was a tad overkill unless they had made a wrong turn and ended up in 17th century France.

The woman approached, her hair tied up into an obscene blonde tower-like structure which he assumed had to be a wig. Across her chest she wore no fewer than three pearl necklaces and a golden lion's-head pendant. On each finger was a ring of varying sizes and metals, each dotted with fine-cut gemstones which reflected the light of the fire like a hundred tiny mirrors. All she was missing was a deathly white layer of powdered makeup and black teeth, otherwise, she was the spitting image of a Stuart-era noblewoman.

Upon seeing Marcus, she broke into a wide smile and threw her arms around him once she was close. Nate and Joel looked at one another both thinking the same thing, she must be another former flame.

"Oh, Marcus what a wonderful surprise, you should have let us know you were coming," she said in a French accent so thick Nate could have pulled a frog out of it. Her tone was one of faux annoyance as she playfully slapped his chest. Marcus chuckled as the pair held one another's arms.

"Apologies, Mary, this all came a bit last minute." She rolled her eyes.

"It's Marie," she groaned, "how many times?" She suddenly turned her head to the side and called a man's name loudly. "Edgar, come see who visits us." Barely a second later a man appeared at the top of the staircase. Dressed slightly less extravagantly than his wife, Edgar wore cotton trousers, a shirt, and a dirty apron stained by countless meals hanging down to his knees.

His face immediately lit up upon seeing Marcus standing below and he descended the stairs two at a time before running over to the group and practically leaping into Marcus' arms laughing all the while. Nate and Joel looked at one another for the third time in five minutes before Nate whispered, "Him too?" jokingly.

"My friend, it is so good to see you again, are you well?" Edgar asked with a noticeable Dutch accent.

Marcus released Edgar from the bear hug, tears of laughter in his eyes. "It's good to see you too Edgar. My friends and I are on an important mission, we wondered if you might have some rooms available."

Marie and Edgar now noticed Nate and Joel for the first time and moved towards them, arms outstretched, as they showered them both with hugs and kisses on their cheeks. Edgar turned back to Marcus, his arms resting across Nate and Joel's shoulders.

"My friend, anything you and your companions need you shall have."

"Thanks, Edgar, now how much..." Marcus began reaching for his coin purse. Edgar and Marie however both gasped as if they had just been dreadfully insulted.

"My friend, you shall not be robbed of one gold piece while you stay under my roof," Edgar replied. Marcus gave him a tired smile.

"Well, I refuse to stay here without giving you something for your trouble." Nate did a quick scan of the room while mentally calculating how much he thought a night here would cost before turning to Marcus and quickly shaking his head.

Marcus ignored him and continued to insist on covering their meals at the very least to which their hosts begrudgingly agreed. Once negotiations were concluded Marie showed the men to their rooms while Edgar returned to the kitchen promising to cook up a feast fit for kings.

Marie led them up the spiral staircase and along a narrow corridor. There were three rooms on each side, one of which was the master bedroom. Nate wondered how the couple managed to keep the place running considering their location, expensive taste, and lack of guests. One by one Marie unlocked three doors and showed them inside until only Nate was left.

His room was no less impressive than the others. A king-sized bed occupied the space between the door and the near wall, while two wardrobes and a large dressing table were situated at the back of the room where a window looked out onto the rather unpleasant and uninteresting side street. In the centre of the room between the end of the bed and the dressing table was a large, metal bath which Marie assured Nate could be filled whenever he wished.

"Dinner should be ready in about two hours, please make yourself comfortable until then," Marie said as she smiled sweetly and closed the door behind her. Nate immediately stripped down to his underwear and dove onto the bed. It felt even better than it looked. The four down feather pillows and modal sheets felt more like clouds than any man-made material. It was therefore no surprise that his head had barely contacted either of them before he was woken over an hour later by banging on his door.

It was the same powerful thuds he had become more than familiar with over the past few months and instantly recognised them as belonging to Marcus. Bleary-eyed, Nate threw on his trousers and answered the door to a dressed-down Marcus. Wearing a buttoned shirt and brown trousers, he looked at Nate with a mixture of amusement and disgust. "You wouldn't last five minutes in polite company." Nate looked down at his skinny yet thanks to months of training, improving torso and backwards trousers but did not say anything.

"C'mon, it's almost time for dinner and I'm sure Marie would like a chance to speak with us all."

Nate nodded and rubbed his eyes. Finding a clean shirt in his army-issued knapsack he quickly washed his face and under his arms before joining the others downstairs.

Marie had changed out of her blue ball gown into a frilly pink dress, although her hair remained ridiculous. She, Marcus, and Joel sat around a dining table which had been prepared next to the fire, the other furniture having been moved elsewhere around the room. There were echoes of laughter bouncing from the walls as Nate groggily descended the stairs.

The laughter had died down by the time he had taken his seat which had already been prepared for him. He had barely time to draw breath before Marie addressed him, barraging him with all manner of questions.

"So, Nate, Marcus tells me you have only recently arrived in our fair city, how are you finding it thus far? What was your world like? Do you miss it? Are you looking forward to your first big adventure?"

Nate blinked quickly as his brain struggled to process Marie's words and form a coherent answer.

"The city isn't so bad, although it is infinitely better knowing a lady as beautiful as yourself is only a day's ride away," he replied, turning on the charm. Joel smirked as he took a sip of wine from a gold-rimmed glass while Marcus rolled his eyes, endlessly impressed by Nate's determination to sleep with anything even remotely female.

"Oooh such a gentleman." Marie squealed with delight as she poured herself a second glass of wine. Nate took a sip of his own, it was sweeter than he expected and hit him with an almost overwhelming taste of cherries. "Marcus here has been ever so secretive about this mission of yours, so why don't you tell me, are you ready to get out there and stuck in?"

This description of potentially killing dozens of human beings was far less refined than he had expected of someone who so evidently prized themselves on poise and gentility and so he was unsure how to answer. Marie sensed his hesitation and did not wait for him to speak. "I know it's all a bit daunting, isn't it? I've never been one for violence myself," she huffed as she took a long drink, nearly draining her glass in one. "But it does seem to make the world go round," she finished.

The three men nodded in silent, solemn agreement. Then Nate spoke, as there was a question which had been burning in his mind since they had arrived and now seemed the best chance to get an answer. "

So how do you know Marcus?"

"Ah," Marie gasped as if she had been waiting this whole time to retell the tale. Marcus simply groaned and assured

Marie she did not need to go over the story he had heard her tell a thousand times before. She ignored him and after topping up her own glass, did the same to Nate's.

"You see, years ago Edgar and I were members of the imperial court if you could believe it." Nate took a quick glance at Marie's hair and the vast collection of esoteric art around him before concluding that he could in fact believe it.

"So how did you end up here?" Joel asked inquisitively, as it was not every day you met a living former member of the imperial court.

"We fled after the Peasant's Rebellion," Marie explained. "Edgar and I had helped many of the refugees fleeing the conflict by settling them on our land."

"Very generous of you," Joel said with narrowed eyes and a hint of disbelief. Marie was oblivious to this and nodded in agreement.

"Indeed, except one day the Seekers came to our estate accusing us of siding with the rebels during the war. They did not even wish to hear our explanation and set about slaughtering the refugees and looting our home."

"How did you escape?" Nate asked, horrified to hear of such barbarity against the helpless but not at all surprised. Marie's face was grim now as she recounted the dark weeks that followed, the most harrowing times of her life.

"We dressed as paupers and fled to Tinelia. Edgar, my love, had the wits to hide some of our most precious gems in the soles of our shoes, with the hopes of buying a property once we reached the safety of the city." Nate took another sip of wine, he had not been a fan at first, but the more he drank the more he enjoyed, which was probably the point of alcohol to begin with.

Marcus however was busying himself looking anywhere other than at Marie, knowing his part in the story was drawing close. Joel seemed to be the only one genuinely not enjoying himself, he sat there with a scowl, biting down on his glass waiting for Marie to incriminate herself, although to him she had done that already. Unknown to the others, Joel had spent many years helping to relocate those same refugees, many tens of thousands of whom had still been displaced decades after the war had ended.

After listening to countless stories of how the common people were treated by their noble overlords, even before the rebellion, he was firm in his belief that they were all guilty of the same crimes against their own people. Marie continued, unaware she was being harshly judged for the crime of association.

"Edgar and I were but a day or so from Tinelia when we were set upon by bandits. They took what little we had, even the clothes on our backs and locked us in cages, ready to sell as slaves." She then looked at Marcus with wild, sparkling eyes as if it had all happened barely a moment ago. Marcus tugged at his collar awkwardly as his body temperature began to rise.

"Then, one night, out of nowhere this lumbering oaf stumbles into their camp." She laughed as she relayed the shared look of surprise on both Marcus and the bandits' faces. "In a flash, he had killed all five of them single-handedly and set us free. He then escorted us to the city and helped us to find this place. Everything we have now is thanks to him," she said, rounding off the story with a smile and fluttering eyelashes as she stared at Marcus like a schoolgirl who had just discovered love.

Marcus immediately added, "Just to clarify, there were only three bandits, and we were all drunk."

"Yep, that is a lot more believable." Nate snorted as he drained his glass. Joel had hoped to enquire into Marie's past further but was interrupted by Edgar who had appeared beside them from the kitchen pushing a trolley laden with food.

"Ladies and gentlemen, it is my pleasure to announce that dinner is served," he said as he overloaded the plates and set them down in front of his guests. Nate stared at his meal and had no idea what he was looking at, but it smelled divine. It was some form of pastry which had been cooked inside a duck, or at least somewhat looked like a duck, stuffed with steamed vegetables, and practically drowned in a sweet, red sauce.

The five of them wasted no time tucking in, the meal being a far cry from the basics Nate would make for himself back at the barracks. Every mouthful was an explosion of new flavours and textures, each radically different from the last. Even Joel had forgotten his earlier resentment of their hosts and happily engaged in the chatter and banter.

It was past midnight when dinner had finally been cleared away and the five lounged about around the fire on the recliners and sofas. Joel and Marcus both snored away having eaten their fill and been overcome with that familiar urge to sleep where they sat. Nate too was drowsy, although much of that was thanks to the five glasses of wine he had finished in the end.

Marie lay across Edgar's lap, not yet asleep but with her eyes closed, enjoying the smells of the empty wine bottles and smoky fire as it climbed its way up the chimney. Edgar was the only one still fully awake, and he smiled contentedly as he stroked Marie's cheek softly with his index finger. Despite it all, losing their home, their wealth, and power, Edgar could not have been happier than in this moment. Surrounded by friends in the comfort of his own home and blessed with the most beautiful wife God could give – in the end, it had all been worth it.

Marie and Edgar were distraught to bid farewell to Marcus and their new friends the following morning. As much as the three would have loved to continue sampling the life of luxury they had a job to do and set off at the crack of dawn. Despite Nate's vehement protests, Marcus had convinced the two of them to slip an extra few coins under their pillows as a thank you to their more than generous hosts.

They would arrive at the outer gate at midday where Ardell and the rest of her host would be waiting. Both Marcus and Nate were pleased to see all signs of potential rebellion had been quelled as they passed by the endless expanses of crops growing on either side of them to which teams of farmers and their farmhands tended tirelessly.

Almost all signs of civilisation had vanished, save for the occasional farmhouse standing tall and nobly in the distance, or the occasional side road which would lead to one of the many thousands of isolated hamlets and villages. Thankfully, the day was much warmer than the previous one and the trio could ride unmolested by the elements except for the gentle caress of the sun which filled them with much-needed energy.

None of them knew what Ardell's plan would be once the ambush had been set, but they were confident in her ability to pull it off. Their only misgivings were about their own ability not to make fools of themselves, Nate naturally feeling the most apprehensive. He wondered if this fight would be like the last, where he had been saved by sheer dumb luck or whether he would, at last, prove himself to not be as useless as he suspected everyone thought.

The three arrived at the outer gate right on time and found Ardell hunched over a table at the roadside. A crowd of around sixty people handpicked for this mission stood in neat rows just a few steps away. Ardell had a detailed map of the confirmed smuggler camp's location and was issuing orders to three officers, each of whom would have one-third of the small force under their direct command.

Marcus, Joel, and Nate all dismounted their horses and took their places among the gathered troops. The two beside Nate were a man and woman, both tall and muscular in thick steel armour barely able to contain their tree-trunk like arms. Their faces were stern and concentrated, their posture rigid and professional.

It was only now the realisation hit Nate. He was not just playing soldier anymore, this was not a videogame, this was serious, and people were inevitably going to die. He looked ahead with the rest of the troop, determined not to have his first taste of action be his last. After a few moments of silence as Ardell and her officers revised the plan of attack, the officers returned to formation just a few paces ahead of the others.

Ardell folded up the map of placed it in her satchel before addressing the gathered troops. This was the first time Nate had seen the captain in her armour. Until now he had only seen it on a stand, which by comparison did it no justice. It was pitch black and hugged her body tightly like Nate's own leather. The chest had a stretch of golden arraignment from the left shoulder to the right, aligned just below her neck. The edges of the gauntlets and shoulder guards were also rimmed with gold patterns identical to the one across the chest. Otherwise, it was black as the void, Ardell's equally dark hair seeming to vanish as it spilled over her breastplate.

It was without a doubt the most impressive piece of metalwork Nate had ever seen – it was fitting, he thought, that it would be worn by an equally as impressive woman. Although its thinness seemed counterproductive as it would take only a glancing hit to penetrate and do serious damage. He was not aware however, that this armour had been forged in the heart of Vendaag, from the metal Divinite, making it almost invincible.

Not that this mattered to Ardell of course, as she made sure her enemies were dead before they even had the chance to draw their swords. As she looked out over the soldiers gathered before her, her face turned into a scowl as if she were disgusted by what she saw. This encouraged them all to stand a little straighter, their eyes unblinkingly staring ahead, as many held their breath in anticipation.

Inwardly however, Ardell could not have been happier. Grand Admiral Lee had accepted her request to take part in the mission on the condition that the attempt was made to bring back as many prisoners as possible.

She squeezed the hilt of her sword to keep herself grounded as her heartbeat quickened at the thought of battle. She had not brought Oath-Breaker with her; instead, strapped to her side was her basket-hilted backsword. The hilt was in the form of a spider, its long, spindly legs wrapping around the users' hand like a fly trapped in a web.

At last, when she felt the men and women before her had been made sufficiently nervous, she spoke. Her voice was loud and commanding, so much so even the civilians who had continued streaming in through the gate had stopped to admire the sight of such a renowned leader.

"You have all been chosen for this mission because your officers have vouched for your skill and courage. So, make no mistake in thinking that this mission is anything other than of the highest priority." A few of the troops smiled to themselves – for many it would be their best chance at recognition, maybe even promotion. For others, it was enough to have their ego stroked by someone they all admired.

Ardell knew what the troops were thinking and while she had no plans on any official reward for anyone, even if the mission was a blinding success, she knew the prospect of it would make them fight with enhanced vigour.

"We shall be marching southwest for the remainder of the day. Once we reach our destination you will be split into three groups under the command of an officer. You will follow their orders to the letter," she said, her voice cold and hard as she stressed the importance of unit discipline and respect for the chain of command.

"We attack at nightfall. Now," she said gesturing towards the gate. "Move out."

Suddenly the whole formation turned on its heel to the right and began marching towards the open city gate, their officers leading the way. Nate did the same until Ardell called out. "Marcus, Nate, a word."

"Shit," Nate whispered as he broke rank and jogged over to where the captain stood, her face contorted into its usual annoyed scowl. Marcus had already sprinted there as fast as he could, taking no chances after the captain's earlier warning. She looked them both up and down without saying a word, exhaling loudly through her nose as if she had spotted something that displeased her. This was most worrying for Nate as she had been looking directly at him when she did so. She clicked her tongue against the roof of her mouth. The pair seemed to be prepared for the task ahead. Their armour was clean, and Marcus looked to be spoiling for a fight.

Nate seemed far more nervous, but she would let that slide this time. All in all, she was pleased, if not slightly disappointed she had no new reason to chastise either of them.

"The two of you will be under my direct command on this mission."

Shit, shit, shit, Nate thought. Marcus too was thinking something similar. "I need to know that you Nate, are capable of following singular, simple commands before I can risk putting you in a unit using multiple complex orders and tactics."

"Yes, Captain." Nate nodded, relieved – Ardell it seemed had gone out of her way to do him a favour. She then turned to Marcus.

"And I need to know you have learned some respect for your captain's orders," she said in the condescending tone one would expect from a schoolteacher punishing a small child who should know better.

Marcus also nodded in acceptance of his fate. She kept the two there a short while longer, her eyes narrowed as she investigated theirs, looking for the slightest hint of dissension. "Do not disappoint me. Either of you," she whispered at last.

"We won't, Captain," they said in perfect unison.

"Good," she replied immediately, "now get back in line."

Nate and Marcus bowed and ran back to their formation which was already out of the gate and marching down the road. Nate barely had time to recognise the momentous occasion as he passed under the massive final gate which separated the city from the rest of the world. This was the first time he had ever left the city; beyond was a complete unknown full of dangers. But he could not allow these thoughts to overtake him now, not when Ardell was watching with keen interest.

From the moment Nate had arrived in Purgatory he had wondered what the world outside the confines of the city looked like. He had gone through phases of imagining desolate, barren wasteland of cracked brown mud and burned-out buildings all the way to picturing the yellow-brick road with happily dancing munchkins along its edge. He was therefore rather disappointed to see it was barely any different from what he had just left behind.

The huge stone walls may have gone, but a town stretching beyond the rise and fall of the main road met him immediately. Even this was protected by a much smaller, although heavily patrolled, wooden wall equipped with trebuchets and ballistae.

It was not until an hour later when they had exited through another gate that Nate did get a glimpse of something non-artificial and unmolested by civilisation. A forest, dark green and thick with plant life, greeted them. Despite the bright sun and clear sky, Nate could barely see more than a few feet into the densely packed woodland. The trees were almost perfectly spaced apart, so they cast an endless, dark blanket across the entire forest floor. What was worse is that they were marching straight into it.

The smugglers had set up their camp well away from any established road network, even the unused ones in case they were discovered. This meant the troop would have to march through the forest itself without the help of roads. Until this point, they had been marching in three close columns, two men wide and ten deep, with their officer at the front. Now they were forced to adopt a looser formation which would allow them to manoeuvre the thick foliage but still respond effectively should they come under attack.

Nobody expected this of course. The Imperium was thousands of miles away and the immediate area of the forest closest to the city was swept daily for monsters. Yet there was always a chance and so Ardell kept them on edge just in case, shouting orders from the back, ensuring everyone stayed in formation and did not get lost.

It was only ten minutes before the world around them had gone dark, the sweeping arms of the forest embracing them, cutting them off from the world. For the first time in months Nate could no longer hear the clamorous noise of the city which had been almost constant. Now, the only sounds came from the crunching of leaves and twigs underfoot, or the occasional hushed curse from one of the soldiers as they tripped on a concealed log and broke formation.

It was not long before their movements had slowed to a crawl. There was no obvious immediate danger, but the threat of it kept them all on edge; even the more experienced of them constantly darted their eyes around the shadows, looking for some hidden threat. From his place near the back of the left column, Nate could see neither Marcus nor Joel, only the occasional bright flash of armour as a rare beam of sunlight broke through.

This timid march continued for the next four hours. All the while the troop remained deathly silent, sweating profusely as the air around them grew ever more humid the further into the forest's depths they delved. Suddenly, the identical landscape of perfect row of trees after perfect row was interrupted by a structure jutting out of the ground at an uneven angle as if it had begun to collapse but then given up halfway through.

"This is it," Ardell boomed from the back making everyone jump. The said structure was an old outpost, abandoned centuries ago. It was made of white stone which had turned green as nature had reclaimed it, choking it with ivy until it could no longer bear the added weight. It was only a mile or so from here where the smugglers had their camp, set up around this tower's twin. Ardell allowed her troops to break formation and rest, but only after setting up a perimeter and some rudimentary defences in the form of logs sharpened into stakes and mounds of earth to act as defence from arrows and fire.

Nate volunteered along with another man to clear out the tower, just in case there were any nasty surprises lying in wait. Luckily though, it was as abandoned as it looked. The stone stairs which led up to the tower's roof had collapsed and all that remained were the rotten splinters of a long-abandoned set of beds and dining tables.

"I'm almost disappointed," the other man grinned at Nate as he sheathed his sword and returned to camp.

Nate threw back an awkward smile and was left alone at the base of the tower. He put away his own sword and breathed a heavy sigh. Outside he could hear the low laughter of the troops and the crackle of a freshly lit fire as it cooked the company's dinner. While before, the forest had been alive with the sounds of nature; insects and birds, loud and proud in their domain rarely disturbed by humans, now, however, there was nothing – no birds chirping, no insects clicking, just deathly silence as if they knew to keep far away.

Nate looked up at a hole in the ceiling, where the tower punched through the choking stranglehold of wood and bark, allowing him to catch a glimpse of a patch of orange sky. It would not be long now, he thought. Not long before Ardell would order them to march on and commit themselves to battle. He laughed, amused at himself and his situation.

He thought of his childhood heroes such as Achilles or Perseus. They had faced far greater threats and never once shown fear. He had always wished to emulate them, foolishly believing he would have acted no differently in their shoes. Now that he was, he could barely prevent wetting himself out of fear. Nate cursed himself for allowing his pride to take charge, he should have told Ardell that he wanted to transfer, not carry on with this madness. But he was here now, and as Ardell had warned, he could not take it back.

His thoughts were then interrupted by the angry gurgling of his stomach which was eager for him to join the others and eat. He did as his body demanded but could not stop his left hand from shaking. The camp was split into more than a dozen groups of chatting and resting soldiers waiting for their turn at the makeshift kitchen where what looked like a pig (except for its long muscular legs and lack of ears or a tail) roasted.

Ardell and her officers stood away from the camp, going over their plan of attack as their map was laid over a tree stump. Nate scanned the crowd for Marcus and found him and Joel, along with a few others, sat near the outskirts, where the light of the fire had limited reach.

Marcus spotted him at the same time and waved him over. Carefully avoiding the many outstretched legs of napping men and women Nate dropped down beside his friends on the grass. "We were just discussing our little bet," Marcus whispered, on the off chance the captain had superhuman hearing. Nate's mind went blank for a moment as he had totally forgotten any former talk of a bet. "You know, about the captain," Marcus added after seeing the utter lack of understanding on Nate's face.

"Oh, that one," he smiled as he remembered Marcus' other claim during the same conversation. One of the men opposite whispered in response.

"It's all everyone is talking about; nobody has seen the captain fight in decades at least. The pool is up to one thousand gold, even the officers are in on it."

Nate's eyes widened at the prospect of such a prize.

"Are you serious?"

"Deadly," the man whispered back. "Whoever guesses the right number of kills shares the jackpot with the other winners. You want in?" Nate felt at the coin purse which dangled from his waist, it held barely ten pieces, and losing it on a bet was not something he could afford right now. But then he glanced over to where Ardell stood. She was studying the map eagerly, holding her chin between her thumb and forefinger, her other hand gripped tightly on the hilt of her sword. For some unknown reason, he was suddenly filled with confidence, not only in Ardell's martial ability, but in her eagerness to get bloody.

"I'm in," he said tossing his coin purse at the soldier.

"I'll add it to the prize," he grinned. "What's your bet?"

Nate thought for a moment, his eyes kept switching between Ardell and the glistening, beady eyes of the man before him.

"Eight or nine," he said at last.

"You're mad," Marcus chuckled, as the rest of the group nodded or scoffed in agreement.

"Probably," Nate shrugged. Suddenly the tantalising smell of meat filled their noses as the first flank of the beast had been cut into.

"C'mon," Joel said, his mouth watering already, "before it's all gone." The others all leapt to their feet and joined the growing queue. Their meal had been delicious, though it was no more than a chunk of salted meat garnished with a few other herbs. Nate could not help himself go back for seconds. By the time they were all finished there was not a speck of flesh left on the animal's bones. The forest was darker than usual now and torches had been erected around the makeshift camp.

"I'd say we have another hour or so before we move out. Ardell won't have us fighting on full stomachs," Marcus grunted as he lay prone on the grass. "Best grab a nap while you can," he advised the rest of the group, all of whom were already in the process of falling asleep. Nate, however, could not relax. While his body enjoyed the pleasant post-meal sluggish drowsiness, his mind would not allow sleep to come. Instead, it replayed the scenes in the warehouse over and over. The knife-like claws of the rat, the shrill cry of the smuggler as he was torn apart and the flash of blood which spattered over him.

He knew this time would be much worse, far more people would die. He looked around at the sleepy, relaxed bodies around him and wondered if it would be any of them. Curiously, he did not feel the same fear for his own safety he had done at the warehouse.

He had extrapolated from Ardell's orders that he would be kept well back from the fighting and given less dangerous orders. His concern was for his friends and companions in the troop. They all seemed so oddly at ease with their situation, as if none of them feared death. Perhaps that was natural though; after all, they were all already dead. Many of them had been here for centuries if not longer and had probably already died once or twice before. Perhaps Nate had simply not been around long enough for his natural fear of death to subside. But even then, the idea of starting over, somewhere completely unknown and from scratch, that thought seemed just as bad.

There was a sudden shout from the centre of the camp as Ardell addressed them. "All of you up, we move out in five, your officers will now split you into your squads."

"So much for your hour," one of the nearby soldiers grumbled at Marcus as they all hauled themselves to their feet. Nate and Marcus both made their way over to the captain, knowing she would be waiting for them. Ardell did not look up as they approached, instead her eyes were still glued to the map in her hands. It had been edited to show an accurate depiction of the smuggler's camp, the tower acting as the camp's centre.

There were two rings of defence. The first would be where they would find most of the smugglers, the inner ring would be where their leaders and contraband resided. Both were protected by a thin wall of spikes, much like those which protected their current camp but nothing significant enough to stop a well-planned assault. She pointed to a space on the map at the camp's Eastern edge. "Nate, I want you to take up a position here."

Nate quickly moved in closer so he could see where the captain was pointing. "It will give you a vantage point over the inner part of the camp. Marcus has told me you're a good shot, so I want you to take your bow and wait."

"Wait for what, Captain?" he asked, already struggling to work out where he needed to be once he was no longer looking at it on a map and additional orders on top of that were already making him sweat.

"I'm going to try and force their surrender – if you see me draw my weapon, I want you to fire a shot at the man closest to me. If you miss or hit me, I will kill you. Understood?" Nate gulped and nodded. She then turned to Marcus.

"Marcus," she began.

"Yes, Captain," he said eagerly, puffing out his chest and straightening his posture. Ardell waited for a moment and allowed him to raise his hopes before she spoke again.

"I want you to remain at camp with a few others. If things go badly for whatever reason, we may need to retreat here. In which case I want more defences to be ready, some deeper trenches and makeshift platforms for archers should suffice."

Marcus' face and heart both dropped, and suddenly his posture was slouched as if he were carrying a heavy load on his back. He wanted to protest and began to speak before abruptly stopping himself.

"Yes, Captain, whatever you say." A flicker of a smile dashed across Ardell's lips so fast Nate barely noticed it.

"Excellent, in which case we had better be off." She folded up the map and placed it in her knapsack once again.

"Sorry, Captain," Nate interjected, "but what do you want me to do afterwards?"

Ardell pursed her lips and thought for a second.

"Just try not to die," she said patting Nate's shoulder gently before moving on.

"I can't believe this," Marcus whispered once Ardell was no longer in earshot. Nate wiped the sweat from his underarms and let out a groan as he tried to remember the orders Ardell had given him.

"Swap?" he joked. But Marcus was in no jovial mood and scowled at the spot where Ardell had stood before turning to Nate.

"Just do as you were told, and don't do anything stupid," he warned, "follow orders and you'll be fine." Nate nodded and the two shook hands before Nate had to race off and join the others. Despite the crushing blackness of the forest, Ardell would not permit any torches to be lit in case they were spotted and lost the element of surprise.

The band of fifty therefore crept slowly through the woods, becoming the very thing they had been afraid of just a few hours earlier. Slowly, they edged closer to the location of the camp until the bleary fuzziness of the forest was gradually illuminated by distant flickering torches. Nobody needed to be reminded of their orders as they carefully, so as not to be heard, surrounded the camp until both its exits to the north and south were cut off.

Nate had until now been following closely behind Ardell, who turned and signalled for him to take his position on the rise overlooking the camp. He did so while keeping as low and quiet as possible, but it was unnecessary. The forest was so dark the smugglers could barely see past their own defences, let alone the force which carefully positioned itself amongst the shadows. It only took Nate a few minutes of searching to detect the gradual incline which he followed until he found himself looking over the camp, his view almost completely unobstructed for the first time since the mission began.

The tower had been built on a small hill in the centre of a large basin – practically useless at surveying the surrounding forest, it was no wonder it had been abandoned. The movements of the troops eventually came to a halt, and they all simply watched with bated breath as the smugglers went about their business, totally unaware of what was about to happen.

The initial scouting reports had been extremely accurate. The smugglers were matched by the ambushers man for man, although Nate personally thought this to be a mistake and that Ardell should have brought more. But Ardell knew her fifty would be more than enough when considering they had the element of surprise and superior firepower – specifically, her. Some smugglers were busying themselves moving contraband from a wagon on the outer northern edge of the camp to the tower in the centre. Most however, were relaxing by one of the many fires that dotted the outer defences, oblivious to the hundred eyes trained upon them.

Within the centre of the camp were at least ten more smugglers rotating between several large tents and the tower. Their leader, Nate assumed, was among them. Nate's heart was pounding in his chest and his breaths were frantic and shallow as he waited for the inevitable signal for the attack to begin, but first he would have to play his part in Ardell's plan.

After ten minutes of waiting Nate began to wonder if the plan had changed, maybe Ardell was going to cancel the attack after all. But just as this thought began to cross his mind, a tall figure with glossy black hair and a sword at their side began walking casually towards the southern entrance. *This is it,* Nate thought as he nocked an arrow onto his bow.

Chapter 12

Ardell was supremely confident in her plan as she swaggered towards the entrance to the camp. She had spent every waking moment for the past fortnight planning every minute detail of every possible outcome. The bonus of her presence just further cemented their inevitable victory. She tapped her fingers against her sword's hilt with anticipation and took in a deep breath of the crisp air. It was an excellent night for a fight.

There were only two bored-looking guards protecting the southern entrance. Leaning on their spears they had barely noticed the woman approaching them before the whistle of arrows as they sped through the air abruptly changed to thuds as they found their mark. The guards fell to the side dead before they had been able to raise the alarm. Ardell simply strolled right past them and up the slight incline to the centre of the camp.

Nobody had seen her despite the number of people piled inside, and why would they? They had been smuggling out of this base for years and not once had they had even the slightest whiff of trouble from the city guards. It was therefore not until Ardell found herself smack dab in the middle of the inner defences, did someone notice something peculiar about the heavily armed woman amongst them whom they did not recognise.

"Oi, who the hell are you?" a gruff voice that sounded like it belonged to someone who had smoked eighty a day for the past two hundred years called out in surprise. Suddenly all eyes were on Ardell, both in and outside the camp, although those smugglers in the lower section still had no idea what was going on just meters away.

Ardell took a deep breath and stood composed as a semicircle formed around her of people brandishing a variety of cruel but poorly maintained weapons. Meanwhile, Ardell's forces began to move in. They slowly descended upon the camp and hid in the ditches below the palisades where they were out of sight of the main enemy force. Nate and fifteen other archers stayed behind, hidden in the trees, arrows noctched, waiting for the signal.

Ardell spent a quick moment eyeing up her opposition before clearing her throat and proclaiming just loud enough for those around her to hear, without alerting the enemy below.

"My name is Captain Ardell of the Tinelian Army, and I am here to announce the official end to your operations. Those of you who submit to arrest now will be treated and tried fairly." The semicircle of smugglers was silent for a moment, throwing each other puzzled, bemused looks before they burst out laughing.

Ardell began to grit her teeth and scratch her sword hilt with impatience, she was not used to being laughed at. Suddenly a man pushed his way through the semicircle until he was part-way between them and Ardell. He was short, his face covered in acne and dressed in expensive blue robes and a yellow cap which sat perched on the crown of his head, while at his side was a small yet menacing-looking dagger.

"What did you say your name was?" he spluttered, desperate to have misheard the first time.

"Captain Ardell," she replied coldly. The man's eyes grew until they took up most of his face and he quickly withdrew his dagger. Ardell tensed as she expected him to charge, as did Nate who was crouched less than a hundred meters away with aching arms as he aimed his arrow at the man's torso. However, the man's next move surprised everyone. He threw down the dagger at Ardell's feet as if it were made of fire and dropped to his knees, his hands behind his head.

"Please," he begged, "I surrender." Those around him were frozen in shock for a moment as they tried to understand why their companion had shown such fear at a mere name.

"Anyone else?" Ardell grinned. Another challenger then stepped forwards, and with an ugly sneer he picked up the surrendered man roughly by the neck and threw him to the ground just past where Ardell stood.

"I'll deal with you later," he threatened as the terrified man scurried off and hid behind some crates which had been stacked just shy of the tower's door. Ardell assumed the man before her was the smugglers' leader. He stood close, with the undeserved bravado of a thug who had never been in a fair fight. He was tall, perhaps six foot three, and muscular, a fact she assumed he was proud of as he wore no shirt despite the cold night. A grave mistake, she thought. On his left arm was a poorly done tattoo of a snake which slithered its way up to his neck, and disappeared within his long, greasy brown hair. His sword hand twitched eagerly on the hilt of a scimitar strapped to his waist and Ardell could taste the stale odour of tobacco carried by the breeze.

"What you doin' out here on yer own, love? A pretty little girl like you should be careful, there are monsters in the woods ya know." The other smugglers cackled, somehow still perceiving themselves to be in control of the situation. Ardell ignored the weak attempt to goad her and shot back a retort of her own.

"A captain does not repeat herself, but perhaps the words I used were too advanced for you so, let me try again. Give up or die."

The previously sneering face of her opponent grew red, and veins in his neck suddenly popped out as rage built up inside him, he refused to be insulted by some girl with an attitude.

"I'm going to fuck your pretty little corpse," he growled as his hand moved to quickly draw the scimitar from its scabbard. A grin then grew across Ardell's face, a grin so devilish one would think she had just tricked a man into selling his soul. Even the smugglers who had her hopelessly outnumbered found it deeply unsettling.

There was a sudden flash of silver, followed by one of red as Ardell ripped the sword out of her scabbard and in one motion sliced open the man's throat. He fell to the ground clawing at the gaping wound in a futile attempt to stop the bleeding. The other smugglers froze for a second time, unable to believe what they had just witnessed. This gave Ardell the precious seconds she needed to assess her situation. There were ten foes in total, covering both her flanks, lightly armed and combined possessing less skill than even the dullest of her recruits. Ten to one were not good odds, not good at all.

For the smugglers.

This was Nate's cue; the enemy closest to Ardell was lightly armed in a leather breastplate similar to his own. She had a small axe in one hand and a shield held close to her body in the other. For a moment he wavered, this was not the same as the Wailing Pits, or even the warehouse. This person had no idea he was there and would have no way of defending herself. His arm was frozen in place, unable to release the arrow. But then a strange feeling came over him, one of duty and responsibility. Ardell had given him an order and was counting on him to carry it out – if he didn't, he was putting her in danger. Without a second thought he released the arrow and watched as it sailed to meet its target.

Ardell had been waiting for the arrow to come as it would signal the beginning of the attack. She had given the same order to three others in case Nate was not up to the task but was pleased to see the arrow shatter the collarbone of the foe to her immediate right, bringing her down as she gasped for air, her lungs rapidly filling with blood.

Immediately following this, the other archers let their arrows loose, raining them down upon the still unaware smugglers manning the outer defences, and few missed. Anarchy now spread through the camp like a plague, confused and agonised screams filled the air as the panicked criminals tried to form some sort of defence against their invisible enemy. After the second volley landed, the rest of the troops hidden in the ditches just outside the camp charged in.

Any attempt at order and strategy within the camp was instantly broken as they were overrun, breaking from their hastily assembled lines and rushing for the exits, only to be faced with more of Ardell's men pouring in. It was now that Ardell went on the attack. She rushed forwards to the man at the centre of the semicircle, he swung low which Ardell dodged by leaping into the air before planting a kick into his chest. His ribcage shattered and caved in on itself, shards of bone skewering his organs, killing him before he hit the floor.

She landed firmly as her defeated foe rolled backwards in the dust. She heard the *whoosh* of a sword slicing through the air and bent her body backwards, the blade missing her head by mere inches. Springing back up she effortlessly dodged another lunge aimed at her stomach, using her opponent's momentum against him she spun out of his path, severing his arm and head with a single swing.

Ardell's face was now speckled with blood, her hair was no longer glossy but sticky with gore, and her devilish grin had only widened. She was enjoying herself. The other smugglers began to feel disconcerted at the ease with which she was cutting them down, yet they still believed their numbers gave them the advantage.

What followed could only be described as the most magnificent, yet macabre exhibition of swordplay Nate had ever seen. From his vantage point he watched with both genuine disgust and amazement as Ardell dealt death with savage and yet beautiful efficiency and style. She seemed to dance around the battlefield, twisting and turning as if the blades swung her way were little more than ribbons, part of a ballet performance in which she was the prima ballerina.

With each flick of her wrist, she ended another life, blood splattered and sprayed across the ground and remaining combatants like paint from a brush, and Ardell was only just beginning her masterpiece. Nate noticed one of Ardell's foes stood still, paralysed with fear yet still clutching his weapon. *Still a threat*, he thought, loosing another arrow which pierced the man's heart. He brought a third target down before deciding the others were too close to the captain for him to risk firing another shot. Instead, he shouldered his bow and ran down from his vantage point, hoping to join the battle below.

Ardell was having the time of her life, smiling like a madwoman each time she dodged a strike or felt the tearing of flesh and explosion of blood at the end of her blade. In her excitement she had forgotten all about her orders to bring in as many prisoners as possible and practically cut a man in half, even after he had thrown down his weapon and his hands into the air. This animalistic lack of mercy encouraged the other smugglers to fight on, despite being so hopelessly outmatched. Ardell had not suffered as much as a split end since the fighting began and decided to up the tempo to her dance of death. With strikes so fast her foes barely had time to register them before feeling the sharp sting of metal against their skin, Ardell began slicing her way through what little opposition remained, savouring every thrust and cry of agony.

At one point she taunted her foes by refusing to fight back and simply dodged each of their strikes with inhuman speed. For her coup de grace she pirouetted, her hair, congealed and red, flailing behind her like the arms of a foul monster spitting blood in every direction. In the same movement she tore open the stomach of one foe, her guts spilling to the floor, while decapitating another. In the end she stood alone, the ground around her littered with corpses suffering varying degrees of mutilation.

Ardell breathed heavily, not because she was out of breath, but because she was disappointed it had all ended so soon. She looked around eagerly for another foe to fight but there was no one, only the shrivelled and snivelling shape of the man in the blue robe who had surrendered earlier, still cowering behind the crates. She was about to descend to the lower level of the camp in hopes of fighting a little while longer but was met by her officers coming the other way, bloody, but with smiles on their faces. The battle was over, and it had been a resounding victory.

Nate had not managed to reach the camp before the battle had ended. As the others rounded up any captives and treated their wounded, Nate had an altogether different task in mind. He marched straight towards the centre of the camp where Ardell and her officers were debriefing and discussing further plans. Moving with purpose so as to avoid being handed a job clearing corpses or cataloguing loot, he soon found himself at the feet of the first person he had killed, her body having not yet been moved. She lay crumpled, a hand wrapped around the arrow lodged in her collar, the other curled upwards like a dead spider in a pool of blood. Her skin was pale and the light from her eyes had left her, leaving behind dark, empty vessels. Her face was contorted into one final expression of agony, her chin and neck drenched as she had slowly drowned in her own blood.

Nate could not help but stare into her lifeless eyes. He expected to be sick, but his stomach was strangely unmoved. Neither did his heartbeat quicken in his chest, instead it was calm, it's slow, unstrained thumping insistent that nothing was out of the ordinary. What Nate did next had not been planned, in fact he found himself doing it without even thinking, almost instinctively. He kneeled, the cold sticky pool of blood soaking into his knee guard, and with one hand, closed his victim's eyes. A sudden hand on his shoulder made him jump up, the connection between his body and the bloody ground severed by a vulgar, wet tearing sound.

It was Joel, who wore a gloomy smile and a small plaster under his left eye where one of the smugglers had glanced him with the edge of their blade. "The first one is the easiest," he said sadly. Nate turned his attention to Ardell who was going about her business as if she were not still dripping with blood. Joel followed his gaze and then added, "for most people anyway."

There was a sudden shout which drowned out all noise in the camp and caught everyone's attention.

"Captain, captain you need to see this," screamed the panicked voice coming from inside the tower where the smugglers had stashed most of their loot. Ardell, along with most of the camp, rushed over and quickly crowded the small door. At first nothing seemed out of the ordinary, the room was stacked high with crates of contraband ranging from weapons to drugs and disassembled machinery. Yet it soon became apparent there was more at play as the man who had called so loudly a moment ago stood quaking in his boots at the mouth of a passage which had been hidden behind some empty crates.

He pointed into the gloom with trembling fingers as Ardell cautiously stepped forward, her hand ready on her sword. The passage itself went underground and was not part of the tower's original design, someone had dug it out and reinforced it with stone since it had been abandoned. The most likely culprits were the smugglers themselves – after all, it would pay to be able to hide your loot in case of capture to which you could return later.

The passage was lit by a single torch and the entrance to another room could be made out. Ardell turned to her officers: "You three with me," she said as she led the way, the clanking and scraping of their armour on the stone walls echoing ahead of them.

It took less than a minute to reach the end of the passage and enter the new room. This room, however, was pitch black and so Ardell cast a spell which resulted in a football-sized orb of light floating to the ceiling. Immediately as the light appeared the eerie silence was broken by an orchestra of angry, vicious snarls, as if the room had been filled by wild animals.

Ardell instinctively jumped back and drew her sword, crashing into her officers in the process who tumbled like dominos down the passage. Ardell gasped, quickly realising she was in no immediate danger, but kept her sword drawn. The room was just like the tower, stacked floor to ceiling, although this time, with cages rather than boxes. In each cage were between six to eight Husks, crammed together, screaming, and raging at Ardell. Her face turned into an ugly scowl as she stormed her way past her officers, out of the tower and towards where the prisoners were being kept.

Bound and gagged they sat on the ground, some still bloody from their earlier confrontation. The prisoners all shuffled away as far as their bounds would allow them as they saw the figure of Ardell approach. They had seen what had happened to their friends who had suffered her wrath and were not eager to draw it upon themselves. She halted in front of the group, scanning them for her target, quickly identifying him by his yellow skullcap.

Without hesitation she dragged him to his feet and pulled the gag from his mouth. Wasting no time, she began her interrogation immediately.

"Why are you capturing Husks?" she snarled. The prisoner blinked innocently.

"I have no idea what you're talking about." Wrong answer. Ardell said nothing as she cut his bonds and forced him to the ground, face first, his right arm outstretched, the point of her dagger resting against his palm.

"Last chance, what are you doing with the Husks?" The prisoner was sweating and shaking with terror, this maniac would never believe that he did not know, even though it was the truth. He panted, trying to think of an answer that would satisfy her. But it was pointless, lying would get him just as far as the truth at this point.

"I don't know," he sobbed finally. Ardell closed her eyes and took a deep breath to hold back her anger but was only partly successful. She pushed the end of the dagger into the prisoner's palm. He screamed in pain as the skin broke and a river of blood began flowing into the dust. Suddenly, another voice spoke up – a prisoner who, unable to stand watching his friend be tortured, had worked his gag free and called out.

"He doesn't know, but I do, let him go and I'll tell you." Ardell raised her eyebrow at the man – was this prisoner, bound and helpless, really giving her orders? She stood, relieving the pressure on the crying prisoner's arm, who quickly pulled it back to nurse it. Ardell took the man who had spoken by the scruff of the neck and shoved him forwards.

He was a similar height and build to her, with dark, almost obsidian-coloured skin and his long, curly hair was tied into a bun. Ardell had him kneel and placed the tip of her dagger under his chin. A bead of sweat from his temple dripped onto the dagger's tip and off its edge, mixing with the blood of its previous victim.

"Speak," she snapped. The prisoner's eyes switched from the dagger to Ardell's eyes, which shone with the same cruelty as her weapon.

"We were being paid to catch and transport them," the prisoner gulped.

"Where, by whom?" Ardell growled back. She hated it when people she was interrogating decided to abandon the normal style of conversation and give out information piecemeal. The prisoner shook his head as much as the steel against his skin would allow.

"We don't know who was paying us, but they wanted the Husks delivered to the border with the Imperium, near a town called Blight. I swear that's all any of us know."

"You had better pray that's not the case," Ardell grumbled as she pushed the prisoner back amongst his fellows. At the same time one of Ardell's officers approached with a piece of parchment in his hand. Ardell snatched it from him before he had the chance to speak, knowing it was a final summary of everything found in the camp. After the unexpected discovery of the caged Husks, this report detailing quantities of contraband recovered was far from easing her growing headache. Quickly scanning the document, she turned to the officer.

"Prepare everyone to move out, we're heading straight back to the city. And someone put down those damned Husks," she said storming out of the camp. The officers immediately set about organising their squads into formation and marching them back to their own camp, leaving behind a small detachment to guard their spoils. Nate found Joel taking his place in the column and marched back to camp beside him, nobody seeming to mind that they had one extra in their troop.

Nate did a quick headcount – as far as he could see they had not lost a single one of their own whereas only thirteen smugglers still lived. "How you holding up?" Joel asked. Killing was routine in this world but that did not make it any easier on the soul, veteran or not. He had worried that after his reaction to the Wailing Pits, Nate would break under the weight of killing another person. Nate shook his head.

"I'm fine," he said, although his eyes were glued to the ground and his brow was creased as if straining to understand a difficult concept. Which in a way, Nate felt that he was. After how he had felt at killing the Husks he had expected to be in a similar if not even worse state now. Yet he felt nothing, no pangs of guilt or raging torrent of thoughts of his victim's families and friends, the lives he had ended. This to Nate was deeply unsettling; he was glad to not be suffering any adverse effects from his actions, but felt that he should be.

Moving at a much quicker pace than before their attack, the troops and their prisoners arrived at their camp in only fifteen minutes. Marcus quickly abandoned his post and rushed over to Nate and Joel, relieved to see them both alive. For the entirety of their absence he had done little more than torment himself with graphic visions of Nate's death without himself there to protect him.

He met them both with slaps on the back and a beaming smile. "Didn't get yourself killed then?" he laughed slapping Nate for a second time, slightly harder than was necessary which left his skin stinging. Before Nate could utter a word, he was approached by a man in plate metal armour and carrying a mace, both of which were dotted with specks of dried blood. It was the man with whom they had been speaking earlier when discussing their bet, which in the heat of battle Nate had completely forgotten about.

At first the man looked angry, his eyes squinted and a hand on his weapon. Nate wondered if he was about to receive a beating for some unknown crime. But the man's hard features quickly softened as he gave a sly smile and slapped Nate hard on the back which almost sent him face first into the ground. "You're one lucky kid," he smirked as Nate straightened himself, rubbing what was now certain to be a hand-shaped welt on his back.

"Yeah, I didn't expect to make it back alive either," he laughed nervously. The man laughed and shook his head.

"Come and see me by the outer gate as soon as we get back, I'll have your winnings then," he said turning away, throwing Nate a single, congratulatory thumbs-up. For a moment Nate still had no idea what he was referring to before it hit him, and he almost tripped over himself.

"Holy shit, did I win the bet?" he practically squealed.

"No way," Joel gasped.

"Looks like you'll be buying the rounds when we get back then," Marcus grinned cheekily. The sudden end to his money troubles completely wiped Nate's mind of the events of the past hour as he now fantasised over how he would spend his winnings. With a new pep in his step Nate helped to disassemble the camp before Ardell ordered them onwards.

The sky was pitch black by the time they exited the forest and found the road leading back to the city. Clouds obscured the usually twinkling sky and even Ardell found herself getting lost more than once in the darkness of the forest with no daylight to guide her. By the time the edges of the city were visible the entire party was exhausted. Their formerly rigid formation had frayed into loose strings whose shoulders sagged under the weight of their armour, their arms and legs aching terribly as they dragged themselves onwards. Only Ardell remained composed; despite her own tiredness she was constantly on alert for any potential danger. Although she was more relaxed than usual, her mind was still back in the battle, replaying every strike, every movement in exquisite detail. She smiled to herself; she was still the best.

The troops practically collapsed on the roadside once they had been waved through the city gate. Some stumbled on in search of a room while others decided enough was enough and set up camp where they lay. Ardell and her officers headed for the nearby barracks which was reserved for those of higher rank while Nate, Marcus and Joel stood around debating where they should spend the night.

While Marcus and Joel argued whether a night in a brothel or an inn would be best Nate noticed the man from earlier, still clutching his bloody mace leaning against a wall. Nate left his friends to their argument and approached the man who replied with a smile and a wave. Checking both ways to make sure Ardell was truly gone, he pulled a large, leather pouch from his bag which jingled with the unmistakeable sound of currency as he tossed it Nate's way.

Catching it with both hands he was surprised at its weight, it was lighter than he expected, not that he was complaining as he hurriedly stuffed it into his bag.

"Had to split it between another lucky bastard but it's all there, you not going to count it?" the man quizzed.

"Nah, I trust you," Nate shrugged, "Plus if you've cheated me, I'll tell Ardell the whole bet was your idea." The man folded his arms and laughed.

"You're alright, kid, I think you'll fit in fine around here. Just make sure you've always got one eye on your back." Nate nodded and the two went their separate ways. Marcus and Joel were still in the midst of their argument when the sound of jingling coins drew their attention.

"I don't know about you guys, but I could do with a soft bed and a steak," Nate said gently swinging his bag so the sound of his winnings could just be heard. Joel and Marcus immediately set aside their differences and grinned.

"A steak sure does sound good," Marcus said.

"Couldn't agree more," Joel added licking his lips.

*

Ardell lay in her bunk on the second floor of the officers' barracks, the gentle flicker of the fire casting a red glow in the otherwise dark room. On her bedside table lay a half-eaten sandwich while her sword, as usual, lay on the floor nearby in case it was suddenly needed. The excitement of battle had now worn off and she was back to her usual brooding self. She had already written her after-action report and re-read it for the third time.

It had been a textbook example of a mission gone right, her meticulous planning and well devised orders having won her a great victory, but the taste of success was a bitter one. For all the goods that had been seized and smugglers put out of action, the discovery of the Husks, caged in the dark, followed by the prisoner's earlier confession, made Ardell feel as if she had missed out on a far greater piece in a much larger game. Furthermore, there had been nothing found linking Massah to the smuggling activity as she had hoped.

Clearly there were other forces at work here, but whom, and what they hoped to achieve, were a mystery to her. Suddenly a thought crossed her mind and she leapt out of bed, heading back to her desk where fresh parchment and ink lay waiting. She might only be privy to the information passed down by her superiors and gathered by her spies, but she knew someone who could make sense of what she had found. She took up the quill and began drafting a letter. It was not often she would ask the Battlemages for help, but for reasons she could not fully explain even to herself, she knew there was something more to this.

She had stumbled upon something sinister, something which needed to be stopped. Ardell signed and sealed the letter before quickly walking over to the fire. Tossing it into its greedy jaws, she watched in silence as the parchment blackened and curled as the flames devoured it. When only ash remained Ardell returned to her bunk, her mind slightly at ease; whatever was going on, she would get to the bottom of it.

A few days later Ardell was once more in her usual quarters, back to the mundane day-to-day activities required of her position. She was scribbling away at a letter when she sensed movement behind her. She had been facing the door all morning as she sat at her desk and nobody had entered, her windows were also tightly locked.

She smiled to herself and lowered her quill. "One of these days, Leridon, you're going to sneak up on the wrong person." She turned and saw a man in a long, dark-blue robe, his features covered by a hood, stood with his back against the wall. He let out a small, deep chuckle and lowered his hood to reveal an attractive face with a square jaw, bright orange eyes and medium-length blonde hair which ended in a braid.

"I'll stop as soon as it stops being fun," he replied. Leridon was not his real name, rather the Grand Masters of the Battlemages adopted the names of ancient sorcerers to hide their true identities. Despite knowing one another for many decades, Leridon had never disclosed his true name to Ardell, and she had never once asked, as she knew better than most the importance of discretion.

"You got my letter then?" she said raising herself from her chair and embracing her friend.

"Indeed," Leridon said lowering himself onto Ardell's bed, his expression turned to one of mild surprise. "I must say this is a strikingly odd coincidence."

"How so?" Ardell replied raising her eyebrow and folding her arms. She refused to believe in coincidences herself.

"Well just moments before I received your letter, one of my agents told me he had heard rumours that Husks were going missing along the border with the Imperium."

"That's not too strange," Ardell shrugged. "Husks are wild creatures after all, they go where they please." Leridon nodded as if to say both yes and no simultaneously.

"Usually, I would have thought the same, except this was no less than the fifth such rumour I had received, and as you know my agents never tell me the same thing twice."

"They are quite good," Ardell smirked, 'good' being a gross understatement when referring to the skills of the Battlemages. Leridon ignored the comment and continued.

"That's not all," he said rubbing the fresh stubble on his chin. "They believe the Imperium is behind these disappearances." Ardell screwed up her face as one would when encountering a bad smell, indicating she did not entirely believe what she was hearing.

"Come now Leridon, I know you lot aren't fans of the Imperium, but why on Gaia would they want to start kidnapping Husks?" The Battlemage sighed and returned to his feet.

"That's why I'm here," he said walking over to Ardell's desk and producing a map which he instructed her to inspect. There were red markings along large swathes of the Imperial/Tinelian border and red circles with intelligible notes hastily scrawled beside them at a multitude of locations, all of which were within Tinelia.

"What's all this supposed to be?" Ardell asked. Leridon began pointing to the red circles on the map.

"Each of these marks denotes a camp similar to the one you found a few days ago. Each one full of Husks crammed into cages all bound for the border." Ardell looked in amazement at the sheer number of these markings – there were at least a hundred, if not more.

"You found all these in less than a week?" she gasped. Leridon could not help but give a smug grin.

"We don't study magic for centuries because it's fun you know." Ardell looked at him and then back to the map.

"This isn't an isolated incident then, something on this scale had to come from the top," she replied. Leridon nodded in solemn agreement – whenever the Imperium set its mind and resources to something, it always spelled disaster for the rest of the world.

"What do you suggest we do?" Ardell asked. Leridon was taken aback.

"You mean to say the great Captain Ardell does not have a plan for this exact situation?" he teased. Ardell rolled her eyes as Leridon spoke again.

"Not to worry, I today received a letter from one of my most capable agents. He claims to have unearthed some extremely valuable information, but for whatever reason is unable to communicate it through the usual channels."

Ardell placed both her hands on the table and stared at the map as if it were hiding a message she needed to decipher.

"I'm guessing that's where I come in?"

"Indeed," Leridon nodded. "I need someone to meet my agent at the town of Cotts, which is to the north-east, just a few miles shy from the border."

Ardell looked at him suspiciously.

"Why can't he just find another way to transfer the information, covert meetings are risky business even in peacetime, and why can't your own people do it, surely, he's far more likely to trust one of his own?"

This time it was Leridon's turn to fold his arms and look suspicious, although not at Ardell, but rather at the situation itself.

"I'm not sure, the agent said it was unsafe for him to perform any sort of magic, even in secret. He also specifically requested to meet non-members for the handover." Leridon shook his head. "To be honest this whole thing reeks, I don't know what to make of it." Ardell let out a long sigh.

"Do you think your agent believes he can't trust the order?"

"It certainly seems that way, but I pray it's not the case. A traitor in our midst could prove catastrophic, which is why I am investigating the possibility, quietly. In the meantime, do you have anyone under your command who is up for meeting my agent, people you trust?"

Ardell thought for a moment, "I believe there may be a few I can count on to get this done."

"Excellent, as soon as they reach Cotts and complete the handover contact me, we will move from there." Ardell raised her head from the map.

"Agr… "She stopped; the room was empty once again. "I hate it when they do that" she grumbled, returning her gaze to the map, its red circles like a pox on Tinelia.

"They'd better not fuck this up."

Chapter 13

The castle was always cold, but the fresh wind which fought its way through every nook and crevice was painful as it bit at Adeneus' bare face and arms. Drawing his thick cloak around him he made his way down the stairs from his chambers and into the main hall where his servants had been preparing breakfast.

The hall was unusually empty, with only Adeneus' general Sir Garrus and manservant Olin present. The hall was usually filled with either soldiers or servants busying themselves with whatever inconsequential tasks had been assigned to them. Glad for the quiet, Adeneus made his way over to the large fire pit in the centre of the room and stood warming his hands, his heavy footsteps echoing on the stone floor.

Olin, meanwhile, set out his master's breakfast at the head of the table, a large bowl of leek soup accompanied by various fresh fruits and sweet bread. After Adeneus was sufficiently warmed through he made his way back to the table. Sir Garrus was wolfing down sandwiches and fruit while Adeneus slowly sipped at his steaming bowl. Garrus let out a belch as he downed half a flagon of mead in a single gulp.

Disgusted at his general's lack of table manners Adeneus turned to him. "Do you have anything to report Sir Garrus or are you just going to sit there ruining my morning?"

The knight put down his drink and turned to face his master. "We captured two caravans yesterday, so you have plenty of new subjects," he said, wiping away the mead which dribbled from his chin.

"Excellent." Adeneus smiled as he took another sip of his soup.

"They should be here in a few weeks, then you can have your fun." Adeneus thought about scolding his general but decided not to waste his breath on someone who could never possibly understand the importance of his work.

"Don't you have work to do? I'm quite sure I recall his holiness commanding you to be my servant not my personal breakfast eater." Garrus nodded and took his leave, tossing half a pear into the fire as he left. As the huge door to the main hall closed shut, whipping yet more freezing air into Adeneus' face, he leant back in his chair. Uninterested in his soup, he beckoned Olin to take it away.

"Do you want anything taken to your lab, my lord?" Olin asked.

"No, I'll be very busy today, don't allow anyone to disturb me."

"Yes, my lord." Olin bowed taking the uneaten food away to the kitchens. Adeneus sat there for a moment in silence before hauling himself to his feet with an exhausted huff. It was barely seven o'clock and he was already mentally drained from the prospect of the task ahead of him.

Returning the way he had come, he descended the spiral stone steps which led to the heavy wooden door of his laboratory, held shut by a thick beam across its length.

Removing the beam with his magic and pulling the door open, Adeneus stepped inside. It was a huge room about double the size of the great hall. There were rows of cabinets and shelves containing hundreds of potions and thousands of books in scattered piles.

It had been a monumental pain relocating so much of his research and belongings out into the sticks, but the goal in the end was worth his current suffering.

Of course, as with all laboratories, there were rows of cages containing prisoners, or as Adeneus liked to call them '*less than willing participants.*' Many were men and women captured from within enemy territory, unlucky victims of Sir Garrus' roaming gangs of thugs. They sat curled up on the floor, filthy and cold, any hope of escape extinguished long ago. Now they wished for nothing more than a quick death. Unfortunately for them, this was unlikely.

Adeneus himself did not enjoy inflicting pain. He was a scholar, after all, and the pursuit of knowledge was his only aim. Yet he understood that ground-breaking discoveries could not be made without a price. If that was the blood of innocent victims, he was happy to pay, it was insignificant considering the potential rewards. He like to pretend to himself that had he been in their situation, he would have understood.

Most of the prisoners, however, were Husks, grey and rotten, who cried and howled in anger and pain. They were the focus of his research, what the Phoenix project was all about. Luckily, he was not starting the project from scratch. There was a wealth of notes from previous Arch-Sorcerers at his disposal. Just months before their work had been put on indefinite hold, a breakthrough had been made.

It had been found that Husks shared a psychic link with humans. It was weak, but if it could be exploited it would be revolutionary. This is where Adeneus found his greatest obstacle, how to not only harness this psychic link, but then control it. He had spent months pouring over old notes, applying potions, and going through an excessive number of subjects in his experiments yet had achieved nothing.

He walked over to his workstation, which was cluttered and disorganised, half-empty vials of various coloured liquids a reminder of his failure. He sighed and spent the next half an hour re-reading the notes he had made the night before. Three participants had been lost for no gain other than to learn humans could not control Husks through simple voice commands and physical prompts, a rather obvious conclusion really. They were not dogs after all.

Irritated, he pushed the notes away and reached for the shelf above him, retrieving a small vial filled with a bright blue liquid. This was a rather common potion that could be bought at a market, although with his own modifications. Its main use was as a truth serum, as when ingested, the potion would target the victim's spinal cord, slowing down the speed of signals sent to the brain, making the act of lying impossible.

However, Adeneus had modified it so that the effects were much more potent. He hoped that this would allow him to control the Husks' movements with voice commands. The logic behind this thinking was that if the subject's brain was sufficiently hampered, then stronger, alternate, auditory signals received via the ears would replace the signals sent by their own free will, allowing him to control the subject with his voice alone.

He approached one of the cages containing a Husk. It was male, the ghostly remains of what had once been a full head of thick blonde hair barely visible, hanging in wisps from its decaying scalp. Adeneus held out his hand and the Husk violently slammed into the bars of the cage, unable to move as the spell gripped it tightly. Pouring the contents of the vial into the Husk's mouth, Adeneus released it from his invisible grip. It fell to its knees before standing once again, its face pressed against the bars as it stared with eyes full of rage at its tormentor.

Adeneus checked his watch; he would wait sixty seconds for the potion to take effect before continuing. The bodies of Husks were severely decayed and so he would not need to wait as long as for a human subject. Suddenly, the Husk went stiff, and stood perfectly straight, its fingers and eyes twitching slightly. Adeneus smiled – the potion was working. He waited another few moments before issuing his first command.

"Step back," he instructed. The Husk did nothing, it remained still, its eyes still twitching. Adeneus gave an annoyed sigh – maybe he had to speak louder, more clearly, the creatures barely had functioning ears after all. He raised his voice just shy of a shout. "Put your arms above your head." There was no response from the Husk, its furious eyes still burning into his. "Bend your knees," Adeneus continued through gritted teeth. The Husk refused to move.

"Dammit," Adeneus cried, hurling the vial away, which shattered near some of his human participants who scurried to the back of their cages in fear of a reprisal.

He was on the verge of giving up, of sending a letter to the Emperor explaining how the Phoenix project was a bust, simply impossible. But then a sudden thought entered his mind. It was a long shot, but what choice did he have?

He strode back to his workstation and frantically rummaged through the mess until he found what he was looking for. In his hand he held a green crystal, three inches in length and two inches deep. Corite, a common gem which could be found in great abundance in most quarries and caves.

It bore no special magical or aesthetic properties and so was mostly ignored by both scholar and merchant alike. Adeneus hoped this would be the key to the project – if not, he had no idea where else to turn.

The ability of metals and gemstones to absorb and trap magical energy was well documented and considered the most efficient way to transport large quantities of raw magic, untainted by human emotions. He wondered if it could trap something else.

He walked over to one of the cages in which a woman was curled up, her knees planted under her chin. She had only been captured a few days ago and was therefore in the best physical condition for the experiment.

Her dirty face was streaked with tears, and she shivered from both fear and the cold. She looked up at Adeneus as he stood with his face only inches from the bars of the cage, his brown eyes filled with a mixture of both guilt and determination.

No matter how he felt about the ethics of his experiments, they had to be done, for the sake of science if nothing else. He said nothing as he once again held out his hand and the woman braced herself for what she knew was coming. But it was impossible to brace oneself for something like this.

This was a spell Adeneus had been working on in his spare time since becoming Arch-Sorcerer. Nothing like it had ever been successfully attempted before and he wondered how his subject would react as she was lifted from the floor of the cage like a puppet on a string, powerless to stop what was happening.

Adeneus curled his hand into a claw, and upon doing so the woman began to shake and contort violently. Veins bulged across her neck and forehead, thick and purple like worms sprouting from the ground after fresh rain. Suddenly, the sickening sound of her bones cracking and splintering under the pressure filled the room. She opened her mouth to scream but could only produce a sick, gurgling sound as white froth formed at the edges of her mouth.

Not a minute had passed since the start of the experiment but for both Adeneus and his victim, it already felt like a lifetime. Just as he began to doubt his methods, Adeneus saw what he had been waiting for.

What started as a faint glow in the back of the woman's throat soon grew to a bright ball of pure, white light. Adeneus' eyes grew wide, he could not believe it, he was the first person in the known world to witness the human soul with his own eyes. Filled with renewed confidence he tightened his hand into a fist, hoping it would be enough to draw out the soul entirely.

By now the woman's features were unrecognisable. Her bright eyes were filled with blood which also streamed from her nose and ears. Her limbs were broken and stuck out at unnatural angles or hung limp as the bones had been turned to dust. With a final cry Adeneus used all his strength to rip the soul free, as he held out the Corite crystal ahead of him which absorbed it like a sponge, just as he had hoped.

He released his grip, which saw the participant's lifeless corpse fall to the ground with a crunch. He could not tear his eyes away from what he held in his hand – even if the rest of the project were doomed to failure, he had still achieved what many had considered impossible.

His legs were weak as he stumbled to his workstation where he collapsed into his chair breathing heavily. He immediately set about scribbling down every detail of the experiment, no matter how trivial. The time of day, the temperature, subject's sex, height, amount of blood lost, everything he could think of.

He once again leaned back and marvelled at his prize. The Corite was now no longer a pure, translucent green, but cloudy as the soul trapped within filled the confines of its prison. It did not look like much, but in his palm, he held the summation of a human being. Everything that made them unique and special in the eyes of God. At last, he had the materials required to achieve his goal, he just needed to uncover how to use them.

He turned to another of his test subjects, their eyes locked. The prisoner knew what was coming and tried his best to get away, hurling himself at the bars at the back of his cage as Adeneus approached with a fresh crystal, stepping over the growing pool of blood from his last victim. There was no doubt or guilt in his mind anymore, this *had* to be done.

*

"Any questions?" Ardell said rhetorically. Neither Marcus or Nate answered, knowing questions meant you had not been listening in the first place and would earn you a beating. "Excellent," Ardell grinned. "You can select your own party for this mission, but make sure they can be trusted, this is extremely important, do you understand?" Both men nodded. Just as Ardell was satisfied that the two understood the gravity of the mission and what was expected of them, Marcus spoke up.

"Apologies, Captain, but are you sure Nate is ready for this? He hasn't been here six months yet." Ardell's eyes darted over to Nate, she quickly looked him up and down while chewing the inside of her cheek. Nate usually would have regarded such interest as a compliment if he did not think she was considering the most amusing ways to kill him. Ardell wagged her finger at Marcus while shaking her head from side to side.

"Nate performed exceptionally well during the last mission; I think he is more than ready for a taste of real responsibility. You can't be a mother hen forever Marcus, one day your chicks must leave their nest."

Marcus' face began to turn red at the comparison and decided to remain silent to save himself from further embarrassment. Ardell looked back at Nate and flashed a grin before getting back to the matter at hand.

"You'll be masquerading as a merchant caravan; you can have some of those fake weapons we confiscated to back you up. The moment you contact the Battlemage I want you to get back here as fast as possible. No stops, no detours, you get back here, and we move from there, understood?" Again, both men nodded silently. "I'll give you two days to assemble your party and then I expect you to be on your way."

Alarm bells suddenly rang inside Marcus' head – two days was nowhere near long enough to go through an extensive vetting process for such an important mission. As the men bowed and were dismissed Ardell called after them.

"Oh, one more thing. This operation is off the books, so I won't be taking a commission." This was already enough to bring looks of excitement to both Nate and Marcus, but Ardell was not finished yet.

"I'll also give you each a ten per cent bonus if you get back by the end of next month." The two men could not stop themselves from smiling now, ten per cent on top of what was already generous pay for the type of job was unbelievable.

Whatever information the Battlemage possessed, it must be vitally important. But neither of them were interested in that right now, all they could think of was striding like kings into the bank to admire their hoard and curl themselves amongst it like dragons. The pressure was now on Marcus, however, as it was his responsibility to assemble a party of capable and trusted individuals and complete the mission. As they left the keep, he wondered out loud why Ardell had trusted *him* of all people to get this done.

"Maybe she likes you after all," Nate teased, gently elbowing Marcus in the ribs.

"Ha, fat chance," Marcus snorted back. "Right," he said as a plan began to formulate in his brain. "I want you at Pedan's no later than six, we have a party to assemble." Nate nodded and set off home astride Bob. Marcus meanwhile rode in the opposite direction; he already had a good idea of who he wanted on this mission if it were going to have any chance of success.

As he cantered on home Nate could not decide what emotion to feel. He wanted to be nervous, it had only been a week since his first battle and the thought of it still set his body shaking. Not from guilt or fear, however, rather from adrenaline as the mere recollection of events excited his body which yearned for more. He could not decide, however, if in this world that was a good or a bad thing. He also could not help but be slightly excited at the idea of venturing outside the city walls again. There was a whole world out there waiting to be explored and he was finally now being given that chance.

Nate was so lost in thought he had not noticed he had already made the journey home and stood outside the door to the barracks. Chen was still in a foul mood with him and had given him a black eye upon his initial return, but tempers had luckily cooled after that.

"What did she want this time?" Chen grumbled before Nate had even fully stepped inside. She was hunched over the bath, furiously scrubbing her dirty clothes. Nate's meanwhile had been left neglected in the same heap they always were, another sign of her lingering annoyance at him. He did not think that announcing he was being sent on yet another mission would do anything to improve her mood.

He rubbed his still bruised eye; he already knew the consequences of lying. He cleared his throat and moved over to his bunk, pulling off his armour until only his shirt and trousers remained.

"She wants to send me and Marcus on another mission," he said, trying to play it off casually while keeping his good eye out for foreign objects being launched at his head.

"Oh, right," Chen said dismissively as if she'd never cared to begin with and continued scrubbing a blouse stained with tomato juice. Nate was taken aback and even slightly disappointed by her response, he had grown fond of jabbing Chen's delicate temper to elicit a reaction. He decided to poke the bear further, rubbing his aching feet and adopting an equally cool tone.

"It's top-secret though, really dangerous, I shouldn't even be telling you really." Surely this would do it, Nate thought as he watched Chen from the corner of his eye.

"Best stop talking then," Chen responded as she carried her now sopping clothes to hang outside without once looking Nate's way.

Refusing to back down now Nate followed her outside, leaning in the doorway as Chen struggled with her short legs to peg up the washing in the glorious sunlight. He folded his arms and sniffed loudly to draw her attention while averting his eyes skywards as if Chen were boring him.

"Reward is unbelievable too, plus there's a bonus if we are back in two months, might find myself somewhere nice with it," he smirked at the sky. He looked back to where Chen had been stood, fully expecting her to be shaking with rage but found her gone. He unfolded his arms and jumped back with such force he almost knocked himself out on the doorframe.

Chen was stood directly in front of him, an evil smile pencilled across her thin lips. "W…What?" Nate stuttered. Chen continued to wear her menacing smile and placed her hands on her hips.

"You've got a party already or not?" The question threw Nate off and he failed to answer, which to Chen was an answer in itself.

"Excellent," she beamed, "guess I'll be joining you then," she said, twirling around and back to her chore.

Nate did not know what to do, he was frozen in place as he replayed the last few seconds in his head. How had he gone from teasing into having her sign herself up for the mission?

He knew she was serious too; she had the twinkle in her eye that meant she had set her mind to something and there was nothing anyone could do about it. He thought about what Marcus was going to say when they both turned up at Pedan's later that evening. '*Shit*' was all he could manage but it still seemed appropriate.

For once Pedan's inn was quiet – it was still early, and most people would not have finished their shifts or shut up shop, the perfect time to get a potential party together and come up with a plan.

Chen had been only a step behind Nate despite his constant attempts to dissuade her from coming along, even going so far as to apologise for his teasing. It was for naught, however, as Nate's promise of a big reward had totally convinced her. A quick scan of the nearly deserted room save for the same few drunk faces that never left showed no sign of Marcus.

"He's on the top floor," Pedan shouted across the room while he wiped a plate with the same rag as always. Nate nodded his thanks and made for the stairs, double-checking nobody was coming the other way, now an unwanted habit.

Chen giggled quietly to herself at Nate's awkwardness and bounded past him. Nate quickly followed, desperate to explain himself to Marcus before Chen could do it for him. But he was too late, by the time he had reached the top of the stairs Chen was already at the top of the second set. After reaching the top floor, he caught Chen already deep in conversation.

At first Marcus' face was one of surprise which then quickly turned to anger as he spotted Nate panting and leaning on the banister for support. He nodded in defeat at Chen to which she smiled sweetly and joined the others who were sat around three tables beside the balcony, half of whom Nate did not recognise.

Marcus stomped over; his hands balled into fists. "Why for the love of Venus would you invite her on this mission without my permission?" Nate tried to defend himself, but Marcus waved his excuses away before they had even left his mouth.

"Next time you want to bring your girlfriend along, ask me first, this isn't a day out."

Nate rolled his eyes and looked over at Chen who was chatting casually with Kyle, his long white robe replaced by a blue gambeson.

Nate wondered why Kyle of all people would be so heavily armoured for a trip to the pub, but quickly noticed he was the least heavily armed among the group.

Joel sat reclined in a wooden chair which seemed on the verge of tipping over at any moment, a polished steel breastplate protecting his chest, while thick, heavy leather boots and armguards covered his extremities.

The other four strangers were dressed in a wide range of armours from samurai karuta to a female hoplite of shining bronze. Marcus began walking away and beckoned for Nate to follow, eager for him to meet his new companions. Dropping himself opposite Joel the two shared a friendly smile and handshake while Marcus took centre stage and addressed them all.

"Everyone," Marcus began in a commanding voice he had picked up from watching Ardell. "I want you to take a look around, the men and women beside you will be the ones watching your back on this mission, so get yourselves acquainted."

Nate looked over at the woman in bronze, who had long blonde hair and a slender but toned frame from countless hours of training in all manner of specialties. She was picking at her nails, her legs crossed as if she would rather be anywhere else, like she was too good for the lot of them.

Marcus began introducing the party members one by one, trying to keep the mood light while also cementing the importance of the mission and its secrecy. Finally, he reached the four strangers and began with the only woman among them, the one Nate had been ogling for the past fifteen minutes.

"The lovely lady before you is Cassandra," he began, and as if on cue Cassandra flicked her hair away and gave each man a quick glance which set all their hearts racing. Chen rolled her eyes and folded her arms; how men fell for that crap every time without fail she would never understand.

Marcus continued. "She's an expert with a bow, sword, shield, spear, and pretty much anything else you can think of. She's got more successful expeditions under her belt than the rest of us combined, we're lucky to have her."

Cassandra let out a giggle. "You're far too kind Marcus, I promise I'm not even half as good as you say." Sensing that every man in the room was about to start showering her with compliments regarding her modesty Marcus quickly moved on.

"This fine gentleman is Jin," he said, holding out his hand in the direction of the man dressed in the karuta. "He's one of the best swordsmen this side of the Vanguard, well, for what we can afford anyway." Marcus grinned. There was a round of laughter, the loudest of which came from Jin himself.

He was relatively short, around five foot four, with dark, cropped hair and a thin moustache which trailed off at the corners of his mouth. Nate could tell however, by the way he was sat and held himself, along with the various scars which marked his face that discipline and swordsmanship were his life. Then came the final two.

Both had broad, muscular shoulders and arms, chiselled square jaws, and flat noses. The only notable differences were that one was fair-skinned with short, sandy hair, while the other had dark onyx-like skin and was bald, with a long, perfectly rectangular beard.

These two were Leo and Said, renowned mercenaries whom Marcus had dealt with many times before. Usually, a mercenary's loyalty was to whoever had the heaviest coin purse, but for Leo and Said, once a contract was accepted, their commitment was unquestionable.

Marcus was pleased with himself, having assembled such a fine party in such short notice. He cast a disapproving glance over at Chen – he could have rejected her the moment she opened her mouth with the intention of joining them.

However, the ache in his jaw where she had punched him said otherwise, and he did not fancy going for a second round. Nate had been sizing up his new companions and was lost in thought when a wooden bowl full of broth and a fresh bread roll were placed before him. Looking up, Pedan was smiling down at him with his nauseatingly yellow teeth.

Nate reached for his coin purse, but Pedan waved it away. "This one is on the house." Nate was shocked. If there was one trait everyone in Purgatory seemed to share, generosity was not it.

"Any particular reason?" he asked. Pedan chuckled.

"It's your first ever expedition, so this one is on me, besides this will probably be the last hot meal you'll have for weeks."

That notion did not give Nate much comfort, but he raised the bread in toast and thanked Pedan for his kindness before breaking it in half and dipping it into his broth.

"Good luck," Pedan wished as he made his way down the stairs and back to his bar. As Nate sat there eating his meal, he felt what very well could have been a tiny shiver of excitement – excitement at the prospect of finally being given a real mission, of finally seeing what this world was about.

He was only a few sips into his broth when Kyle plopped himself down opposite. The others were all mingling and chatting, discussing their skills and how they would benefit the mission. Kyle had a different intention in mind, however, and looked as if he were holding back a secret he could not wait to spill.

Christ, here we go, Nate thought as Kyle opened his mouth.

"How's it going bro? Face is in pretty good shape if I do say so myself."

"Not too bad mate," Nate replied, faking enthusiasm. It was clear Kyle was not interested in small talk and leaned in so that his nose was practically dipping into Nate's food, his eyes shivering with anticipation. "I'm sure Pedan can make you some too," Nate said, only half joking. Kyle ignored him.

"How is your magic coming along?" Kyle asked. With such a hectic training schedule and day to day life, Nate had almost forgotten about the existence of magic entirely. As of now his only experience had been Kyle fixing his broken nose. He had no idea he was supposed to have been training with magic too. He wondered whether he would be whisked away to a school with wands, robes, and questionable hiring practices.

Kyle noticed the puzzled look on Nate's face and gasped as if Nate had said something horribly offensive. "Tell me you've at least had a few lessons to go over the basics?" Nate shook his head as he took another bite out of his roll. Kyle fell back in his chair and huffed.

"Unbelievable, well in that case we need to make up for lost time, come with me," he said grabbing hold of Nate's sleeve and dragging him towards the stairs. Joel immediately swooped in upon the unguarded meal as Nate shot him an evil look.

Outside, the inn had what had once been a seating area with dozens of wooden tables and chairs. However, after countless instances of them being used as weapons during drunken brawls Pedan had decided to cut his losses and replace them with a garden of colourful flower beds.

A steady stream of patrons were now making their way inside as the day drew to an end. It would be dangerous to practice magic with so many people around and so Kyle, still with his hand clasped firmly upon Nate's sleeve, dragged him around to the back of the building.

The rear garden was far less appealing – broken tools and stacks of empty crates littered the ground and the grass was a miserable shade somewhere between dark green and brown.

"Right," Kyle began, finally releasing his grip on Nate. "We can't have you going out there without at least some basic understanding of magic."

"Everyone else seems to manage just fine." Nate shrugged as he thought back to Captain Ardell ripping her way through opponents with skill alone. You would have thought coming from a world where magic did not exist, Nate would be ecstatic at the opportunity, but for some inexplicable reason he could not care less.

He had barely got the basics of combat and survival down and adding magic on top of that seemed like a lot of unwanted extra pressure. But Kyle would not be defeated so easily, he ordered Nate to sit – the grass was damp and unpleasant, but Nate did as he was told. Kyle sat opposite, cross legged, a hand on each knee, palms facing upwards.

"I swear if I have to start humming and chanting, I'm leaving," Nate said. Once again Kyle ignored him. If there was one thing he relished about his job, it was teaching the new priests the magical healing arts.

New arrivals would usually go through a year-long training course with various mentors who taught them everything from combat to alchemy and survival skills. Magic, however, had been off the curriculum for years as the powers that be in the Citadel saw it as a waste of time and preferred the more predictable sciences instead.

"Magic is a fairly basic concept," Kyle began. Nate was tired and in no mood for what could end up being an hours-long lecture out on the cold, damp ground, but he promised himself to give Kyle the benefit of the doubt this one time.

"You see, magic is like any other force of nature, it is constantly surrounding us, waiting to be utilised." As Kyle said this, he gently waved his hand in the space between them and a small but bright light raised itself from his flesh and left behind a brief trail, like a comet while the body remained firmly attached to Kyle's hand as it moved.

Nate nodded in understanding as his eyes remained glued to the bright ball. "Magic is extremely malleable, all sorts of things can affect it, human emotions being one of the most common and helpful tools."

"Emotions?" Nate asked, raising an eyebrow. This was starting to edge dangerously close to the back of a camper van at Woodstock hippie territory.

"Exactly," Kyle replied. "All of our emotions have different effects, but some are more potent than others. For example, the spell I just used requires me to be in a state of either complete calm or utter infatuation. I'll let you decide which," he said with a wink. Nate folded his arms – so far this had not been too complicated.

"So, no special words or wands needed?"

"Not for the basics," Kyle confirmed, "although more advanced spells that you would learn at the universities require raw magic energy untainted by emotion, but we will focus on the really easy stuff for now."

"Right," Nate said, wishing he had not asked. Kyle held out his palm and indicated for Nate to do the same.

"I want you to try and be calm."

"I already am," Nate interrupted. Kyle let out a small sigh and continued.

"The calmest you've ever been, try and block out everything around you, all the noise, the smells, close your eyes if you have to."

Nate sighed. Marcus and Joel were probably right around the corner wetting themselves, what would be next, a naked handstand?

Nevertheless, he did as he was told and shut his eyes. His other senses were immediately heightened to compensate and the low hum of conversations from within the inn soon became a roar.

He could barely hear Kyle's instructions to imagine the same ball of light emerging from his own hand. He tried his best, but his mind was quickly diverted from the task at hand. He found himself thinking about his dinner which by now was surely all gone, about the battle at the smugglers camp, and about Cassandra in her gleaming bronze. He opened his eyes and looked at his palm in frustrated disappointment as no light had materialised.

"Well, this is bullshit," he seethed looking quickly to Kyle to explain why he was not able to do it perfectly on his first try.

"You're not concentrating," Kyle said sternly in a tone which Nate did not think he was even capable of. "You must block everything out, even me. Just focus on the light, control your breathing and it will come."

Nate tensed his shoulders – he hated having to be taught, but this was not the training ground where he could at least try to take his anger out on Marcus, no matter how many times he ended up worse for it. He closed his eyes again; the clamouring from the inn had only grown louder and he wondered how anyone could concentrate in such conditions. But if Kyle could manage it, he was determined to do so as well. He took three deep breaths and tried to distance his mind from the noises that surrounded him.

For a while Nate seemed to be getting nowhere, the inn was as loud as ever and the feeling of Kyle's impatient eyes burning into him, wondering why he could not do this simple task, tested his patience. Then, without warning, the noise seemed to fall away, not gradually but immediately, as if he had suddenly dropped out of existence.

Before him, Nate could see nothing but a dark, swirling mass of smoke far below his feet. He realised this must be what

Kyle had been hoping for and tried to imagine the small ball of light. At first, nothing changed, but then, emerging slowly from the darkness, came a light.

It rose slowly, dispersing the smoke around it before gaining speed as it rose higher. Before long it was shooting towards Nate at lightning speed. It was also large, far larger than the light Kyle had produced, perhaps the size of a basketball. Nate held one hand out and the other over his eyes as the intensity of the light became unbearable.

He felt a sudden force against his palm and opened his eyes. He was back in the garden with Kyle, a huge, mesmerising ball of energy resting on his palm. He and Kyle both looked at one another, Nate with a look of triumph, Kyle with one of utter astonishment. The light was bright enough to illuminate the whole garden in a white glow and both men had to shield their eyes.

Nate was not sure how he was supposed to get rid of the ball he had summoned and instinctively closed his hand into a fist. The light immediately vanished, throwing them back into the gloom of twilight. "Mine is bigger than yours." Nate grinned, a sense of victory flowing through him. Kyle, however, could barely speak, mouthing words but unable to match them with sound. Nate watched in amusement for a moment as Kyle struggled to regain his senses.

"That was unbelievable," he gasped at last.

"Not bad for a first attempt." Nate shrugged, trying to rub his success in Kyle's face even further. Kyle wiped newly formed sweat from his forehead.

"Nate, to create something like that, with no training whatsoever…" Kyle trailed off.

"What about it?" Nate asked – sure, the ball had been much larger than he'd expected, but surely Kyle could do that too if he wanted?

"Your emotions must either be extremely potent, or you've got a knack for magic that I've never seen."

"I'm sure it was just beginner's luck" Nate said, now trying to play it off as a fluke in case he was expected to achieve the same level of success again. Kyle was visibly shaking –

perhaps Nate was right, maybe it was a fluke, there was only one way to find out.

"Ok I want you to try something else, I want you to try to create a flame like you did the light," Kyle said, his voice no longer that of a strict schoolteacher, but more like a zookeeper trying to coax a lion from its den, a unique mixture of respect and fear.

"Let me guess, I need to try and get angry this time instead of calm?" Kyle tilted his head to one side.

"Yes and no, anger can be used to make a flame yes, but so can passion. Try thinking of something you care deeply about, more than anything else."

"Ok," said Nate as he closed his eyes once more. Kyle breathed a quiet sigh of relief. Passion would indeed create a flame, but it would be nowhere near as powerful or destructive as one formed by rage. With Nate's clear abilities still untested it would be inadvisable to make himself angry in case he burned the whole street down.

It was once a common occurrence for gifted but untrained sorcerers to accidentally cause destruction on a mass scale, one of the reasons the Citadel began their move away from it. As Kyle was thinking what course of action would be best for Nate, either taking him to the university to be properly trained or discouraging him from exploring his skill further, he was interrupted by a burning hot sensation on his face and legs.

A flame, around six-feet tall and burning a bright red, erupted from Nate's outstretched palm with a roar. "Shit," exclaimed Kyle quickly shielding his face from the heat with his arms. Nate, upon hearing Kyle's expletive, opened his eyes and quickly broke into a large grin and triumphant laughter.

"Holy shit, this is amazing," he laughed. "But wait, why can't I feel the heat?" he shouted over the roaring inferno. By this point Kyle had risen and taken a few steps back to be at a safer distance should anything go awry.

Even from his new position the heat and light were so intense he still had his face shielded. He had expected the flame to be no larger than that of a candle – even the most rage-fuelled fireball he had ever seen did not compare to what was supposed to be little more than a spark.

"Your own spells don't have any effect on you, go on, stick your other hand in, I promise it won't hurt." Nate was apprehensive at first, but some animalistic instinct urged him to try and get a safe distance away from the flame, and certainly not to put any part of him even closer. But burying his fear and replacing it with trust he thrust his left hand into the fire.

He expected a searing pain and to quickly pull away little more than blistered and charred flesh. But no sensation of the sort occurred. In fact, the only indication that the torrent of flame was there at all was the fact he was looking at it. He closed his fist again and just like the ball of light the fire vanished leaving nothing, not even smoke behind.

"That was awesome," Nate beamed. Kyle could not help but be both amazed and terrified by such power – unchecked, Nate could be a serious danger to those around him.

The final lesson he wanted to teach was healing. This proved to be the trickiest for Nate to master, not because it required any special technique, but instead required the caster to feel total altruism towards the recipient.

Kyle opened a small wound on his finger while Nate attempted to heal it. After many failed attempts and beating himself up over it, Nate finally managed to close the wound. The trick he found was not to feel altruism towards the person you were trying to help, but to instead imagine someone you cared deeply about in the same situation, and the spell did not seem to mind the difference. Satisfied with their results Kyle clapped Nate on the shoulder and smiled.

"It usually takes over a year to learn those spells."

"You're joking?"

"I swear," Kyle said, "you've got some serious talent. I might try and poach you off Marcus once this expedition is over with."

This was by no means a joke, but Nate was unaware of this and laughed it off. The pair decided enough was enough and returned to the inn to re-join their companions, each taking away a far different conclusion to their training than the other. Nate had been happy with his apparent rapid progress, while Kyle was wondering not only what caused Nate to possess such power, but also formulating ways to counter it should things go wrong.

He had unintentionally opened Pandora's Box. Now that Nate had been taught how to cast spells, he could do it accidentally. Like a switch, he and his emotions were now permanently connected to the magical energy around him, with no way of turning it off. All Kyle could do now was keep an eye on him, hoping he did not suddenly explode taking half the city with him.

The inn's warmth and smells of roasting meat were welcome sensations as Nate re-joined the others. His dinner was, of course, gone, while the others had done away with their preliminary small talk and had begun drinking. Joel's idea – it was according to him the only way to really get to know someone.

Once you have drunk your fill and spilled your guts, both figuratively and literally, then topped it off with a fight, you will have cemented a bond that will last an eternity. The group were already rowdy, Chen was playing five-finger-fillet with Jin, a look of steely determination on her face while Said and Leo were showing off their muscles and scars, attempting to impress Cassandra who looked about ready to throw them both from the balcony.

Marcus and Joel sat together going through their fourth beers, casually discussing the plan for the following day before they had to set off the day after. "Let's see what Nate thinks of it," Joel said as Nate came closer to the only unoccupied seat around.

Nate's interest was piqued – it was not often anyone asked for his opinion on anything, not that it stopped him from sharing it anyway. Marcus relaxed back in his chair and let Joel do the talking, sipping from his beer as his vision became blurrier and blurrier.

"What's up?" Nate asked as he searched in vain for a drink he hoped had been set aside for him.

"We were both thinking about tomorrow."

"What about it?" Nate asked, pushing away an empty mug.

"It's the last day before we have to leave and the only chance we will get to prepare." Joel looked at Marcus whose face was obstructed by the bottom of his mug as he drained it. Joel continued, "we were thinking of having the party meet at one of the training grounds and have them practice with one another. So, we can get a real idea of what we've got to work with rather than trusting word of mouth and rumour alone." Nate flinched as he imagined having to fight any of the people sat behind him, well, except maybe for Chen. But as far as a plan went, it was a good one.

Going out on such an important mission without absolute certainty in your party's abilities was asking for trouble. "Not a bad idea, it will get us all familiar with one another's strengths and weaknesses so we can compensate where we need to," Nate replied.

"I guess that settles it then." Marcus burped as he lay down his mug and wiped a trickle of golden liquid from his chin.

"Just one thing," Nate said catching both men's attention. He jerked his thumb behind him to where Jin was furiously stabbing at the table between his fingers as Chen watched on with horror.

"Please don't make me fight him."

The three men laughed just as Chen conceded defeat and pushed a handful of coins in Jin's direction. Nate suddenly abandoned his jovial tone and said with all seriousness, "No, seriously please don't." But this only made Marcus and Joel laugh even harder, not the reassurance he was looking for.

Chapter 14

The next day dawned with a brilliant blue sky and warm rays of sunlight which bathed the world in a radiant gold. Colours seemed brighter, flowers more potent, birdsong sweeter, everything seemed to come alive. At the training ground, however, most of the party were nursing hangovers gained the night before. Shuffling like the walking dead they cursed the bright sky which hurt their eyes and the passionate birds who only caused further pounding of their heads.

It was the same place where Nate had done his combat training with Marcus, who stood in his usual position upon the raised platform, addressing the half-dead crowd below him. Tutting at their state but saying nothing he split them all into pairs to spar for twenty minutes before changing partners. Nate's first partner was Jin.

They all formed a circle around the platform and began their final preparations such as fixing their armour in place or stretching. Many, however, took this time to place their heads between their knees in the hope their nausea would suddenly vanish. Marcus closed his eyes and took a couple of deep breaths as he screamed internally – hopefully, this would not be a sign of things to come.

He gave Kyle a look which plainly meant *'please fix them before I kill them.'* Kyle immediately understood and went to each member of the party and had them drink a sip from his small leather flask. The strange, warm liquid had barely passed their lips when all their symptoms disappeared and they jumped to their feet, full of life and energy once more.

"Great," Nate said to himself as what had moments ago been a very green-looking samurai leaning onto his sword for support, had transformed into an energetic killing machine, twirling his katana between his fingers, and grinning madly. Kyle was the only one not sparring, even Marcus and Joel were practicing, eager to gain eternal bragging rights over the other.

Kyle was on standby to provide any medical assistance as they were all using real weapons, not the blunted ones meant for practice. Marcus had made it clear that he wanted no maiming or serious injuries, but not to hold back. He wanted to see what his new team were capable of.

Kyle took his place at the centre of the platform so he could observe all the participants and reach them easily. Today he wore a thin t-shirt and shorts which revealed yet more ridiculous tattoos plastered across his legs. He gave a whistle which was the indication to begin. Nate had barely turned his head from the platform when he felt Jin's shoulder slam into him. He landed hard on his back which knocked the wind out of him. He looked up in a daze, the point of Jin's katana just centimetres from his face. "Dead." he smiled.

"Great," Nate wheezed getting back to his feet. Jin took a few steps back and allowed Nate to catch his breath.

"You ready?" he asked once his opponent had stopped hyperventilating. Nate raised his sword and nodded. He would not allow himself to go down again so easily. Against Marcus' advice, Nate had abandoned his use of a shield late in their training. He found it difficult to move when his left side was being weighed down and instead preferred a free hand which in some cases could do much more.

He hoped this would allow him more manoeuvrability and speed against heavily armed opponents such as Jin, whose armour consisted of heavy iron plates tied together. Unfortunately for Nate, his opponent was not only far fitter and more used to fighting in heavy armour, but it was far more flexible than one would expect. He easily dodged Nate's slow thrusts and slashes and each time counterattacked with the speed and ferocity of a viper. Nate was barely able to parry one strike before another came from the other direction. The force of each blow against his sword sent jarring pain up through his wrist and into his arm and shoulder. *Perhaps a shield would be helpful after all,* he thought, grimacing as another shockwave of pain caused his arm to spasm.

Despite their duel having only lasted for a maximum of two minutes Nate was already out of breath, sweat was dripping from his hair and nose and his ability to respond to Jin's attacks was rapidly deteriorating. In only a handful more strikes Jin had put Nate on the ground once more, a bruised chin his only reward where Jin's fist had brushed against him.

Despite being in the dirt again, Nate was still hopeful that he would be able to get the advantage in a prolonged fight. Surely even the best swordsman could not fight for longer than a few minutes at a time in such heavy armour, all the while under the boiling sun. He looked up at Jin, expecting him to be reaching the point of exhaustion but was horrified to see he had literally not even broken a sweat.

"You're taking it easy on me," he accused. Jin planted his katana in the ground and leaned his elbow upon the pommel, his bright red armour doing a great job at making Nate think for a moment he had been hurt far worse than was the case.

"You want me to fight you for real?" Jin smiled mischievously. Nate pulled himself up, as even if he was already getting his arse kicked, he did not appreciate Jin holding back. It made him feel like his opponent did not take him seriously, which to be honest, he did not. "Ok," Jin shrugged as he freed his katana from the ground. Taking a few steps forward he waited for Nate to be ready before launching into another rapid succession of strikes.

True to his word Jin did not hold back, so much so Nate was afraid that he was genuinely trying to kill him. The scraping and clanging of metal against metal and their grunts of exertion quickly overtook those of the sparring partners around them. Nevertheless, despite Jin's obvious skill, Nate finally felt he was getting somewhere. He had managed to land two glancing hits, once on Jin's shoulder, the other across his thigh. Although they did little more than cause him to drop back a few steps, they were victories to Nate.

Overconfidence then began to take hold. Believing his opponent to be vulnerable, he began leaving himself more open, taking longer, more obvious swings and attack patterns. Jin waited for the right moment when Nate tried swinging hard from the left and blocked the hit, the force of which sent shockwaves through them both. Recovering more quickly, Jin pulled his blade downwards, catching Nate's hanging left arm. There was a flash of blood and a shout of pain as Nate leapt back cradling his arm, his sword now abandoned on the ground.

The cut was not deep but stretched from the fleshy part of his palm below the thumb, six inches up his arm and was already gushing blood. The pain was like nothing Nate had ever experienced before. Sure, he had occasionally cut himself while shaving or trying to get through a solid chocolate bar he had left in the fridge for a few days, but nothing like this. His whole arm burned as he had expected it to the previous night when he had been messing around with fireballs and the metallic smell of blood was so strong, he could taste it in the back of his throat making him want to be sick.

He immediately called for Kyle who came running over to examine the wound. Taking hold of his arm far less gently than he would have liked, Kyle turned it from one side to the other before offering his diagnosis. "It's not too bad, you'll be ok for now."

"What?!" Nate practically squealed as he fought back tears of pain through gritted teeth. Kyle looked at him with surprisingly unsympathetic and cold eyes.

"You can still fight," was all he said before turning back towards the platform. The sheer callousness of Kyle's words set a fire in Nate's stomach. He angrily snatched up his sword and before Jin had signalled that he was ready, began swinging. He kept his injured arm close to his body, but this only served to throw him off balance and make him less agile.

The fight was now heavily in Jin's favour, not that Nate had had any real chance of winning previously, mind you. Jin casually blocked or dodged each increasingly frustrated and erratic blow, knowing time would do the rest for him. Sure enough, after a few more minutes the colour had drained from Nate's face, his entire lower body painted a thick, crimson red. The fight ended with one last desperate lunge which Jin dodged easily, grabbing hold of Nate's wrist, and pulling him to the ground.

Finally admitting defeat, Nate lay there breathing heavily, the pain in his arm having multiplied tenfold. At last, Kyle knelt beside him, placing his hand gently upon the injury, to which Nate responded with a whimper. In barely a second the wound was gone in the soothing blue glow Nate had become, in his own opinion, too familiar with. Nate tried to thank him but was too exhausted.

"You did well, you almost got me a few times, and I haven't seen many people fight like you did with such a wound, I'm impressed," Jin praised Nate as he helped him to his feet. Certain he was only trying to be nice and was talking out of his arse, Nate appreciated it all the same.

"Thank you," was all he could manage as the pair rested for a while. It was clear neither of them would gain anything from continued sparring and so they talked instead as they had not had the chance to do so the night before.

Nate learned that Jin had lived not in feudal Japan at all, but instead in a modern world like his own. Apparently, he had been an office worker during the early 1990s for a small tech company in Kyoto when a superbug had wiped out large swathes of Europe and Asia. He had been one of the unfortunate victims. His obsession with samurai came from his father, who had told him stories of his ancestors who had been important figures and respected warriors during Japan's many civil wars. As soon as Jin had found himself in Purgatory, he set out to fulfil his childhood dream of becoming the kind of man his father would tell him stories about.

By the time their slot was up Nate felt much better. There was not so much as a scar to indicate he had been wounded and Kyle's spell must have replaced his lost blood too because the colour had come back to his face, and he no longer felt dizzy or sick. Marcus, who claimed to have won his own private competition with Joel, something which Joel loudly dismissed, ordered them all to switch partners.

As Nate was about to move on Jin clasped his arm and shook it. "It was good to meet you, I look forward to fighting by your side." Nate was not expecting such friendliness from the man who had spent the morning kicking his arse and blushed at the compliment.

"You too," he smiled back before moving on, hoping his next opponent would be easier. His next opponent was Joel.

Nate's other fights went about as well as he could have expected. He was eating dirt in record time when facing Joel, while Said and Leo had enjoyed tormenting him, like a cat with its food. They would leave themselves apparently open and then bring a fist or knee up quickly to meet any part of Nate which was vulnerable.

It was all in good fun though, and not once did Nate get the feeling that his new comrades were brutish or bullies as Barrett had been, this was just their chance to show off and they would for all they were worth. In fact, Leo had been overly apologetic, saying sorry every time he landed a strike which got so annoying Nate had to practically beg him to stop and wondered how such a person could have the stomach for the mercenary trade.

Nate's duel with Cassandra had been the worst. He had been practically drooling over her exposed thighs when she responded with a roundhouse kick to the head which almost removed his brain via his ears. Finally, he moved on to face Chen. *At last, someone I can beat,* Nate thought as he rubbed his aching head.

Nate had never seen Chen fight before; he knew she had been on multiple expeditions and so could evidently hold her own. But looking at her, barely standing as high as his chest, with her dainty figure she seemed as fragile as a porcelain doll. Not that it would convince Nate to go easy on her, he had too much pent-up frustration at being beaten so easily in his other fights. Plus, they had both been threatening to kick each other's heads in for months, and now they could finally give it a go.

Chen was twirling a spear in one hand while the other held a round shield, large enough to cover her torso by her side. She grinned menacingly as Nate dragged himself over, still partly dazed. "You want a fight, or would you rather perv at my legs instead?" Chen taunted, pretending to lift her skirt. Her own armour was the same set she used for guard duty, a polished steel breastplate with matching greaves, gauntlets, and leather boots, with a full leather set underneath for extra protection.

However, she had decided to forgo the steel gauntlets and greaves which lay on the ground a few feet away. The combination of the day's heat and vigorous training were causing her to sweat, weakening her grip on her spear. The last thing she wanted was to be the silly girl who could not even keep hold of her weapon the day before the expedition.

"I don't think it would be fair to call this a fight," Nate retorted with an air of arrogance, certain he would have no trouble winning at all. Chen ran her tongue along the edges of her teeth playfully, she had been waiting for this opportunity for months. "C'mon then," Nate shrugged, "I promise not to hurt you too badly." Chen could not help but giggle; the look on Nate's face when she had his head under her boot with a mouthful of dirt would be downright delightful.

The two sparred rather casually at first. Chen would launch probing strikes with her spear from a distance, keeping Nate from being able to use his sword. She wanted to tire him out while convincing him even further that if he could just get close enough, he would have her. Nate meanwhile was supremely proud of himself, deflecting what he thought to be concentrated efforts to bring him down and he looked for a way to get around the spear and bring the fight to a close.

Suddenly, he found one. Having deflected Chen's spear with a strong parry which sent the head swinging far to his left he sprinted forwards. Chen would have nowhere near enough time to bring the spear back down and reposition before he was too close.

That was the plan anyway. What happened was what Chen had intended all along. Rather than trying to fight against the spear, she used its momentum and spun in a full circle. Keeping her body close to the ground, the shaft of the spear had come around and swept Nate off his feet before he had taken more than a single step towards her. He came down with a crash kicking up a dust cloud which settled gently back down on his face and hair like a layer of fresh snow. He coughed and spluttered as some of the dust entered his lungs while Chen simply laughed.

"Oh, I'm so glad you're taking it easy on me," she mocked. Nate sat up, spitting a mixture of saliva and gritty dust onto the ground. He did not bother with a response as he knew anything he said would certainly be used against him in future, especially if he lost again.

Chen, however, was having a grand time. She unwound the straps which kept her shield fixed to her hand and placed it on top of her already discarded equipment. Now armed only with her spear and no other means of protection, Nate assumed correctly that this was another effort to taunt him. This time he would be careful, analyse Chen's moves and only strike when he was confident it was not a trap. Chen was not thinking strategy at all, she did not feel she needed to, she was just focused on having a good time and reminding Nate of his place in the process.

Without her shield Chen's attacks were different; gripping the spear with both hands she would use each end as a weapon. While Nate worried about the bladed end which swung and lunged at his body, he would quickly be reminded of the other by a sharp whack to the side of the head or back of the legs which left a horrid, lingering, stinging sensation.

Every step he took, every swing, Chen seemed to have already seen in her mind and planned for, rewarding him with a smack from her spear for his efforts. Evidently, his current strategy was not working, he would need to think of something else. Then it hit him, the edge of the spear that is, catching his left ear leaving a shallow cut along the lobe. He ignored the pain, however, and waited for Chen's next strike, when he finally had half an idea.

The spear came aimed straight at his abdomen. Instead of parrying it which would have just led to another strike from its wielder, he struck the head of the spear for all he was worth. The wood splintered and the head snapped free from the body. While Chen was still in shock at the destruction of her favourite spear, Nate grabbed what was now just a stick still grasped firmly in her hand.

Pulling hard, Chen stumbled forwards – why she did not just let go of the spear neither of them would ever know. Nate quickly brought his arm around and caught her on the chin with his bicep. The top half of her body fell back while her legs continued moving. There was a loud crunch as steel met earth and Nate moved quickly to secure his victory. He spun around and brought down his sword arm to where he expected Chen to still be lying.

As Chen fell, she foresaw a future where Nate would for the rest of time tell the story of how he defeated her with ease, how she was just a weak little girl who stood no chance against him. This could not happen. She had barely touched the ground before she had rolled away and pulled free the knife from her belt. Usually, it was concealed by her shield and had still gone unnoticed by Nate. With her other hand, she retrieved the head of her spear and jumped up just in time to catch Nate's sword against her dagger.

Nate was beyond surprised to see how quickly Chen had moved and was even more surprised to find the tip of the spear being pressed against his side. Their faces were only inches away from one another, separated by their crossed blades. Chen smirked and blew him a kiss before pushing away his sword and sweeping his legs from under him with a powerful kick. Before he could recover, she placed her boot on his head and pushed him further into the dirt. Nate looked up at her with defeated eyes and stopped struggling, his body limp in surrender.

Chen smiled. She had been right, the look on his face was delicious. As if on cue, Marcus called their training to an end. He had seen enough and was happy that his party were more than prepared for anything they may have to face on their mission. Nate was still useless, but that had been expected, he had spirit at least. If Marcus could rely on the rest of the team to keep themselves alive, he could keep an eye on Nate. Chen helped her embarrassed roommate to his feet.

"Loser buys the rounds tonight," she said pushing him away playfully. Nate looked at his feet, he could not believe he'd lost every single fight – hopefully, alcohol would numb some of the pain, although despite getting his arse kicked, he had enjoyed himself. It was certainly a nice change of pace from having orders barked at him by Marcus from dawn till dusk.

Marcus once again made them all gather at the foot of the platform and issued his latest orders. "Well done everyone, I think it's safe to say we have a strong team here. Now, go and get some rest, we will meet at the main gate at five tomorrow morning, make sure you are all fully prepared." There were a few groans at such an early start, but nobody was bothered enough to officially protest, they were getting paid enough after all. They were then dismissed, and Nate climbed the platform to speak with Marcus.

"Up for a drink?" he asked. Marcus shook his head and Nate was amazed. This was the first time Marcus had ever rejected the offer to get absolutely plastered.

"I've got way too much to worry about".

"That's the point," Nate laughed. Marcus had to try exceedingly hard to control himself but in the end was successful in avoiding a night he knew he would regret the next day.

"I'm going home for some food and then to bed, you should all do the same," he said loudly enough so that any stragglers could hear him.

"Not my choice I'm afraid, I broke the lady's spear, so I owe her a drink at least," Nate said as Chen approached. She thumped him hard on the arm.

"You owe me more than one." Marcus simply sighed, he knew better than anyone that keeping a soldier away from drink was a herculean task, no matter what army he belonged to.

"Just make sure you're there tomorrow, both of you," he said wagging his finger and shooting Chen a suspicious look. Chen was not sure what she had done to warrant this but decided to ignore it – once they were out of the sight and safety of the city, she would show Marcus what a valuable companion she was.

"Here we are, as promised," Nate said as he set down the two drinks. One mead for him, a beer for Chen, who gulped down most of it before Nate had even sat down. She was left with a moustache of foam which she wiped away on her sleeve. The two had been home already, and had scrubbed away the sweat and grime they had accumulated while training and put on fresh clothes. They now sat on the first floor of The Hovel overlooking the floor below, the mouth-watering scent of roasting beef wafting its way up through the building from the firepit.

"So, you excited for your first real mission?" asked Chen. Nate raised his eyebrow.

"I have already been on one you know. It was pretty intense too."

Chen scoffed and rolled her eyes so hard they almost left her skull.

"What?" Nate said, hurt that his contribution to the battle at the smuggler's camp was not being taken seriously.

"Oh please," Chen giggled, "You went out there with Ardell, that's not a mission, that's work experience where you sit back and watch a real warrior." Nate was silent as he leaned back in his chair and took a sip of his drink while he contemplated Chen's words.

"She was incredible, I have to admit."

"I know!" Chen gasped excitedly as if she were a teenage girl discussing the members of her favourite boyband, catching Nate off guard.

"You've seen her fight before?" he asked. Chen shook her head in disappointment.

"No, but I've seen her train with her bodyguards. She does it at night when there is nobody around to watch, but I just so happened to be patrolling the fort one night and I saw her in the courtyard. She fought all of them at once, they didn't so much as scratch her."

"I can see someone is a fan," Nate grinned over the edge of his mug as he brought it to his lips once again. Chen replied with a groan which indicated the person she was talking to was a clueless idiot, in this case a fair assumption.

"Have you seen any other female captains around, even heard their names mentioned, what about generals?" she asked with more anger in her voice than she intended. Nate did not notice; however, he was so used to being spoken at in angry tones they barely registered anymore. But he had to admit Chen had a point, Ardell was the only woman he knew of with any real authority.

"Women are looked down upon so much by the Citadel it's a joke. Sure, there are no laws preventing us from doing whatever a man can do, but if one of us wants to be a captain or anything remotely political or powerful you can guarantee it won't happen."

"So how did Ardell get where she is?" Nate asked not entirely believing Chen's tale of systematic oppression. "The other captains and lords respect her from what I've heard." Chen raised her eyebrows as if to ask, *Are you an idiot?*

"Can you imagine what would happen if someone tried to cheat Ardell out of a promotion she earned? Anyway, I heard Grand Admiral Lee appointed her to the position personally."

"Makes sense," Nate admitted as he remembered with vivid detail Ardell cutting her way through a small army as if they were made of paper. "Hold on," he said swallowing a mouthful before pushing his mug towards Chen, as he still could not finish a whole one yet.

"What happened to the whole 'ooh violence is bad; ooh I hate war' crap thing?" It was a fair point, one moment Chen was spouting her hatred for the bloodshed that dominated every part of this world, and the next she was signing up for an expedition and gushing over someone whom Nate considered to be an unhinged killer. Chen folded her arms, but not before downing the rest of Nate's drink and shrugged as if to say she needed no explanation.

"A girl's got to make a living somehow."

Nate smirked as he realised Chen was not at all as complex as she pretended to be. In the end, she was the same as everyone else, willing to do whatever it took to keep her purse from running dry. He joined her in folding his arms and staring out over the balcony at the patrons below. Until now he could only imagine the kind of stories they could tell. Hopefully soon, he would have some of his own and would no longer feel so out of place, still like the boy who dropped out of the sky one day into a world unknown.

After a brief silence, Nate looked at Chen, her shiny black hair resting comfortably on her shoulders, while her bright eyes scanned the room below as she unconsciously bit her lip. She did that when lost in thought. It occurred most often when she was concentrating on her books or pretending to listen to whatever nonsense Nate was spouting that day. "I'm glad you're coming with us," he said at last. Chen's attention was immediately caught.

"You need someone to make sure you survive till the end," but her words were softer, less toxic than her usual jibes and she quickly turned her face back to the floor below, praying Nate did not notice her blushing cheeks.

Nate could hardly sleep that night due to constant worry about not only what they might find outside the city, lurking in the forests and untravelled paths of the world, but also about his own ability and whether he would be a functioning member of the team. The last thing he wanted was to get someone hurt or killed because they were having to babysit him. Once he had managed to shake these thoughts and drift off, he was plagued with nightmares.

He saw the face of the woman whom he had put an arrow through in the battle a few nights ago. He saw her writhing on the ground, coughing blood, begging for help that would never come. He would wake sweaty and shaking, expecting some vengeful apparition to be waiting for him, but one never met him in his waking. Only the soft glow of the dying fire lit that evening.

After three repeats of this cycle, the sun was beginning to brighten and probing rays of light slowly worked their way through the room. Nate watched them grow until they were shining directly upon Chen's body, who, wrapped in her duvet, was still dead to the world. Her hair was a mess, stuck to her face and sticking out at multiple angles, her nose squashed against her pillow.

Nate had meant what he said, having Chen along for the mission would make the whole ordeal much easier. She was strong, much stronger than she looked, but more than anything she was dependable and loyal. Nate felt lucky to count her as a friend. Why that had caused her to blush so much he had no idea.

Anyway, he had better get moving otherwise there would be hell to pay. Turning up late on the first day of your first mission was not how anyone wanted to start their career. He drew himself a bath as quietly as he could; there was no reason Chen needed to be awake for this, he would rouse her later once he was safely clothed. Of course, in accordance with sod's law, Chen woke up just as Nate was sliding himself into the steaming water and got a full view of the moon.

"Christ, I didn't need to see that first thing in the morning," she groaned through bleary eyes crusty with sleep. Nate practically cannonballed into the bath at the sound of her voice, sending water spilling over the sides and onto the floor. Chen made nothing more of it, she was still far more comfortable with their living arrangement than Nate. Spending a year posted on the edge of the known world, surrounded by ice, and sharing a room with fifteen other people would do that.

She made her way over to the fire and stoked it back to life so she could make tea and porridge. Catching herself in the mirror she squinted and pawed at her face before turning to Nate.

"Don't take too long, I look even worse than you for once."

They ate a double helping of porridge topped with blueberries and what Chen called a hujo – a soft, round, red fruit about the size of an orange but which had its own unique sour taste. Nate was not a fan, but Chen insisted he eat it for its slow-release energy that would keep him going until the end of the day if necessary. Once breakfast was concluded they rushed to don their armour and double checked they had everything they needed for the mission as they had no idea when they would be back.

Chen was instrumental in helping Nate with his preparation, telling him what to pack and what could not go with them. To his dismay she would not allow him more than two pairs of spare underwear, her logic being if he couldn't kill something with it or eat it, it was not necessary. Mostly, their packs consisted of spare multi-purpose tools such as knives or small hammers, non-perishable food, a sponge for cleaning their armour and weapons, and lastly, a map just in case they got lost. Nate grunted as he lifted the heavy pack onto his shoulders before helping Chen with hers.

"I hope we don't have to carry these things the whole way," he complained.

"That's up to Marcus, hopefully, we won't be walking," Chen replied as they gave one last look at the barracks, double-checking they had everything they needed before locking the door, their return not guaranteed.

The rest of the party were already assembled at the Gate when Nate and Chen arrived. Marcus was making final preparations, loading food, weapons and other supplies onto a wagon which was drawn by two gorgeous chestnut-brown horses.

Joel was busy sharpening his longsword on a whetstone, while Cassandra was repeatedly drawing back on her bowstring, testing the tautness. Jin, Leo, and Said were all hard at work carrying yet more supplies, loading them into the back of the wagon which reminded Nate of the wagons from old western films, except the fabric acting as a roof was a camouflaged green rather than white.

Marcus looked glum and serious as Chen and Nate neared – he had never led an expedition before, and the stress was already getting to him. He gave them a glance that lasted barely a second before turning his attention to a hastily scrawled checklist on a crumpled and torn piece of parchment. "Chuck your bags in the wagon, we will be moving soon."

The pair breathed a sigh of relief and hauled their heavy packs from their shoulders and onto the wagon's wooden base. For a mission where they were only pretending to be merchants, Marcus was taking no chances. The wagon was nearly full of neatly arranged sacks and crates, mostly containing confiscated goods which Ardell had permitted be requisitioned for the mission.

Hidden amidst the junk were the party's real equipment, tools which would ensure the success of the mission and hopefully keep them all alive long enough to claim their reward at the end. After pushing their packs towards the front of the wagon Nate hoisted himself up and was about to take a seat and enjoy the ride when a meaty hand closed around his ankle.

"What are you doing?" Marcus asked, genuinely puzzled. "We're walking."

"Ugh, you've got to be kidding me," Chen moaned, slumping her shoulders, and tilting her head back like a stroppy teenager. Nate jumped down and looked to where he had left Bob tied to a post nearby. Marcus read his mind and instantly killed the thought before Nate could voice it.

"No horses either, we're walking." Turning his back to indicate this was not up for debate he addressed the others, who had only just finished their preparations and were catching their breath.

"Right, that's it, everyone, let's get moving. Nate, you come up here with me. Cassandra, Jin you take the left flank. Joel, Chen you take the right. Leo, Said cover the rear. Kyle, take the reins and try not to set anything on fire."

There was a laugh as everyone got into their respective positions. Nate joined Marcus at the front about fifteen steps ahead of the horses. Marcus was in his full legionnaire attire including his large shield emblazoned with four golden wings sprouting from the centre on a red background and the letters S.P.Q.R. written at the bottom.

"Isn't that going to be annoying?" Nate asked.

Marcus took a long look at his shield and smiled before answering. "This thing has saved my life more times than I can remember. As long as it's by my side, nothing can kill me," he said with a mischievous smile. Marcus had strategically placed Nate at the front of the formation so he could keep an eye on him. It was also statistically the safest place for him to be as it was uncommon for bandits or monsters to attack head-on, preferring flanking attacks from the concealment of the trees instead.

It would still take them a few days to reach the outermost gate, but Marcus wanted them marching in proper formation the whole way. That way, by the time they left the city for good, they would already be familiar with it and their expected roles. Nate threw Chen a final smile and thumbs up to which she responded with a sullen look – she was going to have blisters on her feet by the end of the day and she was not looking forward to it. Dark clouds suddenly closed ranks over the sun and a light rain began to fall. "Great," Chen sighed as Marcus signalled for them to move on.

A few days and popped blisters later, the party arrived at the huge iron gate separating them from the rest of the world. For the rest of the group, this moment was nothing special, they had been stood in this same spot hundreds of times before. But for Nate, he could not help but feel nervous butterflies in the pit of his stomach. Kyle pulled the horses to a stop while Marcus showed the guard a permit, written and signed by Ardell herself stating that they were merchants journeying east.

Kyle was the only one who had not yet had to walk a single step of the journey and was the target of much jealousy from the rest of the group who had sore feet and aching legs. Yet there was no chance to voice their displeasure as Marcus returned a few moments later, followed by the loud scraping of the heavy portcullis being raised. Nate once again saw the large town stretching well into the distance. This time, however, he would be going through it rather than around before finding himself on the quiet, dangerous roads which would lead them to their destination of Cotts.

But before they set off, Marcus retreated to the back of the caravan and emerged a few moments later with something long and wrapped in brown cloth. He approached Nate and offered it to him. Nate took it gingerly, looking confused. The confusion did not last long, however, as Nate recognised the familiar shape and weight of a sword.

The wrappings fell away, and Nate was left holding a blade fresh from the forge, its edge razor-sharp and gleaming in the sunlight.

It was a kopis, a Greek short-sword, unmistakable for its broad, arched body which began to curve downwards slightly halfway along the blade. Its grip was polished wood, wrapped in leather. The guard was thin steel that arched downwards on one side to form a handguard, almost like a cutlass as the pommel was a bronze upwards arch that ended in a blunt point on the same side, which glittered brilliantly as the light caught it.

"For you." Marcus smiled. "Joel and I thought you deserved a proper weapon to celebrate your first expedition instead of that old thing," he said pointing to the sword the army had issued strapped to Nate's belt. All Nate could do was gasp and admire what was beyond doubt the most beautiful gift he had ever received. He knew this would have set them both back no small amount, a sword like this would not have been cheap.

He clasped Marcus' hand firmly and thanked him while also giving Joel a thankful nod which he returned with a proud smile. "Just try not to lose it," Marcus joked as he retook his position at the head of the formation and ordered them all to continue moving.

Nate quickly broke rank to deposit his old sword in the wagon while attaching the new one to his side. He felt like a new man entirely, just from this small change. No longer did he feel like a hanger-on or liability, sponging off the success of others. No, he felt part of this team, like he was valued, wanted even. He did not stop smiling even as the safety of the city melted behind them and the open road lay ahead.

Chapter 15

The Emperor finished the letter and folded it neatly before passing it to Nestor to be immediately archived. Adeneus had sent an update of his progress on the Phoenix project but had evidently done so in a fit of hysteria. Most of the letter had been unintelligible to anyone without knowledge of advanced theoretical magical principles.

Luckily, the Emperor had got the gist of it. While it had been extremely difficult at first, Adeneus had confirmed the possibility for a human to control not just one, but dozens, if not more Husks telepathically at once. Further tests and therefore funds and materials would need to be provided by the Imperial treasury first, however. There were mixed reactions from the Congregation as the Emperor relayed the contents of the letter.

Elias was the most vocal in opposition, twirling his moustache as he decried Adeneus' attempts to control the physical embodiment of sin, claiming it to be blasphemous and against the principles of the Seeker order. Sir Bryce was also disturbed by the news, although more out of fear for his own position than any theological concerns. If an army of Husks could be controlled by just a handful of men, what need would the Emperor have for him, for the armies he had spent centuries drilling into the ultimate fighting force?

Rohm, however, was more optimistic about these developments. He cared little for the notion of controlling armies from afar but was supremely interested in other potential uses for this newly discovered magic, especially in his own field of espionage. Good spies were both expensive and hard to replace, but if one had the ability to listen in on a conversation half the world away with one's own ears, the very thought made him lick his lips.

Nestor meanwhile was on the fence about the whole thing. He agreed that if a great threat was coming, having an army of expendable killing machines would potentially save millions of lives. Where his reservations lay, however, was the question of who would be trusted to control these armies, and what would happen if they decided to turn against the Imperium.

Only Sarah did not voice her opinion. She sat poised and elegant as usual on her pristine white throne, but her eyes were fixed on the far wall, her mind still wading through the hurt and the pain her husband had caused her at their last meeting. The voices of the Congregation mixed into one low drone until at last she was brought back to attention by the Emperor repeating her name. She blinked slowly as if having been woken from a deep slumber and looked around the room to see all eyes were on her. She looked lastly at the Emperor.

She had only recently returned from her tour of the countryside, visiting those villages which had refused to cast votes in the last election. The Emperor had planned to go with her, but she had left without him a day early. Overall, the trip had been an unparalleled success. All five of the villages she had planned to visit, the sixth having been sacked by bandits just a few days prior to her arrival, had welcomed her with jubilation. Word of her kindness and sympathy had spread across the country, and it seemed a new era of good relations between the crown and its poorer subjects had begun.

Yet for weeks she had avoided her husband at all costs. Locking her bedroom door at night, taking alternate routes home, even changing the time of her classes at the last minute much to the anger of her students. But now she was trapped, bound by obligation to attend whenever the Righteous Congregation was called. A part of her wondered if it had been the Emperor's last-ditch effort to draw her out, so he might see her once more and try to apologise for what he had done.

"I'm sorry, I was miles away," she smiled sweetly, instantly melting the heart of every man in the room, except for Elias of course who glared at her disapprovingly. If there was but one benefit to coming to these meetings once again it was just to see the look of pure disgust on Elias' face each time she took her throne at the head of the table and he was forced to address her, a woman, as his superior.

"Please do not feel you need to apologise, your majesty," Rohm soothed as he intertwined his fat, sausage-like fingers and rested his hands on his belly. "I too would rather be sat in one of my orchards on the coast, sipping wine in the sun."

"Well, I'm sure we could arrange someone to take your place my Lord, I would hate for the affairs of the realm to keep you from your wine and sandy beaches," the Emperor said, drumming his fingers on the table. Rohm chuckled softly which sent ripples through his chins, which sat like rice paddies on a steep slope.

"Oh, I'm far too invested to quit now your Holiness," he replied.

The Emperor turned his attention back to his wife.

"We would like to know your opinion on the matter, of turning Husks into soldiers and forming an army for the defence of the realm."

He repeated the most vital parts of the letter, so Sarah was up to speed. The more he read, the more Sarah's brow creased with concern. Once the Emperor had finished Sarah looked at her hands, her nails a ruby red and glossy after a morning of being pampered in preparation for this very event, the injuries she had sustained at their last meeting having long since vanished.

Each man waited patiently for her response, all hoping she would be in favour of their own point of view. Even Elias dared to hope that for once the two might agree on something.

"I think whoever you choose to control this army needs to be unquestioningly loyal, the last thing we need is to be betrayed by our own in the midst of a crisis."

Rohm smiled to himself; the Empress had never once been content with playing the part of the beautiful but dim-witted wife of a powerful man, unlike the other noble ladies whose only concerns were the latest fashion trends and how much allowance they received. She had chosen her answer carefully, to appeal to the greatest number of those around the table. She understood that even the wife of the Emperor needed allies.

"I agree," the Emperor nodded, "which is why I was considering Sir Bryce, the leader of the Chosen; Phalon, and a handful of nominees from each." Sir Bryce breathed a sigh of relief and was about to thank the Emperor for his generosity and trust before Sarah cut in.

"From what I recall, you mentioned Adeneus believed strong psychic links were required for reliable control of the Husks?"

"Yes, what of it?" the Emperor asked. He was not well educated in magic and found the specifics both boring and overcomplicated. Sarah looked over at Sir Bryce.

"My apologies Sir Bryce, I know your loyalty to his Holiness and I, and the Imperium itself is unwavering. I am simply concerned that as you have not studied arcane arts, you may not have the necessary ability to control such an army. I believe only an extremely powerful sorcerer can perform such a deed."

Once again Sir Bryce's heart sank, but Sarah was right. His skill in battle had cost any aptitude in magic whatsoever, he could not even cast the simplest of healing spells.

Elias could not resist a jibe. "I thought your area of expertise was insects your majesty, I did not realise you were also an expert on magic."

Sarah clenched her fists beneath the table and gritted her teeth, her jaw becoming visibly tense. She composed herself and smiled kindly, she would not allow Elias to coax her into another outburst so easily.

"Reptiles my Lord, but luckily even a novice at the university could tell you powerful spells require powerful casters. But do not fret, I am sure when some peasants need burning alive you will be able to offer us some expert insight."

This time it was Elias who clenched his jaw in anger, but he did his best to remain calm. Sarah might have a sharp tongue, but he had the Order of the Seekers and divine authority at his back. It was not worth losing his patience and drawing the newfound anger of the Emperor over a trumped-up whore, no matter how many titles or accolades she awarded herself.

The Emperor intervened before the two could continue their war of words. "Her majesty speaks sense, fine. We shall offer this opportunity to the most talented minds of the Imperial University with titles and wealth for those who take part and succeed."

"And what if there are no volunteers?" Rohm suggested, his booming voice reverberating from the stone walls as if the room itself were presenting the question. It was Elias who answered, smiling cruelly, and staring directly into Sarah's viperous eyes as he did so.

"Then I suppose that is where my expertise will come in handy."

The Emperor returned to drumming his fingers along the table, the deep crevasse where he had struck it in anger at the previous meeting still present. It ran along the entire length of the table, like a canyon carved into the earth from a now long-extinct river. The rest of the room fell silent and waited for him to speak. In the past, he would have sanctioned whatever force Elias had deemed necessary to fulfil his goals. But now, with Sarah beside him, her revulsion at his mere presence palpable, that was no longer an option.

He looked at her, hoping to catch some inclination of the right path in her expression, but she immediately turned her gaze away, still unable to bear looking into his cold, heartless eyes. This was an answer in itself and the Emperor nodded as if he had been posed a question.

"It will be volunteers only, if none or too few come forward…we will look for peaceful alternatives. We cannot just experiment on our people without their consent."

He turned again to Sarah and saw it. It only lasted a second and was almost concealed behind the curtains of her blonde hair. But it was there, the corner of her mouth twisted into a smile before quickly fading away. It was then the Emperor knew; she was not lost to him yet.

Chapter 16

Nate knew perfectly well what he was leaving behind. A warm bed, decent food, baths, not having to worry about his head being ripped from his body at any moment. What lay ahead of him, however, was a complete unknown. The vast corridor of buildings that signalled the final stretch towards the city of Tinelia had melted away into the horizon. He was now left with nothing but a dark, dense forest on either side of a well-travelled dirt road.

In keeping with the theme, the road into Tinelia was huge, easily as wide as a motorway. But this had narrowed the further they ventured from home until it was little more than a countryside path. The wagon was only just wide enough to avoid slipping into the ditches on either side. Those guarding the flanks, however, were forced to trudge through brambles and mud, all the while keeping their eyes and ears out for any sign of danger.

Their destination of Cotts would mean passing by the city of Sundered Crown, so named for the battle which took place there between the ancient Queen Sabel and the united tribal kingdoms. Legend stated that Sabel had challenged the twelve tribal kings to a duel and slain them all. The crown of the alliance leader, supposedly split in two by her blade, was now on display in the city temple. Other than that, there was nowhere else worth mentioning along their path. They would pass by many small towns and hamlets, but none worthy of more than a passing glance.

The day was warm, and the wind was gentle. The scent of wet grass and pine trees wafted through the air, reminding Nate of times he had gone walking through the woods near to his home before he had died. The forest itself was eerily quiet. Expecting it to be full of birdsong and the various chirps and clicks of insects, the silence filled him with an unease which crawled up his skin. The only sounds Nate could hear were the clinks of armour and the footsteps of the horses and other party members.

For a world meant to be bursting with life, the forest felt dead. Before long they were plunged into the same darkness as during their excursion against the smuggler camp. Looking up Nate could see the sun desperately trying to break through the leafy canopy which blanketed the sky, with little success.

"Keep your eyes ahead, Nate," Marcus said in a serious tone. They might have only just left the outer limits of the city but that by no means meant they were safe.

"Sorry," Nate replied, snapping to. He tried to focus on the road, which held the scars of countless similar expeditions. Deep ruts where wheels and feet alike had trodden over the millennia guided their way. Occasionally they would see discarded items at the roadside, whether abandoned on purpose or left behind as the owners fled in panic no one knew. There were also a dozen or so travellers coming in the opposite direction and the parties would exchange nods and words of greeting as they passed.

The first few hours went by without incident. It was only when Nate was starting to feel more relaxed, his hand no longer itching to reach for his sword, that Marcus ordered them to stop with a raised palm. About thirty meters ahead was a Husk. It was shuffling across the road and had not noticed the party. It wore a robe like Kyle's white priest's robe, yet it was stained with blood.

Marcus looked at Nate. "Do you want this one?" Not long ago Nate would have felt faint at the mere thought of killing. Now, after Marcus' brutal training, and then a further explanation of the origins of Husks, he felt nothing at all as he wet his new blade for the first time. He tossed the corpse into the ditch at the roadside and took his position beside Marcus, who was impressed but trying not to show it. "At least you can say you didn't come back from this empty-handed now," Marcus joked as they continued marching. Nate nodded, with a swing of his sword – his vault at the bank had got just a little bit more crowded.

The solitary Husk attempting to answer the age-old question of why it was trying to cross the road was the only excitement the party encountered on their first day. Despite Marcus' strict training regimen, which had resulted in Nate being in the best shape of his life, he was still not used to spending almost the entire day on the move.

His legs ached and his feet were sore. His armour had once again become one with his skin as the sticky heat of the humid forest threatened to boil them alive. He took a sip from his canteen, the now warm water still a blessing as it passed over his parched lips. Surely, they would not have to keep going for much longer.

The sun was fading now and even Marcus looked shattered. His eyes stung from the sweat dripping from his forehead, unsurprising seeing as he was essentially a walking oven plastered in all that metal. His usual strong footsteps were now scraping along the floor as he lacked the energy to lift his feet fully clear of the ground. Yet he was determined to push on, this was his chance to prove to not only Ardell that he was capable and trustworthy, but to himself also.

In the end, Joel had to force Marcus to rest. The sun had almost entirely faded now and was beginning its transition. The forest was pitch black and the party had been relying on Kyle's magic to light their way. Torches would have only added to the still unbearable heat.

As it was too dangerous for anyone to risk opening an inn in the middle of the forest, the party would find no real shelter for a few days at least. However, over the centuries, countless impromptu 'pit-stops' had been formed every few miles, not far from the roadside. They were easy to spot as the trees around them had been felled and a patch of short grass ranging to tens of meters in diameter had been established. Luckily, there was one of these 'pit-stops' nearby and the exhausted party practically collapsed once the caravan had been safely concealed.

Thankfully, the air was beginning to cool as night drew near and a fresh gust of chilled wind washed over their bodies. Joel and Marcus had both walked another mile up the road to check for danger before returning. Somehow looking even more exhausted than before, Marcus rested himself against a tree-stump while the difficult decision was made to light a fire.

All except Kyle kept their distance from the flames, which were small but still too much for them to handle while the air remained hot and heavy. As he had used a spell to summon the fire, it had no effect upon him as he set about cooking his dinner. A roasted squash along with various nuts and small slices of fruit hardly seemed a fitting reward for such a taxing day, but Nate was too tired to give Kyle grief for his culinary preferences.

They then took it in turns to prepare their meals. Joel went last as he kept watch for any nasty surprises coming their way. Nate was ravenous by the time his chicken legs had cooked and he almost choked on the bones as he vacuumed them down. Before leaving the city, Kyle had done the painstaking task of going through everyone's food packs and casting a freezing spell on any meat or other perishables so that they might last longer.

It was not as good as keeping them in a real freezer, but they would last at least until they could buy more. Once they had all gorged themselves Marcus gave Kyle an order that Nate did not understand until he saw him carry it out with his own eyes.

Standing in the very centre of their makeshift camp, Kyle stretched his arm above his head and just as Nate thought he was going to break out into a dance, what appeared to be a fountain of deep blue water erupted from his palm. It rose five meters into the air before raining back down and encircling the camp forming a dome. The water then settled – no longer did it ripple and shimmer, now it was smooth like glass before it vanished entirely.

"What the hell was that?" Nate asked, amazed, as he reached out an arm to feel where the dome had been but found nothing.

"Invisibility barrier," Kyle said as if it were the most normal thing in the world.

"Nobody should be bothering us tonight, but we should set up a watch just in case," Marcus instructed. He tried to take the first shift himself, but Jin, seeing Marcus' sorry state, demanded he take first watch. Without the energy to argue, Marcus wrapped himself in a thin, scratchy blanket and was asleep in seconds.

Kyle also offered to take an extended shift once Jin had finished. Seeing as he had been driving the wagon all day, he was the least exhausted of the group. Perching himself on a tree stump he kept one eye on the road and the other on the spells he was practising to entertain himself.

At first, he tried rapidly growing and controlling the roots of the trees which rose from the ground like veins. However, the furthest he got was sprouting a few extra shoots and leaves. Quickly growing bored he turned his attention to the spell he had been experimenting with for years without an ounce of success. He plucked one of his newly grown leaves from its lifeline and set it on the stump. Holding his hand over it so that the leaf was no longer visible, he began to concentrate hard.

First, he tried all the range of emotions that he hoped would elicit the desired result, then switched to more advanced manipulation of magical energy once that had failed. He had done this routine thousands of times, and yet the result was always the same, and his disappointment was never any less. He lifted his hand away to find the leaf completely unchanged. He had hoped there would be two.

The search for a spell that could endlessly and reliably duplicate objects was the most sought after yet ridiculed field of magic. Alongside teleportation, it had been argued for millennia to be impossible and a waste of time and magic energy. It would have been in the same class as alchemy if that had not already been mastered and formed part of the bedrock of magical theory.

Kyle did not believe his critics, however. Nearly all the magic now taken for granted across the known world was once dismissed as impossible. Now most people could barely live without it. He was determined to be the one to discover the secret of duplication. The fame and fortune that would come from such a discovery would put him on a par with emperors and kings. But that was not his motivation.

Kyle enjoyed magic for its mystery, for the puzzles yet unsolved. He also knew something as powerful as duplication could save countless lives in future. Famines, droughts, shortages of any kind would be a thing of the past. That would be its own reward. For now, however, he would give up. Tonight was evidently not the night he would change the world.

While Kyle carried out his shift the other members of the group either settled down for some much-needed rest or continued eating. Nate found Chen near the edge of camp removing her boots and rubbing the painful sores on her feet. The grass along the outer periphery under the shade of the trees was damp and Chen sighed with relief as the cool sensation met her steaming feet. She curled and uncurled her toes, spreading the water between them. There would be few moments of real comfort on an expedition, so you either had to suck it up or make your own.

"I thought I could smell a dead animal somewhere," Nate teased as he crashed down beside her. He was exhausted, his arms heavy, his legs and feet sore. He was desperate for sleep but the combined excitement of it being his first night outside of the city, and the fear he could be attacked at any moment kept him awake.

"Strong words from the guy who turns our barracks into a gas chamber every time he eats beans," Chen replied. She was exhausted too but was able to summon enough energy into her tone so that it did not sound like she was trying to start an argument. "How did you find your first day then? You're a tried and tested adventurer now," Chen smiled.

They both knew full well their journey so far had been about as stressful or dangerous as a pillow fight. Nate yawned and rubbed his eyes which were beginning to feel like lead. He waved his wrist as if shooing her away.

"Oh, this is easy. I have no idea what everyone keeps fussing about."

Chen had to stop herself from laughing and exhaled loudly through her nose instead.

"Just you wait until you're in a real fight and can't hide half a mile away," Chen grinned. "I've got five gold on you shitting yourself, literally."

Usually, Nate would have brushed off such a comment as a poor attempt at humour. But after seeing how the people here would bet on anything, including how many people an individual would kill in a fight, he was not so sure it was a joke after all. His eyes darted between his companions and wondered who had started it before shrugging and lying his sweaty head on the cool ground.

In the clearing, he could, at last, see the sky, not that there was much to see though. The sun had long since faded and the moon had taken its place. Its ghostly light did little to ward off the darkness, and the party was now glad for the flames of their fire. Nate had barely rested his eyes for a moment when he was being shaken awake by Cassandra.

"Your watch," she grumbled as she released his shoulder from her death grip. Nate lay there for a moment, watching longingly as Cassandra walked away – even in this simple action she was seductive. He had been asleep for at least six hours and the moon was beginning its slow illumination into the brilliant sun.

There was fresh dew on the ground and a thin layer of fog rested at ankle height. It would be about another hour or two before the dawn when Marcus would insist they be on the move. Nate, brushing the sleep from his eyes with the back of his hand, found the stump which marked the edge of their camp. He sat there for a while, playing with his breath that rose like clouds from his mouth as a child would.

He would occasionally rise from his log to exercise his legs and check either way down the road, just to find the same empty grey stretch as always. After the first hour, Nate decided to venture onto the road itself, just for a change of scenery. He passed the borders of the camp and onto the dusty path which crunched beneath his feet.

He looked left, the way they would be heading. The fog was thicker further down and gave the impression that a blanket had been pulled over that part of the world. He sighed and rubbed his arms which were exposed to the cold air and had broken out in goosebumps. He decided to return to his stump and perhaps spend a minute or two by the fire, nobody would notice. But when he turned back to where the camp had been, there was nothing there.

The clearing was visible despite the fog, but the wagon, the fire, his companions – they were nowhere to be seen. Just as he was about to panic, thinking he had been left alone in the woods to die, he remembered the invisibility barrier Kyle had cast the night before. Now he could see, or rather not see, exactly how effective it was. There was not a single shred of evidence anyone had been in the spot for weeks. This made Nate think of all the other clearings they had passed on their journey already, and wonder whether any of them had also been occupied but invisible to their eyes.

It was no longer the pitch blackness of midnight, but Nate stretched out his arms as one would having found themselves in a dark room, desperately searching for a light switch, or at least something solid to cling onto. Planning each step carefully, he slowly edged back towards where the camp had been. He knew nothing of magic and did not know whether he would be able to re-enter the camp once he had exited the barrier. Or if it would electrocute him or better yet, vaporise him.

When he did at last cross the threshold of the barrier there was no warning. No piercing of a veil by his fingertips or sudden violent electrocution as he had feared. Rather simply, one moment he was observing an empty space, unremarkable in every way. The next it was filled with sleeping bodies, the wagon and the small fire which still clung to life.

Luckily, the only soul to observe Nate's song and dance attempt at re-entering the camp was Jin, and Nate did not feel he was the kind to gossip. Rather, he nodded his head in acknowledgement and went back to his unhealthy breakfast of a jam tart and salted beef. Everyone was new once, there was therefore no reason to make Nate feel bad for not knowing the ins and outs of everything there was to know. Nate returned to his tree-stump and remained there until the early morning sun had beaten the shadows into a retreat.

Before long, the various grumblings and movement which indicated the rest of the camp was awake filled the previously still air. It took around ten minutes to pack up their things and get the wagon back on the road. There was an unofficial rule to keep the campsites clean and tidy for the next lot of weary travellers. Marcus did one last check to make sure they had left nothing behind before ordering the party onwards. Nate may have been more alert than the rest of the group having already been awake for his shift, but his legs already ached and there was much walking to do yet.

"How was your first night?" Marcus asked, keeping his eyes firmly planted on the road ahead. Nate ran his hand through his already greasy hair, catching a whiff of his odour gained from yesterday's blistering heat and smoke from the campfire.

"Wasn't too bad. I'd prefer a five-star hotel tonight though if that's not too much trouble."

"I'll see if we can find you a nice bear den," Marcus replied.

The cool morning breeze was bliss as the memory of yesterday's thick air which had stuck in their throats was still fresh in their minds. After an hour, what had started as a single-track road had begun to split off in multiple directions. At one point there were as many as six paths, some wide, others even narrower leading off into the forest which never seemed to end in any direction.

Luckily, Marcus knew the way from memory and was able to lead them on without having to consult his map. The party were making good time. Their muscles were already strengthening from the previous day and their pace was naturally quicker. Their luck would then only continue to improve as the sound of rain lightly drumming against the canopy above turned into a downpour.

It was the closest thing to a bath the party would find in the woods and so nearly all ruffled their hair hoping the rain would wash away at least some of the accumulated grease and grime. They also took to holding out their canteens. Going back to the wagon for water would have broken their formation which Marcus would not allow while they were on the move. The rain then suddenly stopped, as if a great cosmic tap had quickly been shut off just before the party were soaked through entirely. Thankful for the relief the downpour had brought to their hot and aching bodies the group continued, reinvigorated.

There was a bend in the road up ahead which Marcus ordered them all to take cautiously. Slowing to a crawl the party rounded the corner with Nate and Marcus at the head. Everyone assumed Marcus was only being so cautious due to this being his first leadership role. But once they spotted the overturned carriage conveniently blocking the road, they were glad they had not come thundering round the corner for the whole world to hear.

The carriage lay on its side, its wheels facing towards the party. It was not the extravagant kind one would expect royalty to travel in but was small and plain with enough room for two people and a driver. The walls and roof were made from a thin, black material and were dotted with medium-sized holes and tears.

Marcus ordered the group to stay put while he, Nate and Joel investigated. Nate was no expert, but even he knew there was no way the carriage had not been placed there deliberately. Instinctively he prepared to draw his sword at the slightest notice and scanned the forest around them. But the shadows and thick trunks and tangled masses of shrubbery and roots made seeing anything at all a difficult task.

They reached the carriage without issue, although Marcus kept his shield raised higher than usual just in case an arrow came his way. Quietly, he ordered Nate and Joel to round the flanks. The carriage was low enough for him to climb onto the body without issue, and if there was anyone lying in wait on the other side, they would not expect an attack from above.

Nate's heart was pounding so hard his hands were shaking. He dreaded to think what could be waiting to ambush him on the other side of the carriage. At least in the next few seconds, he would not need to worry either way. He drew his sword as silently as possible, although it still made the unmistakable sound of steel being run across leather. Looking to Marcus who replied with a quiet nod, he darted around the corner, the heavy thump of Marcus' steel-clad frame summiting the carriage in his left ear, deathly silence in his right.

To his utmost relief, the only thing waiting for them on the other side was the same dusty, compacted earth of the road.

"Well, that's legitimately disappointing," Joel sighed sheathing his weapon. Nate was about to do the same when he heard the *whoosh* of something moving at great speed, followed by the thud of it striking something solid. All three men looked to see an arrow lodged just centimetres from Marcus' foot where he stood on the carriage, still vibrating vigorously from the force of its impact.

Nate did not need to think about what to do next, his instincts did it for him. He dove back around into the cover of the carriage just as another two arrows thudded into the wood beside him. "You were saying?" Marcus grumbled to Joel as they also took cover. He waved a signal to the wagon which indicated they were under attack. Now Marcus would get to see how well his strategy would work. Kyle, Said and Leo would stay behind and guard the wagon. The rest would come forward to support their allies under fire.

Nate, Marcus, and Joel, now supported by their reinforcements, prepared to move out, but not before Marcus had confirmed what they were up against. Carefully, so as not to catch an arrow in the eye, he peered over the top of the overturned carriage. He feared that their assailants would remain hidden in the trees, content to riddle them with arrows before moving in to pick off the stragglers.

Luckily, however, their foes were not the intelligent kind. Closing in on them were at least a dozen skeletons. Ranging from bleached white to dusty grey the reanimated piles of bones knew nothing but an insatiable urge to kill. Marcus smiled; this was going to be easy. Nate noticed this newfound glee at their situation and asked what was so damn great about getting shot at. "It's just a bunch of bones," Marcus replied, much to the relief of the others who suddenly became less tense. Having no idea what Marcus was on about Nate peered around the corner to see the living dead shuffling towards him.

"Jesus Christ," he gasped, throwing himself back into cover far harder than he intended. Cassandra placed a calming hand on his shoulder, the first nice thing she had done for him since they met.

"It's easy," she reassured him. "They're stupid and one hit is enough to put them down, just keep your eyes open and don't take on more than you can handle, ok?" Nate still had some serious doubts that this was going to be as easy as the others claimed, but he could hardly back out now.

"Ok," he nodded.

"Alright then, let's go," Marcus ordered. The party split left and right around the carriage and sprinted forwards to engage the enemy. Those with shields held them out to protect their torsos, while those without simply had to be more careful. Luckily, there only seemed to be a single skeleton with a bow, the rest were wielding either crude axes or spears which were little more than sharp rocks tied to sticks. Still, they were enough to kill.

While Nate was focusing on the foe nearest to him, a greyish-green skeleton which looked as if it was growing mould, an arrow flew past his head, missing him by inches. Slowing momentarily in shock at avoiding death by such a small margin, Chen raced past him. She went for the same skeleton Nate had been charging at, and with a sweep of her spear, had split it in two. The skeleton became instantly lifeless and reduced to a pile of inanimate bones. Marcus had been less delicate. Aiming to take out their biggest threat, the sole archer, he slammed his shield into it, his body acting as a battering ram.

Splinters of bone flew in all directions as the skeleton shattered like glass. With their main threat gone, the rest of the party could relax a little. Nate was determined to take at least one enemy down, but his companions kept getting in the way. The lightning-fast movements of Chen and Cassandra had all but wiped out the foes on the right flank. Marcus, Joel, and Jin were slower, but had also left little chance for Nate to get involved. Just as it seemed to be over, with Jin pulling his katana free from an enemy's skull, Nate noticed at least four more skeletons emerging from the roadside nearest to him.

One swung at him, its axe slicing through the air beside his left ear. As Nate staggered back, he wondered how a creature with no muscles or brain was able to summon such force. Their faces may have been hollow, their eyes nothing but empty black sockets, their mouths gaping pits. But Nate could still feel their hatred and anger towards the living, radiating from them like heat from a furnace.

Copying Chen's earlier example, Nate swung the edge of his blade against the skeleton's spine. He missed and ended up catching its ribs instead which cracked like plaster at the strength of the blow, collapsing the skeleton entirely. It was strange Nate noted that once a weapon struck one of the skeletons, no matter how lightly, the skeleton would practically explode. Each of its joints suddenly became separated from whatever magic held them together. This indeed made them easy to dispatch as Cassandra had said, and Nate had much fun taking down the other three with little more than half-hearted taps with his sword.

When the battle was over the road looked like a graveyard. Bones in various stages of decay and destruction lay scattered across the area. One skull had even managed to find its way at least three meters up a tree, resting between two branches, missing the lower part of its jaw. "That hit the spot," Cassandra exclaimed happily as she cracked her neck and back. Within half an hour they were all back to marching after clearing away the debris and pushing the carriage into a ditch.

As they resumed their usual task Nate received compliments from just about everybody. Taking on four skeletons alone was no miraculous feat for an experienced warrior, but Nate had done so as a novice and come away without a scratch. Even Cassandra had nodded her approval which left Nate feeling giddy for the remainder of the day.

Nate wanted to know more about the skeletons they had defeated, where they came from and most importantly, how much each was worth. Marcus, with nothing else to do anyway, was happy to educate his young apprentice. As far as anyone knew, skeletons could be one of two things. First, and most likely; they were just people who met an unfortunate end and whose corpses were used by necromancers as labour.

The manipulation of the dead was a taboo school of magic and while not officially outlawed in Tinelia, you would be hard-pressed to find anyone who would openly admit to practising or supporting it. The Imperium took a harsher stance and burned necromancers alive as blasphemers and heretics, which had resulted in an influx into Tinelia. Often, they would take up residence in abandoned mines or villages and continue experimenting.

The other possibility was that they were just another monster sent to test them. Either way, they were worth ten gold at best, but this could fluctuate depending on how many were kicking around at a time. Nate was slightly disappointed; he had hoped they would have bagged him at least a three-figure reward. Now he knew he had barely scraped two digits for his efforts he wondered why he had bothered putting himself in danger to begin with. *Oh well*, he thought, there would be plenty more opportunities to come.

The next few days were a repeat of the first. Hours upon hours of marching in weather which could not seem to make up its mind. One moment it was so hot they could have cooked an egg on one of their breastplates. In others, it was a mix of freezing rain or hail so violent they were forced to halt and take shelter under the trees until the stinging barrage of ice had stopped.

At night those in the group who were not utterly exhausted would sit and chat. The main topics of conversation were past adventures and what they were planning on buying with the pay-out from this one. And of course, the most favoured and unique topic to Gaia; how everyone had ended up there in the first place.

Nate's confession about the bus had gone about as well as he could have hoped, he only got the one snigger from Chen who laughed no matter how many times she heard the story, and an eye-roll from Cassandra as if to say everything about him suddenly made sense. He knew Marcus had died while fighting in Germany during the Roman invasion, and Joel had been aboard the HMA Shropshire which had been sunk by Japan in 1944. Although Joel had never heard of a Mr Hitler.

Everyone else had suffered far less exciting deaths. In fact, Cassandra was the only one who had not died because of some sort of plague, although she refused to say what had brought her down in the end. Everyone assumed that due to her skill with a weapon it was something she was embarrassed to discuss, as most warriors were more than proud to recount how they had heroically fallen.

On the night before they would reach the city of Sundered Crown Nate awoke with a start, breathing heavily. Only moments ago, he had been dreaming of Cassandra, she had been laying across his lap while he stroked her hair, which was like spun gold. Now he found himself in darkness, the small campfire his only source of light.

Dawn was clearly still a long way off as the moon was bright and the sky was filled with stars. He looked around hoping to see the sleeping Cassandra nearby, but she was gone. And upon closer inspection, so was everyone else. Had he somehow rolled out of the barrier in his sleep, or had he been abandoned for real this time?

He pulled himself to his feet and immediately noticed something was off as the grass felt warm and sticky to touch. In the dim light of the fire, he could not see what, but something thick and oily now coated his palms. As he edged closer to the flames, he could finally make out his hands clearly and had to stop himself from screaming.

They were dripping with blood, a deep, almost unnatural red which stank of iron as it pooled beneath his feet. His heartbeat was quick now, his breaths short and panicked. He looked for his friends, for any sign of life at all but could see nothing. He thought about calling out their names but stopped himself. He had no idea what was out there in the woods at night. His mind swam with images of glistening fangs, red, hungry eyes, and jagged claws.

At first, he thought it was his imagination, his mind playing tricks in the depths of his desperation. But then he heard it again, and again until it was unquestionable. Cassandra was calling to him, but from where? He spun in circles until he felt sick, trying to pinpoint exactly where the noise was coming from. Even when he did, at last, obtain a general idea of her location, it made no difference, he would still have to venture into the woods.

Past the limited reach of the fire, there was no light, just the towering shadows of ancient trees which now looked to him like gargantuan creatures with long, twisting arms, waiting for him to make his move. Desperately needing a source of light to explore the forest, Nate attempted the illumination spell Kyle had taught him a few days previously. However, in his current state of fear and anxiety, it was impossible for him to reach the necessary level of calm required to cast it.

Growing increasingly frustrated and panicked he created a makeshift torch from a thick branch and rags which he tore from his own shirt. Using the campfire to ignite it he began his descent into the forest, as Cassandra's voice grew ever weaker and harder to follow.

Even by the light of his torch, the dense thicket of trees was almost impossible to navigate, and Nate quickly lost his sense of direction. Already he had lost sight of the weak glow of the campfire and was relying on Cassandra's voice alone to guide him. He was not moving quickly, but the inability to see resulted in branches scratching against his face and arms, and more than once he would lose his footing and stumble over a root.

Cassandra's voice was now getting louder, however, so he was going the right way. It was strange though; her voice did not seem strained or panicked as one would expect of someone calling for help. Rather, it had the same sense of urgency and tone of calm as if she were calling him from across a crowded room, not fearing for her life.

Nate did not think too deeply about this though and pushed forward. With all the noise he was making, snapping branches, crunching leaves, and swearing each time he tripped over something on the forest floor, he could only pray there were no monsters around. He would be the easiest meal they had eaten in weeks.

Without warning, the thick mass of trees gave way to a wide, open space. The knotted mess of shrubs and branches by his feet had been replaced by pristine white marble, its sheen bright in the moonlight. Stunned by the sudden unlikely change in scenery Nate kept back, wary that the marble floor could be some sort of trap.

That was until Cassandra called out again. Now, at last, he could see her clearly, stood in the centre of the strange scene. She wore what looked like a wedding dress, albeit with a rose-pink tinge, complete with veil and train. But it was Cassandra without question, her long, silky hair as bright as fire in the moonlight. Her voice, soft and soothing, called Nate's name once again and without hesitation, he stepped out onto this bizarre new landscape. As soon as his boot contacted the smooth, slippery surface a shadow appeared beside Cassandra. It sprouted from the ground like a spring and grew rapidly until it stood a few inches above her.

Nate's heart practically stopped beating and he held his breath in case the slightest movement on his part would result in harm to his companion. But it was too late, the shadow swirled like the same vortex which had brought Nate into this world, and when it relented, a man stood in its place. At least Nate thought it was a man, his build was tall and muscular, but his face seemed both masculine and feminine at once.

It was as if every detail of this individual had been handcrafted to perfection, they were without a doubt the most objectively beautiful human being Nate had ever seen. Like Cassandra his hair was long and golden, but so golden, so pure, it was as if it were a different colour altogether, one so perfect it was not meant for man.

He held out his hand which Cassandra took without hesitation. Lifting her veil Cassandra revealed herself to indeed be dressed for a wedding. Her complexion was perfect, lipstick the colour of blood painted her lips and her long, black eyelashes stood out against her pale make-up. Nate did not understand what was going on, but he knew, felt it deep in his heart that the man before him was evil, that Cassandra needed to run. He tried calling out to her, but his words lodged in his throat. He tried to run to her, but his legs would not respond, all he could do was watch.

Watch as slowly, gently, Cassandra and the stranger's lips met. The kiss was brief, lacking in passion, but it had been enough. The stranger chuckled quietly, yet the ground seemed to shake at his doing so. He then released Cassandra's hand and disappeared into the same shadow which had delivered him. Now Cassandra turned to Nate. She was smiling madly, unnaturally, as if the corners of her mouth were being pulled apart by fishhooks. Tears began to run down her face, smudging her make-up and leaving long watery trails.

Then, without warning, flames burst to life in a circle by her feet, trapping her. With his legs still unresponsive, all Nate could do was hold back tears as Cassandra, now crying out in agony, was consumed by the flames. Yet not once during this tortuous ordeal did she stop smiling. When the flames finally retreated there was nothing left. No bones, no dress, not even the smell of charred flesh. Cassandra was simply gone, as if she had never existed at all.

This time when Nate awoke, he was beyond relieved to see his companions in various locations dotted around the camp. Cassandra was snuggled close to the fire, her blanket wrapped around her and bunched up near her face. Nate breathed a sigh of relief as he wiped the cold sweat from his brow.

He had never had nightmares back in his own world, but now they came to him frequently. Perhaps it was remnants of his brutal training with the Husks bleeding into his subconscious. Or maybe it was just a result of being out in the wilderness, surrounded by danger with only himself and his friends to rely on to keep him alive.

He rolled onto his side to try and go back to sleep, but the rumblings of his stomach and the gradually brightening sky were not going to let that happen. Marcus would be up soon anyway, ordering everyone about, he was almost as bad as Nate's old boss. Therefore, he may as well get first dibs at breakfast before everyone else was trying to use the fire.

He was spoilt for choice but decided in the end to go for porridge and hujo. It was not the most tantalising meal for the tastebuds, but Chen was right, just half a hujo had been enough to keep him going nearly the whole first day of their journey.

Nate had just finished spooning his porridge into his bowl when Marcus plopped himself down beside him. The two had barely had a chance to speak since the expedition began. Marcus was too busy planning each step of the journey, and Nate was focused primarily on trying to keep himself alive.

"Hey," Marcus said as he filled his own bowl with porridge – Nate always made far too much and so did not mind Marcus pinching some. "Sorry we haven't had much chance to talk, this whole being in charge thing is stressing me out a bit," Marcus said. Nate's mouth was full and so he responded with a shake of his head, which Marcus knew meant not to worry about it.

In truth Marcus had been impressed with Nate. He had planned this mission expecting to have to watch his back at every turn. But he had proven to be surprisingly competent over the last week. Nate swallowed his porridge which left a pleasant warm feeling as it slid into his stomach. "What's the plan once we reach Sundered Crown?" he asked.

Marcus had been wondering this himself. Going around the city would take longer, but they would be less conspicuous. Going through the city would be quicker and allow them to restock on supplies but would put them at greater risk of being discovered.

"Haven't decided yet," was his answer as he slurped up the last of his breakfast. "We will burn that bridge when we get to it," he said getting to his feet.

"Wise words." Nate grinned as he too rose and stretched his still sleepy limbs. They should arrive at the gates of the city within three hours, they would be able to make their decision then.

Chapter 17

Nate had expected Sundered Crown to be like the city of Tinelia, at least the size of a small country. He was therefore extremely surprised to find that it was barely a large town. Its walls were high and thick, but from them you could see from one end of the city to the other. The buildings were much more modest also, most being only a single storey or two at a maximum. The only exceptions were the fortress and the cathedral, which were titans in comparison.

Marcus had hoped to bypass the city, but the closer it came the more the rest of the party wished to visit, if for nothing more than real beds, fresh food and most importantly, a bath. Reluctantly Marcus had caved to their pressure and agreed but said they would be staying no longer than two days to resupply and recuperate.

Further differences between Sundered Crown and Tinelia could be found in its abundance, or lack thereof, of travellers. The roads were sparsely populated, and the party did not have to queue at all to gain access. The city itself began immediately past the gate, every spare inch was utilised, and there was not a blade of grass or tree in sight, only the murky brown of old wood and mud, into which the road had descended almost immediately until it was little more than a slimy puddle.

Even the people seemed different. In the Vanguard it was not uncommon for people to conduct their business in expensive doublets, fancy hats, and colourful dresses. Here however, almost everyone was dressed in the same off-green, splattered with mud and worn with age.

Even the guards' armour seemed rusty, and their weapons chipped. The idea that Nate had been secretly living a far better life than these folks, unbeknownst to him, made him suddenly feel incredibly grateful for his luck. The others were unphased at their surroundings, there were people far worse off than this. These people at least had roofs over their heads and high walls to keep them safe. Deeper into the countryside, you had to fight for everything you had, and nothing could be taken for granted.

As Joel had put it on one of their many long days of travelling, only those lands within Tinelia's ever-growing walls were considered worth protecting. Everyone outside of those borders was effectively on their own. They might be claimed by the Citadel, but that awarded them no protection no matter how dire their circumstances.

At first, Nate had found this cruel, while Joel had argued it would be impossible for any nation to defend borders that were forever expanding. In a limitless world, there was not any point in trying. Nate had then wondered why anyone would want to go so far away from safety. Joel's reply had been equally as logical. That is, there are those who were drawn to the unknown, who wished to spend eternity exploring and discovering things long forgotten – for them, they were already in heaven. For others, they just wanted to be left alone, free from governance to spend eternity as they pleased.

From where Nate was standing, amongst the squalor and bleak faces of the people, this seemed about as far from heaven as one could get.

"Right," said Marcus as he ordered the wagon to a halt. "I want to see everyone at the eastern gate at dawn the day after tomorrow, understood? Oh, and we are travelling merchants, remember?"

With that, the party then split off in separate directions, towards whichever comfort they currently needed most. Nate was stood in a daze; he had no idea how to best use his new freedom in such an unfamiliar place. Marcus noticed this and placed a hand on his shoulder while pointing down an alley to their immediate left.

"Down that way is a pub that does excellent food for cheap. Down there," he said now shifting his finger in the direction of the monstrous cathedral, "is an excellent inn with soft beds and strong mead." It was funny, Marcus was far more worried for Nate's safety now that they were behind well-defended walls than he had been for the whole of their journey.

"Don't worry, Marcus," Chen chirped from behind. "I'll keep him alive for the next few days." Nate frowned at the comment, he thought he had been doing a good enough job thus far to avoid such jibes, evidently not. Marcus thanked Chen and set off with Kyle in search of a stable that would take the wagon.

"What do you want to do first then?" Nate asked. Chen took a big breath of air, which stank of sweat, mould, and shit, but she loved it. It reminded her of home. She stuck out her arm, her index finger extended towards the cathedral.

"First time in Sundered Crown, that has to be your first stop," she smiled.

"Ok." Nate shrugged as Chen led the way, a curious spring in her step. As she led him through the streets closer to the centre of the city, the surroundings became more familiar. Evidently, not everyone here lived in squalor, as he soon caught glimpses of colourful hats and other ridiculous fashion trends only the wealthy could afford to care about.

Nevertheless, he could not shake the feeling that there was something wrong with this city, as if it were rotten, decaying from the inside out. Like a Husk. If Nate had thought the cathedral was huge from a distance, it was practically gargantuan now as they stood directly outside. It was impossible to see the tips of its many spires from here without craning one's neck to breaking point. Its doors were at least as tall if not taller than the buildings which surrounded it. Luckily, the doors were already open, otherwise, Nate doubted they would have been able to get inside without a battering ram.

Within lay without a doubt the most ornate and beautiful architecture he had ever seen. Statues of marble, bronze and gold stood every few meters, depicting all manner of gods and goddesses. The level of detail was remarkable, from the tiniest dimples and fairest of age lines to even individual strands of hair indistinguishable from the real thing. Nate could almost feel the emotion of the sculptors radiating from their work. And yet there was far more to see.

Above them hung crystal chandeliers which reflected the light from the massive, stained-glass windows which showered the room in a rainbow of colours. Most impressive of all, however, were those contraptions resembling angels and other winged beasts such as Pegasi which drifted through the air, high above their heads. Whether this was achieved by magic or engineering Nate was unsure, but either way, it was marvellous to behold.

He doubted anywhere in his own world even came close to its craftmanship and otherworldly beauty. The air itself seemed to shimmer like gold and Nate had to stop walking so he could fully appreciate what his eyes were showing him. Chen stopped too and was thoroughly enjoying the looks of wonder and amazement as they took turns upon Nate's face.

"Pretty, right?"

"Pretty?" Nate scoffed "I think that's the understatement of the year."

"Come on," she giggled while beckoning him forwards, "you haven't seen the best part yet." Wondering how anything could possibly best what he had already seen, Nate continued full of eager anticipation. He was not disappointed with what Chen showed him. In the centre of the cathedral stood an altar so intricate it must have taken centuries at the very least to complete.

A variety of precious metals formed its structure, while the events which had led to the creation of the city in which it stood were depicted in masterful detail. It showed armies clashing in battle, banners rippling in the wind and the dead piled high. Its centrepiece depicted a woman, supposedly Queen Sabel, standing tall over the corpse of what must have been a giant, his crown split in two beside him. The face of the victorious queen had been damaged, however, and her features were unrecognisable.

Why someone had felt the need to commit such an unwarranted act of vandalism towards such a masterpiece Nate did not know. In the centre of the altar, placed upon a rather plain wooden pedestal, was the crown for which the city was named. Nate had expected its extravagance to at least match that of the cathedral which housed it, if not surpassing it.

However, it too was rather plain, with a thin band which looked as if it would have been equally suitable on one's wrist, and six small points which rose like daggers around the front. The only other feature was six small rubies spaced between each point along the band. The crown sat in two pieces upon its pedestal, close enough together that you could see how it would have looked upon a king's head, far enough apart that the story behind it could not be forgotten.

"Please step back," said a gravelly voice which belonged to one of four guards stood at the corners of the altar, which Nate had not noticed until now, so enthralled was he by his surroundings. The four guards were all men, tall and strong, dressed in steel so well polished they seemed to generate their own light. Upon their heads were helmets in the shape of broad arrowheads, decorated with a plumage of which each man had a different colour – red, blue, green, and yellow. Nate had no idea what they were supposed to represent and thought they looked like Power Rangers in training.

"Sorry," Chen said on their behalf as she dragged Nate away and past the altar towards the very back of the cathedral where a large crowd was gathered.

"What's this way?" he asked, surely there could not be anything that would outdo what he had already seen.

"The Oracle," Chen replied, almost whispering. *What the hell is an oracle?* Nate wondered as Chen, with her hand still wrapped tightly around his wrist, pulled him to the back of the crowd. At first, he imagined a young woman, wrapped in thin veils twisting and writhing among incense as she hallucinated before charging gullible fools for the pleasure. He then imagined a condescending old woman with dreadlocks holding a tray of freshly baked cookies.

When they had finally reached the front of the queue, after discovering quite quickly that barging through a crowd does not actually work in real life, Nate was disappointed to see his first guess had been the most accurate.

Sat upon a golden throne was a woman. She did indeed wear the luxurious silky veils which obscured her face, while her arms would have been bare had it not been for the hundreds of gold and silver bangles which draped them from wrist to shoulder. Chen explained that an oracle was simply the term for a female prophet, someone who received visions from the gods and could read your future.

This oracle was considered the most powerful in the known world. Most prophets and oracles only saw short glimpses of the future, of great, calamitous events obscured mostly by darkness and metaphor. This one, however, could see in perfect detail an individual's life hundreds of years in the future.

However, Nate was not convinced. One would think, considering he was in Purgatory, wielding magic and only a few days ago fighting against reanimated skeletons, that he would be more open-minded. The cynic in him would not go down so easily though. The Oracle turned to him now – all he needed to do was present a few coins and she would begin her ritual which the crowd never grew tired of.

However, this time something was different. Even behind her multitude of veils Nate could see the bright, amethyst-coloured eyes burning through his own. He wanted to look away, so intense was her stare, as if she were seeing the sky for the first time, but he could not. Something about her drew him closer, until he was unknowingly climbing the stairs leading to her throne.

Suddenly a violent force threw him backwards into the crowd. One of the Oracle's guards had stepped in, believing Nate to be a threat. Recovered now from his trance Nate sat on the stone floor and watched as without a word the Oracle rose from her seat and retreated into her quarters, surrounded by her guards.

"What the hell was that about?" Nate asked Chen as she helped him to his feet and the others in the crowd groaned and threw him insults after he had ruined their chances to have their fortunes told. Some of them had travelled half the world just for this.

"Yeah, what the hell were you doing? The guards could have killed you," Chen scolded. Brushing himself off Nate looked back to the now empty throne – he could still see the amethyst eyes, feel them piercing through his skin.

"I…I don't know. I feel like…. like she was trying to tell me something."

Dismissing Nate with a roll of her eyes, Chen whacked the back of his head.

"That's her job you fucking idiot, there's no way we will get to hear our fortunes before we have to leave now. Thanks a lot," she said storming off. She made it about halfway out of the cathedral before realising Nate would have no idea where he was and so waited for him to catch up. However, she led him straight to an inn after that and only spoke to express her annoyance, ignoring his attempts to explain or apologise for his actions.

The inn was smaller than he was used to back in the Vanguard, only two storeys and with small rooms just large enough for a bed and a bathtub. The innkeeper had mentioned something about having a girl come and help him with his bath for an extra charge, but Nate rejected him. He knew how to fill up a bath on his own. Marcus had been right though, the bed, although small, was soft and seemed to mould to his shape. He had barely sat down after drying himself off after his bath before he was asleep.

It was not long however, before he was woken by a voice calling his name. A woman's voice. For a second, he was afraid he had re-entered the same nightmare from the previous night. The one where Cassandra had been engulfed in flames while he watched helplessly. But this time when he opened his eyes he was still in his room. The single candle he had lit earlier cast an eery glow which did little to combat the darkness which surrounded him.

He swung his legs over the side of the bed when he heard his name called again; the voice was soft yet authoritative. Nate did not bother getting dressed and entered the hallway in only his trousers, his bare feet cold on the wooden floor. The hallway was lit by candlelight, and Nate could sense that he was not alone which made him feel uneasy.

The voice called to him again, more clearly this time but still slightly muffled. He crept along the hallway slowly, not totally convinced a masked serial killer was not about to jump out at him from one of the rooms which flanked him on either side. He breathed a sigh of relief when he managed to reach the front door without being stabbed to death. He flung it open and almost plummeted to his doom but was able to catch himself on the doorframe first. The world had gone and in its place was an endless black void, below him were grey clouds which writhed like worms.

While he caught his breath from avoiding his demise once again, the voice called his name. This time it was clear as day and much, much closer. He turned his eyes from the swirling mass beneath him and saw her. The Oracle. She stood only a few meters away, her feet planted firmly upon the darkness as if it were solid ground.

This time however, her face was unobstructed. She had long, bleached white hair, so perfectly straight it appeared more like an artificial headpiece. Her facial features were small and pointed, except for her eyes, which were large and round, her amethyst pupils swimming in the milky sea which surrounded them.

"I have waited a long time for this day, and yet it was never certain you would come," she said softly, just loud enough for Nate to hear. He wanted to reply, he had a few questions of his own but found his voice would not come. "Return to the cathedral. On its western side you will find a door reserved for the clergy, it will be open. Come to me."

She did not give Nate time to respond. As soon as she had finished speaking, she vanished into the blackness and Nate awoke again. This time, for real. This dream had felt no different to the others. Equally as real, equally as foreboding. This time however, he felt compelled to believe it had been more than a dream, and to follow the instructions he had been given. He threw his clothes back on and rushed out the door, his damp hair sticking out in every direction like a hedgehog.

It took him longer than it should have to get back to the cathedral. While it was clearly visible from anywhere in the city, the night made it that much harder to navigate. He found himself twice at dead ends down dodgy-looking alleys before quickly doubling back. Once he had gathered his bearings after recognising an amusing cobbler's sign which he had passed earlier of a goblin's bare backside being kicked by a well-crafted boot, he was able to jog the rest of the way.

There were very few lights in the city at night, just the odd solitary oil lamp hanging from a well-to-do business. Otherwise, the only lights came from patrolling guards, or from within the buildings themselves and they too were mostly black as their residents slept. It therefore took a great deal of fumbling and straining of his eyes in the fuzzy darkness before Nate could make out the shape of a door.

It was tall, its frame curved into a leaf-like shape. More importantly, however, as the Oracle had claimed, it was unlocked. Nate did a quick double-take before daring to go inside. The last thing he needed was to be accosted by the guards as to why he was sneaking into the cathedral at night. He would be a thief at best, an assassin at worst. To his relief, there was no one about and he quietly slipped inside.

The door took him to an entirely new part of the cathedral he had not seen on his earlier visit. It consisted of a short corridor with two doors on either side before reaching a much larger door at the end. Luckily for him, the doors were labelled. *Clergy's quarters, kitchen, toilets, crypt.* He doubted he would find the Oracle behind any of these and tiptoed his way past them.

His breathing was rapid and shallow, and he was terrified he might be caught at any moment. He kept his fingertips outstretched so that they glided along the cool, stone walls. Something to keep him grounded as his nerves became ever more frantic the closer he came to the large door at the end of the corridor: 'Quarters of her Lady Worship'. *'Bingo,'* Nate thought to himself. The handle to the door was large and heavy and desperately needed oil as it cried out when Nate turned it. He winced, expecting guards or priests to come bursting through the doors behind him to investigate the noise. Nobody came.

Nate allowed himself to breathe a sigh of relief as the door politely opened without so much as a creak. What followed was an agonisingly tall and twisted staircase that Nate had half a mind to give up on before he had even climbed a third. Surely the Oracle could at least have met him halfway and been waiting as soon as he entered the cathedral.

Winded and cursing under his breath he finally reached the peak and momentarily rested himself against the door which separated him from the Oracle's chambers. It was no wonder she was so thin having to make this climb every day. As he reached for the doorknob his hand froze and his confidence wavered. For reasons unknown he knew that once he went through this door, once he had heard what the Oracle had to say, everything would change.

There was no logical reason for him to feel this way, but it manifested and grew within him, resting at the pit of his stomach, reaching out and placing an aching grip upon his heart. The problem was he knew he would not get this chance again and whatever knowledge the Oracle planned to confide in him would be lost forever.

He knew he would spend the rest of his days wondering what it could have been she wanted to speak with him so urgently about. Could it save him from disaster, make him rich or even save someone he cared about? If she were the real thing, if she really could see the future, he could not allow this opportunity to pass.

He swallowed his trepidation and gently nudged the door open. What lay beyond was a rather underwhelming bedroom, certainly not what he had expected for someone of such standing within local society. There was a large fireplace of which only embers remained of a recent fire which still filled the room with its warmth. A few wardrobes whose doors were open and most of their identical contents of sequined veils and sashes scattered about the floor. A large dressing table which took up perhaps a third of the room and a four-poster bed upon the edge of which the figure of the Oracle sat.

"You took longer than expected," she said, her tone reserved and drowsy, as if she were half asleep. Nate immediately had to shield his eyes as the Oracle only had a single thin, almost transparent piece of cloth covering her upper body. The Oracle seemed to take offence at this, although her tone of voice did not change.

"Is the sight of my body so dreadful that it offends you?"

"Of course, not," Nate replied, his eyes still fixed to a particularly captivating spot on the far wall. "I'm just not used to…" he trailed off.

"Not used to the sight of a woman?" the Oracle said in a way which made it impossible for Nate to distinguish between an insult or genuine question.

"I have hoped for millennia you would come to me one day," she said at last. Nate ignored the millennia part and skipped straight to the bit he was interested in.

"Well, your invitation was difficult to ignore. How did you do that anyway?" He had finally turned his attention away from the wall and was fighting the age-old struggle of maintaining eye contact. The Oracle tilted her head to one side as if to dismiss her abilities to enter people's dreams.

"I could not have done it were you not a prophet" she lied.

These words did not resonate with Nate as perhaps they should have. As they would have done with almost anyone else on Gaia. His eyes narrowed and he chewed on the inside of his lip as he waited for some sort of punchline. Because surely, she was joking.

"You don't believe me, I understand," she replied, almost hurt at the mere suggestion from her own lips.

"It's not that," Nate said. "I mean…it's just…" he trailed off again. He was not sure what you were supposed to say to someone who claimed not only they, but you also were a mouthpiece for the gods. He folded his arms, clearly there was something to this woman, she had appeared in his dreams and given him an order after all. But for all he knew, this was one of the ways she made her money, tricking gullible fools into thinking they were special too.

The Oracle could tell Nate was having doubts by his not-so-subtle body language and the look of mistrust in his eyes. She was used to it though. Many great scholars and theologians had attempted to debunk or challenge her abilities. All had failed.

There was much she wanted to say and little time, she would have to prove herself quickly and beyond any doubt, although she had a fine line between guidance and interference to tread. "You can save her." Nate's ears pricked up and his interest was caught.

"Who?" he asked. The Oracle felt a pang of guilt as she used Nate's own feelings against him to gain his trust. In the long run, however, it would be vital.

"The woman in your vision. The one with golden hair who you watched be devoured by fire. Her fate is not yet sealed, you can save her."

The room seemed to suddenly drop by ten degrees as shivers ran through Nate's body. His face drained of colour entirely. The Oracle decided to double down. "I was there, I saw it."

"How?" Nate began before the Oracle cut him off. She stepped forwards and placed a gentle hand on his arm which was now limp by his sides. She spoke with a tremble in her voice.

"I have seen things Nate, things I am sure were meant for you."

"What things?" Nate replied, his own voice now a whisper.

The Oracle placed her free hand on his other arm and squeezed, desperate to divulge all she knew. Yet she dared not. The two locked eyes, hers shimmering as she stared unblinkingly into his own, a distant blue. She said nothing, but Nate could sense the maelstrom of thoughts rushing through her mind.

"I hope I don't have to pay extra for this," he croaked. The Oracle did not laugh. She squeezed him tighter with surprising strength for someone her size.

"You are man, imperfect by design. I cannot tell you more without influencing events to come. Just know, your choices carry weight, even here. Ensure you make the right ones, for all our sakes."

"I don't understand," Nate protested as the Oracle released him and returned to her bed. She ran her hand along its silk sheets and wondered for how much longer she would live in such luxury.

"I'm sorry, Nate, but I cannot risk telling you much more. You must understand that you hold great power within you. Do not ignore your visions as they show you the choices that are to come. Be the man I know you can be. Do not allow your own evil to prevail."

My own evil, what the hell does that mean? Nate thought to himself. But the Oracle would hear nothing more and stubbornly refused to answer his questions. She feared she had said too much already, enough to divert history from its present course to one which she had not yet foreseen.

In the end Nate left more confused than before, stomping his way out of the cathedral without a care for who might hear him. The only thing the Oracle had said which made any sense at all was that he was a prophet. Yet Nate doubted even this as she had not elaborated on what this meant and simply expected him to go along with it. He muttered complaints to himself all the way back to the inn and drifted off in his bed, angry, but unable to shake the memory of the Oracle's bright eyes and warnings of evil from his mind.

Tonight, there would be no more dreams. For once Nate was well rested when the signs of daybreak were unleashed. The shouting of vendors in the streets, the calls of various domesticated animals to signal the new day. This would be his only full day where he was free to explore the city and do as he pleased before they would need to set off once again.

He initially thought about returning to the Oracle to demand more straightforward answers. However, he doubted he would be any more successful than the first time he'd tried to approach her in public and so decided to let sleeping dogs lie. Instead, he met up with Chen who had cooled off significantly from the previous day and she ended up giving him a tour of the city which took up most of their free time.

Apart from the cathedral and fortress, there was not much else of note in Sundered Crown. It had once been a thriving city renowned for its guild of blacksmiths and metalworkers. However, as the city of Tinelia had expanded, and the distance between the two cities shrunk, most of the local artisans had either left for Tinelia or gone bust. Now all that remained were subsistence farmers, mercenaries, travellers, and of course, the Oracle.

Ultimately, their day was uneventful. They had both made a quick stop at the bank so Nate could confirm for himself that he had indeed been rewarded for his heroic dispatch of the skeletons a few days prior. Chen had also run a few errands such as buying new arrows and stocking up on food for the rest of the journey. In the end, they both found themselves back at the same inn, munching on an assortment of fruits and cheeses as the last rays of daylight retreated into the night.

Nate decided to casually bring up the previous night's escapade with the Oracle to which Chen simply laughed. "Oh yeah, right, and I'm secretly Queen Sabel in disguise." Nate sighed, disappointed, and went back to his food. This threw Chen off who expected him to come clean about the joke. Now, examining him more closely, his vacant, troubled eyes and restlessness as he played with his fork led her to believe that he was in fact, telling the truth. She chewed on the thought for a moment.

Prophets and oracles were not that rare an occurrence, even after the imperial purges, so that part of Nate's story she would happily believe. It was the idea that he was important enough that the most powerful oracle in the known world would meet him in secret offering such a warning. Nate was nobody, he commanded no armies, and held no influence anywhere; how could he of all people be such a vital piece in whatever game the gods were playing?

Nate could sense the mood between them had changed and looked up to see Chen examining him as if he were a new species. "We should talk to Marcus about this," she said, at last, deciding it would be foolish to dismiss such a clear warning from the Oracle. This did little to lift Nate's spirits, he would have much preferred it had Chen confirmed his earlier suspicions that it was all a moneymaking scam. Her decision to inform Marcus only more tightly wound the knot in his stomach.

Wasting no time, Chen held Nate by the collar and practically dragged him the whole journey across town to where Marcus was keeping a close eye on the eastern gate. He had spent most of his stay working out the best time for the party to leave unnoticed, a task made difficult by the seemingly random schedules of the townsfolk. He was not at all surprised to see Chen holding Nate by the scruff of the neck before him. In fact, he was shocked it had taken this long.

"Sick of him already?" he asked while keeping one eye on the gate from his room on the first floor. Finally, Chen released Nate from her death grip.

"Tell him," she ordered. At first, Nate was unwilling, he felt he had blown this all way out of proportion and was now more concerned about looking like a fool than any prophetic warning he may have received. Marcus, however, was too stressed by his mission to waste his time with this and so demanded Nate spit it out. Like a scolded child Nate sheepishly retold the events of the night before. All the while Marcus said nothing, occasionally throwing Chen a glance as if to say, *and you believe all this?*

When Nate had finished, Marcus went back to observing the gate from his window, mulling over how, if Nate were telling the truth, it would affect their mission. Suddenly, an idea came to mind, one which would settle this debate once and for all.

Finding Kyle was not a difficult task, they just found the cheapest, dirtiest room in the city and lo and behold, there he was, lying on the floor, surrounded by dozens of various glass bottles, some half-empty, some drained dry. The room stank of stale sweat and urine, whether that was all Kyle's doing or the room itself was impossible to determine.

Kyle awoke from his drunken slumber after a few courteous prods and then a kick to the leg, although still bleary-eyed and unsteady as the alcohol was still heavily present in his system. He looked at his three companions for a moment, suspicious and on edge, until he suddenly recognised their faces and his whole demeanour changed. "Morning already?" he asked as he felt around for an unfinished bottle. Marcus was unimpressed and growled softly to vent his frustration so that he did not have to kick Kyle again to make himself feel better.

"We think Nate might be a prophet, any tests you can do so we can be sure?" Marcus asked. Pausing in his search for more alcohol Kyle looked first at Marcus, then at Nate. The expression on his face was one of doubt, then of interest.

"What makes you think Nate's a prophet?" Kyle asked as he unsteadily got to his feet and put his face barely an inch away from Nate's as if there was some tell-tale physical sign that would give them the answer.

Nate almost gagged as the stench of various boozes better not mixed filled his nostrils and was forced to back off a few steps before offering Kyle more information.

"The Oracle told me….in a dream." Nate decided he would keep his little adventure in her bedchamber to himself.

Kyle raised his eyebrow – oracles and prophets, powerful ones anyway, could enter others' dreams at will. But this did not give them the power to know who else was a prophet and who was not. It would go some way in explaining Nate's natural aptitude for magic, however. Prophets of all kinds were incredibly powerful sorcerers, whether they knew it or not. Either way, it would be good for them to know if they had such an asset in their party.

"Ok," Kyle began, wiping his mouth on his shirt. "There's a pretty simple test for this sort of thing, it'll get us to the bottom of it."

Kyle took a few steps back and raised his right hand to face the wall. From his fingertips sprouted green tendrils which instinctively, like a living thing, sought their way to the nearest surface. They soon found the wall opposite and latched on, detaching themselves from Kyle and wrapping themselves around one another until they had formed a writhing, shapeless mass. After a few seconds, the writhing stopped and in its place was a perfectly formed, although slightly off-green, smiley face that took up most of the wall.

"I don't get it," Nate said as Kyle turned to face him.

"Me neither," Chen added. Kyle ignored her and answered Nate.

"Do you see it?" he asked, excited. Nate took another look at the face on the wall and shrugged, still confused although now slightly frustrated.

"If you mean the big green thing on the wall then yeah, otherwise you've lost me."

That was the answer Kyle had been hoping for. He slapped Nate hard, too hard, on the back and beamed like a proud parent.

"He's a prophet alright."

"I still don't get it," Nate and Chen said in unison, leaving it up to Kyle to explain the whole process.

"That," he said pointing at the wall, "is a message, a magical one that can only be read by either the person it was meant for, or..." he said turning back to Nate, "a prophet."

"That's why we can't see anything, Chen," Marcus added. Nate looked first at Chen, then at the wall where the smiley face was now a permanent resident, then back to Chen before grinning.

"Wait, so you can't see what Kyle said about you?" Chen's eyes grew wide as her muscles tensed.

"Piss off," she growled.

"Cut it out," Marcus scolded as he gave both Nate and Chen a whack on the back of their heads. Of all the things he had expected Nate to turn out to be, a prophet was not one of them. He allowed his mind to wander while Nate and Chen bickered like children and Kyle went back to searching for more booze.

As far as he could tell, Nate being a prophet would not impact their mission. It might even turn out to be of use if Kyle could properly instruct him on the use of magic. Yet this would make his job of keeping Nate alive much harder. If Nate's status became widely known, he would be their enemy's first target during any engagement. Even worse, however, was the idea that upon returning to Tinelia, Nate would be shipped off to either a temple or the Citadel, to be hidden away from the world while the state made full use of his powers. Marcus was not going to let that happen.

"Alright, listen," Marcus said, bringing the bickering to a halt. "Kyle, I want you to keep a close eye on Nate, tell him everything you know about prophets, then tell me. I don't want any surprises while we are still on mission."

"You got it boss," Kyle replied with a mock salute.

"In the meantime," Marcus continued. "Nate isn't a prophet; he never met the Oracle, and he can barely light a match, let alone be a master sorcerer in the making, understood? The last thing you need is the wrong people to find out about this," he said shooting a finger at Nate. The other three agreed not to mention it again. Although Nate had no real idea why being a prophet would be such a bad thing, deep down he still felt that nothing good could come of it.

"Right, we had all better get some rest, we are leaving early tomorrow," Marcus said heading for the door. Nate did the same, but Marcus held him back. "You're staying here, you and Kyle have a lot to discuss before morning." Nate looked back at the urine-soaked floor and peeling walls where the sickly-green smiley face looked strangely apt. He winced as Chen left him with a thump on the arm.

"Have fun" she smirked. Nate let out a heavy sigh as the door slammed behind him and he was left alone with Kyle.

"Let's get this over with," he groaned as he tried and failed to find a place to sit that was not already wet.

The next morning Nate and Kyle arrived late to the east gate where the rest of the party were already waiting for them. They had spent almost the entire night discussing what it meant to be a prophet, everything from what powers Nate could expect to develop, to an oral history of important prophets over the past few thousand years. The only aspect Nate really had any interest in, other than innate magical aptitude, was the ability to see the future through visions.

Kyle had explained that they often came in the form of dreams and were therefore difficult to distinguish. Some extremely powerful prophets and oracles, however, could summon visions merely through touching certain magical objects or during moments of extreme physical or mental duress.

Unfortunately, Kyle had not been any help in trying to understand what the Oracle had meant by overcoming his own inner evil. He had been more useful, however, in deciphering what she meant by Nate needing to make the right choices. While prophets and oracles were powerful, and their visions had helped countless people, they were not set in stone.

Rather, a prophet or oracle would see one of an almost infinite version of events that may or may not come to pass. Whether the visions did come true depended on the choices of the vision's subject. Whatever the Oracle had seen required Nate to make the correct decisions when the time came.

"I don't understand why she didn't just tell me what her vision was so that I could do everything to make sure it came true," Nate complained as they finally re-joined their companions. Annoyingly, Kyle had an answer for this.

"I doubt it's that simple. What if by actively trying to make it happen, you prevent it from happening altogether? That's why she wouldn't tell you anything more, she has no way of knowing what could influence the outcome." Nate kicked at the dust in frustration as he double-checked the straps on his armour. He would really appreciate it if for once, he could leave a conversation with more answers than questions.

"That's enough, no more talk until we make camp," Marcus hissed as the streets slowly began to fill with a trickle of peasants and soldiers. There was a sudden, sharp pain in Nate's side as Chen hit him in the ribs which caused him to double over.

"Some prophet you are," she giggled quietly as she took her previous position in the formation and the gates of the city opened onto the winding road once more. One of these days Nate was really going to give it to her, he just needed a few centuries more training first.

Just as the party passed the threshold into the wilds once more, a guard called out to Marcus, the clear leader of the group. Marcus ordered the rest of them to halt while he and the guard conversed. From where he stood, Nate could see a look of concern on the guard's face, a look which quickly latched on to Marcus. Their conversation did not last long, and Marcus returned scratching his head, his gaze directed at the ground.

"What did he say?" Joel asked just in earshot of Nate. Marcus was still looking at the ground but looked up to answer once he had gone over the conversation a few more times in his head.

"He said to watch out heading east, said something isn't right."

"Nothing is ever right within one hundred miles of the Imperium," Joel scoffed. "What is it this time, bandits, marauders, beasts?". Marcus shook his head.

"Nothing," he replied. Joel's brow furrowed at such a strange answer.

"Nothing wouldn't make your face look that way," Joel said curiously. Marcus was never one to mince words and it was vital that a party knew what they were heading into before an expedition. So, it struck Joel as odd that Marcus would brush any sort of warning off as nothing. However, Marcus quickly set the record straight, shaking his head in his frustration at not being able to come up with an explanation for himself.

"He said there's nothing out there, the forest is empty, not even a Husk between here and the Imperial border."

Joel was shocked, he had never heard of entire regions being totally devoid of life, not outside of the Imperium anyway.

"That's not possible," he whispered, not wanting the others to hear and potentially panic. Marcus agreed entirely, yet this is what he had been told. He gazed in the direction in which they had to travel. The dark shadows of the forest were taller than before, the wind like a growl as it passed over them.

"I have a bad feeling about this," Marcus said softly so that only Joel could hear. A sentiment he now shared.

Chapter 18

Adeneus was restless. Despite his countless hours without food or sleep while he toiled in the laboratory, he could not find comfort in rest. If anything, it was little more than an annoyance which kept him from his work. Work that would revolutionise the world. Work whose goal still seemed so very, very far away.

After much tossing and turning, he decided that he may as well turn from one fruitless endeavour to another. Throwing on the same clothes he had worn for the past few days, he navigated the dark passages through the keep to his laboratory. Most of the torches had burned themselves out and ghostly wisps of smoke stalked the narrow passageways.

Perhaps it was just his tiredness, or maybe being so far away from civilisation, out here in the wilds where all manner of dangers still lurked, but something in the air made Adeneus feel uneasy, unsafe. His strides were more timid, purposefully silent as he descended the stairs to his laboratory. He may have been one of the most powerful sorcerers in the known world, but here, all sane men were afraid of what lurked in the dark.

As he neared his laboratory door, which remained locked and undisturbed, he could hear movement from the other side. Not the usual shuffling or groaning of his test subjects, but quick, purposeful footsteps and the unmistakable scrunching and shuffling of paper. Adeneus' eyes grew wide, his fear of the unknown now replaced entirely by fear of failure in his mission. A fear well-founded as he quickly unlocked and threw open the heavy door to find a man, tall and stocky, dressed in the blue cloak of a Battlemage standing over his desk with an armful of his notes.

The two men immediately froze in shock. Adeneus' mouth was open, but no words escaped it. His heart and mind were too busy racing to recover his research as quickly and peacefully as possible. He would not risk their destruction for anything, even a millennia-old ideological struggle between the Battlemages and the Imperium. At this moment such things seemed trivial.

The Battlemage too was unsure how to proceed; he had not expected to be discovered and so had, despite his rigorous training, no contingency plan. For a moment the world was still, even the air seemed too afraid to move should it set off a destructive chain of events.

The two men stared at one another. The Battlemage's face was covered by a cloth mask pulled over his nose, but his eyes were a brilliant emerald green, and they worked frantically to find an escape route. Adeneus was trembling with adrenaline at this point and with a hand raised in peace, took a careful step forward, still hoping to resolve this standoff without violence.

The Battlemage, not wanting to get himself into a drawn-out struggle against such a powerful foe, also hoped to resolve this quickly. He suddenly pushed his free hand in front of himself, expelling a transparent spear that grew from his palm like the stem of a deadly flower. It flew towards Adeneus at a fantastic speed, aimed straight for his heart.

Even at such a speed, there was little chance the spear would strike its target; indeed, before it had covered half the distance between them, it had shattered into a million shards as Adeneus cast his own spell. However, the Battlemage was not interested in a fight to the death and simply sought to escape, rushing madly for the wall to his left.

Adeneus was faster, however, shooting a thick, blue bolt of lightning between his foe and freedom. The Battlemage barely dodged the spell's scorching touch as it brushed past him, arching and twisting before contacting one of the many occupied cages at the back of the room which then exploded in a shower of metal, bone, and blood.

Avoiding the fiery touch of death caused the Battlemage to lose his footing, and he stumbled backwards, the notes he had stolen flying free from his grasp and spilling across the floor. Knowing he would not have time to retrieve them, he decided all traces of this evil magic must be destroyed.

Rolling onto his feet like a skilled acrobat, he extended both of his palms outwards to form a huge fireball. This was of no real concern to Adeneus until he realised that he was not the intended target. The fireball shot across the room towards the desk where much of his work still lay. He was only able to save it by forming a magical barrier at the last possible moment.

Now, filled with anger that a fellow sorcerer would risk denying the world such knowledge, Adeneus lashed out. After all, to destroy someone's work was far worse than to steal it, Adeneus could have forgiven him for that. Whipping his left arm around, Adeneus caught the Battlemage with a blast of telekinetic force which knocked him off his feet and sent him flying into the adjacent wall.

This burst of emotion, however, was a mistake on Adeneus' part, as the Battlemage utilised the magic they were best known for, turning his body from solid to ethereal and passing through the wall without injury, his escape now complete.

The room was now quiet once again, apart from Adeneus' laboured breathing and the exhausted, pitiful cries of his captives, who were agonising that they had not been lucky enough to have been dealt such a quick death as their fellow prisoner. The smell of charred flesh and molten metal hung in the air while thin wisps of smoke trailed skywards.

As if on cue, Adeneus' guards rushed into the room; weapons drawn, they shielded their master with their bodies from the enemy, who no longer posed a threat and was perhaps already on his way back to a nearby Battlemage chapter house. As the guards stood there uselessly, Adeneus pushed his way to the scattered papers the Battlemage had nearly escaped with.

Luckily, they were all undamaged and he breathed a sigh of relief as he returned them to his desk. Everything else seemed to be in its rightful place – clearly, the Battlemage had not known what he was looking for and had instead tried to take whatever he could get his hands on.

At that moment it looked as if disaster had been avoided, until, upon closer inspection, Adeneus realised something was certainly missing. His journal, one of many, was gone. Frantically he checked every inch of the room –perhaps the battle had caused it to land elsewhere. No, it was gone, and the Battlemage had taken it.

This journal, while not filled with notes specific to his experiments, was instead filled with his day-to-day accounts. These included the ultimate aim of his mission and perhaps rather foolishly, estimations of how it could be used to effectively overwhelm their enemies. A cold sweat formed on his forehead as he realised the potential consequences of the Imperium's enemies gaining hold of that journal. He quickly turned to his guards who were standing idle, poking at fleshy lumps with their swords, all that remained of his earlier subject.

"What are you still standing around for you idiots? Get out there and bring me back my journal!" Adeneus screamed with the desperation of a man who could now be accused of failing his Emperor.

The guards jumped to attention and scurried from the room, none of them having any idea who they were looking for or even where to start. "Shit, shit, shit," Adeneus cursed as the last of the guards sprinted up the stairs to alert the rest of the castle and nearby villages.

He held his head in his hands and pulled hard at fistfuls of hair. He had to fix this, and he had to fix it now – there would be no need to mention any of this to the Emperor, however. He was certain he would get the journal back and nothing would come of it, his mistake would remain a secret.

At last, however, it seemed all his energy had been drained and he slunk off to bed, finally embracing the warmth of sleep. Tomorrow he would restart his experiments with renewed vigour. After all, if the Battlemages were interested in his work, clearly, he was onto something. That was enough to motivate him to continue, despite the challenges which still lay ahead.

The very next night Adeneus felt another wave of unease so strong it woke him from a deep sleep. With great caution, as a child would do to avoid alerting the monster under the bed, he raised himself into a sitting position. The few still burning candles cast just enough of a glow for him to see exactly what he had feared.

Stood at the end of his bed was the unmistakeable robe of a Battlemage; clearly, the thief had returned to complete his mission and finish off Adeneus for good measure. Despite this, Adeneus did not call out for help or immediately begin casting offensive spells to scare off his assassin, because for whatever reason the Battlemage did not attack either.

Immediately Adeneus realised this was not the same man who had tried to steal his research. His eyes had been green, while those which looked back at him now were sparkling gold. He carefully pulled down his hood and greeted Adeneus as if he were an old friend.

He was completely bald except for a small patch of fluff under his bottom lip, even his eyebrows had been shaved clean off. The man smiled, revealing at least half of his teeth to be silver.

"It's been a long time, Adeneus," the Battlemage said amused, at Adeneus' forlorn attempt to place the face he was sure he had seen before.

"What do you want?" Adeneus demanded, sick to death of his nights being interrupted by pretentious pricks too lazy to do their own research. It was almost as bad as working at the Imperial University.

"Don't tell me you don't recognise me, even after all these years?" the Battlemage replied doing a great job of trying to sound hurt. Adeneus squinted through the gloom trying desperately to remember where he had seen this man before. Then it hit him. Before him sat the former Lord Philip Thorn.

One of the brightest minds ever to have stepped foot in the Imperial University and one of the most insufferable twats Adeneus had ever met. You had to be to adopt a second name and choose 'Thorn' of all things. Philip had mysteriously left the university one day centuries ago never to be seen again. It made sense he had joined the Battlemages considering his own expertise in offensive and illusory magic.

"Philip?" Adeneus gasped to which Philip grinned in satisfaction; he had not been resigned to the dustbin of history quite yet it seemed. The surprise had quickly worn off for Adeneus however and he repeated his question, although this time somewhat less eloquently.

"What the fuck do you want, Philip?" This immediately soured Philip's dramatic return and he considered not involving Adeneus in his plan at all before thinking better of it. He might hate the man, but there was no denying the Arch-Sorcerer was light years ahead of the other academics he had considered and the only rational choice.

Philip gritted his teeth and decided this would be far less painful if he just got on with it. "A friend of mine told me that he paid you a little visit the other night and that he may have taken something of yours. Is that correct?"

This simple, loaded question was enough to send a shot of fear coursing through Adeneus's veins. How could this have happened so quickly? More importantly, why was Philip, a Battlemage and sworn enemy of the Imperium, here discussing it with him? Philip could tell exactly what Adeneus was thinking by his now rigid posture and the air of arrogant confidence settled upon him once more. He intertwined his long, gloved fingers and adopted a condescending tone as if he were speaking to one of his pupils.

"I was hoping, perhaps we may be able to help one another."

"Whatever you need," Adeneus blurted out. At this moment he could not care less what Philip was planning, all that mattered right now was that he got his journal back.

"Excellent." Philip smiled cruelly as he withdrew a parchment detailing the exact locations of dozens of Battlemage safehouses and handed it over to Adeneus. "Your journal should be in one of these locations. I'll be in touch when I have need of your skills."

By the time Adeneus had looked up from the parchment, Philip was gone. He looked back to the parchment immediately, there were many potential locations where his journal could be hidden, but one stood out. The town of Cotts, barely a few days' ride into Tinelia. Sending soldiers directly into Tinelian territory was out of the question, but luckily, he had a few men who could get in and out undetected while completing their mission. Nothing would come between him and retrieving that journal before the entire world descended into a madness of his making.

Chapter 19

For four days the party had travelled along the road which led to the town of Cotts, and for those four days, they had heard and seen nothing. At first, they had been in high spirits, the apparent lack of any sort of creature willing to do them harm had led to many good nights of sleep and better overall mood. However, after Nate had un-sportingly pointed out the complete lack of any sort of life at all, from birds and squirrels to even spiders, the group had been on edge.

Cassandra had seen a similar phenomenon before, usually before a volcanic eruption or earthquake. Surprisingly, this also did little to improve morale as everyone now expected to be incinerated or swallowed by the earth in the blink of an eye, even if there were no volcanoes for thousands of miles. Naturally, however, it was Nate who took the brunt of abuse for ruining their until now, almost pleasant countryside stroll.

Marcus was the exception – from the very beginning he had worn a scowl, one that had only deepened with each passing day without some sighting of life. Now, after four days he could practically kiss a Husk if he could just find one. What worried them the most was that they had not even seen travellers or merchants coming in the opposite direction.

The Imperium and Tinelia might be at war in all but name, yet that had not stopped a thriving trading relationship. With Cotts being one of the closest towns to the border, it was beyond strange to have not seen anyone by now.

Whatever this was, clearly it had been going on for a while as the road was poorly maintained and the forest had in some places reclaimed it entirely. Nate had spent at least two hours on the fifth day cutting brambles and branches which had blocked their path, making it impassable for the wagon. He was sure Kyle could have cleared the way in a matter of seconds if he had just used his magic, but the excuse of not wanting to burn the whole forest down did little to ease the pain of the blisters dotting his palms.

Not long after progressing past the blockage Marcus decided he would allow the party to camp for the night. It was close to dusk and while a relatively chilly day, their earlier task had exhausted them and drenched the party in a thick layer of sweat. Further evidence that they had been the only travellers for some time was the lack of any sort of clearly defined stopping place, usually abundant at the roadside. Instead, the party with great difficulty, managed to traverse the wagon through the woods until they had found a rocky alcove not too far from the road which would offer them adequate shelter.

Few had the energy to talk as they set about making camp and they went about it in a tired and irritated silence brought on by their aching, sweaty bodies. Nate stuck to the one task he was not totally useless at, gathering firewood. Alone with his thoughts at last as he tossed aside the mostly wet or rotten branches, Nate looked back on the events of the last few months.

He knew that he was still way out of his depth and there would be a lot more learning and failures yet to come; however, he could not help but feel proud of himself. If only his childhood bullies or his old boss could have seen him take on those skeletons or cast spells, perhaps then they would have respected him more.

Nate tried to remember their faces, the people who for his whole life had put him down, made him feel worthless. Yet no matter how hard he scoured the recesses of his mind, they remained elusive shadows, and before long were replaced entirely by the faces of his companions and others he had met here in Purgatory. This brought a slight smile to his face.

Those people whom he had detested so much and considered the bane of his existence were barely memories now, replaced by trusted friends and people who, at least for now, did not resent his existence.

The sudden snapping of a twig not far in the distance brought his reminiscence to a halt and he stopped, like a deer in headlights. His eyes darted from tree to tree, rock to rock in search of the perpetrator of the noise, but he could see nothing, and no further indication, sight or sound came that suggested there had been anything there at all.

Nate waited another few moments just to be sure he was alone before turning back. When he returned Kyle made him light the fire with the spell he had learned before they had begun their journey. It was much harder the second time around with so many eyes on him, but after a few attempts sparks burst from his fingertips, followed by a jet of flame that quickly caught on the fuel they had assembled.

Barely had the first lick of flame touched the open air before a queue had formed of hungry people eager to cook whatever they had bought for themselves from Sundered Crown. Nate saw Leo and Said setting up their bedrolls along the wall of the alcove and decided to do the same before all the good spots were taken.

It only now occurred to Nate that he had not spoken a single word to either of them since their journey began. The pair were distant, spending almost all their time together and interacting very little with the rest of the group.

It was nothing personal of course, it just made their lives easier if they did not get too attached to their companions; after all, you never knew who you were going to be paid to kill next week. Nevertheless, Nate doubted a little conversation would hurt and forcibly engaged them in whatever idle chitchat he could while he waited for the fire to be free.

That night was bitterly cold. Frost-tipped wind hammered the walls of the alcove forcing the party to huddle up into one large mass. The fire could not stand the onslaught and had died long ago. Nate found himself squeezed tightly between Said and Leo, desperately trying to leech any body heat he could as he shivered in his thin bedroll.

No matter how hard he tried, however, he could not get his body back to sleep once the cold had set into his bones, he was simply not yet used to such conditions. The rest of the party sleeping contentedly did not help either.

With bleary, aching eyes he lay on his back and stared at the ceiling, hoping the mixture of boredom and darkness would fool his body into rest. Barely a few seconds after attempting this strategy, he froze in fear. It may have been pitch black outside, but Nate could still clearly make out a shape crawling along the ceiling above him.

He watched for a moment, praying that it was just a hallucination brought on by tiredness. As it crawled closer however, Nate could see hallucination or not, it had teeth. Rows and rows of dagger-like bared teeth, with saliva dripping in large globules. This thing, whatever it was, had no eyes, no ears, and no hair. Just a huge, gaping mouth and a wolf-like snout. Its skin was white and its arms and legs at least twice the length of a normal person's.

Slowly, like a bat it lowered itself from the ceiling until it was upside down, barely a meter from where Nate lay, still paralysed with terror. It was then Said made the mistake that would cost him his life. He turned on his side, still asleep and unaware of the danger. The creature instantly turned its nose in his direction and pounced, its claws and teeth at the ready.

The creature landed on Said with a thud, followed by a pair of screams – the creature's as it tore into its prey, and Said's as his flesh was ripped from his bones. This immediately awoke the rest of the party into a state of panicked frenzy as they realised what was happening and they did whatever they could to get the creature off their friend. Nate had not moved however, he lay there, barely inches from the creature as he was splattered with Said's blood and rocked in his bedroll by their thrashing.

After what felt like hours there was a pained scream as Jin thrust his katana into the creature's back before Cassandra followed up by removing its head. Said had long since ceased his struggle by now and lay, barely recognisable, his features torn apart. Kyle dove to his side hoping by some miracle he could be saved, but he quickly realised it was too late.

Marcus, realising Nate was still prone, hoisted him up and shook him, hoping to release him from the clutches of fear.

"Get it together Nate, there may still be more," he said, placing Nate's sword in his hand.

Marcus had been right, barely a second later the battle began. They came like insects, crawling along the outside of the rocky outcrop before leaping to the ground as if the height was nothing. There were six in total, but their speed and ferocity made it feel like many more. Each time it seemed like a strike would land, the creature would leap several meters into the air before landing dangerously close to another member of the party.

One had latched itself onto Marcus' shield. Its long arms curled around it like a spider as it attempted to swipe at his face. Luckily Joel was close at hand, and he skewered the creature so violently he could not retrieve his weapon, forcing him to turn to his dagger.

Teamwork was the key. The party split into pairs, and while one worked as a distraction the other would attack from behind. Luckily the creatures were not smart, and the battle quickly turned in the party's favour. Nate paired with Cassandra, who acted as the distraction while he charged, determined to make up for his earlier failure which had resulted in Said's death.

The creature went down as the tip of Nate's sword protruded through its chest, although as its last act it swung an arm out wildly, just catching Nate's side, tearing a jagged hole in his armour, and leaving a deep gash in his flesh.

This was Nate's first real injury in the heat of battle, and it was worse than anything he could have imagined. He would gladly take Barrett's fist to his nose a dozen more times over the pain he was feeling now. He fell to the ground clutching his side, hyperventilating, and shaking as if death was certain to come. He pulled his hand away slightly to see hot blood steaming in the night air and immediately regretted it.

Cassandra stood close by but did nothing, her attention already focused on another of the creatures. Nate shot out his hand and grabbed her ankle, pleading for help. She turned, a disgusted look on her face before shaking him off and running into battle, leaving Kyle to come to the rescue. Despite the monstrous cries of enraged and savage enemies, the sloshing of blood on the ground and various other sounds of death, Kyle was strangely unperturbed. He had been amid much worse and Nate was relieved to feel the familiar warmth of Kyle's healing spell as it sealed his wound in a matter of seconds without leaving so much as a scar.

By the time Kyle had helped Nate to his feet, still woozy but uninjured, the battle was over. Luckily, Said had been the only casualty and the group was left unsure what to do next, still reeling from the sudden surprise attack. Some set about cleaning their weapons and the battlefield of the dead, others tended to their injuries. Nate however, had a totally different idea in mind.

Furious that Cassandra had left him to die, he walked towards her as fast as his still-painful side would allow and shoved her in the back while she was wiping blood from her sword. She fell to the ground, kicking up dust and scraping her knees. The sudden, random act of violence surprised everyone, not least of all Cassandra who spun around expecting to see another wave of creatures but instead found a red-faced Nate.

She hesitated for a moment before punching him square in the jaw. It was nowhere near as hard as she could have hit him if she had tried, but Nate did not know that and now angrier than before, went in with a fist of his own. Before the two could properly brawl, however, Marcus stepped between them, Joel grabbed hold of Cassandra by the waist, while Jin did the same to Nate, pulling them apart.

"What the hell are you two doing?" Marcus bellowed, the mixture of adrenaline and pain of losing someone under his command rising within him until the veins in his neck threatened to burst.

"Ask him, he just attacked me," Cassandra screamed trying to break free of Joel's grasp so she could show Nate what a real injury felt like. This was true, Marcus had seen the whole thing but could not believe Nate would attack another member of the party like that without an excellent reason. He turned his attention to where Nate was also struggling, albeit less ferociously to get at his opponent.

"What happened?" Marcus asked, less angrily but still clearly with little time for such idiocy within his own ranks. At least now he could relate more closely with his captain.

"She left me. I was injured and she left me," Nate said now clutching his side where Jin had roughly held him. Marcus turned to Cassandra now who did not show the slightest sign of remorse – instead, she shook her head and laughed.

"Is this true?" Marcus asked, eyeing the obvious tear in Nate's armour, disturbed that a member of his party would not help another when clearly hurt.

"It was barely a flesh wound, he would have been fine; anyway, Kyle was there, and the monsters were still attacking." Marcus quickly weighed up the arguments and decided that Nate was in the wrong – the wellbeing of the many came over that of the few.

"Nate, you may not like it, but you can't always save everyone, even if that everyone is you. Cassandra did the right thing." This was not the answer Nate had expected and he scowled, not quite able to believe what he had just been told.

"If you *ever* assault someone under my command again, I'll tell Ardell you're good for nothing but cleaning out latrines. Do you understand?" Marcus added.

Nate gritted his teeth and nodded. "Good, now both of you get to work clearing this mess up, we need to get out of here now." Begrudgingly the two walked away from one another in search of a task to perform.

Jin, Kyle, and Marcus were all busy examining the things that had attacked them. Turning one over with his boot, its gangly limbs now passive, Jin looked on with disgust.

"What the hell is this thing, you ever seen anything like it, Kyle?"

Kyle rubbed his beard and thought back to his hours in zoology class so many years ago. Kneeling and getting his face much closer to the creature's still dripping jaws than anyone else would have dared he wracked his brains. Just as he was about to admit defeat, a memory came back to him.

As a third-year at the Tinelian university, there had been a short course on magical corruption and its effects. If he was not mistaken, the creatures that had just attacked them were Husks, in this state referred to as Stalkers, corrupted by dark magic banned in the civilised world. However, only an exceptionally powerful sorcerer at the top of their field would be able to perform such a feat.

This explanation did little to comfort the others who now wished to revert to the mundane quiet of an otherwise deserted forest. Nate decided to return to where it had all started, and found Leo already there, standing over the body of his friend. "I'm really sorry," he began but Leo shrugged and smiled sadly.

"We always knew it would happen eventually. I just don't think either of us expected it to be like this," Leo explained. By now most of the others had gathered around, unsure whether they should offer condolences or move the body.

"Did he have any requests if this were to happen?" Marcus asked. Leo could not help but let out a choked laugh as he recalled the exact same conversation many years ago when he and Said first started their partnership.

"Yeah, make it look more heroic than it was," he smiled.

"We can definitely do that," Joel replied with a glint of mischief in his eye. By the time the remainder of the party had packed up and were ready to continue travelling, they had arrayed a glorious final stand for Said, placing his sword in his hand and dragging the corpses of the Stalkers so that they formed a semicircle around him.

At first, Nate found the whole idea gruesome but quickly understood why it was so important not just for Said and Leo, but for everyone else too. Honouring a companion's final wishes was something they had all been forced to do countless times and it was in a way, their final chance to be together.

By some miracle, the horses had been left untouched by the Stalkers and amid the darkness, the party moved on. Despite the difficult loss of Said, they had suffered far fewer losses than Marcus had expected, something he naturally did not share with the rest of the group. Soon they would reach Cotts, and this nightmare could finally end.

Chapter 20

Cotts was a small town that reminded Nate of the country village he had grown up in – no more than a hundred houses yet a different pub or inn at the end of every street. After their harrowing ordeal of losing Said the previous night, the party were in desperate need of some R&R. However, they were held up for nearly an hour at the gatehouse, the only western entrance to the town.

The guard in charge informed them that some shady looking people, possibly imperial spies had been spotted in the surrounding area and so each of them would need a permit to enter or leave. After faffing around with paperwork, the party were finally permitted to enter, after a thorough search of their wagon of course.

Once passing the threshold into the town the group breathed a collective sigh of relief, they were safe for now. After parking the wagon in a rather overpriced stables that did not offer contents insurance, Marcus had the group meet outside a tavern called 'The Cheeky Goblin' where he discussed their plan.

He, Joel, and Kyle would meet with the contact at 'The Queen's Purse,' another inn towards the other end of town. The others were to do as they pleased so long as they kept their heads down and their eyes out for anything suspicious. If they felt as though they were being watched or followed, they were to head straight for the Queen's Purse and find Marcus.

However, after coming this far Nate protested and pleaded for Marcus to let him tag along to their secret meeting. Eventually Marcus surrendered and agreed, it would be easier to keep an eye on Nate this way anyway. After the last time he did not need him wandering off and discovering he was the rightful king of Tinelia.

With that the party went their separate ways, although Cassandra and Chen along with Leo and Jin went off in pairs, deciding that would be safer with potential unfriendly eyes watching them. Kyle, however, was unphased by the potential danger and decided he would leave the shady meet-ups to the professionals and headed off in search of the cheapest liquor he could find, much to Marcus' anger.

"Fine," Marcus said rubbing his face with frustration as Kyle sauntered off into the distance. "Come on you two, let's find our man," he said to Joel and Nate as they navigated their way to the Queen's Purse. Thankfully, Marcus had been given some information by Captain Ardell to go on and only had to ask the innkeeper for a 'room with a sea view' and he would be directed to their contact.

This all seemed easy enough and while their mission was urgent, Marcus did not want to be seen as acting too suspiciously so soon after arriving. Therefore, upon reaching their destination he ordered a well-deserved meal and drinks, to which Joel and Nate quickly followed suit.

They allowed an hour to pass, all the while keeping a watchful eye on everyone entering or leaving the building. Thankfully, nothing seemed to be out of order and just as dusk began to fall Marcus approached the barkeep with his request.

"Room number six," he replied without looking up from the pint he was pulling. Pleased that everything was going off without a hitch Marcus turned away to fulfil his mission. But the barman's next words made his blood run cold. "Awful lot of people wanting a sea view today," he mumbled to himself, just loud enough for Marcus to hear.

His eyes immediately grew wide, and a sickly feeling appeared in his stomach. Without a word he ran for the stairs, caution be damned.

Nate and Joel, alarmed by the sudden change of pace leapt up from their seats and followed Marcus up the stairs. By the time they burst into the room Marcus was already face to face with the contact. Tied to a chair in the centre of his room, his body mutilated beyond recognition, very much dead.

Marcus' heart had virtually stopped beating, surely this could not be happening. If they had just arrived a day sooner... Thoughts were racing through his mind as to what to do next, did he contact the captain immediately, or try to hunt down the perpetrators?

Joel meanwhile had locked the door so nobody could accidentally stumble upon the grisly scene and was examining the body. Nate was simply trying not to be sick; he had seen far too much gore over the last few days and sat on the bed with his head in his hands.

Marcus was now pacing about the room mumbling to himself, paying no attention to the mess before him, and why would he? The contact was of no interest to him in this state. However, Joel was disturbed by the cruelty in the way that their man had been killed.

From what he could tell, the killers had started by removing fingernails, followed by the fingers themselves which were scattered about the floor. His ears had also been set upon, but the killers had made a hash of it and only partially removed them, perhaps after realising their victim could not answer any questions without the ability to first hear them. Finally, one of the eyes had been removed and was nowhere to be found, the other, once radiant green, now glassy and lifeless.

A sudden crash made Joel and Nate jump as Marcus threw a chair at the wall. "I can't fucking believe this," he fumed, "Ardell is going to kill us." Joel could not help but agree; considering the room was in an orderly way, he could only assume that the killers found whatever they had been sent to retrieve.

Nate, finally deciding to brave a look around, immediately caught his eye on the victim, or more specifically, the space beneath what remained of his right hand. It seemed to be giving off a strange orange glow.

Trying his best to keep his dinner down, he inched closer to the body and carefully lifted the bloody stump. Lo and behold, branded into the arm of the chair was a message, almost identical to the one Kyle had demonstrated back in

Sundered Crown, although this one was rather more informative and burned a fierce orange.

Nate could not help but gasp with amazement before quickly setting the stump back down and rushing to the window; throwing it open he leaned out far enough that he was on the verge of falling. Joel and Marcus watched, perplexed – was Nate about to launch himself from the window rather than return to Ardell a failure? Perhaps a wise move.

Neither could believe what happened next. After stretching as far as his body would allow Nate pulled himself back and in his hands was a small leather bag, and in it, a small, red journal.

"No bloody way," Joel gasped as Marcus pushed past, snatching the journal from Nate's grasp.

"I can't believe it," Marcus said flicking through the pages. This was it, what the mission was all about. He quickly placed the journal within his own knapsack and slapped Nate on the back triumphantly. "What do you say we get the fuck out of here?" The trio left in as orderly and inconspicuous fashion as they could, unaware of the pair of eyes that had been watching them from the moment they had arrived in town.

The next day, spirits were high. The rest of the party did not need to know the details, just that their mission was complete, and they could go home. After quickly stocking up on more supplies, the party left at first light. Luckily the town guard was too busy dealing with a murder to worry about guarding the gate, nobody arrived anymore anyway and so the group were able to leave uncontested.

It was a beautiful autumn day; the sun was bright and the leaves on the trees were all browning while a refreshing breeze rustled through them. Marcus could not have been in a better mood, and of all people, he had Nate to thank. He could not believe his luck. If Nate had not been a prophet there was no way anyone would have seen the message left by their contact in his final moments. Perhaps Nate would turn out to be his good luck charm – regardless, he had earned himself a drink when they returned home.

"I heard we have you to thank for this little adventure being a success," Chen said walking side by side with Nate. He could not help but smile and reply smugly.

"All in a day's work for a hero." Chen giggled and gently prodded him with the end of her bow. Nate may have been an idiot, but at least he was not a useless one. Suddenly the party came to a halt and Nate, still talking to Chen, crashed into the back of Marcus who was standing tense and motionless in the road.

"I was walking here," Nate joked, but nobody else laughed and the sound of a sword being drawn immediately snapped him to attention. Looking past Marcus, about one hundred meters down the road was a blockage. Except this time, it was not undergrowth or fallen trees, it was a group of at least ten, heavily armed and spaced out so that nobody could pass. Nate's heart began to race as he drew his own sword. At last, Marcus addressed them.

"Keep calm everyone, let's not do anything stupid just yet."

As they neared the roadblock everyone was on edge. Chen had already nocked an arrow onto her bow and everyone else had drawn their weapons, though at this stage nobody wanted a fight. Once the distance between the two groups was roughly ten meters Marcus ordered them to stop again. He approached the other group who then sent out one of their own to meet him.

They were wearing riding leathers beneath a steel breastplate and their face was covered by a hood; however, the short sword at their side was clearly visible.

"Morning." Marcus said casually, testing the waters. At best this would be a group of renegades, at worst an imperial scouting party.

"A beautiful one at that," the figure replied, the pitch of their voice clearly female. She pulled back her hood, revealing herself to be extremely beautiful with medium-length brown hair and rosy cheeks brought on by the hours she had been stood in the cold.

"Off anywhere nice?" she asked, nodding towards the wagon.

"Just to Sundered Crown, hoping to do a little trading," Marcus replied, still unsure of how this would play out.

"Ah, ok," the woman nodded; her lips pursed as if she did not believe his story. "Mind if we do a quick search?"

"Under whose authority?" Marcus replied. The woman shrugged.

"Just my own curiosity I suppose." Marcus gave a weak smile.

"Well, you know what they say about curiosity," he replied slowly bringing his hand down to the hilt of his sword. The woman gave a slight smile of her own in reply. Then there was a sudden shout from behind.

"Marcus!" It was Nate's voice; Marcus really did not have time for him now and so ignored him.

"Well, it's been lovely talking to you."

"Oh, hasn't it just?" The woman interrupted just as Marcus was about to suggest she kindly get the hell out of their way. Another shout suddenly caught his attention, this time from Joel.

"Marcus get away from there, look at her men!"

Marcus allowed himself to look away from the woman for a moment and immediately realised what had Joel sounding so alarmed. The men blocking the road were not men at all. They were dressed in armour and carried weapons, but their skin was grey and rotten, their eyes black and soulless. They were Husks.

Marcus did not have time to consider the implications of what he was seeing before the woman lunged with her sword. Only by the skin of his teeth was he able to withdraw his own and block her. An arrow suddenly whizzed past and struck one of the armoured Husks, bouncing harmlessly off its thick breastplate.

The parties charged forwards, leaving Marcus to duel with the mysterious woman. The shock of facing Husks in such an unimaginable scenario threw everyone off and they struggled in what would usually have been an effortless task. These were like no Husks anyone had ever seen, swinging weapons with great force and accuracy, blocking attacks sent their way and most astoundingly of all, using teamwork.

Despite being outnumbered and shaken by their foes, the party put up a decent struggle. Nate got the best of one Husk after severing one of its legs, quickly bringing the tip of his blade into its brain as it lay on the ground. However, he soon found himself facing two more who quickly disarmed him and threw him to the ground, one kneeling on his neck while the other ran to support its comrades.

This only added to the madness. Husks did not take prisoners, yet they were going out of their way to take as many alive as they could. With his limited mobility, Nate could see Chen, Jin, and Joel all in the same position.

Marcus was not doing much better in his duel either. His foe's speed was almost inhuman, and he was struggling to keep up. Each time he thought he had caught her out she would dash around him or to the side and it would take all the skill Marcus had to keep himself alive.

Leo then appeared at his side, drenched in the black blood of a Husk as he charged the woman, swinging wildly. This forced her to take her attention away from Marcus for the time being. Although this distraction was only momentary, exploiting an opening in her opponent's erratic movements she ducked and with her free hand withdrew a dagger from her thigh that she used to slash Leo's throat as she sprang back up.

Leo fell, now drenched in his own blood. He did not last long enough for Kyle to reach him, who himself was then quickly apprehended by yet more armed Husks who had appeared from the flanking forest. The shock of seeing his companion fall so quickly caused Marcus to freeze – it was only for half a second, but it was long enough. When he turned back to his opponent, he found himself staring down the wrong end of a sawn-off shotgun.

Realising his situation was hopeless he dropped his sword and placed his hands on his head. "Glad we could get that out of the way," the woman huffed, both tired from the fight and annoyed at herself that she had killed a hostage, that was one less bounty for her.

Marcus was then, along with the rest of the party, bound and searched before being thrown unceremoniously into the back of his own wagon. With the look of pure joy on his enemy's face when one of the Husks brought her the journal, one would have thought she had won the lottery.

Which in a way, she had. Adeneus was offering enough for its retrieval to set her up for a long time. The only comfort Marcus could draw from was that he had not lost more of his party – while they were bruised and demoralised, at least they were alive. Although, as the mysterious woman signalled for the caravan, driven by one of her Husks to take a little-known route out of Tinelia and towards Adeneus' castle, perhaps death would have been the better alternative.

Chapter 21

The Journey into the Imperium was long and uncomfortable. Their captor, who called herself May, had taken the caravan guarded by around thirty armed Husks through the countryside and around anywhere that showed signs of life. It had taken weeks but at last, they had crossed over the border and were only a few hours from Adeneus' castle.

The novelty of being some of the first people to face this new threat of semi-intelligent Husks had yet to wear off. The creatures did not need to eat or sleep and so stood guard over their hostages twenty-four hours a day. May would not even allow her prisoners to go to the toilet privately while under guard, and so they were all forced sooner or later to go in full view of the others, their final humiliation complete.

Unfortunately, there were no other people for May to converse with, from whom the party could steal snippets of information. All they knew was that they were heading into the Imperium and as May had so kindly informed them, their dead friend Leo was the lucky one.

Nate had expected to immediately recognise the Imperium once they had crossed the border. He had envisioned forests of dead, scorched trees, fields of black soil and starving peasants. He was therefore shocked to learn his prejudices had been entirely unfounded after only discovering they had entered Imperial territory three days after the fact. For all intents and purposes, it was indistinguishable from anywhere in Tinelia. Rolling fields of strong and healthy crops, wide, sparkling rivers and the occasional village were the only sights on their long journey.

Perhaps the only difference between the two sides was that the local people barely blinked at the sight of people trussed up in the back of a wagon like animals, escorted by the creatures they had spent millennia killing for a quick payday. Adeneus' castle was located on the outskirts of a town called Blight, a reference to an unknown disease which had killed crops and people alike in their millions many centuries ago.

Otherwise, it did not live up to its name. From their limited view in the caravan, the party saw people going about their daily business, farmers toiling in their fields and merchants bellowing at the top of their lungs in the market. The only thing out of the ordinary was that every soldier patrolling the town, of which there were hundreds, were all Husks.

"Ok, this is getting out of hand now, what the hell is going on?" Cassandra whispered. Nobody could answer, even Kyle after all his years studying magic had no explanation for what they were seeing. The caravan made a sudden turn and began a steep climb up the road to the castle which sat on a hilltop overlooking the town.

"What do we do, Marcus?" Nate asked. Over the course of the last few weeks, he must have been asked that question a thousand times, and yet he still had no answer. He had no idea what they were heading into and so could think of no way out of it. They would have to wait until they knew more about their situation before they could formulate any realistic sort of escape. He remained silent as the caravan pulled beneath the portcullis of the gatehouse which slammed into the dirt behind them.

After what had seemed like years the caravan finally stopped, and the party were dragged out and marched into a stone building not too far across the courtyard from the keep itself. Nate's joints were sore after being in such cramped, uncomfortable conditions for so long, but he got no sympathy from the undead guards who jabbed him with the blunt end of their spear to keep him moving at an acceptable pace. Nate made sure to get a good look at his surroundings before he entered the stone building, determined to memorise every inch for their inevitable escape.

The building was small and cramped, certainly not fit for habitation, and was most likely used for storage. However, inhabited it was, as at least eight other people were already there, crammed into cages just big enough for a person. Despite their ultimately futile protests, each of the prisoners was forced into their own cage and when the last key had been turned in its lock, the party were left in total darkness.

"Well, this sucks," Nate complained, fumbling in the blackness for some miracle escape route, perhaps a man-sized hole in his cage the captors had not noticed.

"Kyle, can you help us out here?" Marcus asked trying to keep himself calm in the hope that everyone else would attempt the same. The room was suddenly filled with a soft white light as Kyle produced four magical orbs that floated at head height. Now that they could see, the party could get a better idea of how to escape.

The room had no windows. Solid stone surrounded them apart from the single thick wooden door which they had entered through. Their cages, as to be expected, were solid iron, free from rust and too sturdy for any man to break. Luckily for them, they had not been checked for sorcerers within their ranks, a common practice when taking prisoners. Imperial standards must be waning, Marcus thought as he gave Kyle and Nate their orders.

It took many hours, but eventually, Kyle and Nate had used their mastery of fire to melt the locks and free everyone from their cages. Nate of course had made a state of most of his attempts and molten clumps of metal dotted the floor around the cages he had worked on.

Kyle had managed to leave the locks almost entirely intact, helpful if someone decided to check on them. This was only the first step, however. The party, now bolstered by the eight other prisoners, who were beyond grateful to be freed, needed to work out how to escape from the castle grounds unnoticed.

Some of the other prisoners had been there for weeks already and informed the rest that their captors had only started using this room as a prison recently. Before that, the prisoners were kept in a sort of dungeon below the keep, where they knew for a fact, there was a hidden escape route.

This was not the kind of breakthrough Marcus had been hoping for. The only plan more dangerous than trying to get out of the castle unseen, was trying to get in. Nevertheless, it was the only plan they had – after all, the keep itself was possibly less defended with so many Husks patrolling the walls and nearby town. Also, if the portcullis was still down, the dungeon was their only option.

Over the coming hours, a plan was decided. Around midnight the party would break out of their prison and head for the keep. There they would scavenge any weapons they could and try their best to enter the dungeon unnoticed. If they were caught, the plan remained the same – fight their way to the dungeon or die.

Thankfully, nobody came to deliver food to the prisoners – never having been so glad to be victims of a human rights violation, the party awaited their time with bated breath and pounding hearts.

At last, midnight came, and through cracks in the door, the party could see the ghostly glow of the moon and hear the calls of nocturnal animals. Marcus nodded to Kyle who with laser-like precision, used his magic to cut the door's lock. Straining every inch of his body to be as quiet as possible, Marcus pushed the heavy door open. As far as he could see in the grim moonlight the only guards were the ones in the gatehouse at the opposite end of the courtyard. The fact that they had been left totally unguarded shocked him; clearly whoever was in charge was not a seasoned military man.

Gingerly, the prisoners exited the building, in single file, their backs crouched, keeping as low to the ground as possible. Silhouetted against the keep walls as they crept closer, they looked like a trail of mice, hunting for whatever scraps they could find.

They reached the keep doors without being spotted – amazingly, these were also completely unguarded. Someone was clearly extremely confident in their defences. Nate was right behind Marcus and Kyle behind him just in case some emergency magic was needed. After checking for a final time that they had not been spotted, Marcus led the way into the keep.

They were all immediately hit with an invigorating warmth from the huge fire in the centre of the room which almost made up for their aching joints. This is where Marcus had most expected the plan to fall apart, walking in on the main hall filled to the brim with soldiers looking directly at him.

Yet there sat only a single person in the room. With her back turned to them, May had her feet up on a table and was reading a novel. They would need to deal with her quickly and quietly. While the rest of the group tiptoed their way around the edges of the hall, hugging the walls, Marcus approached May from behind.

Like a snake, Marcus wrapped his burly arm around May's neck and squeezed while using his free hand to keep her from reaching her sword. Taken entirely by surprise, May choked and kicked as her breath ran out. But Marcus held her firmly in place, the chair rocking and groaning under the desperation of the struggle, her shotgun falling from its holster just out of her reach.

Nate had stopped his circumnavigation and now stood motionless watching the scene unfold, unable to look away from the terror in May's now bloodshot eyes as each second brought her closer to death. Just as it looked like she was about to succumb, with a final, heroic effort May managed to reach the dagger strapped to her thigh and plunge it into Marcus' leg. With an agonised cry Marcus fell to the floor clutching his wound, while May fell in the opposite direction, gulping down air and coughing furiously.

May spun around, sword drawn, her thoughts consumed with a ravenous bloodlust. Yet by the time she had regained her footing and turned to kill the helpless Marcus, she was faced by Nate, threatening her with her own shotgun.

Nate had never held a gun before, and it was far heavier than he had expected. Having to hold it with both hands he aimed it at May's chest, where there was no chance even he could miss. Kyle rushed over and immediately began working on Marcus' leg. After a few seconds of silence interrupted only by Marcus' groans of pain and May's breathless panting Marcus was back on his feet, although unsteadily.

"Nice one, Nate," he praised snatching May's sword from her hand as Kyle retrieved her dagger.

"Now what?" Nate asked, his own breathing shaky as adrenaline rushed through him. May kept her hands up at chest height but was clearly thinking of a way out.

"Can't take her with us," Marcus stated matter-of-factly.

"I know but she's unarmed," Nate whispered.

"Sorry, Nate but there's no other way," Marcus said, reinforcing that May was not getting out of this situation alive. Realising she had nothing to lose she filled her lungs with air and called out as loudly as she could.

"GUARD…"

The boom of the shotgun cut her short and catapulted her across the room, her body crashing into a table, reducing it to splinters. Blood oozed from the dozens of small holes where the pellets had penetrated her armour and shredded the tissue beneath.

In the stone halls, the already loud explosion was amplified until it sounded like a cannon. Everyone froze in shock, only snapping out of it when the thunder of a hundred boots could be heard heading their way. Grabbing Nate by the shoulder and pulling him along Marcus followed the other prisoners who knew the way to the dungeon, praying they could still make a clean getaway.

Sprinting as fast as their limited knowledge of the keep would allow, the prisoners descended the spiral stone steps leading to the dungeon. Unable to lift the heavy beam, Marcus threw his body against the door before Kyle was able to blast it open with telekinetic energy. There was no point in trying to be quiet anymore. Spilling over one another into the room like a colony of ants the prisoners only advanced a few steps before recoiling in horror.

Two Husks stood side by side in the centre of the room, armed with long blades and an excuse to kill. But that was not what had appalled the party, it was what the Husks were guarding. Sat between them in a wooden throne was a man. Adeneus.

Emaciated, his skin droopy, almost falling from his bones. His complexion was milky white, his lips slightly parted, his eyes a glowing purple. Upon his head was what looked like a crown, although it was huge and sat more like a cage upon his shoulders, three cloudy green crystals its centrepiece. From it, a light humming and cracks of magical energy could be heard.

Nate took care of both Husks with the final cartridge in his shotgun before tossing it aside and taking one of their swords for himself, Cassandra taking the other. Most of the party simply dismissed Adeneus as another victim of the Imperium's many atrocities and began searching for the passage out, although Kyle and Marcus had different priorities.

Barely affording Adeneus a glimpse, Marcus' eye was caught by a solitary red notebook on an otherwise empty desk. Rushing over with a smile on his face he was ecstatic to find it was the same journal he had been tasked to retrieve by Ardell. The mission was not yet a failure.

Kyle was more interested in Adeneus himself, however. Despite the growing echoes of more Husks close behind, Kyle could not help but sate his curiosity. He examined the headpiece Adeneus wore, the cloudy green crystals fixed upon it that buzzed angrily. He had seen them somewhere before, but not used like this. Lastly, he stared directly into Adeneus' glowing eyes, trying to make sense of it all.

No, it was impossible. Such a thing was beyond even the greatest sorcerers in the world. No matter how much Kyle tried to tell himself these lies he could not deny the truth. In a panic-stricken voice, he called out to the others who had ripped a bookcase from its hinges to find the way out.

"It's him!"

The others did not even acknowledge this and had already begun their escape.

"He's the one controlling the Husks!" Kyle screamed again.

This caught Marcus' attention. Rushing over he looked first at Adeneus, this withered, hollow version of a man, and then at Kyle, the disbelief evident in his face, which had gone completely white. Without a word, Marcus thrust the point of May's sword into Adeneus' heart.

There was a soft gasp as Adeneus' last breath escaped him before his eyes went dark. The sound of stomping feet behind them immediately ceased. A few seconds later the human screams of terror began.

The passage was long and dark but led far from the scenes of carnage at the castle and town of Blight. The Husks, free from the control of their master had turned on the people, slaughtering those they had moments ago protected. Emerging into the glow of the moon, deep into the forest the party did not stop, running almost the whole journey back into friendly territory.

After many weeks of travel, avoiding all roads, clinging to the shelter of the forest, the party arrived home, by some miracle, having lost nobody else.

In their brief moments of respite, Kyle had explained what he believed to have transpired with Adeneus, and delving into his journal would only confirm these theories. Chen had been the one to ask the question nobody dared pose.

"Do you think he was the only one?"

"God help us if he wasn't," Joel would answer.

Chapter 22

Three months after their dramatic escape from Adeneus' castle, Nate and Marcus stood before Captain Ardell in her quarters. Her eyes were glued to a spot on her desk while her mind raced, her hands cupped around her mouth and nose.

The moment they had returned nearly a month ago they had sped straight to her and presented Adeneus' journal. After reading it she had delivered it to Grand Admiral Lee personally. Now she had one more task for the pair who had brought these events to light. A task she had angrily refused to take part in.

"Believe me when I say I do not wish to make you do this," she said pulling away her hands and leaning back in her chair. "But the Admiral believes you and your companions deserve to be present after all you have done."

Nate and Marcus looked at one another sheepishly — surely, they were not to be punished after all they had gone through?

"There is no doubt the Imperium intends to conquer us, conquer the known world." Ardell paused, not quite able to form the words they left such a sour taste in her mouth. Eventually, she continued.

"Admiral Lee believes we must prevent this from happening, and so a force has been assembled to knock the Imperium out of the war before it can begin. You two will be part of that force."

Marcus grinned but Nate did not see the funny side. He was not sure he was ready to be thrown into action again so soon, he was still having nightmares from their earlier mission. "I'll be taking you to meet with the Grand Admiral myself in two days," Ardell added.

Nate and Marcus could not believe their ears. During his short stay in Tinelia Nate had created quite a mental image of the man everyone in the city seemed to revere so much. To meet him in person was a great honour for anyone, let alone a lowly recruit.

"Also, before I forget," Ardell said straining to pick something up from the floor beside her desk. "I heard you had your weapons stolen, so consider this your bonus for a successful mission."

As she straightened herself, she brought with her two swords. One was a gladius very similar to Marcus' former weapon, although a clearly far newer and finely crafted one. The other one was an arming sword, a common enough type of weapon, although this one had come from her personal collection. "Nothing fancy I'm afraid, but I have a feeling you will use them well."

Nate and Marcus could not decide what to be more surprised about; their meeting with Grand Admiral Lee, their new swords, or the fact Ardell seemed to be smiling at them without visions of torture behind it. They spluttered a thousand thanks before being dismissed and naturally celebrating by getting the drunkest of their lives.

Their hangovers had only just passed by the time Ardell summoned them for their journey to the Citadel a few days later. Nate had never been closer than the Vanguard to the nation's seat of governance until this moment. Passing through the rich Warrens where most of the country's nobles had residences was a much different experience from the Vanguard. Each street was paved or had cobbled roads; parks and green areas had been strategically placed rather than allowed to spring up naturally, and of course, the prices in the shops were beyond astronomical.

Yet even this was nothing in comparison to the Citadel. From the moment you entered through the gate, it was like stepping into a huge garden. Innumerable species of flowers denoted every path and walkway. Nate was amazed, he had never seen anything so beautiful in all his life. Then there was the Citadel itself. From the base it was impossible to see the top, which was more like a mountain than something made by human hands. From every rampart hung hundreds of noble and national banners, a reminder that there was a world outside these walls, a world worth protecting.

After receiving a message that morning, Ardell led the pair to the docks where Grand Admiral Lee and the mighty Tinelian fleet were waiting. Making use of the river which ran directly beside the Citadel, the trio disembarked their small, wooden ferry and found the Admiral. He was not at all how Nate had imagined him. He had tanned, leathery skin but bleached white hair. Furthermore, he did not have the physique of a warrior or king, being no taller than Nate and with not much more muscle to boot. In all honesty, Nate was disappointed. Marcus, however, was beside himself with excitement to meet his leader.

Lee was speaking to another man about their upcoming operation but smiled warmly as he saw Ardell's companions. Nate and Marcus instinctively stood to attention, to which the old Admiral laughed. "No need for that, boys, hell I should be saluting you for what you've given us." Nate was unable to place his accent, stuck somewhere in the Baltic Sea between Swedish and German.

"The chance to commit war crimes?" Ardell replied sarcastically, not even giving her commander the satisfaction of her gaze. Lee shot her a disgusted glare and snarled back at her.

"Did I ask for your opinion, oath breaker?"

Nate and Marcus were shocked at the viciousness of the remark and stood looking awkwardly at one another. More than anything they were surprised someone could take such a tone with Ardell and continue to live, regardless of their status. Quickly regaining his composure, Lee turned back to them with a wide, triumphant smile.

"This is our chance to deal our enemies such a blow they will never think to wage aggressive war again". Ardell mumbled some vague curses under her breath before Lee addressed her. "Why are you still here? Get out of my sight."

"I'm sure you'll feel much better once you've slaughtered some peasants, my lord," she growled. Nate caught her eye as she boarded the ferry once again, the look on her face one of anger and pity. Anger at her commander, pity for Nate. Her words had not reassured him much either, but there was no time for discussion as Lee led them down the gentle slope to where their ship was waiting.

Built in a style very similar to that of European ships of the line, the Tinelian navy filled the ocean as far as they eye could see. With three huge masts and hulls full to the brim with cannons they were a truly formidable sight. Atop each mast would usually fly the blue and gold of the Tinelian naval flag; however, this time it was curiously absent from every ship.

Lee led the men onto the deck of their ship where the rest of their companions were already present, Kyle notably absent, having rejected the opportunity. Shaking Marcus and Nate's hands with a firmness of appreciation he wished them success on their mission.

"You're not coming, Admiral?" Marcus asked, daring to hope he would be able to retell the story of when he and commander took the fight to the Imperium side by side. Remorsefully Lee shook his head.

"I wish I could son, but the other lords simply won't allow it. I'll be the first one here for your heroic return though, you can count on that."

Marcus could not help but beam with delight at the prospect and after standing to attention once more as Lee left the ship, turned to greet his companions. Nate soon found Chen leaning against one of the masts, clearly not happy with their current situation.

"I thought you were up for this?" he said jokingly, "kicking some imperial arse that is." Chen had been chewing on her nails and spat one aside. "Charming," Nate grinned. But Chen did not respond with her usual playful self. She shook her head and started on another nail.

"I dunno, I'm starting to get a bad feeling about this," she said as the pair watched a huge, black spherical object be loaded onto the deck by a crane and then carefully positioned below deck. Before Nate could share his own doubts about the vagueness of their objective the planks and walkways leading onto the ship were pulled away. Suddenly, the ship began to shudder violently.

Nate looked up to see from the tip of each mast, four metal blades, flat and long, extending and then spreading out like feathers on a wing, each equally spaced apart. Before he could put two and two together, the blades began to spin, slowly at first but rapidly gaining speed until they created a deafening rush of wind.

"What's going on?" he shouted to Chen. She wrapped her arm around the rigging of the mast and shouted back. "Hold on." Nate had barely managed to fling himself towards her, wrapping one arm around hers and another around the rigging before the ship pulled itself free from the water and took off into the sky.

It was an incredible sight, thousands of wooden ships cutting through the air on rotor blades like some Frankenstein combination of ship and helicopter. The noise was still deafening hours later, but by now Nate had become used to it. He stood on the starboard side enamoured at the masses of identical ships flying in formation.

He did not dare look down again but knew they were now well above the clouds. What had started as a pure blue both above and below them had steadily turned orange. It would not be long before these ships would be invisible to the naked eye, hidden against the backdrop of a black sky.

Most of the others had gone below deck to escape the noise and perhaps get some rest before the action started. Nate could not bring himself to be pulled away from such a sight, however, one he never imagined he would see. One he might never get to see again.

It was another few hours before the lights of the Imperial City were visible in the distance. In the darkness, they had been easy to spot and now the deck was full of people busying themselves in preparation. Nate was soon joined by the rest of his companions, some looking well-rested and fresh, others such as Chen a clear nervous wreck.

"What's wrong?" Nate asked, concerned by the clear distress in Chen's body language as she hugged herself. They were rapidly approaching their target now; in a few seconds, they would be directly over the heart of the Imperial City itself. Chen said something but it was lost as the ship suddenly halted and hovered in the air like a huge bird of prey. They had reached their destination.

"This is wrong," Chen repeated.

"What?" Nate asked, recovering from the sudden cessation in movement.

"They can't do this," Chen said with tear-filled eyes as the rest of the party leaned over the side of the ship like they were at a spectator sport. Nate was about to reply expressing his confusion but immediately got his answer with the sudden shifting of weight as the bilge of the ship, along with thousands of others opened, releasing the huge metal bombs they had been carrying upon the city below.

Chapter 23

The Emperor awoke to the sound of rapturous thunder and lightning, great bright flashes bursting through his thick curtains. Reluctantly, he dragged himself into a sitting position and rested against the headboard, letting out an exhausted sigh. Was he doomed to suffer eternity without a full night's sleep? The storm continued, creeping closer like a predator upon its unsuspecting prey. Deciding some fresh air would help alleviate the stuffiness of the room and perhaps result in a better chance of comfortable rest, he threw off the bedcovers and headed towards the balcony doors.

As his hand reached to pull them open, the whole room shook, and a deafening roar filled his ears. Paintings fell from the walls, the ceiling cracked, dust cascaded down like snow. The Emperor was knocked off balance and stumbled into his dressing table, knocking the wind from him. Adrenaline poured into his veins as he leapt back to his feet and ripped the balcony doors open, as all the while the whole palace shook.

Laid out before him was a scene torn straight from his nightmares. A firestorm engulfed the city, thick plumes of smoke visible even against the darkness of the sky filled the air. With each passing second more massive explosions could be seen ripping through the streets and homes below. Another rocked the palace, sending chunks of masonry falling just shy of the Emperor as he watched in horror.

Yet he could see no soldiers in the streets, no invading armies come to lay him to waste. Only panicked citizens desperately trying to put out the fires destroying their homes, screaming as more explosions tore them apart or burned them alive. He did not understand how this could be happening and looked to the sky in desperation, as if expecting divine intervention to save his people from this vision of hell.

But no intervention came, no bright light to dispel the darkness, no great flood to douse the flames. Instead, barely visible against the black sky the Emperor could make out hundreds of large shapes moving slowly over the city. Below them, explosions slaughtered indiscriminately. The Imperium was indeed under attack yet had no way of defending herself. Accepting the painful truth that there was nothing he could do for his people, his mind turned to Sarah. He had to find her and make sure she was safe.

As he turned to retreat, his bedchamber doors burst open, and his personal guard stood in the doorway. "Come your holiness, we must get you somewhere safe!" he screamed over the bombs which fell like deadly hailstones. Usually, the guard would never have seen the Emperor without his mask, and so would have counted this moment as the luckiest of his life. Yet there was no time as his sense of duty overtook him and keeping his Imperator alive was all that mattered.

"We must find my wife first," the Emperor ordered as the pair ran from the room. All around them chunks of rubble fell from the ceiling, crashing onto the tiled floor of the palace's reception. The guard held his shield above his head to protect the Emperor from any falling debris as they sprinted along the balconies and corridors to Sarah's bedchamber.

Everywhere there was chaos, as servants, and nobles alike all ran screaming for their lives, paying no attention to the half-dressed Emperor running at full pelt, vaulting over rubble. Sarah's bedchamber was only a few minutes away, situated in the east wing of the palace. The Emperor decided to cut through the ballroom as this would shorten his journey considerably.

He was panting heavily at this point, each breath containing more dust and plaster than air. Remarkably, despite being fully clad in steel, his guard was still close at hand. The thuds as chunks of stone and metal bombarded the shield above his head were like the beat of a deadly drum.

The door to the ballroom had already been reduced to splinters as the men rushed inside. What was once an example of elegance was now nothing but broken glass and rock. Luckily, the two sets of stairs placed opposite one another, meeting in the middle, were still intact. Just as the Emperor was about to descend, to his delight Sarah, accompanied by her own guards, appeared atop the other set of stairs.

His heart swelled with joy and relief at the sight of his wife unharmed. Sarah's face too beamed a relieved if not terrified smile as their eyes locked. For that moment, despite all the chaos and destruction, all was well with the world. Nothing had been lost that could not be rebuilt or replaced. Although this momentary relief was short lived.

Time seemed to move at a fraction of its normal speed as an explosion erupted beside them, a thin wall their only protection. Like pellets from a gun, brick and stone shot forth, followed closely by a raging inferno. The Emperor could do nothing but watch as Sarah, her eyes still locked with his own, was buffeted by debris and engulfed in flames, her body thrown violently across the length of the room.

Despite the best efforts of his guard, a small slab of stone struck the Emperor in the head, knocking him down the flight of stairs. As the world slowly went dark around him, the last thing he saw was Sarah, her body aflame, lying on the cold ground as the world collapsed around them.

The Emperor awoke a few hours later, back in his bedchamber which had fortunately been spared most of the destruction, although dust lay across it like a blanket, while shattered glass and stone had been brushed aside. At his bedside sat Nestor and Elias, both of whom jumped up with relief as they saw the Emperor's eyes open.

"Your holiness," they both gasped, each rushing to help as the Emperor tried to sit. He lifted his hand to where the debris had struck him.

"Don't worry, your holiness, the physician has already seen to you," Nestor assured him.

"We were attacked, your holiness; we know not by whom or why, but we are all hard at work to uncover the truth. Rest assured we will find the filthy heretics who did this," Elias added.

"Sarah," the Emperor whispered, his voice hoarse after inhaling so much smoke and dust. Nestor and Elias both looked at one another with concern. Neither wanted to give the

Emperor the news and were pressuring one another with increasingly violent stares. "Where is my wife?" the Emperor shouted. At last Nestor capitulated and placed his hand upon the Emperor's. An act which immediately filled his heart with dread.

"She has been taken to the infirmary your holiness. She was gravely injured in the blast."

It broke Nestor's heart to give him such news, his admiration for Sarah was second only to the Emperor's.

"Take me there," the Emperor demanded as he tried to stand. While he no longer suffered a physical injury, his body was still in shock and was reluctant to move. Elias quickly moved to stop him, placing his hand against the Emperor's chest.

"Your holiness, you are not yet fully healed, you need to rest." The Emperor pushed his arm away.

"Do not try me Elias, not now," he growled, the threat in his voice very real. Nestor continued speaking as he helped the Emperor to his feet.

"The royal infirmary was destroyed in the attack your holiness. A makeshift one has been set up in the palace courtyard, her majesty is there."

The Emperor nodded in understanding, gripping Nestor tightly as he helped him dress. Before long they were following a similar path to the one he had taken the previous night. Over the half-ruined bannisters, he could see the result of the attack in full daylight. Bodies still lay in the reception, uncovered and with their final expressions of fear and pain forever carved across their faces. Many walls had collapsed or been blown apart, while sunlight poured in through holes in the ceiling where the first bombs had fallen.

Supported slightly by one of his guards, the Emperor tentatively descended the many hundreds of steps leading down to the reception and out into the courtyard. Even now, people halted their work to bow before him as he made his way through the rubble of his home. The main palace doors had remained undamaged and had been left open to allow the stream of engineers and medics to do their work. The engineers were using every tool they could find, including their hands, to clear debris, daring to hope they might find survivors buried beneath. The medics, meanwhile, rushed around with gurneys, carrying those with lesser injuries to the field hospital, while treating those with more serious wounds where they lay.

At last, the Emperor and his entourage found themselves in the courtyard, the true scale of destruction wrought upon the city now visible. From where he stood, he could not see a single structure that either had not been gutted by fire or reduced to rubble. Only the mighty golden spire of the temple of the One stood seemingly untouched, like a beacon of hope through the carnage. Before him were hundreds of makeshift beds, upon which lay the injured, shielded from the elements only by ugly green oilskin fabric tied between poles. Beside them sat their friends and loved ones, either weeping or tending to their wounds as the vastly outnumbered medics rushed between beds.

"This way, your holiness," Nestor instructed as he led the way between the rows. All around them, people screamed in agony, many of them burned beyond recognition. The sick smell of cooked flesh dominating the air forced the Emperor to cover his nose and mouth. Quickly the Emperor noticed a large screen surrounded by guards on the edge of the makeshift hospital. Realising this must be where Sarah lay, he rushed forward, pushing past Nestor. Medics and civilians jumped aside as he took up the aisle with his muscular frame.

Pulling back the screen with vigour he darted inside, desperate to find his wife in better condition than those around her. Yet the reality was far worse than he had expected. Lying in her own bed, was Sarah, almost her entire body burned and blistered beyond description save for the right side of her face. Her left arm was withered and twisted like a spent matchstick, with white spots where her nightgown had fused with her flesh dotted across her torso. Her thick golden hair, within which the Emperor had sought comfort countless times, was but a wisp.

Beside her stood her personal physician, frantically applying potions to her burned skin, his hands glowing all manner of colours as he cast spells of healing. None of which had any effect. The Emperor rushed to her bedside, sinking to his knees, and gently taking hold of her right hand which was mostly unharmed. The physician stood back in both shock and respect, bundles of potions spilling from his arms.

"I am here my love," the Emperor whispered, ripping off his mask. Tears welled up in his eyes and a lump formed in his throat. Slowly Sarah turned her head to face him, leaving behind a bloody imprint on her pillow. She tried to smile but most of her lips had been burned away, revealing black and bleeding gums.

"You're late," she croaked, her own voice barely audible. The Emperor tried to summon a chuckle but instead it caught the lump in his throat and tears began streaming down his face.

"Look what they have done to you my love," he finally managed, gently stroking her right cheek. He turned to the physician, bursting with rage. "What are you doing?" he boomed. "Why haven't you healed her?"

The physician knelt opposite the Emperor, tears running down his own face.

"I'm sorry your holiness, but whatever material was in those bombs is unknown to us. I have healed the rest of her wounds to the best of my ability, but unless we know exactly what caused these burns, we cannot heal them." He paused for a moment to wipe his eyes before continuing. "I have every available alchemist working to identify the make-up of the material, but I fear that could take weeks."

This could not be true, the Emperor refused to believe it. He frantically began applying his own limited knowledge of healing magic to no effect. His heart sank. He sat there, staring at the physician with wide eyes and quivering lips. Suddenly Sarah squeezed his hand and his eyes shot back to her. She could sense fear and hopelessness overcoming him, and while she knew her time was short, her only concern was for the well-being of her husband.

"Do not mourn for me, my love, I will not disappear from this world forever. Whatever happens, wherever I find myself, we shall see each other again."

The Emperor squeezed her hand in response, sniffing back tears. "I swear to you, I will find you. I will scour every corner of this world until at last, I have you in my arms once more." Sarah tried to smile, tears beginning to roll down her scarred cheeks. "And I promise I will find the ones who did this to you and make them suffer as you have suffered. As I suffer now, the world will burn for what it has done," the Emperor continued.

Sarah gently shook her head and raised her hand to hold her husband's face. "No, my love, you are no monster, do not allow your enemies to make you one."

The Emperor clasped her hand and kissed it, even now Sarah refused to give in to hatred and anger. It made him realise all the more how much he depended on her. "I love you," he sobbed.

"I love you more," she replied attempting a smile. "Although I'm so tired," she groaned.

"Sleep," the Emperor cooed, "I will be here."

True to his word the Emperor sat for three days and nights by his wife's bedside. He did not eat or sleep and would suffer no visitors save for the physician. All the while he held Sarah's hand firmly against his cheek. On the morning of the fourth day, Sarah's shallow and laboured breathing halted entirely, her hand slipping from the Emperor's grasp. With no tears left to cry, no prayers left to say, he stood, staring one last time at what had once been his beautiful wife, and what his enemies had done to her. Silently he left the room, a cold, steely expression on his face.

Yet to his surprise, awaiting him outside were gathered thousands of people in total silence, most of whom were peasants, dressed in their scruffy work clothes. At first, the Emperor believed them to be opportunists, hoping to catch a glimpse of his face and anger began coursing through him at the thought. However, a man stepped forward, his hair and clothes as caked with dirt as the fields he worked. The guards who had kept their post since the attack moved to intercept the man. But the Emperor stopped them and beckoned him forward.

Removing his hat, the man bowed before speaking, his voice trembling yet full of sincerity. "We are truly sorry for your loss, your holiness. Her majesty was a kind and generous soul who always had time for the likes of us. We will mourn her passing for many years to come, and we hope we can be of service to you, in the hope of honouring her memory."

The Emperor was suddenly overcome – never before had he experienced or expected such kindness from those whom he had always treated with disdain. He stepped forward, and took the man's hand in his own, causing all those present to gasp in amazement.

"I thank you from the bottom of my heart for your kind words. Sarah would have been touched to hear them. But I was not the only one to suffer from this cowardly attack. It is my solemn promise to you that all those who have suffered these past few days will be avenged."

The man bowed again as the Emperor moved past, barely able to comprehend what had just happened. His path was suddenly blocked by a woman, her face bandaged and bloodied.

"Please your holiness, my home was destroyed, and I have no money for a healer. Please show me mercy." Sarah's words reverberated within the Emperor, and he smiled as he placed his hand on the woman's head. A soothing blue light coming from his palm glowed briefly and the woman was healed. She immediately burst into tears of pure joy and fell to her knees in reverence.

Suddenly the Emperor was swarmed by hundreds of bodies, some asked for blessings, others to be healed. Most, however, wished only to shake his hand, to know that he was flesh and blood like them. A man who suffered the same pain they suffered, and who would lead them through the coming darkness. The Emperor, far from being disgusted or uninterested in his people's plight, took pity on them. For too long they had been absent from his thoughts; now, however, he felt obliged to listen. Soon Nestor appeared from amongst the crowd with a host of guards who positioned themselves between the Emperor and his subjects.

"Your holiness," he gasped, unable to believe the scene playing before him. "Her Majesty?" he asked, sheepishly peering behind towards the screen where Sarah lay. The Emperor responded by placing his hand on Nestor's shoulder. Immediately he understood and broke down in tears. The Emperor, however, lifted him up and embraced him.

"We will avenge her," he whispered; his voice filled with malice. With that, the Emperor left accompanied by his retinue of guards, headed for the temple of the One. As he passed through the ruined streets of his city rumours of his kindness had already spread. Before long he had a huge train of people following him through the burned-out streets. After just over an hour of walking they reached the temple of the One, the Emperor signalling for his guards to deny entrance to anyone until he returned. He climbed the steps alone, the weight of an empire on his shoulders.

As the heavy doors slammed behind him, he looked around at the intricate beauty of the temple. Barely a single surface did not shine with gold or precious gems. Stained-glass windows which depicted him in all manner of holy roles decorated every wall. The crusader with his shield held high, defending the weak from the forces of the Fallen One. The monk, clad in his humble robe deep in prayer. The king sat upon his golden throne, his subjects kneeling before him and many more. None of which had ever resonated with him. No matter how much pomp and ceremony or fancy words Elias draped over him to cement his image as an instrument of God's will.

The Emperor slowly proceeded down the main aisle, the empty rows of pews and his own statues his only company. At the far end of the temple was the altar on which the Grand Seeker would offer sacrifices of gold and silver to the Lord, along with the most magnificent of the harvest's bounty. It is here where the Emperor sank to his knees, his body and soul drained. His armour scraped and clanged along the stone floor. He looked up at the image of the Lord looking down at him, his piercing eyes cold and uncaring, full of harsh judgement.

The Emperor's own eyes were red and bloodshot, and despite his best efforts, his body was too exhausted to summon a single tear. Instead, he bowed his head and spoke, addressing his God directly, running his hand along the smooth surface of the altar.

"What hellish torment must I now suffer, Lord? To have that which I love beyond measure be held beyond the reach of my senses, yet not lost to them. To have all that is good and pure snatched from me with no justification. To leave me in a world of darkness and evil. Why must I suffer this, Lord? Why have you forsaken me?"

The Lord did not answer, and no enlightening vision came to him. No soothing words to console him, to reassure him that this was all part of a divine plan. The silence was deafening, and it filled the Emperor with an insuppressible rage. He could feel his blood boiling and in a single movement he lunged forward, striking the altar with every ounce of his strength which remained.

At the very moment his fist contacted the cool stone, a new vision flooded his mind. He was back in the cavern below the palace, although this time something was different. The door located in the right palm was slightly ajar, not tightly shut as it had been previously. Tentatively the Emperor crossed the room, almost tiptoeing should any excess noise cause the door to slam shut and the opportunity be lost.

To his relief, the door remained open as he placed his hand on the handle. His whole body was trembling, his stomach performed somersaults and his heart was ready to burst. All the while the same feeling of immense power called to him, seeping into his skin. Whatever was behind this door, he felt neither ready nor worthy to see it. Nevertheless, he summoned the last of his courage and pushed the door open fully. Before him was a sight of beauty beyond mortal description. A garden in full bloom, flowers of every colour and type as far as his eyes could see. Fruit-bearing trees lined the way down a path of emerald grass, which led to a small cottage of pure white with a thatched roof and smoke rising from a single chimney.

In all his years he had never seen an image of such perfection. Yet this place was immediately familiar to him as if his entire life had been little more than a journey back to this place. Back home. Suddenly a vision of himself appeared, naked yet giving off a glow that could only be described as angelic. Barely a moment later a similar apparition of Sarah appeared beside it, they locked hands and smiled at one another. A wave of elation and infinite love, incorruptible and pure crashed over the Emperor as he watched. A feeling the likes of which he had never experienced, that he did not know was possible to experience. The two visions, hands intertwined, turned their backs on him and continued down the path. The door to the house opened, it was waiting, and they had both been expected. The Emperor tried to follow them, his foot not making it over the threshold before the vision immediately vanished and the door slammed shut.

In that instant, the Emperor found himself back in the temple of the One, the altar shattered to pieces beneath him. He fell onto all fours, each detail of his vision still pristine in his mind. At last, he understood what had to happen, the Lord had shown him his destiny. Nestor, having managed to talk his way past the guards now stood frozen in place at the back of the temple. Witnessing the Emperor obliterate a slab of solid stone with a single strike, made him reconsider approaching him, wary in case the next blow was in his direction.

"Your holiness," he whispered drenched in fear. His voice echoed through the temple until it was a roar. Slowly the Emperor stood, and with his back still to Nestor, replied in a voice filled with true godlike enlightenment and authority.

"Gather my Chosen, Nestor. We're going to find my wife."

END

Lightning Source UK Ltd.
Milton Keynes UK
UKHW010650071222
413498UK00003B/103

9 781803 695242